P9-CNA-847

The Case for Participatory Democracy

THE CASE FOR PARTICIPATORY DEMOCRACY

Some Prospects for a Radical Society

EDITED BY *C. George Benello*

AND *Dimitrios Roussopoulos*

GROSSMAN PUBLISHERS

New York   1971

The editors wish to express their gratitude to all contributors, publications, and copyright owners for their cooperation in the preparation of this volume. "Toward Freedom in Work" by James Gillespie appeared in *Anarchy* 47, January, 1965; "Toward a Liberatory Technology" by Murray Bookchin appeared in *Anarchy* 78, August, 1967; an early version of "The Cybernetics of Self-Organizing Systems" by John D. McEwan appeared in *Anarchy* 31, September, 1963; all are reprinted with the permission of *Anarchy*. Murray Bookchin's "The Forms of Freedom" is reprinted with the author's permission from *Anarchos* II, Spring, 1968. A portion of "Revulsion and Revolt: Revolution in Our Times" by John R. Seeley appeared in *Daedalus,* and is reprinted here with the permission of *Daedalus*. Gerry Hunnius's essay, "The Yugoslav System of Decentralization and Self-Management," appears here for the first time with the permission of the author and of The Information Exchange Project of the Cambridge Institute. "The Movement: A New Beginning" (Staughton Lynd), "A Left Wing Alternative" (Greg Calvert), and "An American Socialist Community" (William Appleman Williams) all appeared in *Liberation,* and are reprinted here with the permission of the editors of *Liberation*. Any errors or omissions that may have inadvertently occurred will be corrected in subsequent printings upon notification to the editors.

To Michel Chartrand

CONTENTS

1
Components of a New Society

II
Strategies for Social Change

Part I

COMPONENTS OF A NEW SOCIETY

INTRODUCTION

The phrase "participatory democracy" has been taken up by many politicians and political agencies in both the United States and Canada. However, their definition of this concept, which falls within the prevailing political lexicon and society's prevailing public philosophy, is unacceptable to us and to its originators. Those who uphold the status quo, in order not to disclose their intellectual and ideological barrenness, have usurped New Left rhetoric in an effort to swing with the style of ideas now emerging from the base of society. A book on the real meaning of participatory democracy is long overdue.

It is appropriate that the first effort at conceptualizing the nature of participatory democracy should be a collective one. We need such intellectual task forces evaluating the work of contemporaries as well as the concrete experiences in the movement for radical social change. What we hope to achieve in this volume is a vision of participatory democracy placed squarely in its proper intellectual arena, and we hope to spell out the points around which serious debate on the subject is now taking place. In the course of the book, it will become clear to the reader that the debate goes beyond the concerns of liberalism, social democracy, and the authoritarian Old Left. The thrust of the thinkers represented is to seek for structural changes in a system that is closing out true democracy and that is robbing people of a chance to have politically meaningful identities within their culture. All this is not simply a question of programs and ideologies, but of the prevailing institutions themselves.

People's desire for a community in which they can control the decisions that affect their lives has been, from the beginning, part of the very nature of society. This desire is also central to the new revolutionary movement; far more than a vague idealistic yearning, it arose as a profound reaction to the steady process of depersonalization pervading advanced industrial societies in a period of tumultuous transition.

The transition has been from market capitalism to neocapitalism. Partly initiated by extraordinary technological innovations, it has accelerated occupational specialization, accentuated interpersonal competition, and generated both a growing authoritarianism and a passive attitude that accepts all this as necessary. Politically, technological advances have concentrated power in the hands of self-appointed elites. But more importantly, these

elites and their corresponding institutions exercise a highly centralized social control. If, as it is said, technology conquers nature, then to do so, it
must first conquer man. The disappearance of overt political coercion
should not blind us to this fact.

The authors represented in this book do not accept the belief, held by
liberals and most socialists, that technology has within it a self-correcting
mechanism. On the contrary, they believe that while the economic base of a
society can determine the orientation of its technology, no society yet established has developed checks on the deforming drives of a "technotronic"
superstructure, once it has come into being. Technological advances affect
the societies in which they occur in ways so extensive that they cannot help
but be political. The self-appointed elites who manage technology make
decisions that have far-reaching effects on the shape of the urban landscape,
on the management of resources, on where people work and live. Refusing
to recognize the extent to which they are political, the political system of
liberal democracies has consigned these decisions to the private sector. Participatory democracy seeks to reintroduce the concept of democracy from
the ground up, which means introducing democratic process into the major
organizations of society, public *and* private.

It is here that examples from abroad are relevant—the Israeli *kibbutzim,*
the French communities of work, the experiences of community and worker's control in Yugoslavia. In the United States, the experience of community development corporations, short though it is, marks an important step
in the movement to democratize from the ground up. While the Yugoslav
efforts have focused on the work place as well as the basic geographical
units, in the United States the effort has been to create community development corporations, based on the belief that urban blight and ghettoization
have created a potent base for organizing around the issue of seeking
greater power to meet community needs. Hence the twin themes of worker's
control and community control are fundamental to any idea of participatory democracy, and appear in a number of forms throughout this book.

The New Left's early concept of participatory democracy and its applications was developed in terms of community organizing in poverty areas.
With the failure of these efforts to create a truly mass movement, the New
Left has gone through a number of contortions, resulting in the rise of authoritarian and vanguardist fads. The experience has burned a number of
young people as they found their early definitions of participatory democracy wanting in political effectiveness. By now, however, the movement has
come almost full circle, and the most urgent debates are no longer over

program but over structure. The sides line up: revolutionary movement versus revolutionary party; Leninist vanguardism versus collectives, affinity groups, or communes. Interestingly, the debate within the New Left movement is a paradigm of a debate about the nature of power and society itself; although describing their efforts by a variety of names, the first generation of New Left activists have, in effect, undertaken a formal re-examination of the underpinnings of participatory democracy. This development is encouraging, but it derives more from a direct perception of the failures of the American social system than it does from the development of a theory. However, both are necessary: an experience of the ways in which elitist institutions dehumanize people, and a theory of how such institutions can be reconstructed in a democratic fashion.

Western liberal democracy has dealt with only some parts of the problem of power. For the Founding Fathers, there was little organized power to deal with outside the government, so they devoted themselves to creating an elaborate system of checks and balances within the government. In the Constitution they did not acknowledge the existence of corporate entities, hoping to isolate those who governed from the impact of social power. Their method was to enfranchise a limited electorate of the propertied class, and give to their representatives maximum freedom from popular pressures. Their ideal can be described as Platonic: to create an elected class of philosopher-kings, whose wisdom would ensure good government.

As corporate power quickly developed with the industrial revolution, a pluralist theory replaced that of the Founding Fathers, arguing that as long as no single organized group achieved a preponderance of power, freedom was guaranteed by competition among different groups. This theory of veto groups holds only to an extent; we have a kind of pluralism of the powerful, but those who are not organized and who lack access to wealth and power have no voice in the pluralist cacophony, and it is precisely these constituencies that most need to be heard. The system thus perpetuates the inequities of the status quo and, hence, is essentially conservative. The philosophy of participatory democracy, by confronting the realities of organized power in the society, would ensure that all constituencies be formally represented in assemblies at the relevant level—local, regional, or national.

In a participatory democracy, decision-making is the process whereby people propose, discuss, decide, plan, and implement those decisions that affect their lives. This requires that the decision-making process be continuous and significant, direct rather than through representatives, and organized around issues instead of personalities. It requires that the decision-making process be set up in a functional manner, so that constituencies significantly affected by decisions are the ones that make them and elected delegates can be recalled instantly, doing away with self-appointed elites whose decisions have a broad political impact on the society, but who are accountable only to themselves, or to interlocked groups of their peers.

Participatory democracy assumes that in a good society people participate fully, and that a society cannot be good unless that happens. Participation and control must be *one*. Furthermore, the democratic process of participation and control must be used in the movement for social change from the start; thus the means employed for change must be democratic. This does not imply that strategies should be limited to electoral politics, or even based on it. Rather, a politics of creative disorder is indicated, at once oriented to unveiling the inequities of the present, and to building a counter-system that is participatory from the ground up. New, participatory institutions must be built in all social spheres and, as they develop, will claim legitimacy and recognition as being genuinely democratic and accountable to their constituencies.

An analysis of the concept of participatory democracy can lead us to a new and liberating vision of our own society and its technology. It can also suggest a number of tools by which to arrive at a new critique. For instance, research is needed on inter-personal dynamics, on the sociology of organization, and the self-aggrandizement implicit in bureaucratic organization. Such an analysis has its roots in the democratic tradition of socialism, in Marxist humanism, and in anarchism. Primarily a socio-political critique, it does not in itself deny the importance of the economic base of a given society, but supplements that focus in needed ways. It speaks to the sense of powerlessness that prevails not only in the work place, but also in the ghetto, the atomized suburban community, the school, and the university.

Up to now the Left has believed that the nature of society would be fundamentally changed if its economic base were socialized and nationalized. This has not proven to be the case. The Chinese Marxists have admitted that contradictions do not evaporate after a socialist revolution, and, moreover, that class conflict persists. Mao Tse-Tung's Cultural Revolution represents an appreciation of this question unprecedented among Marxists. However, Mao's solutions, ironically, are conceived in "idealistic" terms. The Cultural Revolution is more of an attempt at psychological exhortation than an attempt at profound structural change leading to a non-authoritarian, non-repressive society. Hence the primacy of chant and ritual.

The deliberate transformation of technology would be one of the first crucial tasks confronting the movement for participatory democracy. Much of the elitism and inequity of the present system rests on the myth that centralized control is a prerequisite of efficiency. Democracy is considered a luxury that can be practiced in public governance, but in the critical areas where technology and production are involved, the experts of management must prevail. As a high official of the National Association of Manufacturers commented, "democracy is all right for politics, but in business, we have to be sure things get done." This ideology is self-serving and ensures that those who control also get a lion's share of the profits. It perpetuates distinctions of class, education, and wealth, and, moreover, perpetuates a system where unskilled work is so alienating that it results, in more cases than not, in mental illness.* This approach to technology must be challenged at its roots, by citing the growing body of evidence that participation in policy-making is essential if work is to have integrity, and in no way detracts from efficiency. The social organization of the work place should not take on a mechanical form dictated by the machine; instead, the machine can and must be altered to conform to the dictates of humanistic social organization. All that is lost is the fragmentation and specialization of job function that ensures that control can be maintained from above. And that is precisely what must be eliminated.

Robert S. Lynd stated in his foreword to Robert Brady's *Business as a System of Power:*

> Liberal democracy has never dared face the fact that industrial capitalism is an intensely coercive form of organization of society that cumulatively constrains men and all their institutions to work the will of the minority who hold and wield economic power; and that this relentless warping of men's lives and forms of association becomes less and less the result of voluntary decisions by "bad" or "good" men and more and more an impersonal web of coercions dictated by the need to keep the "system" running.

A movement for participatory democracy must combat the present ideology, which claims that technological and industrial advance can be maintained only by the present style of coercive social organization. Businessmen argue, not that democratic work organization is anti-American—we are all for democracy—but that it won't work. To prove that it will requires the development of counter-institutions that differ fundamentally in their structure from present work organizations. When these demonstrate that

* Arthur W. Kornhauser, *The Mental Health of the Factory Worker* (New York: Wiley, 1964).

they can get the job done as efficiently, and at far less social cost in the form of worker alienation, pollution of the environment, dislocation of jobs and families, they will then be in a position to press their argument strongly.

In addition to exposing the depradations of the present socio-political system and its allied institutions of the military, the corporations, the foundations, the educational system, and the public bureaucracies, a movement for particapatory democracy presses for local and decentralized control, for non-alienating work, for non-regimented study, for a decent environment, and for restriction on the powers of non-accountable and self-serving elites in both the public and private sectors. However, its attack on the exploitation and elitism of the present system will be firmly based only when it can point to working examples of how the key functions of the society—work, education, and community life—can be successfully carried out by non-elitist and non-exploitative forms of social organization. For it is a salient characteristic of the present system that, underneath the variety of products and services that are produced, the organizational forms are everywhere the same. People are aware of the social costs of the system, but it is a system that, after all, does deliver the goods along with the costs. In the absence of alternative systems that could deliver the goods without the costs, it is unthinkable to reject this one. Once such alternatives have been firmly established, it will be possible to give resistance and struggle a positive meaning for the many who suffer from the depradations of the system, but see no way to change it.

A movement that builds participatory democracy from the base is committed to the full dissemination of power, whether political, bureaucratic, or corporate, to those affected by it. It also involves the creation of organizational forms whereby shared power can be used for the good of all. Since the ownership of property and, in particular, industrial property is an important form of control, the democratization of such ownership must be a central feature in a program of participatory democracy. Participatory democracy is, thus, socialistic in its demand for the democratization of property so that all affected can have a voice in its disposition. But it is also anarchistic in its recognition that more than the democratization of the means of production and of industrial property is involved. All the institutions of the society must be democratized, not simply the work place.

In order to realize such a vision we need a movement that lives it. The implications of building such a movement are revolutionary, for it confronts the basic institutional structures of the present society. Confrontation is not without implications of violence when demands for participation are met with repression; but it is also a non-violent revolution since its confrontation is on the basis of an alternative vision that seeks expression in counter-institutions that adequately express the vision. Such counter-institutions can act, both as paradigms and experiments embodying a new social vision, and as sustaining bases for continuing resistance and confrontation.

The two wings of such a movement—resistance and counter-institution building—must keep in step with each other. This means that counter-institutions that do not politically challenge the institutions of society will be irrelevant: free schools must confront the public school system, community controlled enterprises must challenge private enterprise. However, a movement that limits itself exclusively to contestation cannot demonstrate concretely that it possesses a realizable vision, and, hence, is unlikely to grow. One of the major strategic problems is how to build a movement that can effectively combine both contestation and counter-institutions in such a fashion that out of the daily struggle over particular issues can come long-lasting and relevant structural changes. Such a combination, in our view, amounts to social revolution.

A NOTE ON STRUCTURE

Not every contributor to this book accepts the total perspective just outlined. Each, however, covers an essential aspect of the whole. We have organized the essays in such a way as to present a more or less coherent case for participatory democracy, and also so as to mimic the sequence in which a participatory democracy might arise.

By definition, a participatory democracy cannot be imposed from above, but must be built from the ground up. Three things are essential for this kind of growth: (1) a viable social and historical tradition, (2) a set of men capable of working from that tradition in (3) small groups that are themselves participatory. Woodcock's essay explores participatory democracy's historical roots. Calhoun shows that emerging psychological theories, which attack the cynical view that men are selfish and incapable of self-government, make a society of participation possible. And Benello offers insights into the dynamics of face-to-face groups, and shows how they can be the building blocks of a new society.

Community and Workers' Control. A society of participation must begin with daily life, with community control and workers' control. Perry and Kanter apply the theory of groups to community control, and, in particular, to the community development corporation. Already signs of change are appearing in the neighborhoods, as people organize to buy food and other items on a community-wide basis.

With community control, workers' control is most important to a participatory democracy. Gillespie discusses the organization of work on the factory floor, and Hunnius, by looking at modern Yugoslavia, shows how workers' control might affect the larger society, and how it must lead to workers' self-management. One of the lessons of the Yugoslav experience is that workers' control does not make for full participation unless it is wedded to community control. It is in making this possible that Bookchin's article on the decentralization of technology is essential.

Organizational Analysis. Again, however, the mere presence of the appropriate social structure does not guarantee participatory democracy. The organizations—the communities and the work places—must themselves be participatory. In the language of cybernetics, organizations must be self-organizing; that is, they must not be dependent upon divisions of responsibility and labor, as giant corporations are, for example. The characteristics of self-organizing systems and the ways to insure that organizations do not bog down in hierarchies are the topics of McEwan's essay. Benello's, in turn, discusses the relationship between organizational goals and structure, and human motivation. Finally, Chickering indicates that one key to making groups participatory is keeping their size down.

Socio-Political Structure. Once participatory organizations have been built in the community and the work place, the question of political superstructure can be considered, and it is to this topic that the last four essays in Part One address themselves. Communitarian social forms are preferable to class-based ones, an hypothesis that Bookchin puts forth. Bay deals with the nature and limits of freedom, and Oppenheimer cautions us against some managerial theories of freedom. This section concludes with an essay by Ward, which illuminates the relationship between political and social structures.

Inevitably there is some overlapping here, but there is also a movement from the individual to the group, from the group to organizations made up of groups, and from there to broad questions of the organization of society. All the writers share a concern to get beyond a politics of the possible, which assumes that the only realistic framework for the study of social reality is the existing system. They do not hesitate both to question prevailing assumptions and to suggest alternatives. It is in the serious consideration of alternative modes of social organization that our social and political theory is weakest, and, we hope, it is here that the real contribution of this collection lies.

Democracy, Heretical and Radical

George Woodcock

"When we use the word democracy we do not or should not mean any particular form of political structure; such matters are secondary. What we mean or ought to mean is the completely open society . . . We have in fact no choice at all; we have to adapt ourselves to an open society or perish." Such words do not seem out of place in the 1970's, but they were spoken in 1941; the speaker was the poet, W. H. Auden. Both facts are significant. By 1941 the dream of the thirties had died as a major casualty of the Spanish Civil War, and among the first to realize the implications of this destruction of an almost purely political ideal was the poet who had once seemed its laureate.

Auden's brief statement prefigures a vital shift in the way we now regard democracy, a shift with implications that began to manifest themselves clearly in the 1960s. Until the mid-twentieth century, the heart of the democratic ideal was supposedly that it put political power in the hands of the people. From this limited preoccupation arose movements for majority rule and universal suffrage, concerns radical in appearance but conservative in effect. "Universal Suffrage is the counter-revolution," cried the French socialist Proudhon, and where universal suffrage has been that and nothing more, events have usually proven him right.

Whenever the right of the people to rule was considered, too few theorists considered the relevance of the question: "What shall the people rule?" The rule of people over persons—the rule of the majority over a minority—is surely, as anarchists have always argued, a special form of tyranny. It is the rule of people over things that is true freedom. Radical democrats are at last becoming aware of this fact, in the latter half of the present century. We have reached the point when radicals and revolutionaries can, without inconsistency, all begin thinking of themselves as democrats, a point at which the great socio-political currents of the past—liberalism, libertarian socialism, anarchism, pacifism—can at last be united in a conception of democracy that, in all its aspects, embraces nothing less than

the open society of which Auden spoke. On the other hand, not to reflect on
those currents from the past that led to the democratic ideal would be tragic
nihilism. We need to know all they can teach us, as well as all our own
inventiveness can conceive, if we are to salvage from the undirected technological and social revolutions of the modern world a society worth living
in—or any society at all.

Seen from the historical point of view, the development of the notion of
radical democracy is a history of heretics. It is the history of a vision of
freedom always emergent, never complete, and above all, never tied to the
merely political. Auden contrasted narrow political democracy with the
open society; today the contrast is most frequently described as being between representative democracy and participatory democracy. I prefer Auden's phrase as the more inclusive, but both conceptions assert a growth
and broadening of democratic conceptions. They also presage the flowing
into the idea of democracy, like tributaries coming into some vast Amazon-
ian river, of many doctrines, theories, intuitions, and experiences of a libertarian nature that even a quarter of a century ago might have been regarded as outside and even opposed to it.

In the gentler mountains of eastern Switzerland lies the Canton of Appenzell. Its capital is a former village with the cozy reek of cow-dung still
hanging in its streets. Here political democracy survives in its most pristine
form. Appenzell offers its few thousand citizens something more, and less,
than representative democracy: it offers direct democracy. On the last Sun-
day of every April, around an ancient lime tree, the male Appenzellers over
the age of twenty meet, as they have done most Aprils since 1408, in a
plenary assembly to determine their laws. A council is elected to wield the
executive power over the coming year, and to recommend laws for the assembly to accept or reject. Any citizen of Appenzell can also propose a law
and have it put to the vote by the assembly.

The advantages of the Appenzell system over a representative democracy
are obvious. Government lies far more securely in the hands of the people
than in either the federal United States or parliamentary Great Britain. But
the limitations of democracy in Appenzell are equally evident. The people
meet only once in a year, so initiative rests mainly in the hands of the
council. The fiat of the majority is still imposed on the minority, no matter
how large that minority may be. Women have no part in deciding the laws
that will affect them. Finally, although the constitution of Appenzell pro-

vides for political democracy, notions of social liberation and regeneration have no place in it.

Appenzell represents in fact a high point of medieval democracy; it is a relic of one of the few successful peasant revolts, preserved almost unchanged for five and a half centuries. In 1408 the people of Appenzell wanted to rid themselves of their overlords, regulate their own affairs, and having shed their tax burden, prosper on their farms. Land was plentiful, and the society was industrially and technologically primitive, so there was no need to complicate their constitution with social overtones. Mountain barriers, good farming, and the steady flight of the young to the cities have enabled them to preserve, almost untouched, a political idyll, a beautiful fossil of a former struggle for liberty.

Appenzell stands a little less than a quarter of the way back in time to classical Athens, where our ideas of democracy were first articulated. Despite the eighteen centuries that divide Appenzell's original rebellion from the high point of Athenian democracy, the two have much in common. The Athenians had a modified form of direct democracy, with considerable power reserved for an assembly of citizens, while political officeholders rotated according to a system of lots, which avoided some of the grosser flaws of the elective system. To the women who in modern Appenzell are second-class citizens, the Athenians added a great company of slaves who had no hope of becoming citizens. Athenian democracy was strongly territorial, as Swiss cantonal democracy remains, and at one time in Athens only those who could prove the local descent of both parents were allowed to vote.

But in spite of its xenophobia, its caste system, its anti-feminism, Athenian democracy did find a reasonably successful solution to a major problem that concerns modern theorists of democracy. Though many Athenians were hard-working farmers or craftsmen, there were others for whom slavery had eliminated toil, as machinery and technology promises to free us. For these, Athenian democracy, within its limitations, was able to provide outlets for creative leisure. Their masterpieces survive, fragmentarily but still magnificently, in philosophy, history, political thought, and such great dramas as Aeschylus' *Prometheus Bound* and Sophocles' *Antigone,* which still speak in clear voices to modern man of the difference between justice and human law, and of the right of the individual to oppose his conscience to arbitrary power. Civil disobedience, which we today recognize as an essential mechanism of true democracy, found moving expression in these tragedies performed more than two thousand years ago. The voice of Antigone still strikes our hearts when she cries out, "I cannot share in hatred but in love," and dies in defiance of a vindictive political authority.

The five centuries from the time Appenzell came into being in 1408 and now have been a period of increasingly rapid socio-political evolution. Compared to them, the centuries from Athens to Appenzell seem like a broad desert in the history of freedom, spotted with scattered oases, traversed at immense distances by small rivers that lose themselves in the sand. To these we now turn.

In Rome in the third century, B.C., the plebeians gained some measure of political identity when, by massive civil disobedience, they won a Tribunate of the People. But the real governing power still lay with a patrician oligarchy that survived to the despotism of the Caesars. In Greece the schools of Stoics, Epicureans, and Cynics put forward egalitarian and internationalist doctrines that criticized both the institution of slavery and the xenophobia of Athens. The Cynics mounted an anarchist attack on the rigidities of political institutions in general, and taught that a true philosopher must opt out of politics and live beyond the law. But such doctrines influenced only a small minority, and certainly did not bring about the abolition of slavery, the destruction of the state, or international brotherhood. In fact, it was during the period of these schools that Macedonian and Roman rulers carried an insanity of power to the extreme of declaring themselves gods as well as kings.

Probably a more solid advance in the direction of human liberation was made, not by the philosophers, but by the mystery religions that emerged from the East and the more primitive regions of Greece to provide the poor and disaffected with cults that did not bow to god-kings or the interests of the privileged, as did the city cults. In these mystery cults, the only real distinction was between novice and adept; once initiated, citizens and foreigners, slaves and women, were regarded as equals. The story that Nero was refused initiation into the Eleusian mysteries because the fact that he was Emperor did not compensate for his moral wretchedness may be apocryphal, but the very fact that it was told indicates that social iconoclasm of a kind was a recognized feature of the mystery religions.

Of these mystery religions the greatest was Christianity, which borrowed from the Orphic cult a recognition that all men were equal, in the sight of God, from the Stoics internationalism, and from the Essenes a stress on brotherhood, community, and mutual aid. Christianity also added a dynamic of its own, the hope of Heaven, which broke the ancient world's obsession with cyclical time and set men's thoughts forward to the millennium instead of backward to an ever-repeated Golden Age.

For centuries the spirit of egalitarianism, brotherhood, and internationalism implicit in Christianity remained encysted in monastic orders, while its forward-looking dynamism was astutely diverted by Saint Augustine into a search for the spiritual City of God. But the chiliastic dream of an earthly kingdom of God, of a literal fulfillment of Revelation's promise that Christ would rule for a millennium, held its own. As the Church attempted to crystallize the medieval social order, the most powerful heresies were always those that promised more freedom to the downtrodden classes. By the eleventh century the great Catharist movement had swept westward from the Balkans into the heart of Europe. The Catharists objected to the episcopal power structure of the Church and to the hierarchical political structure of the feudal kingdoms. Their criticism of contemporary society passed from the political to the social when they denounced the materialism of their age, and advocated either a holy poverty for all men, or a simple communitarianism where work and goods were shared. Because of the Inquisition's assiduous suppression of every trace of Catharism, we know very little of the links between this movement and later religio-political movements of rebellion. It may well be, however, that the tradition of democracy in the post-Greek world had its obscure roots among the Catharists.

Catharism stimulated a flowering of culture in medieval Provence, but it vanished underground in the bloody repression of a Crusade led against the heretics by Simon de Montfort in the name of the Pope and the kings of Europe, who feared for their very existence if the movement were allowed to spread. But by then the medieval order itself was beginning to decay, and by the fourteenth century the disintegration was well advanced. The feudal lords forgot their obligations and became mere despots; the Black Death and the flight of peasants from the countryside to the free atmosphere of the cities eroded the institution of serfdom, and the desire for freedom began to take on multiple forms.

Ancient Greece was rediscovered, and Renaissance humanism fostered a cult of the individual in direct contradistinction to the medieval caste-system. Once men were regarded as individuals, the temptation to think in terms of their political and even social equality was irresistible, and a fine fruit of this renaissance humanism, in the late sixteenth century, was Sir Thomas More's *Utopia*. More tried to reconcile the individual's demands for economic equality with his social responsibilities, within a communitarian structure. To a modern libertarian democrat, the political framework of More's *Utopia* will seem pretty rigid (as will that of any utopia except William Morris' highly permissive *News from Nowhere*), but it was a landmark in recognizing that social, economic, and political rights are interdependent. If its negative inheritance has been the welfare state, its positive inheritance has been the long tradition of intentional communities where human beings have experimented flexibly with human relationships. In his day More was an intellectual writing for a very small audience of peers; but he died ironically as a martyr in the cause of a chivalric order whose decay he had recognized.

As the feudal order decayed, a new element of secular revolt—actual proto-democratic movements—were added to the religious radicalism inherited from the Catharists. During the English Peasant's revolt of the fourteenth century people chanted the jingle,

> When Adam delved and Eve span
> Who was then the gentleman?

Although the jingle had biblical reference, because at the time the Bible and history were synonymous, it also embodied quite independently a conception of social equality. And even if John Ball, who incited the rebels, was a heretic priest, the fragment of his famous speech that Froissart quotes shows him as a social agitator putting forward demands for a democracy at once political and social. "Things cannot go well in England, nor ever will, until all goods are held in common, and until there will be neither serfs nor gentlemen, and we shall be equal." Freedom, equality, community—in other words, the basic elements of modern radical democracy.

Until the eighteenth century there were no important movements of social or political rebellion, no advances in democratic ideas that did not borrow a great deal of their driving force from the dynamism of heretical Christianity. Thomas Muenzer, who led the German peasant revolt, was a religious chiliast, but at the same time he was politically concerned enough to establish, when he ruled Muhlhausen, an ultra-democratic constitution with a senate elected by universal suffrage but directly responsible to the forum of the people; in fact, something very similar to the direct democracy of the Appenzellers. At times the spirit of religious millenarianism perverted the political element, as in Münster when Jan de Leyden proclaimed himself King of Earth and set up an oligarchy of "saints" to usher in the second coming of Christ. But elsewhere radical religious belief went hand in hand with a deepening social and political radicalism. The modern use of the word *dissent,* with its political connotation, records accurately the debt that radical movements today owe to the Reformation and its religious sects with their constant tendency towards fragmentation on the left. Yet by the seventeenth century the most significant, in socio-political terms, among these dissenting sects were the ones that went beyond religious fundamentalism toward deistic rationalism.

At this period the Civil War of the 1640s in England became another source of democratic ideas. The war was fought over the issue of absolute monarchy, though of course the leaders of the parliamentary cause were oligarchs rather than democrats. They sought a political order in which landowners and merchants could order the world to their convenience, and the upshot was the first modern dictatorship under the rule of Lord Protector Cromwell and his major-generals. But on the heretical fringes of the Parliamentary movement—here was a radical and truly democratic thrust. Three men personified it: John Milton, John Lilburne, and Gerard Winstanley; each demonstrated the extent to which dissent had become political rather than religious.

Milton reveals the shift in perhaps its most ironic form. He spent his old age writing a poem intended to "justify the ways of God to men," but instead he made of Satan a Promethean hero, passionately rebellious, defiant of arbitrary authority, and a symbol of glorified individualism, to be taken up later by Byron and Blake and the whole Romantic school. Milton was probably more aware of being of the Devil's party than Blake imagined, certainly when he campaigned for the right to divorce and above all when, in *Aeropagitica,* he made the first great plea for freedom of speech and the press, the very foundation of the democratic process.

"Honest John" Lilburne was the leader of the Levellers, an extreme political left wing of Cromwell's New Model Army. While the generals were content to establish the principle of parliamentary government (which they shortly abandoned to set up the Protectorate) and had no intention of extending participation to any but men of property, large numbers of the rank and file of the army and even several younger officers—Lilburne was a colonel—believed that in a true democracy all men should take part in government. These people shared with later liberals the illusion that universal suffrage—the right of all men to vote—would ensure this. In fact, the Levellers anticipated the Chartist workingmen-reformers of the nineteenth century in demanding for every man maximum participation in a representative democracy, but only a few of them went further to speculate on the relationship between economics and freedom.

At the time, this fell to a group who called themselves the True Levellers, but who have become better known as Diggers. Their leader and principal theoretician, Gerard Winstanley, was a small merchant who had been ruined by the Civil War and whom poverty had set to thinking like a religious and political radical. Winstanley carried his radicalism so far as to declare that God was none other than Reason.

> Where does Reason dwell? He dwells in every creature, according to the nature and being of the creature, but supremely in man. Therefore man is called a rational creature. . . . This is the Kingdom of God within man.

It was this indwelling reason, according to Winstanley, that should dictate a man's social behaviour:

> For Reason tells him, is thy neighbor hungry and naked today, do thou feed him and clothe him, it may be thy case tomorrow and then he will be ready to help thee.

God was reason, but He was also "universal liberty," which led Winstanley to broaden his concept of democracy and attack economic power as well as political power. He also attacked power politics in the family, warning fathers and husbands that "their wives, children, servants, subjects, are their fellow creatures and have an equal privilege to share with them in the blessing of liberty." Finally, as clearly as any nineteenth-century socialist, Winstanley recognized how property oppresses and how it destroys freedom. He wrote his most important pamphlet, *The New Law of Righteousness,* in the beginning of 1649, and in it opposed to the world he saw around him the vision of a society where none would lay claim to property or rule his fellow man.

> But every one shall put their hands to till the earth and bring up cattle, and the blessing of the earth shall be common to all; when a man hath need of any corn or cattle, take from the next storehouse he meets with. There shall be no buying or selling, no fairs or markets, but the whole earth shall be a common treasury for every man, for the earth is the Lord's. . . . There shall be no lords over others, but everyone shall be a lord of himself, subject to the law of righteousness, reason and equity, which shall dwell and rule in him, which is the Lord.

This anarchist communist vision, which would have warmed Kropotkin's heart if he had read it, Winstanley and his followers almost immediately tried to embody by peaceful and direct revolutionary action. They went— forty of them—to a piece of unused waste land in Surrey, dug and sowed it, and called on the local people to join them and the landless men of England to imitate them. The story of their persecution, their obstinate passive resistance, their final failure, has been often told. The Diggers vanished so completely into the anonymous poor that even the date of Winstanley's death is unknown. But the vision he and his followers had and tried to practice was the most radical and far-reaching notion of democracy that appeared in his time and for generations after.

Unlike the British, the American Revolution was essentially a war of national liberation, and its leaders were much too enamored of fusty visions of the Roman Republic for much of importance in democratic theory to emerge. The principle of federalism (which may yet become the saving element in American political life) was introduced largely as a political expedient to reconcile conflicting interests among thirteen very different ex-colonial societies. And, as events have all too often shown, the powers given the executive have militated against the emergence of a mature and effectively functioning democracy in the United States.

The French Revolution, too, was primarily a political event, a power struggle in which the warring factions were little concerned with democracy as we must conceive it today, though they had their effect, no doubt, on the perversion of democracy over which General de Gaulle presided. Men like Saint-Just and Robespierre created a current of authoritarian, anti-democratic revolutionism that continued through Babeuf and Blanqui, and was incorporated, in various adaptations, by both Leninist communism and fascism.

The people's life in revolutionary Paris was far more truly democratic, and left a more interesting heritage, than the Grand Guignol in which the leaders strutted and bloodily vanished, since it was centered on the Commune, which embodied the principles of federalism much more directly than the American constitution. Paris was divided into sixty sections, in each of which citizens could meet in general assemblies to regulate and administer their affairs directly. Where delegation was necessary, it was done by appointing special commissioners subject to close scrutiny and recall. The institution of the French general assembly has echoed down through French radical history. It inspired the later and more celebrated Paris Commune of 1871, which hoped to establish a federalist society to replace the centralized bureaucratic order that has always negated France's pretensions to democracy. It was taken up by Pierre-Joseph Proudhon, the greatest of French socialists, as the basis for a theory of society where coercion from above would be supplanted by a federal organization developed from the simplest local level upwards, through communes and associations in which the people most involved in a problem would have the right to solve it themselves. In other words, the experience of the Paris Commune of 1793 was translated into the first clear theory of participatory democracy by Proudhon, writing in the 1860s.

In Great Britain, the reaction among writers on the left to the authoritarian excesses of the French Revolution was not to reject the democratic ideals with which the revolution had begun, but to find a way to effect social change without violence and coercion. The most brilliant and monumental theoretical work to emerge as a result was William Godwin's *Enquiry Concerning Political Justice,* published in 1793. *Political Justice* has long been regarded as one of the canonical works of anarchism, but it has a wider relevance. As one of the most exhaustive studies ever written on the evils of coercive government, it deserves to be recommended reading for all democrats.

Godwin had some extraordinary insights. He foresaw the technological revolution and realized that it might well bring, in his words, "something like a final close to the necessity of human labor," and he regarded this as a liberating trend. He followed Winstanley (though unaware of the fact) and anticipated later libertarian socialist and anarchist movements in recognizing how "accumulated property" helps perpetuate authoritarian politics. The merits of democracy over other known political systems he also recognized:

> Democracy restores to a man a consciousness of his value, teaches him by the removal of authority and oppression to listen only to the dictates of reason, gives him confidence to treat other men as his fellow beings, and induces him to regard them no longer as enemies against whom to be upon his guard, but as brethren whom it becomes him to trust.

Up to now, however, Godwin argues, democracy has clung to elaborate institutional mechanisms. He pleads for progressive simplification, for local governments united in a kind of federalism of autonomous parishes, with juries of arbitration as their only governing bodies, and with national assemblies convened as rarely as possible to deal with matters of common interest to the parishes. Little government, and that directly from the people in their own communities, was Godwin's idea of democracy.

But Godwin remained the theoretician, aloof from the practical task of creating the democracy he envisaged. Robert Owen, to some extent Godwin's disciple, was, on the other hand, an experimenter, and served as a catalyst for a number of movements that sought to give democracy a social and largely non-political base. Owen was disillusioned with the parliamentary reform movement in early nineteenth-century England, but unlike the Chartists, did not regard universal suffrage as the cure-all for political and social ills. He believed that men must begin immediately to build a new society within the old. After experimenting with enlightened factory management in Scotland, in 1825 he funded one of the most celebrated of American intentional communities—New Harmony. Owen believed that such experiments might spread by example and become the nuclei for a new social order.

Except for a few isolated examples, like Winstanley's seventeenth-century experiment, such communities, conceived as a means to change society, have been nineteenth and twentieth-century phenomena. Religious communities, of course, had existed before, and in the form of Christian and Buddhist monasteries, and among such dissenting groups as the Hutterites, still do. But those that survived were the most austere and authoritarian; in them, an over-riding desire to withdraw for the sake of personal salvation led to a way of life quite other than the norm of *l'homme moyen sensuel*. These communities were sustained—making it possible for those within to live and work together under a rigid but voluntary discipline—by an over-riding religious purpose that went far beyond the simple desire to live together amicably. Community was to them a means, not an end, and they took it in their stride as that.

The politically oriented intentional communities of the early nineteenth century were most frequently conceived by European social prophets, such as Robert Owen, and the French socialists Cabet and Fourier; but it was in the United States, where free land was still available, that most of the actual experiments were made. In all, between two and three hundred American socialist and anarchist communities were founded, some as late as the Depression of the 1930s, and many thousand people lived in them. Some communities collapsed within a few months; others survived into a second generation; but the only ones that still exist intact today are those originally inspired by a religious motive, which held the people together and in some measure insulated them from the outside world.

Three instances of intentional communities that have appeared in the present century perhaps deserve special note. The *kibbutzim* of Israel—the first one was founded in 1909 and still exists—are probably the most celebrated and undoubtedly the most successful of all intentional communities, for reasons we shall come to. Somewhat later, during the Spanish Civil War, many villages in the anarchist regions of Catalonia and Andalusia formed communes, socializing all property, abolishing the internal use of money, and sharing their produce. In one province alone, Levante, there were five hundred such communities, and there may have been thousands in Spain. Their history remains to be written, nor can their achievement be easily judged, for after two harvests most were overrun by Franco's armies.

The third notable example of a community movement arose at the outset of the Second World War among English pacifists. More than two hundred communities were attempted, varying in membership from three or four people to more than a hundred. Some lasted only a few months while others survived the war. I lived in two of those communities at the time, and visited many others. My experience and observation lead me to believe that most of them failed for a combination of reasons. The majority were agrarian, but few started with enough funds to farm even half-way efficiently. Few chose their members well, so they usually included some people temperamentally unfit for living in groups, some physically unfit for manual work, and others who were conscientious objectors and regarded the community merely as a refuge. Frugality, even when unnecessary, often became a fetish, and many communities were inefficient simply because of malnutrition. Privacy was virtually non-existent; people slept in dormitories, ate in common dining rooms, and were rarely alone. Generally speaking, the outside world was hostile, which created a feeling of intense isolation. This in turn forced the community to face inward, which, with the lack of privacy, meant that personal incompatibilities were dramatized and resentments became formidable. The bitterest feuds started over trivia that would have passed unnoticed in a normal life.

The communities that lasted longest, I noticed at the time, were those that made the greatest effort to keep in touch with the outside world. In Wales, for example, people were sympathetic to war resisters, and so the communities often succeeded in establishing good local relations. It also helped to develop some strong aim other than merely trying to live together peaceably; groups with a real enthusiasm and a practical aptitude for farming did much better than those who tilled the fields as a kind of discipline in the cause of a better way of life.

Here we come to the reason why the *kibbutzim* have, on the whole, been more successful than other intentional communities. They were conceived not as ends in themselves but as a way to build a whole society. Far from being detached from their immediate world, they existed in a climate generally favorable to their efforts. In all, it seems that at the right time and in the right way, intentional communities may be able to take their place within a larger society, but only if they set out with wider ends and with adequate practical resources, of which dedication to work at this stage is probably the most important.

Returning to the nineteenth century: New Harmony was one of the least successful of hundreds of intentional communities that were established in the United States and Canada then and after. To this day the small intentional community has remained a recurrent feature of libertarian radical movements. But New Harmony's failure did not disillusion Owen, and when he returned to England in 1827, he plunged first into the nascent cooperative movement, and then, in 1834, founded the largest of the early worker's organizations, the Grand National Consolidated Trades Union of Great Britain and Ireland, with a half million members.

In an essay of this length, the history of the cooperative and trade union movements cannot be sketched even roughly, but a few important points can be made. Owen was an impresario, not an originator, in these movements. Both originated among groups of working men, and so represent the arrival in the nineteenth century of the common at what Proudhon called their "political capacity." Not only did the cooperatives and early trade unions run parallel to existing political institutions; they had more than merely ameliorative aims. They cannot be lumped with modern trade unions or cooperative stores, which have become vested interests and are essentially conservative. The early cooperators saw their modest little shops as generating a spirit of mutual aid that would eventually permeate the whole society. As for the Grand National Consolidated Trades Union, its Rules and Regulations say it intended to bring about "A DIFFERENT ORDER OF THINGS, in which the really useful and intelligent part of society shall have the direction of its affairs, and in which well-directed industry and virtue shall meet their just distinction and reward, and vicious idleness its merited contempt and destitution." Like later labor movements, these early cooperatives and trade unions educated their members, this at a time when state schooling was in its most rudimentary stages. Thus they undertook one of the most vital functions of a mature democracy.

An equally innovative step forward took place in 1864 when English trade unionists, who were distant followers of Robert Owen and French mutualist workingmen, who in turn were direct followers of Pierre-Joseph Proudhon, came together to establish the International Workingmen's Association, better known as the First International. Contrary to a stubborn legend, Karl Marx was not one of its actual founders. But the First International collapsed in 1872 when its libertarian elements—the English trade unionists and Latin anarchists—refused to accept an exclusively political direction from Karl Marx and his central European followers. Marx, despite the recent tendency of the New Left to think otherwise, has a negative place in the history of democracy. It is true that at times he is ambiguous and can sometimes be interpreted as advocating a democratic way towards socialism. But on looking at his actions and those of his followers at the First International, this interpretation becomes impossible. The First International broke apart when Marx attempted to restrict it to political action while the membership had pluralisic ideas which have become an invariable feature in theories of radical democracy ever since.

In fact, since the breakup of the First International it is mainly outside Marxist movements that we must look for the flexible pluralist trends which alone seem viable alternatives in the world of modern technology. They are trends that emphasize means rather than ends, leaving the future open to those who must eventually shape it. Among them were the trade unionists and syndicalists, who, by insisting on their right to strike, proved that democratic procedure could lie nearer to home than a parliament elected every four or five years. Also the suffragettes and conscientious objectors of the First World War, who showed that civil disobedience could give powerful expression to the views of a dedicated minority, must be included. Then there is Gandhi, who made out of this a weapon to bring about political change in India with a minimum of violence and hatred; and Peter Kropotkin, the anarchist who considered the problems of urban congestion and rural devastation, which concern us so deeply half a century later, and who suggested means of integrating rural and urban living. In the early stages of the Spanish Civil War factory workers in Barcelona and the peasants of Andalusia expropriated and efficiently managed factories, transport systems, and rural estates, proving that the management of production by the producers was a feasible form of industrial and agrarian organization. Finally, long before the beats and hipsters came on the scene, the anarchistically inclined artists and writers of the 1890s, so-called decadents, asserted the individual's right to explore experience and develop forms of expression without censorship, whether from government or society. The rapid liberation of literature and art from the shackles of convention has indeed been of prime importance to the evolution of democracy, opening the way to a corresponding liberation in manners and morals. For example, recent legislation in Great Britain concedes the individual's right to certain forms of homosexual behavior and to abortion.

In the last decade, we have at last seen emerging on the Left a pluralist attitude that recognizes the apparently dissident currents of the past as less contradictory than they once seemed. This awareness underlies the heterogeneity of contemporary protest movements, in which socialists and anarchists, liberals and pacifists and Fidelistas, squares and flower children, work together for a variety of causes from civil rights to Viet Nam: causes espoused by a conscience awakened to the fact that in our time rigid orthodox democracy must give way to heretical democracy. "As for adopting the ways which the state has provided for remedying the evil," said Thoreau, greatest of all American heretical democrats, "I know of no such ways. They take too much time, and a man's life will be spent."

The sense that society must become open, so that groups within it—now most urgently blacks and the young—can be accepted on their own terms and forge their own futures, has become integral to the notion of radical democracy. But this sense is only a beginning; the rest belongs to the future, on whose frontier this essay, being concerned with history, ends.

It is no accident that authoritarians, elitists, and liberal democrats gener-
ally share a cynical view of man. To seriously propose a participatory de-
mocracy, we must seek another vision.

Calhoun's critique of the sociological and behaviorist approach to hu-
man psychology raises key questions about human nature. It is an indica-
tion of where we are that more questions are raised than answered. Yet the
direction is clear. Society must become more open on all levels before there
can be effective participation on the political level. When men are condi-
tioned to be passive by repressive social institutions, the elitists' fear of
general political participation is probably justified. To speak to these fears,
a society of participation must start with close inter-personal relations, work
up through the institutions of the neighborhood, and, most critically, re-
structure the institutions of work.

That participation is directly related to mental health has been shown
by Erich Lindemann in The Urban Condition *and by Bruno Bettelheim in*
The Empty Fortress. *Ghetto residents lapse into apathy and passivity as a*
result of their pervasive sense that nothing can be done; personality inte-
gration does not take place, and there is no sense of connection between
sustained action and the achievement of worthwhile goals. For the infant,
it is not a question of simply being provided with the necessities of life, or
even with the necessary affection; if food, caring, and love are not related
causally to the infant's manifestation of his needs, he fails to develop the
sense that he can affect his environment. This failure to develop a sense of
causal efficacy is strongly correlated with a lapse into autism and total fail-
ure to respond.

The development in the New Left, and especially in the Resistance, of
various forms of group action and solidarity show an awareness of how
changed personal relationships have a bearing on the achievement of
broader goals. Affinity groups first developed among the anarcho-syndical-
ists in Spain; they are a common unit of organization in the "movement,"
among the more communitarian-minded. Also, Resistance communes have
developed out of a need for mutual support in opposing the military draft.
Here, people experiment consciously with new life styles, out of a sense
that they may be achieving not only freer, more committed personal lives,
but also showing the way to a juster, less violent and oppressive society.

No theory of radical democracy is valid unless it can counter the wide-
spread sentiment that "people can be trusted so far and no further." Along
with some of the other contributors, Calhoun demonstrates that there are

new insights in psychology that challenge the notion of passive, obedient man, incapable of self-determination. He draws on a number of theorists, in anthropology particularly. Konrad Lorenz, Raymond Dart, and Robert Ardrey maintain the "mark-of-Cain" theory of man; Ashley Montagu and Leslie White, on the contrary, react against crude Darwinism and ask us to consider the concept of harmony as an ideal of human relations. The latter seek to substantiate the cooperative nature of man.

The Human Material

Don Calhoun

There is little point in talking about participatory democracy unless we have reason to believe human beings are capable of it. At first glance, it hardly seems likely. Radical democracy presupposes a capacity for cooperative social behavior of a kind that history has only rarely revealed. From marriage to the international society of nations, man appears but barely able to hold his existing social groupings together in the face of inner disruptive forces. His best achievement appears to be a sort of precarious antagonistic cooperation. Voluntary communities, the specific model for a participatory society, seem for the most part to exhibit people's inability to get along with each other. It seems justifiable to suspect that participatory democracy is beyond "human nature."

But despite the apparent evidence, I do not believe this is the case. A proper perspective on the nature of man will give us a basis for going ahead with visions of a more personal and democratic society. Hope seems to rest on a re-examination of the cohesive forces in man (which can hold a participatory society together) and the disruptive forces (which can tear it asunder). And a reasonably hopeful assessment of these can be derived after examining four major views of human nature: (1) Judaeo-Christian, (2) sociological, (3) Freudian, and (4) Reichian.

The heart of the Judaeo-Christian view is that man is the inborn bearer of both love and original sin. The first will draw and bind him to his fellow beings; the second impel him to use, hurt, or destroy them. But man was not always so split. In the Garden before the Fall—when he tasted of the Tree of Knowledge—he was innocent and free of sin. Adam fell, says the Judaeo-Christian ethic, and his sinfulness was transmitted to all his descendants. The implication for participatory democrats is not much different from that drawn by John Adams: "Whosoever would form a state, and make proper laws for the government of it, must presume that all men are bad by nature."

The Jew, it is said, endeavors to submerge his sinfulness in the struggle for the Kingdom of God on earth. The Christian tries to become a new man, to erase Adam's sin, by taking up the cross of Christ. In neither case, however, is the wickedness really eliminated. Faith and commitment may enable love to secure an uneasy upper hand, but sin is still there, forever threatening to erupt and disrupt. Love may save one's individual soul, but it is not likely that the world can really be made much better. For man remains, at heart, "bad by nature." In the words of Reinhold Niebuhr, hardly an apologist for social inaction: "There is no force in human culture, no technique in government, and no grace in the human spirit which can completely overcome the power of human egoism. . . ."

The sociological view of man starts from quite different premises. To the Judaeo-Christian view, human nature is inborn and hardly touchable by social experience. To the sociological view, on the contrary, experience is virtually everything. Man is a Lockeian blank slate, on which life may write what it will. Or, one hopes, what *we* will. If man is bad, it is because society has made him so; and what society has done, society can undo. This is the view that inspired the Enlightenment and the French Revolution. It is the premise of behaviorism, and of the Dewey-led revolt against "instinct," which found human nature to be rooted in "conduct" rather than in inborn drive. Although its hold has somewhat weakened, it is the predominant view of sociologists.

The sociological view underlies the whole Marxist framework of thought, with its faith that everything in man can be remade by proper conditioning. Lenin's view is worlds removed from Adams': ". . . freed from capitalist . . . exploitation, people will gradually become accustomed to the observance of the elementary rules of social life that have been known for centuries and repeated for thousands of years in all school books. . . ." This view underlies a large part of democratic socialist thought, and is probably the underlying view of human nature held by participatory democrats. In my view, it is only half (or, perhaps, three-fourths) true.

With Freud, the viewpoint of human nature shifts from social creation back to innate drive. The key concept is the libido, or life impulse. The libido has its specific genital goal, but it also affects all energy "cathected" to love and work, indeed all energy oriented to the outer world. It is the binding force in all social relationships, but it is also the source of disruptive and destructive impulses. For human civilization, in Freud's view, requires "the non-gratification [suppression, repression or something else?] of powerful instinctual tendencies." The ensuing hostility and aggression always threaten social relationships. Moreover, as Freud saw it, there is a conflict between objects of love. If one loves his mate and family fully, he exhausts most of his capacity for love, and has little left for other social groups. If he devotes himself (perhaps as a participatory democrat) to wider groupings and loyalties, he must sacrifice the more intense experience of family love. In either case, there is frustration, conflict, and further hostility.

Furthermore, said Freud, frustrations of the love impulse are not the only source of disruption: ". . . men are not gentle, friendly creatures wishing for love, who simply defend themselves when attacked, but . . . a powerful measure of desire for aggression has to be reckoned as part of their instinctual endowment." All group life must contend with this explosive force, which cannot be essentially diminished by any social improvement. With Freud we return to the Judaeo-Christian doctrine of original sin, restated in terms of observable biological drives and sociological conflicts. As with the orthodox version, the social prognosis is cheerless. With Freud we have only the hope that love will somehow be able to "maintain himself alongside of his equally immortal adversary."

In Wilhelm Reich, we swing back again toward sociology, but with a difference. We do not give up biology. Reich's sociological view recognizes the body. Man seeks primarily for "love, work, and knowledge." His search is expressed in a bodily striving for free functioning, and ultimately in the urge to unify the body in loving, orgastic surrender. Man is also plagued by overwhelming urges to destroy. These are not, however, innate, but the product of social frustration. They originate in the repressions of childhood, but also in the work frustrations of an exploitative economy, in the difficulty of sexual gratification in crowded urban tenements, in an almost total confrontation with a life-denying culture.

These frustrations give rise to *biopathy*—a crippling of the life function on the deepest social-psychological-biological level. The victim becomes physically "armored" against his culture and against his own urgings, trapping himself in an unrelieved muscular tension. The autonomic processes, which regulate the elemental life functions, become permanently deranged. The concept of biopathic derangement encompasses the "original sin" of Judaeo-Christian theology and the "death instinct" of Freud. The derangement in man can be healed, but only if we will recognize the depth of man's frustrated needs, and the truly radical magnitude of the cultural revolution necessary to gratify them. "Only the liberation of the natural capacity for love in human beings can master their sadistic destructiveness," Reich concludes.

Most of the central issues of the study of human nature are posed by these four views. Taken together, what do they suggest to us about the cohesive and disruptive elements in man?

There cannot be much doubt that the cohesive force, love, is the deepest element in human beings. Life seeks harmony with its environment, and experiences disharmony as tension and pain. In fact, life may be seen as the dynamic reaching-out of matter toward its environment. Let us look at this search under several aspects: (1) play, (2) symbiosis, (3) mutual aid, (4) empathy, and (5) commitment.

The most elemental cohesive life activity is *play*—spontaneous, purposeless satisfaction in engagement with one's environment. Before work and purpose enter, living organisms move, leap, gambol, manipulate, explore, sing, dance—all spontaneous outgoings of self toward the world. Everything else grows out of this.

Play, like all life activities, involves *symbiosis*—interdependence with other life, and with non-life. We begin life in the womb as part of another, we continue at the breast, and we can never be separated from our environment. According to Kinsey, the first impulse of any living organism, upon touching another object, is to press against it. The libido, said Freud, presupposes a second person as its object. An isolated living being is a self-contradiction and an impossibility. To live is to experience some kind of mutual relationship, distorted though it may be.

One aspect of symbiosis is *mutual aid*. Kropotkin has told us that social animals depend for group survival upon patterns of cooperation. Man, physically one of the most vulnerable of species, yet dominates the planet, largely because of his habits of mutual help, his propensity for meshing his actions and goals into those of his group.

Because life is an inseparable part of its environment, its experience is always one of inescapable *empathy,* not only with its own species but with everything else. On the deepest level, we imitate internally the responses of our environment. There is no exposure to joy without some internal experience of joy, no exposure to pain in others without some internal experience of pain. As poets have known, empathy applies not only to life around us, but to inanimate nature also. The empathic response is there even if the object of empathy is present only symbolically in picture, story, or news account. Donne referred not to a special spiritual state, but to an elementary biological and psychological fact, when he told us that "any man's death diminishes me, because I am involved in mankind."

The empathic involvement of man in mankind is a force for *commitment,* the impulse to reduce life's total pain and increase its joy. Here is the core of religious insight: one can realize himself only as he makes mankind's, and the universe's, cause his own. There is no other way. In the words of Augustine, "our hearts are restless till they rest in Thee." Commitment, like empathy, is not a special act above and beyond ordinary life. It is rather the realization of our deepest nature as biological, psychological, and social beings living in a society and a cosmos.

When we consider love as a force in society, we are prone to speak almost apologetically, as though it were something etherial, or sentimental, and not quite part of the guts of life. On the contrary, the outgoing and binding forces, from the spontaneity of play to the deepest spiritual self-commitment, are the very center of life. Love is life itself, and all else ultimately serves it, or substitutes for it.

How far the latent cohesive impulses develop in a person depends upon his social experience, and in particular, his experience in specific groups. As a beginning, Charles Horton Cooley described clearly the way the cooperative "group-nature" aspect of social life arises in primary groups:

> It is the nature which is developed and expressed in those simple, face-to-face groups that are somewhat alike in all societies; groups of the family, the playground, and the neighborhood. In the essential similarity of these is to be found the basis, in experience, for similar ideas and sentiments in the human mind. In these, eveywhere, human nature comes into existence. Man does not have it at birth; he cannot acquire it except through fellowship, and it decays in isolation.

Not all primary groups, however, develop a really social nature. Later studies have stressed the role of family and peer-groups in shaping either cooperative or disruptive personalities. The famous "authoritarian personality" studies showed how a loveless and anxiety-ridden family environment can cripple the social qualities. Recent studies by political scientists have indicated that institutional adult groups may be as important as primary groups. Gabriel Almond and Sidney Verba, in a study of political participation in five countries, found that a positive attitude of trust and confidence in one's social environment is correlated with childhood participation in family decisions, participation in school decisions, participation in job decisions, and participation in political life. Cohesive forces seem to be nurtured by participatory democracy, as they in turn nurture it.

On the other side of the picture, there is no good reason to think, with Freud and the doctrine of original sin, that hostility exists in man *for its own sake*. It is obvious that there are hostile, divisive, and destructive impulses that have reached a form so virulent that they may destroy man. But these all originate in impulses whose purpose is to serve life, and love, by protecting the individual's existence or interest, and that of his group. Aggression is not a primary drive, but the servant of the cohesive forces. Even the most distorted forms of disruption and violence originate in the impulse to protect or expand life.

The whole question of the disruptive impulse is hopelessly obscured by sloppy use of the term "aggression." All kinds of things that have only the remotest connection are lumped together under the term, and the most dubious generalizations drawn. It is well to point here to the fact that the all-purpose term, "aggression," may refer to at least seven clearly different forms of activity, and no doubt many more:

(1) simple self-assertion—the tendency of organisms to move *toward* or *against* their environment;

(2) food-getting activities, which may involve objective violence but not necessarily subjective anger or hostility;

(3) angry violence, whether by individuals or groups;

(4) active non-violence, by individuals or groups;

(5) depersonalized violence, which makes up a large part of modern warfare;

(6) neurotic self-aggrandizement at the expense of others;

(7) sado-masochistic destructiveness, neurotic or psychotic, whether by groups or individuals.

Clearly any discussion of the man's readiness for participatory democracy, should distinguish among these different forms. Such distinction would guard us against generalizations like Robert Ardrey's, that modern juvenile delinquency and war grow directly out of the fact that man's evolutionary predecessors hunted with clubs. We could more easily reject the assumption that the proclivity of infants for temper tantrums informs us on the causes of Belsen or Hiroshima, or the equation of defending one's grandmother from rape with the napalming of jungle villages.

Obviously our human material always contains inborn potential for disruptive behavior. The sympathetic branch of the autonomic nervous system, in concert with the endocrine glands gears the body for various forms of "aggression." Aggressive responses are instigated or channeled through centers in the brain, some of which have been experimentally located. Writers like Ardrey and Konrad Lorenz, in his best-selling book *On Aggression,* have described some elemental social functions of the "aggressive" mechanisms: (1) fighting behavior among animals tends to equip them for defense against out-groups; (2) competition for mates may select strains best fitted for group defense; (3) fighting may be a way of establishing one's status in the group "pecking order"; (4) fighting may be a way of defending group or individual territory, which appears to be a natural tendency of animals.

It is questionable, however, how relevant such primitive concepts of "aggression" are to the problem of disruptive behavior in the modern human world. The fittest, even for most military jobs, are not likely to be recruited in hand-to-hand combat. Simple fighting behavior has little to do with modern national defense. The fact that competitive status systems are relatively absent among the most primitive human groups suggests that aggressive status-seeking is not universal "human nature." The increasing reliance on the military draft indicates that the spontaneous impulse to defend territory is a declining factor in modern war. We shall apparently have to look elsewhere to explain the prevalence of disruptive behavior today.

Does the answer perhaps lie in our reactions to the uncertainty, brevity, and frustrating quality of life itself? Paul Tillich and others have suggested that our life situation as such gives rise to an existential anxiety. Can it be that this expresses itself also as a free-floating, existential hostility? Perhaps, but observation of real people raises doubts. Happy, gratified individuals do not usually express their sense of existential tragedy in disruptive, destructive behavior, but in compassionate identification with their fellow-travelers in life. It is those who do not, or cannot, enjoy what life does give who become "existentially" hostile about what it does not.

Perhaps the answer lies in the inevitable frustrations of social life as such. Freud believed that the culture requires progressive sexual frustration, and thus increasing hostility, and that unused sexual energy is sublimated into cultural tasks. Reich's answer makes more sense: the sexually happy person is the most productive person, and all sexual frustration must be reflected in work disturbances. Freud's claim that family ties conflict with ties to the larger society is based on a similar error. It is true that everyone has a limited amount of time and energy, and it is often difficult or impossible to give as much as one would like to both family and other responsibilities. However, it is again clear that a happy family life is the soundest basis for constructive social participation, and that without it social activity is likely to be disturbed.

Where we most need to look seems obvious: at the frustrations peculiar to our society. Although he did not draw all the implications, Reich's genius lay in pointing up the depth of the collision between the needs of human beings and an authoritarian, life-negating culture. This he was able to do because his emphasis on the somatic basis of the conflict led him far deeper than either the "sociologists" or Freud—or even, in many ways, than the religionists. We can expand on Reich and name five critical aspects of this collision, which are responsible for a tremendous amount of disruptive hostility.

(1) *Work experience in a class society.* Where the means and products of one's livelihood are owned or controlled by someone else for his own private gain, the result is alienation from one's work. Alienation from work cuts to the heart of life itself, since work makes up a large part of life, and should be one's major way of expressing one's identity as a creative human being. It makes no substantial difference whether the controlling class be a capitalist bourgeoisie or a communist bureaucracy. The followers of Max Weber contend that alienation is inevitable in any industrial society, and is not merely a result of class division. Industrialism as such certainly poses problems that a participatory democracy must face. But as we get people's livelihoods out from under any exploitive controlling class, they will begin to feel that the work process and its results are *theirs.*

(2) *Alienation from nature.* This is most clearly dramatized in our drift toward a completely urban society. Life in a steel-concrete-glass jungle is not compatible with the rhythms of living organisms. We have begun to study scientifically the direct psychological and physiological results of air pollution, noise, and physical crowding upon man and other animals. There is already evidence that both crowding and noise may directly produce destructive behavior. These are certainly only part of the disruptive elements in urban living.

(3) *The garrison state.* Military conscription disrupts the life of every boy and man on a deep level, for it robs him of his essential right to self-determination. It introduces an element of helplessness into the life of every parent. The nuclear age has introduced a totally new element into human

experience: for the first time, mankind has become exterminable. As object, man lives within the target sights of nuclear weapons that can be unleashed by political forces beyond his control. As subject in a military nation, he is forced to pay taxes for genocidal military ventures and perhaps for nuclear armament which pursues the national "interest" through the blackmail threat of ending human history. The disruption of the life process is incalculable.

(4) *The food supply*. Emotional health and stability depend upon adequate nutrition. A statement by Linus Pauling suggests that a good deal of mental illness may actually be a cerebral scurvy, a cerebral pellagra, or a cerebral pernicious anemia. Despite the rising standard of living, adequate food is becoming increasingly hard to get. In our urban civilization, food becomes a commodity. Food is almost universally packaged, processed, refined, and adulterated. Half of the calories in the American diet now come from nutritionally incomplete white flour and white sugar. Mechanized farming produces huge yields but the food values of the product decrease. Modern farming poisons its growing yields with insecticides and other chemicals which usually cannot be completely removed. DDT offers a well-documented case of widespread poisoning by a substance known to produce nervous disturbance.

(5) *Sexual frustration and repression*. Freud claimed that the sexual function of civilized man is "seriously disabled." We are passing through a sexual revolution, which has lessened the sexual repression and ignorance of children, increased pre-marital and extra-marital sexuality, and removed some of the barriers to a frank discussion of sex. But it is doubtful that the basic sexual frustrations have been overcome for people over thirty, and it is unlikely that many young people actually achieve gratifying sex experience, for our culture still remains at heart anti-sexual, and sexual experience continues to be a deep source of disruptive and destructive impulses.

What can we conclude? As the great religions have all told us, love and commitment are the strongest force in man. But the orthodox view of original sin is static, mechanical, and inadequate. The sociologists are right in seeing the origins of "sin" primarily in social misarrangements. They are shallow in ignoring deep innate needs in man whose frustration produces "sin." Freud furnishes a corrective, but, like the religious versions of original sin, his view is too static. It is based upon an essentially puritanical antithesis of sexuality and culture, and passes too lightly over the remediable frustrations in present culture. These Reich places in opposition to a human organism deeper and more complete than Freud's. He lays the groundwork for, although he does not complete, a rounded confrontation of man with present culture.

The cohesive and disruptive forces in the human material are, then, a function of the kind of society participatory democracy seeks to revolutionize, and of the kind of society it hopes to construct. To succeed as human beings we require a self-governing social order that returns work to the workers, returns everybody to a life closer to nature, eliminates the centralized military state, restores natural nutrition, and liberates sexual love. We also require, as we have seen, participation in decision-making in both childhood and adult groups.

In the beginning, we must work against the distortion of human nature by social authoritarianism and suppression. As we succeed in relieving that suppression, we will find the human material becoming more cooperative and malleable. The ultimate problem is not an intractable human nature; it is how to raise corrupted man by his bootstraps long enough to change the institutions that have corrupted him.

The argument presented in this article, that groups must be the basic socio-political unit in a society of participation, derives fundamentally from the belief that it is only in the face-to-face group that the process of decision-making can be found in its complete form. A connection is also made between the idea of the group as an essential element of participatory democracy, and the ideas that undergird this notion at the level of individual psychology. When the false antithesis between the self-realization of the individual and the demands of group action is broken down, it is possible to see how a society can be reconstituted along cooperative and synergistic lines. Only when society is reorganized at its basic level and groups are given the functional relevance they deserve, can the broader problems of a participatory democracy be dealt with.

In other words, organizations must be re-structured from the inside before they can legitimately be made part of an overall socio-political system that is itself democratic. Otherwise the familiar arguments against participatory democracy would obtain: that if one decentralized in the South, for example, this would simply increase oppression of the blacks, and that decentralization of itself does not necessarily mean more democracy.

It may seem that the extensive problems of our present social and political system cannot be solved simply by reforms of the structure of that system. But further insight into the ways in which structure determines how organizations and institutions function can be derived from the critique of present organizational style in Benello's other article, "Organization, Conflict, and Free Association." The principle underlying this sort of structural analysis is that in the long run the goals, programs, and day-to-day functions of organizations are inseparable from their structure. Organizations whose structure permits free interplay of human purposes are at the same time organizations capable, as organizations, of realizing those purposes; organizations that coerce by virtue of their bureaucratic rigidity serve organizational goals that themselves are usually anti-human and destructive.

Benello's examples of revised socio-political structures are intended to be no more than suggestions; their value is the value of models that embody the principles of participation and show how they can speak to some of the more unattractive deformations of the present system. It is ridiculous to believe that socio-political analysis should limit itself to reforms that are clearly conceivable in the short run, for many reforms that seemed utopian and inconceivable in one decade have been enacted in the next. It is un-

likely that the sort of structural reforms advocated in this article are just around the corner, however. Democratization of the internal stucture of the great corporate baronies and their feeder institutions is likely to come about only through revolution, or from an intensification, far greater than anything presently imaginable, of disenchantment with the society produced by the great corporations.

In the meantime, if grass roots strategies oriented to community-building can recognize that structure and functioning are closely interconnected, they can devote their energies at once to attacking the issues of urban blight, corporate and municipal irresponsibility, rascism, and exploitation, and show how in the long run these can be cured only by new structures of community and corporate control. Thus strategies that are seemingly reformist (in that they focus on specific and manageable issues within existing communities and in the work place) can, at the same time, be radical when they relate the needed substantive reforms to changes in organizational and community structure.

Group Organization and Socio-political Structure
C. George Benello

While the problems of advanced industrial societies have received a good deal of attention, solutions that in any way represent structural alternatives are not considered with the same degree of interest, in part because it is felt that the obvious issues of racism, war, exploitation, and inequality are the ones to deal with, and in part because revolution is seen as the only therapy to the more structural problems. The attempt in this essay will be to focus on some socio-political principles having to do with group organization, and to show how they are relevant to the problems of advanced industrial societies.

Only a dialectical view of the relation of man to society is adequate to an understanding of the social order. Where Hobbesian or other individualist views are taken, or where Hegelian statist and collectivist views are maintained, the central features of social existence are lost. In the dialectic of man and the social order, the key problem is the meeting point: there must exist the possibility for individual goals to be enlarged and more fully realized by integration with social purpose. Che Guevara and many of the new Marxist humanists have pointed out that man has more opportunities for self-realization and for freedom when his own welfare is closely linked with that of his fellow men.

Collectivist visions, which deify the state, and individualist views, which emphasize the automatic harmonization of self interest, ignore the dialectic between the individual and the collective as well as its locus. The locus for the harmonization of individual purpose and social purpose is fundamentally the face-to-face group, which stands as an intermediary between the individual and larger forms of association. However, to conceive of the group only as this is to lose sight of its primacy. Interactionist psychology, starting with George Herbert Mead and John Dewey, has stressed the social nature of the self and with it the fact that what is given primordially is not the individual, from which society is then constructed, but the self and society as correlative terms. As Mead has shown, the self evolves out of interaction with others; moreover, it is not simply influenced by that interaction, but is the product of it.

However, when the self develops a stable sense of its own identity, it is because of the stability and continuity of ongoing face-to-face relationships with family, peers, friends, and community figures. As the child grows into adolescence and adulthood, affective relationships develop. Beyond these, personal growth requires the development of competencies, and also a capacity to identify with spheres of reference beyond family and home. For this to happen these immediate groupings must be functionally related to the broader areas of the social order. Moreover, groups exist not simply for the sake of sociability; if they are to be growth-promoting they must also be the locus for significant activities of work, politics, culture, and education.

The crucial fact about most advanced industrial societies, and certainly about our own in North America, is that the key activities of the society are carried out by large, impersonal, bureaucratized organizations, where personal relations lack the quality of wholeness found in small functional groups. Hence local associations such as the church, the fraternal association, kinship groups, or voluntary organizations, become primarily places where a weak sociability is maintained. The sociability is weak because significant relationships are built most naturally on joint involvement in significant common purposes; to the extent that local associations no longer have this power the relationships they engender are trivial.

What is engendered by the large bureaucratic organizations that dominate our social system is an inflexibility of purpose and a vested interest in the status quo. Relationships between the various institutional orders—and consequently between individuals—thus become a matter of conflict or at best, compromise, rather than a matter of harmonization of interests. This in turn reinforces the ideology on which our society is based. It may be called an ideology of the market system, and its thesis is that social purpose arises automatically out of the pursuit of selfish interest. In economics the thesis is reflected in competition based on the laws of supply and demand. For the mature corporation, as Galbraith has shown in *The New Industrial State,* these laws no longer operate; nevertheless the model is maintained. No other system of harmonizing private incentive with social purpose is considered possible, much less useful.

In its broader ramifications the market ideology is much less noticed. Yet the approach to politics is basically the same as the approach to economics. The liberal individualist's view of political man, deriving from nineteenth-century thought, sees him as a passive political consumer, casting his vote in the market place of political figures and ideas, much as economic man is viewed as a passive economic consumer, seeking to maximize his gain. Social interaction is seen in terms of trade-offs and bargaining between interest groups and individuals whose interests are ultimately irreconcilable and capable only of being compromised. Collective bargaining between labor and management is based on this model, and, in a slightly different way, so is the legal system, with its structure of conflict between irreconcilable opponents. Moreover, pluralist theories on the safeguarding of political freedom through stalemates between major interest groups, also presuppose the same irreconcilability of interests. It is a dismal view, a zero sum vision of the societal game, and one that contradicts the individual experience of essential love and friendship.

For the self to develop fully out of the dialectic of the individual and the social order, the possibility of reconciling individual need with social purpose must exist. But the social order seems alien and dehumanizing, and so the individual often remains isolated, his social self embryonic and stultified. The value of the face-to-face group, hence, lies in its ability to nurture and integrate individual needs rather than, as in the case of bureaucratic schools and factories, reshaping the individual to meet the needs of the institution. Worthwhile group action not only nurtures the social nature of the self, but carries forth significant human tasks requiring the coordination of joint efforts. The capacity to reconcile individual need with social purpose has been called synergy; involved are the individual needs for status, recognition, and achievement. When a group is synergistic, it has the capacity to create a situation in which the private world of need, dream, and desire and the public world of social reality are harmonized. The realization that the two worlds can be harmonized is a key experience in the process of psychological growth.

The process of self-formation and development, which the group alone renders possible, may also be viewed in psychoanalytic terms, for the group becomes the matrix wherein the basic battles for self-existence can take place. The Oedipal conflict is now generally seen as the problem of coming to terms with authority; the group, by providing an authority basis that is neither arbitrary nor alien, can allow this conflict to be settled. Further, the individual can learn to identify with larger areas of social purpose and in the process lose his fear of a consequent loss of personal identity, of being swamped in the larger whole. As the individual learns that he need not only be acted upon but can act upon the group and influence it, the bridge between Self and Other is crossed, and the possibility of identification with larger wholes is experienced. Next, (and this is much less recognized), the possibility of transcendence is encountered. This is the positive side of identification, where the individual, far from being engulfed by the larger whole, experiences the enlargement and consequent transcendence of his original narrow self in a sphere of shared value that transcends self interest.

In addition to providing a forum wherein the individual can exorcise his subjective demons and in the process develop into selfhood, the group also enables an individual to exorcise a false social consciousness. When the conditions for psychic growth are present, the native initiative of infancy is maintained, and the individual becomes conscious that social constructs experienced by the child as absolutes, since he has had no hand in shaping them, may in fact be altered by the impact of his will.

For many, however, the attainment of this level of awareness is impossible, because the general conditions for growth are absent through some form of psychic deprivation, or because the social institutions specifically resist the possibility of active roles, especially on the part of the young. Schools encourage passive acquiescence and demand obedience to rules the child has had no hand in shaping. Other social institutions are equally authoritarian.

As a result, a negative dialectic of enslavement evolves. The new generation sees its proper relationship to the social order as passive and social constructs are reified as absolutes, unchangeable features of the social landscape. This consciousness is then externalized and passed on, and in the process the real dialectic in which men shape their social institutions as well as being shaped by them, is lost. The end result is a pervasive sense of powerlessness. This cycle is a powerful force for maintenance of the status quo, and to change it is not easy; where people are psychically deprived, an attitude of dependency is created, and the social order is reified. The institutions reinforce this by their own authoritarian structure.

Task groups, if capable of organizing so as to address themselves to social issues, can liberate people from their sense of powerlessness, for isolation is an essential ingredient of the sense of powerlessness and the reification of social reality. People remain stuck in a milieu, as Mills has suggested, and fail to see that their personal problems reflect social issues. When such people come together to form a group, they perceive that their problems are in fact shared problems, about which something can be done. Thus the image of the individual helpless against the all-powerful forces of society is replaced in the member's minds by the image of the group, working from a shared sense of social need, and capable of modifying the social environment that has caused the problem. But for the group to be effective it must develop a sense of the political dynamics that affect it—the workings of local power structures, and ways in which they can be moved. In the development of common purpose, and of an awareness that it can act back, the group becomes an agent of change, freed from its bondage to the status quo.

Once the newly acquired dialectical consciousness is acted on and even a slight modification of the institutional pattern is achieved, the perception of the relation of the individual to the social order is changed once and for all, and the social order is de-mythologized. The individual is made aware of a new-found freedom, is aware that he can act back, and that what he had considered norms—which came into conflict with his own needs for spontaneity and self-expression—were in fact false consciousness. Thus, in addition to gaining a new perspective on the social order, the individual gains a new perspective on himself, and new energy to act on the social order.

When institutions, laws and customs are perceived as man-made, to be judged by their capacity to fulfill human needs, then their legitimacy can be called into question. Where legitimacy is understood as having necessarily to do with the capacity to fulfill human needs, the encrustations of tradition, legality, ideology, and religion can be called into question, and the institutions can once more be returned to man.

In all likelihood, new and powerful group movements will arise in society as centralized technological advance erodes traditional institutions and depersonalizes the population. Such movements will be highly ideological or messianic, perhaps semi-religious like the Japanese Soka Gakkai or the Black Muslims. They will be successful to the extent that they provide an overall critique of the society and provide an antidote to fragmentation by creating an interrelated cell structure of groups. Such movements will possess an inherent power derived from intense commitment that is far greater than such loosely organized institutions as the church, labor unions, or political parties. In Japan the Soka Gakkai, with a membership of well over one-tenth of the nation, commands far more resources, greater commitment, and more members, than any of the conventional institutions.

The ideological-religious cast and intensity of commitment in these groups threaten the presuppositions of liberal democracy, which depends, according to orthodox pluralist theory, on the trade-offs of various interest groups, none of which enlist the total commitment of its members. And yet, as De Tocqueville saw, the fascist potential of modern mass democracies is an inherent, not accidental, feature of them, since it is based on a liberal market ideology, which sees freedom primarily in negative terms—freedom from outside interference—and does not confront the problem of social purpose. Built into this ideology is an unwillingness to exercise direct authority; this creates a power vacuum based on the inherent psychological need for a more coherent and comprehensive framework of orientation and devotion. Social purpose is then forged on the level of the nation-state through grandiose space races, neo-imperialistic designs, and mobilizations against alien ideologies. The fragmentation of the nuclear structure of society is compensated for by various forms of spurious unification and pseudo-*gemeinschaft* engendered by the state.

As the nuclear structure is eroded and the legitimacy of existing institutions brought into question, a climate of lawlessness develops. The basis of the social contract breaks down as people see that the society is incapable of responding to legitimate demands. When the game turns out not to be worth playing, the rules are abandoned, in individual acts of lawlessness as well as in acts of organized disobedience. The response of the state to the breakdown of the social order is clearly seen in the rule of the emperors in

Rome: repressive legislation developed rapidly, and attempts at enforcment led to a reign of terror that accelerated the breakdown of social order and trust. The breakdown was stupendous: the major cities of the empire were left almost totally depopulated as people fled the totalitarian repression to live in caves and in the forest as the civilization crumbled.

When the state is incapable of combating the disintegrative forces of the society, the process of deinstitutionalization caused by technology, and the resulting alienation of the masses, then totalistic group movements of the sort mentioned can be expected to arise. While serving deep psychological needs of their members, the new power groups liberate them from one set of social absolutes in order to replace it with a more coherent and comprehensive but no less authoritarian alternative. Yet, in the case of the Soka Gakkai, a great part of its surprising power derives from its capacity to speak to basic needs. It does so through the creation of a network of institutions—social, cultural, religious, and political—which together create a major social reality in which the individual is located as an integral part. Even though the organization is not formally participatory in any real sense, its group structure provides for integral participation of members in a variety of activities within the framework of a common ideology, and hence creates a high level of commitment.

Before indicating how a society can be formally participatory as well as capable of providing for integral participation through group structure, it is necessary to examine the nature of group decision process in order to understand the basis for formal participation. Effective group decision-making arises as people come to know that the group is capable of significantly enriching their lives, both through the solidarity that it provides and through the performance of tasks that are important to its members. As this process evolves, the possibility of consensus also arises with it. The experience of successful problem-solving by the group brings with it a sense of confidence and trust on the part of its members. As this grows, members come to sense a group identity that has integrity and continuity.

Before this happens, when a conflict arises between the majority decisions of the group and an individual member, the member may question the continued value of the group for him. But as long as the group continues to fulfill its members' needs, it is possible for a member to take the longer view, so that where individual instances of divergence between the group decision and the member's decision occur, the member maintains his belief in the group's continuing capacity to respond to his own needs. Out of this the possibility of consensus arises, not because every member is at all times aligned with the majority decision, but because every member is aware of his continuing impact on the group, and is thus capable of accepting occasional decisions in opposition to his own views.

A further requirement for consensus is a genuine confrontation of perspectives. Where conflicting views exist, it is possible to compromise by taking a middle position, but this satisfies neither antagonist. Only through the use of imagination can creative syntheses be developed that embody the key features of opposing views. Presupposed here is a degree of basic agreement as to values and goals, since where values basically diverge, the same sorts of opposition will continue to recur. But part of the group process itself involves the harmonization of values, so that differences increasingly center around means, not ends. Take for example an editorial committee discussing a given article. One set of editors rejects it, while another set favors it. On that level compromise is impossible—and this is often the nature of decisions faced by groups. The synthesis takes place when the editors collectively agree on modifications of the article which make it acceptable to all. Alternatively, reasons why the piece does not fit in with the general objectives of the periodical may be clarified to the point where all editors agree.

If, moreover, a basic agreement as to values and goals is required for consensus to occur, the nature of consensus becomes clarified. It is often believed that consensus is an operating procedure, to be adopted as an alternative to majority vote. When this is done by a group that has no history, what is usually achieved is a tyranny of the majority resulting in manipulated consensus, or alternatively, a series of stalemates leading to a disintegration of the group. But the description of consensus given here shows that it is in essence a developmental process, made possible only at the point where a group has developed fundamental agreement and trust among its members. It can be achieved either by working from majority rule toward consensus, or more idealistically, when inaction can be afforded, by a refusal to act in those areas where consensus is not yet possible.

As a task or action group evolves, ends become clarified both for the members of the group and for the group as such, and the continuing concerns of members of the group become clarified and can be dealt with. Out of this emerge techniques for reconciling individual concerns: a more accurate understanding of what can be expected from members of the group and skill in relating members functionally to the changing requirements of the group tasks. As confidence increases in the capacity of the group to comprehend the needs of its members, and to relate them functionally to the group's tasks, group identity is strengthened.

Group identity, however, can be negative or positive. Negative groups define themselves in terms of opposition to other groups, their social environment, or a set of social goals. (These views indeed may be justified where the environment is objectively oppressive. Such a group, though in opposition, is positive because it strives for positive values). The truly negative group derives its force from the unleashing of negative emotions, which results in the projection of subjective aggression onto a scapegoat who is perceived as responsible for all the problems experienced by the members. Such groups are incapable of relating functionally to other groups except those that share their own biases. Hence, as they unite, they also fragment the broader social fabric into racial, ethnic, religious, and national antagonisms. But the internal dynamic of such groups is also negative, and their structure is usually authoritarian and undemocratic. When groups operate in a synergistic fashion, it is far more likely that they will be capable of relating effectively to other groups, across racial and ethnic boundaries, for example.

A central problem in the achieving of group purpose is the role of the expert within the group. Since real groups (as opposed to laboratory groups, where a great deal of largely irrelevant study of group decision-making processes has taken place) are involved in various kinds of social decisions, technical knowledge is often involved. Yet the very fact that social questions inevitably involve value components as well as technical components means that the values represented by the various members of the group must be integrated into the decision process. While the decision as to where to build a highway through a township involves technical decisions about costs, terrain, and so forth, it also involves social decisions centering around what kind of property to go through, whether to go through public land or private land, whether the wealthy can better afford to lose part of their property than the poor, and so forth.

One major implication here is that social decisions cannot be made for people by an expert. The group decision process is essential if the multiple perspectives of those involved are to be consulted. The balancing of the many trade-offs involved in social decisions can only be achieved by those most directly affected by such decisions. The role of the expert is to present the consequences of various lines of action clearly, while leaving the discussion of value consequences to the group. The major fact to be grasped is that there is no single correct technical solution to social questions. Customs, norms, ethical and social considerations inject themselves at every point, and groups made up of those affected are the only valid interpreters of such norms and values.

The fact that there is no solely technical solution to social problems is often obscured by those who wish to limit the problem to technical considerations in order to avoid messy questions of social values involving the differing perspectives of different people. Out of this arises a myth of technical efficiency as the dominant consideration, and the enshrinement of the expert. But the experience of worker's control in Yugoslavia has laid the myth to rest; workers' councils have proved capable of dealing with information about costs and profits when they are translated into non-technical terms, and their explicit involvement with a variety of social purposes extending well beyond profit considerations has in no way bankrupted enterprises or made them less efficient.

In general, then, task groups can function effectively when the integrity of group decisions is preserved. When personal relationships involving trust and openness have developed, when every member knows that he will be heard, when members know that their perspective forms a continuing part of the group decision process, when experts are utilized but do not dominate, then group integrity can develop and be maintained. The group then becomes a vehicle for the expression of individual creativity, and justifies itself by clearly proving itself superior, as it proceeds with its various tasks, to the capacities of any single member within the group. Achievement of this type creates a solidarity based on real success in meeting needs, rather than on simply the growth of sentiment within the group.

Having established—I hope—the viability of groups as basic elements in a socio-political decision process, it is now possible to turn to the question of relating them. At present pluralism is the political philosophy that most adequately comprehends the group structure of society. However, it contains a number of critical weaknesses, which shed light on the way the socio-political structure needs to be transformed in order to allow for a democracy of participation. Pluralism recognizes organized groups as significant political forces, but because it shares with liberalism an image of man and of human relationships based on self-interest and the consequent playing-off of the self interests of groups, it tends primarily to enshrine the inequities of the status quo, rather than accommodate itself to new definitions of social purpose as they arise.

The kind of power bargaining that is based on trade-offs takes place outside of government (between labor and business, for example), between government and a power bloc (business for example), and within government, where congressmen bargain with each other for support of their pet projects. Unfortunately this process legitimizes the existing system of interests, so that labor, for example, while recognized by law, at the same time is relegated to a subordinate role *vis à vis* business. New interests find difficulty in being recognized, and when they do, their recognition is proportional to the amount of power—in terms of numbers or money—that they can muster, not to the justice of their cause. Certain key public interests remain largely unrepresented because they do not specifically profit any given group, but rather belong to the interest of the whole. Auto safety, for example, received little attention until Ralph Nader appointed himself a one-man crusader for the public interest, while pollution was hardly noticed until it began to endanger life.

Moreover, the most powerful vested interests remain largely uncontrolled—the oil industry is a prime, but by no means exclusive, example of this—so that their influence with respect to the government is largely one way; the regulatory agencies remain a joke. This points to a basic flaw in representative democracy, which is that the constituency remains unorganized and hence a mass, united only by marginal geographical interests. Within such boundaries, powerful interest groups exist—corporations, local chapters of national associations, entrenched and wealthy families. These groups exert disproportionate influence on congressional representatives, largely because they control disproportionately the financial resources required for election and re-election. Other groups, whether or not they represent key segments of the public interest within the electoral district, may not be heard from at all if they lack access to the required financial resources. Thus the National Rifle Association concentrated its resources in one Congressional district to defeat a candidate who had spoken out for gun control.

In the present system, representatives are free to listen only to those segments of their constituency that can buy re-elections. It has been likened (by Christian Bay) to a system wherein medical treatment is given first and foremost to the healthiest, and only last to the most ill. When power, not need, is listened to, the political system is exactly that. The only way to be heard in such a situation is to create substitutes for existing power, following the formula that one is heard precisely to the degree that one's capacity for disruption and disturbance makes it expedient to respond. Hence a politics of violence and disruption is not only successful, given the existing manner of determining priorities, but actually required. Despite the distance of such a politics from any hope of seizing power, it remains successful in a reformist sense, because it is the only kind of politics that accords with the system of trade-offs based on bargaining from power. If you cannot buy your way into sufficient power so as to have a voice, you had best threaten your way in.

Given this outline of the way the present political system works, it is necessary to sketch out how a system of participation based on the formal recognition of organized groups as the basic socio-political units would speak to the problems indicated above. It may seem that such a scenario is utopian and unrealistic, but it is curious that we accept scenarios when they are of the doomsday type, and are willing to calculate how many mega-deaths we can absorb and maintain the socio-cultural fabric, but are unwilling to conceive that positive scenarios have any relevance. The fact is that they are central in providing critical perspective on the present system and a guide to the development of a strategy of change. Here we will limit ourselves to model making, and will leave the strategic implications to others.

A politics based on the recognition of groups, not the individual, as the basic socio-political unit has been called coercive. But this points to the need to re-constitute groups into basic units of participation and synergy rather than maintaining them as bases of bargaining and trade-offs. Where groups have lost their functional relevance to the areas where power is exercised, they become either the locii of a weak sociability divorced from relevance, as in the rituals of the Shriners, Elks, and their ilk, or they become defensive groups, defining themselves by their differences from others, as with such far-right groups as the Ku Klux Klan. But groups that are tied to the broader socio-political processes are thereby made relevant for their members, who in the present system suffer from isolation and political alienation.

Such groups do encourage participation and can be synergistic and thereby healthful for their members. Nor do they coerce, since the principle of group organization is not that every citizen must belong, but rather that where there are natural groups within the socio-economic structure, such groups should be both internally participative and externally linked to the socio-political structure. Such a principle would destroy the arbitrary division of society into social structure and political superstructure, the latter partially democratic but also in significant ways irrelevant to the former, which is elitist and often harshly coercive. A necessary requirement for such a group-organized socio-political structure is that the citizen have free access to groups, and that access mean a share in the decision-making.

It is clear that the decision-making process in its most complete form is found in the group. The processes of planning, discussion of alternatives, consultation, integration, and implementation are, *in toto,* group processes, for reasons indicated already. As group processes, they break down individual stereotypes, since the group is a forum for many ideas, and as discussion and action proceed, people are forced to confront the consequences of their beliefs. Studies by Almond and Verba of the correlation between group discussion and the prevalence of informed political opinions verify this. In the existing state of affairs, the government is generally more liberal than the electorate in matters that pertain specifically to the public interest such as welfare and aid to depressed areas. Part of the reason is that the electorate has no continuing say in the decision process, while organized interest groups, via lobbying, do.

A further reason lies in the differences between a politics based on genuine group organization and the present pluralist politics of interest groups. The problem with the present system is that powerful groups—the oil interests, the National Rifle Association, the American Medical Association, to say nothing of the Pentagon—possess large numbers of lobbyists and command vast financial resources. But a system that enfranchised groups would cure such inequities. If groups were represented at a system of national and regional assemblies, such representatives would really be delegates, inasmuch as their mandate would clearly be determined by the groups they represented. Rather than pursuing politics as a system of trade-offs with each other, they would be forced to report to their respective group constituencies. This follows from the fact that the locus of decisions of such organized groups would be in the groups themselves, and would not rest with their delegates. The delegates would then function as communication channels between their constituency groups and the assemblies of delegates. Moreover, if groups representing all organized interests were formally recognized—the professions, industry, ethnic groups, the religions, and so forth—their role would also involve legislative control. Today such control is left to the regulatory agencies and is useless, or almost so. But explicit recognition and consequent control would create the possibility of levels of social planning that, though essential, are at present inconceivable.

Viewed from the perspective of the present, it could be argued that an assembly of delegates would still simply represent the interests of their groups, and that the existence of more groups might create a continuing stalemate. But any system that represented all organized groups would also represent every sector of the population, poor and rich, black and white, white collar and blue collar. The ideology of special interests is fed by the existing system of *sub rosa* power interests—predominantly big business— which lays disproportionate claim to the ear of Congress. Moreover, a whole spectrum of critical decisions regarding the use of natural resources, the disposition of the work force, the uses of investment capital, are placed beyond formal political control because they are decisions that are in the hands of corporate enterprise alone. This *sub rosa* government with its public-be-damned attitude is a major factor in destroying the national capacity to plan in the public interest, and beyond that, the public faith in the legitimacy of political institutions.

Where a local assembly represents the totality of local interests, the habit of thinking in terms of the public interest is maximized, since, classically, this is where the sense of public interest and responsibility flourishes. As the Yankee-City study has shown, it is when a local enterprise is taken over by absentee owners that all sense of local responsibility and public interest is lost. When the habit of thinking first of the public interest develops locally, however, it can then be passed on through a delegate system which links local assemblies to regional and national assemblies by whatever number of links are needed. The public interest may then be conceived of as the totality of private interests, mediated and transmuted through the process of group discussion and decision. But the basis for such mediation is the essential ingredient for the transformation of individual need into social purpose, and at all levels this means the face-to-face group, involved in the full process of decision-making.

A further objection that pluralist thought has raised to the idea of group organization as the basis of the socio-political structure is that it tends to be totalitarian. In the pluralist view, man joins groups essentially out of narrow self interest, and hence sees commitment to any single group as limited. Out of this view comes the notion of participation in a variety of interest groups, jostling and bargaining with each other for a larger slice of the pie. The possibility of integration between individual needs and social purpose, conceived as a dialectical process whereby need is transformed through a process of identification with the purposes of the group, is not admitted. But in messianic movements of the sort alluded to earlier, commitment to the group, and beyond it to the movement of which the group is a part, does take the form of identification; this transcendence of the ego-goals, also suggested earlier as a possible result of the group experience, has an important liberating function for the individual. Through transcendence the individual can mature through identification with social purposes that unite him with broad social visions, and thus escape the solipsism of purely egocentric relationships.

In part the pluralist fear of totalitarianism results from the fact that where pluralism and self interest is the rule, movements such as the Soka Gakkai, John Birch Society, Black Muslims, and Communism (in certain cases) do represent a threat. They are ideological, they allow for and in fact require identification with their goals, and as a result of this they stand opposed to both the view of human nature and of the social order posed by pluralism. Pluralism fears the power of such movements with their *gemeinschaft* character, capable of reintegrating the various aspects of human life under a single overarching ideology, and through this enjoining commitment of an order impossible within the pluralist vision. It envisions such a movement gaining control and imposing its vision on the rest of society, thus destroying the possibility of freedom for others. And, given the ideology and politics characteristic of many such movements, the fear is a very real one.

The question to be asked is this: is it possible to preserve the individual freedom that pluralism, along with liberalism, considers paramount, and at the same time recognize the reality of groups as the basis of social organization? The outlines of the answer can be derived from the sketch of sociopolitical organization that has been made. As indicated, messianic movements use ideology and group structure to replace the fragmentation of *gemeinschaft* that has been induced by advanced industrial society. They substitute an imposed ideological system for the process whereby group identity is developed out of the history of the group. The various processes that have been described above, which lead to integration and the development of social purpose within groups, are essentially functional and experiential, not ideological. Through them groups develop identity as a result of the concrete experience of successful problem-solving and through this forge social purpose.

This is not to deny the important critical function of ideology in developing an awareness of the nature of the existing social order with its elitism, authoritarianism, and commitment to violence. Nor is it to deny the importance of ideology as vision, both for a movement of social change and as an aid in renewing the utopian dimension of social thought, which is badly needed. The sketch of socio-political structure, while based on psychological and sociological analysis, is itself an embodiment of such vision. The importance of such a vision is twofold: first, it serves as an essential vantage point for a critique of the existing social order, allowing one to understand the structural reasons for the failure of the existing institutions; second, it foreshadows the building of a movement for change. This is especially true if one believes that a movement for change must embody within it its own goals, thus healing the dichotomy between means and ends that is one of the salient features of existing political behaviour.

However, an understanding of the nature of the group basis of socio-political organization can make clear how totalistic thinking is not and need not be an inherent ingredient of groups. Where integration is existential, not ideological and imposed, ideology is freed to perform its function as critic and guide. In a socio-political order so structured, ideology would continue to perform a critical function (precisely the reverse of the function attributed to ideology by Mannheim), but vision would arise primarily as the articulation of social purpose derived from group experience. This would then constitute the utopian function of ideology, once the necessary socio-political structures had already been created.

The pluralist fear of group organization is in part dishonest, a product of *mauvais foi,* to use Sartre's notion. The fear of domination by groups neglects the other side of the coin, the fact that the enfranchising of groups also allows for the possibility of control of groups, and through this, harmonizing them into broader visions of the public interest. The pluralist fear is dishonest in a deeper sense, too, since it is the total freedom enjoyed by powerful vested-interest groups today that allows them to function as *sub rosa* governments, manipulating people and social resources in uncontrolled, selfish, and destructive ways. Such vested interests rightly fear that a socio-political structure that took explicit cognizance of them would also curtail their freedom. However, since such interest groups themselves must be restructured, they would thus be relieved of their problem.

In part, the kind of politics called for is a politics of reconstruction. A number of presently employed strategies already point in its direction; to the extent that community groups, community corporations, and the like, seek to create autonomous regions wherein participatory control is developed involving local institutions, the outlines of such a politics are present. To extend it and fill it out, it is necessary for such institutions to press for legitimacy and recognition, to band together into a movement, to press for both the libertarian and participatory values they embody, and to advance the kind of overall socio-political structure sketched out here.

Another aspect of the politics of groups is a politics of dissolution. Here the insights of the anarchists are relevant. The relating of groups into assemblies, viewed from one perspective, can be seen as the art of linking the significant institutionalized organizations of the society in such a way as to create a functional politics. Questions of ecological and geopolitical boundaries, basic societal units, the integration of unit planning with overall planning—all would be involved. Yugoslavia has conceived of the commune as the basic socio-political unit; it exemplifies a minimal unit in which the major educational, social, and economic institutions are to be found. But in the process, what would be brought about is the dissolution of the political superstructure, seen as a separate set of institutions, set apart from the social institutions of the society. From this dissolution the concept of socio-political structure would take on its full meaning. Rather than a party politics involving party machines and the paraphernalia of conventions, party hacks and so forth, politics would be restored to its classic function of having to do with all aspects of public life and public interest.

The functional approach to politics does not dissociate power from significant function, and sees this power as primarily a product of organization. Where politics is dissolved into the social structure, issues arise out of the organized constituencies making up that structure. Rather than the vapidities of party rhetoric, there would be a continuing debate within the assemblies of issues as they arose. Thus electoral politics based on party appeals to the electorate would give way to a politics of continuing group discussion and decision. The important thing to note is that the system only works where there is internal democracy, and this is the basic reason we do not have it. If our major institutions were internally democratic, it would be functional and natural simply to have assemblies constituted of delegates from them. Liberalism saw the solution to authoritarian and anti-democratic institutions in terms of bypassing them by creating a democratic political structure. But this resulted inevitably in simply one more bureaucratic elite, setting up coalitions with the others. There is no shortcut to a society of participation. Either one makes the basic institutions internally democratic, or one is blessed with political institutions that take on the coloration of their surroundings. A society gets the politics it deserves.

The two forms that participatory democracy has most often taken are community control and workers' control. In the United States the community development corporation is the most comprehensive example of the effort to achieve community control; the CDC is therefore one of the most significant social innovations in this country. Their value lies in their capacity to fill obvious social needs, and at the same time to employ a novel institutional form. As Stewart Perry's article indicates, the form itself is no guarantee of its success. But it does create a structure within which exist possibilities for extensive community participation, which are absent in conventional community organizations. The community development corporation may be thought of as a sort of nucleus, relating economic enterprise to community development, and thus bridging a gap between the private sector and public sector. In doing so it opens up possibilities not simply for community development, but for an ongoing process of social integration within the community, based on locally created funding for community needs.

The various possibilities for social integration and participation are explored in the article by Rosabeth Kanter, which follows this. But the basic idea of the community development corporation is that, by marking off an area in which the elements of community already exist, it can build on these elements by making them functionally relevant to major concerns of the inhabitants. Where a community development corporation is successful in creating jobs, needed community institutions such as day care centers, health clinics, schools, and also succeeds in making itself a vehicle for community participation, a neighborhood can develop into a true community. It can do so because what is created is more than a set of discrete services, no matter how important. The community development corporation can be the basic neighborhood institution—social, political and economic—thus integrating services, governance, and work.

Participatory democracy must start at the local level, involving people where they work and live. A major problem here is to define the unit in which the change to a more participatory system can most effectively take place. One possibility is to take each institution separately and try to either rebuild it or create it anew. But this ignores the fact that institutions function best when they are locally controlled. When local control can be wedded to an overall local development plan that is economically, socially, and politically relevant, it has the best chance of success. Community development corporations, by dealing with the neighborhood as a single unit, have the capacity to create an overall socio-political system that is both participatory, because community controlled, and relevant to the needs of the community. Thus they can at once address issues and change structures. In doing so, they may be able to create significant change.

A Note on the Genesis of the Community Development Corporation
Stewart E. Perry

Almost unnoticed, a new social institution has been born in this country, the community development corporation. It arose in the efforts of the disenfranchised and the alienated to find a meaningful way to participate in the important social and political decisions of their times and neighborhoods. The CDC has its American roots in earlier forms of organized common effort upon common economic problems. Some of these roots go back even to the earliest history of the American colonies;[1] other roots might be traced to later economic development institutions, such as the city booster corporations of thirty or forty years ago. But whatever the derivations from our traditions, the CDC represents a contemporary struggle against very current and troubling problems: the drive of the poor and of minorities, especially blacks, to achieve a new and significant place, a respected place, in the American society.

In this essay I want to explore tentatively some of the forces and conditions that were a part of the evolution of this new institution in order to see what opportunities or limitations the CDC has had and will have as an instrument for participatory democracy.

The CDC takes various forms, but any CDC will ordinarily exhibit all the following features:

(1) It is an institution focused upon developing a specific territorial neighborhood or area. It is concerned with peculiarly local problems, usu-

ally within a limited inner city area, in which the pride of locality and territoriality is a major motivation.[2] In fact, a threat to the physical locality—as in a highway or an urban renewal project—may be a trigger for more than a fight against the outside invasion. In East Boston, for example, a neighborhood struggle against airport expansion has been the basis for organizing a community development corporation.

(2) Its corporate structure offers shares or membership primarily to residents of that selected area. If shares or membership are offered to nonresidents, the offering is such that control remains with the residents.

(3) The goals of a CDC are multiple, but they always include the creation of new economic institutions—fiscal, industrial, or business. Because the CDC spans the civic interests of an entire neighborhood and offers shares or memberships to all residents, there is generally a clear preference for community ownership of the economic institutions. However, most CDC's also provide services or capital for privately owned businesses of residents. The CDC aim in building new institutions or strengthening old ones does not restrict it from using any ownership approach.

(4) The new economic institutions are designed to promote the multiplicity of goals. For example, while its businesses strive to be successful, profits are explicitly restricted by local community priorities such as a need for increasing employment opportunities, or for providing previously unavailable services such as convenience shopping, or for other generally useful facilities. The CDC ordinarily plans to reinvest profits not just in further economic activities but also in human or welfare services. For example, New Communities, Inc., of southwest Georgia hopes to be able to provide educational facilities as part of its program.

(5) The constituency of the CDC is most often economically and socially disadvantaged. Therefore the aim of the CDC is to change those societal institutions that maintain the economically and socially disadvantaged position of those groups. The community development corporation was originally a product of the black people's civil rights movement. The earliest forms were started by Negroes in urban areas, but the idea has been taken up by other disadvantaged groups, including Mexican-Americans in the Southwest and elsewhere, Appalachian whites, and others.[3] It is important to understand these roots in the civil rights movement, because it helps to illuminate the fact that the CDC is not simply a business development instrument. It is a means of enhancing the whole range of political, social, and economic opportunities for the groups involved.

What makes the CDC different from earlier attempts to improve the status of the poor in America? Is this just another name for the private and public anti-poverty efforts of the past? Why should the CDC be considered different from, for example, the Community Action Agencies, the poor people's organizations sponsored under the programs of the Office of Economic Opportunity? Is it not true that many of the CDC's today are supported primarily by OEO funds, just as the CAA's have been? All of these questions and others must be answered in order to recognize what the CDC may mean in the years to come.

First, it is not possible to understand what the CDC's really represent unless one considers the *institutional* impoverishment of the neighborhoods and groups from which they arose. It can fairly be said that the poor and the blacks, the Spanish-Americans, and certain other minorities have suffered not only from a debased status within our society but also, most excruciatingly, from the absence of their own institutional resources—local, self-developed, and meaningful—to challenge the more comfortable majority to cede them a rightful place. The lack of institutional resources is especially grave in the economic sphere. Businesses, banks, credit facilities, industries, and the like, are rarely controlled by minority group members and even those under outside control are scarce in the areas in which minority groups live.

The people of the ghettos and barrios, the depressed rural counties, and forgotten mountains of this country have had to make do with a few organizations and resources that came to them from that very outside which had never given them a fair shake. It is no wonder then that the underclasses, as Michael Harrington has called them, have not managed to improve their position dynamically, for the available energy ordinarily came from without and was rarely mobilized from within. The CDC departs from that pattern. That is the new promise of the innovative institutions that have begun to emerge. The community development corporation, an indigenous innovation of the poor themselves, a self-developed instrument for their own mobilization, may be the means by which they will fundamentally change their relation to the rest of us. The CDC thus should be seen not just as an environment of institutional resources for the area residents but also as an instrument by which further new institutions can be built.

A second significant orientation for understanding this new institution is that the CDC's are not inherently a part of, nor did they arise from, the federally sponsored poverty program or other outside sponsorship. This fact is instructive on two counts. First, it means that these new institutions are truly a creation of the people whom they are designed to serve. Second, they are, therefore, likely to be more precisely directed to the needs of their constituencies, and more clearly expressive of exactly what the people they represent consider to be important.

Nevertheless, historically, it seems likely that the origins of the CDC's can be traced, in part, also to activities generated by the poverty programs, but in a very special sense. For example, the Community Action Agencies offered assistance and hope to a growing and evolving leadership in the poor communities, but at the same time clearly frustrated much of the aspirations of those communities. The development of new human resources together with the frustration of the neighborhood leaders probably stimulated the evolution of the new institutional form of the CDC.

On the one hand, the local poverty programs offered crucial jobs in community organizing to a considerable number of people who had informal influence within their neighborhood (or who developed that influence in their new jobs).[4] It also provided the poor with a certain experience in dealing with the established power structure by the institutional and procedural means of that structure. These means included the CAA's themselves and the panoply of rules of the game, in relation to the Federal government, to local city or state officials, and to other local majority community leaders in business, welfare, health, and so on.

In short, through the medium of the CAA's a short generation of poverty community leadership has been subsidized and taught how to deal with the structures that had been closed to them in the past. Thus, in fact, help from the oustide provided a means for mobilizing their own people. For example, it was no longer necessary for a woman to earn her living as a domestic and have only a small amount of energy and time to work for the betterment of her neighborhood, to organize neighbors for better garbage collection from the city, for instance; instead, she had a chance to be *paid to do just that sort of organizing*.

So the poverty program did in fact offer certain resources.[5] On the other hand, the experience of the emergent leadership from the poverty program activities was not all that encouraging. For one thing, the success of the poor in changing their status and environment has not been outstanding, to say the least. For another, the CAA was not the instrument exclusively of the poor; it was, as its name clearly denoted, the instrument of the community —the *whole* community, including the rich and the middle class. It was in fact *intended* as a meeting place and common mobilization point for the entire community; of course, it was to be an organization including the poor and for the benefit of the poor, but certainly not exclusively *of* the poor.

Sometimes, the CAA's would encourage the initiation of subsidiary groups that were composed entirely of poor people, and occasionally these were effective groups, but they still operated within the context of the overall vehicle of the larger community—the CAA.

Thus, the interests of the poor were commonly compromised in the arena of negotiation, within the CAA's themselves, presumably as other interest groups compromised with the poor. That indeed was the name of the game —to get the rest of the community into contact with those who had been effectively ghettoized and isolated from significant relations with the majority world, and by so doing to lay the groundwork for getting more resources and changes in the outside world that would be to the advantage of the poor. The poor learned, however, that the CAA was not their instrument, no matter what the rhetoric was. Yet they also learned how useful an organizational instrument might be; and they learned of the basic significance of the business sector in everything that happened.

Out of this experience, then, came the new vehicle, the CDC, that could represent the poor neighborhood exclusively, express its priorities only, advocate its own goals—without the immediate compromise that participation in the CAA requires. Moreover, this new vehicle for self-determination could seize upon the means that meant real power and change in the neighborhoods—the economic muscle of business development.

Early examples of the CDC in Rochester, New York, and Cleveland, Ohio, suggest that the ambitious goals may have arisen out of a sharply increasing recognition of the significance of outside influences in the affairs of the neighborhood. Many leaders had in the past recognized the destructive meaning of institutions that had no allegiance or commitment whatsoever to their neighborhoods and yet determined what happened there; but enough general recognition among residents awaited major conflicts with some of those outside influences. In the one instance, it was a mayoralty campaign after a major civil disturbance; in the other, it was a dispute with a major local corporation. In both instances, after a successful conclusion of the conflict, neighborhood leaders moved aggressively into a larger, more ambitious campaign to bring about full local control through community control of economic resources. And that required a new institution, the CDC.

The community development corporation is, however, a form, the substance of which depends upon the basic strength and mobilization of the community, and upon the strength of its leadership. The mere existence of a

CDC is not an indication of community unity, energy, and strength of purpose—especially today, when increasingly, the idea of the CDC may take on the aura of a panacea to be initiated without any prior community organizing.

The publicity that this institutional form has received in low-income areas has led to the creation of many such corporations. Some of these may go on to important work; others will disappear without having accomplished anything. Yet together with political energy and sophistication, the CDC can provide a new and powerful means for the unrepresented poor of our society to begin to make themselves felt.

If the CDC is to do the ambitious job that it was designed to do—to set priorities, plan, and execute plans—for the revitalization of a whole neighborhood or sub-area of a city or for a rural district, then it cannot be simply another organization. It has to be broadly representative of its entire constituency, to bring together the leadership from all of the different community interests and groups in the immediate poverty area for a coalition that would make overall planning possible, and that would, moreover, provide a united front to the outside world in economic and political negotiations.

Coalitions, sometimes explicitly under a name such as Black United Front, have of course grown up in a number of urban areas to provide a spokesman to deal with outside representatives, especially other political figures. These coalitions could, as in the case of FIGHT and FIGHTON, or Hough Community Council and Hough Development Corporation, provide a political base for the economic development activities of an associated CDC. Employment in the businesses of the CDC also offers important resources for building political power, so long as the need for patronage as well as the social and humanitarian goals of rehabilitation of the locally unemployed and underemployed are judiciously interlaced with the other goals of the organizations.

In what are the two oldest and most evolved CDC's, FIGHTON and HDC,[6] the potential for success in the delicate task of interweaving the multiple goals of the citizen groups, the business development activities, and the political coalitions, might be measured, in part, by the degree to which the CDC's obtain outside resources on their own terms—or at least on fully acceptable terms in a negotiation process. They have obtained already a total of perhaps three million dollars in equity capital, gifts, loans, services, and other assets from government and private sources for development work. Yet this measure of success cannot substitute for long-term viability of the subsidiary institutions established—the businesses, the community organizations, and the service programs. And the viability of these institutions will depend upon whether they will in fact meet the special need that gave rise to the CDC's in the first place: the need of the CDC area residents for a sense of real participation in the affairs of their immediate world.

NOTES

[1] See, for example, an unpublished paper prepared for the Center for Community Economic Development by John McClaughry and Patricia M. Lines, "Early American Community Development Corporations: The Trading Companies."

[2] The significance of neighborhood turf for lower-class and working-class groups has been described by a number of writers. An early report may be found in Marc Fried and Peggy Gleicher, "Some Sources of Residential Satisfaction in an Urban Slum," *J. Amer. Inst. Planners* (1961) 27:305–315. See also Gerald Suttles, *Social Order of the Slums* (rev. ed.); Univ. of Chicago Press, Chicago, 1968.

[3] A directory prepared by the Center for Community Economic Development reveals the wide distribution of groups that are experimenting with the CDC or related institutional forms. Incidentally, the Center, located in Cambridge, Massachusetts, was organized to study and promote such forms of community-based economic activity. It, together with the National Economic Development Congress, which at this writing is just in the process of incorporation, are the two specialized organizations that offer supportive services to the CDC movement.

[4] It is instructive to note that so many of today's leaders of the minority communities even if they no longer participate or even believe in the utility of the poverty programs got support from CAA's or other OEO programs at some early point in their careers.

[5] Once the first CDC's appeared, sympathetic outsiders in the government recognized their significance and sought to make federal resources available. In an interesting but unconnected convergence, in June 1968, a group of legislators introduced the "Community Self-Determination Act," to provide governmental support for organizing and funding CDC's, and the Office of Economic Opportunity made its first grant to a CDC, under what it came to call its "Community Capitalism" program. This double encouragement was undoubtedly an immense stimulation to the development of the idea in local communities at a very early stage of the CDC movement. While the legislation remains in draft stage, the OEO grant program has expanded from an original $1.5 million to about $25 million—still very small in national terms but significant in terms of the individual grants made.

[6] FIGHTON and HDC were both organized in 1967. The Bedford-Stuyvesant Restoration Corporation was organized about the same time, but since it was explicitly the result of efforts of sympathetic outsiders (especially, of course, Senator Robert F. Kennedy and his staff), it did not originally fit the model of the CDC as described in this chapter.

In this essay on the community development corporation, several themes are presented that are touched on elsewhere in this volume. The critique of voting as an effective form of participation applies equally to the more traditional corporation, as well as to electoral politics. Full participation is far broader than mere voting. It includes various ways of working and sharing together; participation is an ongoing process, not as an occasional expression of opinion.

Moreover, the essay shares the conviction with other essays in this volume that the only complete and effective form of participation is through small groups. Here the decision-making process can involve everyone in meaningful ways, and people are vitally linked to the ongoing activities of the organization. For the writer, it is through group process, community contact, and shared goals that the CDC can become an effective organization. It is not enough to create an organization that is formally under community control, and the lesson to be learned is that the specifics of organizational structure are what make or break an organization, making it either elitist or democratic, ridden by class divisions or egalitarian, impersonal and bureaucratic or sensitive to member's needs.

The rest of the paper raises questions concerning the role of CDC's in a community. Underlying many of them is the tension between the requirements of economic efficiency, and the broader needs of people in the community. Given the anomic quality of contemporary community life, the CDC when introduced should be used to speak primarily to the community's need to create greater integration, even where this functions at the expense of productive efficiency. It tells us something about human nature that is ordinarily overlooked: that people hunger for community and shared goals as much as for economic gains, and that gains in efficiency may be at the loss of community.

Perhaps what the essay leaves us with is a sense of the enormous distance we have to go before we become effective as social planners in any way that even distantly approaches our skills as industrial planners. Yet the CDC must function in a market environment, where it must compete with the conventional corporate forms of enterprise, geared to their narrow definitions of efficiency. Whether the CDC can do this and at the same time achieve the broad social goals suggested in this essay remains to be seen.

Some Social Issues in the Community Development Corporation Proposal

Rosabeth Moss Kanter

One of the primary aims of the Community Development Corporation proposal is to provide the poor with "meaningful participation" in their own institutions. The question arises: what is meaningful participation, what is its importance to the CDC's as organizations and the members as individuals, and what does one do operationally to bring it about? Meaningful participation may be defined as occurring when a person has a sense of his involvement in a total enterprise, a sense of where his effort fits into an overall plan, when he identifies with the collective goals, has a feeling of efficacy with respect to the accomplishment of the goals, and has a stake in the results of the total enterprise. As outlined, the proposed CDC's provide meaningful participation primarily in the last sense: a private and social or shared return on investment of money and time if the corporations do well; little that I can find in the organizational rules for the CDC's necessitates meaningful participation in the other senses.*

Meaningful participation is important for several reasons. From the point of view of the corporation, it generates commitment to the goals of the organization. When commitment to organizational goals is lacking, organizations face high member turnover, alienation and dissatisfaction, waste (such as petty theft) and inefficiency, and the possibility of dissenting factions arising, which deflect time and energy from the pursuit of shared goals to the waging of internal conflict. Big business can better afford to absorb these consequences of having non-committed participants than can a fledgling community corporation with a shaky financial position. When people

* This article was written in response to a proposal for a "National Community Self-determination Act" made in 1968 by Gar Alperovitz and John McClaughry.

are committed to a total enterprise, on the other hand, they work harder, are more satisfied, less rebellious, less antagonistic, more willing to change or try new things, less likely to engage in internal power struggles by non-legitimate means, and they will go to great lengths to prevent the organization from falling apart.

From the point of view of the person, meaningful participation contributes to his psychological well-being. He feels that he is "in control" of his world, that he understands events and his part in them. He feels competent and efficacious, with a sense of dignity and personal worth, a sense of making a contribution.

BUILDING MEANINGFUL PARTICIPATION

As outlined, CDC members are stockholders and voters. These two things by themselves do not constitute meaningful participation; stockholders have the most minimal kind of involvement in their organizations and are interested only in profit, and the fact that most Americans vote does not seem to be decreasing alienation. Not only do voting and holding stock by themselves not significantly build commitment, but if the CDC holds out the promise of meaningful participation without fulfilling it, widespread disaffection, often a function of the failure to meet rising expectations, may result. Furthermore, the CDC plan contains no precautions to prevent the corporation from becoming just another impersonal bureaucracy in which the bureaucrats happen to be also members of the community; no structures or mechanisms exist to prevent administrative exigencies, red tape, a leadership hierarchy, and clogged communication channels from destroying whatever sense of meaningful participation the individual might have had because he owns a piece of it and because it takes care of his children.

The CDC proposal should suggest or establish programs that ensure high member involvement. Participatory democracy by itself is not enough, when the decision-making body meets twice a year and may consist of 500 to 3000 people. The CDC should develop full participation, community contact, and shared goals. A variety of possibilities for doing this can be envisioned:

(1) *Full participation.* In order to join the CDC a person might have to be employed by it, and vice versa: to work for it you have to be a member. (This requirement could be waived for temporary employment of persons possessing necessary skills not found within the membership.) This ensures that CDC members do more than hold stock, it prevents them from becoming an "ownership class" that employs but does not do the work itself, and it means that there is no one working for the corporation who does not also share in its proceeds. Another possibility is that when members join for $5 they must also agree to spend a certain amount of time on CDC projects, in addition to their other employment. Ideally, there should be opportunity for every member to make a contribution. This might mean that what the CDC does is determined, at least in the beginning, by what skills members already have; that the business ventures and social projects undertaken are those that make the widest use of skills, talents, and abilities of the membership, and do not require too many special skills or advanced technical knowledge. It might be more important to start with what members can already do rather than to try to get technologically advanced things done. People should be able to make the kind of contribution most characteristic of them. This has both obvious and profound implications. It means, for example, that a CDC in the black ghetto might be better off forming a record company than an electronics firm. To some extent, full participation might be valued above financial profitability (given break-even operation) in the goals the communities set for themselves. Whereas the government's primary motivation in enabling the establishment of CDC's might be economic, community participants might have a different set of motives, and it is possible that quality of life through full participation might be more important than economic advantage. Many social psychological studies indicate, for example, that given certain minimum levels people work not for money but for other kinds of satisfactions. The implications of all of this for the CDC proposal are that (a) CDC's may not always be profit-making organizations, and, in fact, it might be detrimental to their serving other social functions to assume that they should be; (b) the CDC plan should avoid structuring things in such a way that it is to the CDC's advantage to choose financial goals at the cost of social goals.

(2) *Community contact.* Identification with a collectivity is one of the important sources both of commitment and of personal identity, as well as a defining aspect of meaningful participation. Again, there are many ways to build this into a CDC. Communal work efforts are a possibility; many CDC projects—possibly even aspects of the business ventures—could be community-wide efforts, such as the harvest in a farm village when everyone turns out to help everyone else. In such a case, task and social functions intermingle; group achievement and strong interpersonal ties are both enhanced. There are neighborhood projects like this today: street sweeping Saturdays, for example. I think these could be extended to encompass more

activities, including economic enterprises. They are a prevalent feature of successful work communities like the *kibbutzim*. A large number of things can be defined as the responsibility of the whole community, and the whole community can make some contribution to them: make posters for advertising campaigns, visit the sick, clean the schoolyard, and so forth. As with participation, the examples are simple but the implications profound. Such activity occurs in limited form—car pools and the like—in middle-class suburbia; to what extent is it a part of the life of the poor and alienated?

Community contact can also be enhanced if the CDC is organized into small groups, such as neighborhood subgroups. The leaders of the subgroups could also be part of another group that meets very regularly with top leadership in the community. Thus, there would be a number of people who bridge the gap between the membership at large and the top leaders, easing communication both upward and downward. Ideally, everyone should belong to some group and be able to speak confidently to someone he knows well who will pass the message up the line. These small groups can serve many other functions, but their existence is crucial, I think. These groups can prevent bureaucratization of the CDC, provide a forum for grievance, foster intimacy, and offer a chance to express shared values. At the same time, to the extent that community leaders themselves participate in small group interaction, it can serve to break down status and hierarchical distinctions. It would be valuable both for the community and for the individual if, in addition, the groups served functions of an intimate personal nature, as in Oneida's mutual eroticism and Synanon's "games." (The Model Cities plan for Boston includes a provision for self-help groups for addicts, I assume along the Synanon model.) What such groups can promote is both sensitivity to the standards of the community and individual self-reliance.

Other ways to promote community contact come to mind. The CDC headquarters could serve as a neighborhood center, with meeting rooms and recreational facilities. CDC's could be encouraged to use available funds to buy, rent, or build a camp outside the city—a vacation site for the community, a place for children in the summer. Retreats, training sessions, and other community functions could be carried on there. Whatever is valuable to a community in the intimate atmosphere and close contact of a *kibbutz* or a utopian community could be generated in part there.

(3) *Shared goals.* This is something, of course, that communities tend to define for themselves, without outside intervention. To the extent that communities must define themselves in order to establish a CDC, shared goals should arise or be expressed in the process of organizing. But there

are strategies that might be used to ensure that shared goals exist, that members identify with and are committed to them, and that they feel they are making a contribution to the attainment of the shared goals. For example, there could be a provision in the CDC charter that a certain percentage of profits must go into tangible community-wide projects. (There is already a provision that only 80% of the business profits can be distributed to the CDC; this would be merely a further extension.) Such projects would be concrete signs of the collective endeavors, and would represent tangible achievements, the benefits of loyalty and hard work. This should be one aspect of a sense of over-all planning for the community, of which business planning is only a small part. The CDC could have planning divisions: business, education, housing, neighborhood improvement, social problems, recreation, and so forth. Members could study community needs and desires, existing facilities, and innovations in these areas and make reports to the total community. It could be required that these planning committees represent a certain percentage of the community. Instead of one elected board of directors, or in addition to and subordinate to them, there could be elected directors for all relevant aspects of community life.

Without provision for full participation, community contact, and shared goals, a CDC could degenerate into just another bureaucracy. But with it a number of other organizational and social problems would be solved.

OTHER ISSUES IN THE ORGANIZATION OF THE CDC'S

(1) There is a danger of creating elites or a managerial class. Already in the proposal, the management of the businesses is somewhat insulated from community membership. If focusing on business success means an emphasis on expertise and technical knowledge, the members of the community who are somewhat better educated and more skilled could either take over the CDC or participate in it more fully than the less skilled, pushing out the people at the bottom. Since it is those at the bottom the proposal wants to help, this could be a serious problem.

(2) There is tension between meaningful participation (community, value expression) and efficiency. There are many expressions of this. For some purposes strong centralization of power and decision-making is more efficient, but at the same time works against meaningful participation. The creation of specialists and professionals who know one job well and only that and have a stake in defending their territory of expertise may be more efficient for some purposes, but again militates against the kind of meaning-

ful participation discussed earlier. A similar argument might be made with respect to the hiring of outside labor. This is a problem faced by *kibbutzim* today. With the Israeli government demanding certain rate of productivity, the *kibbutz* finds that it must be more efficient. At the same time, however, it wishes to avoid bureaucratization and retain the communal values that make it worthwhile for participants. *Kibbutz* planners are now at work trying to develop organizational strategies which resolve this dilemma. Among the solutions: to ultimately provide every *kibbutz* member with management training and rotate managers to avoid creating professionals. This dilemma has already arisen in one of the communities that is a potential constituency for the CDC program, Roxbury, in Boston. Roxbury is trying to organize a Liberation School, but members seem more interested in sharing values than in developing administratively feasible, let alone efficient, plans. They are more interested in doing things that indicate agreement with common values, that provide community contact and sense of involvement in a distinctive black culture, than in implementing tactics that would permit the school to operate well. (My informant is a black Harvard Business School student who has attended their meetings.) Often people refuse to do the most efficient thing because it violates other needs and values. CDC planners should be aware not only of the tension between these two pulls in social life, but they should also realize that by stressing economic goals they may be weighting the scales in favor of efficiency to the detriment of community or may be creating pressures that members of certain groups wish to resist. This relates to the next point:

(3) The danger of imposing outside criteria of success on a community. Material prosperity is only one measure of success, and communities serve many other worthwhile social functions. In fact, there is a strong relationship between financial success and the dissolution of American utopian communities, possibly because prosperity indicates attention to efficiency, which interferes with community. It is important to ask communities what *their* goals are and what *they* mean by success. While the CDC proposal is admittedly very non-directive, one should be aware of the implications of rewards and contingencies and perhaps build in rewards to the communities for the establishment of certain kinds of social programs that meet internal rather than external definitions of importance.

(4) What is the community's right to exclude people from membership? What problems arise from this question?

(5) There is a tension between high member identification and relations with the outside. It is conceivable that CDC members could have a great

sense of meaningful participation within and still feel very alienated from the rest of American society. How would the government feel about this possibility? How much independence would be permitted?

(6) What is meant by "local autonomy"? I am worried lest the desire to promote community control mask a laissez-faire attitude on the part of the government. In at least one Job Corps Center, for example, the notion that participants should be responsible for their own social organization provided an excuse for the staff to remain quite distant and uninvolved and provide little guidance or help. I think training programs for community leaders are extremely important, and that many suggestions should be offered as to the possible development of the CDC's. The trained leaders could then set up their own training programs for other members.

With some exceptions given current values, the commitment mechanisms I outline in "Commitment and Social Organization: A Study of Commitment Mechanisms in Utopian Communities" * could serve as a "how-to-do-it" manual for planners of similar experiments. But these kinds of practices never arise at once and *in toto;* they develop over time, and members agree to each step. The CDC's certainly cannot suddenly spring into being with the kinds of activities described in that paper or mentioned here. But they can start small, with just a few programs, and gradually extend their activities and their projects, if the government will turn over more and more control to them. The proposal could include provisions that after a certain amount of time if certain conditions are met, money or other incentives will be available for other programs.

The CDC's have a great deal of potential, but there are also a great many problems. The economic details of the endeavor appear to be well conceived; the social implications deserve similar attention.

* *American Sociological Review,* Vol. 33, No. 4 (August 1968) 499-517.

No society can be participatory if its workers do not make economic decisions. With community control, workers' control is at the heart of a participatory democracy. A management consultant, James Gillespie has had wide experience with the operation of small groups on the factory floor, which he presents in the essay that follows. To be sure, the kind of industrial democracy discussed in the article is one of co-management, not one of self-management. It involves control of the assembly line and work place, but not control of policy making. However, the experience is important, since it illustrates that worker control of the work place can be more effective precisely because it is more democratic.

A clear indication of the necessity to democratize management as well as the work place is given by Seymour Melman, in Decision-Making and Productivity. It becomes rapidly evident that unless the two-class worker-management system is abolished, and the values of group work made to prevail, the competitive orientation will continue to dominate the production process:

> Within the management hierarchy the relationships among the subsidiary functionaries are characterised primarily by predatory competition. This means that position is gauged in relative terms and the effort to advance the position of one person must be a relative advance. Hence one person's gain necessarily implies the relative loss of position by others. Within the workers' decision system the most characteristic feature of the decision-formulating process is that of mutuality in decision-making with final authority residing in the hands of the grouped workers themselves.

Competition within management hierarchies thus follows a zero-sum game model: one person's gain is the other's loss. This sort of psychic economy of scarcity pervades the work enterprise and the society as well. Where mutuality exists, the game is not zero sum, since through collaboration all members of a group win. The group basis of work is at the heart of Gillespie's argument.

Gillespie speaks of the necessity of free groups, and of the inability of joint councils to bridge the gap between management and the work floor. This parallels the Yugoslav experience, where the trend is toward making work units primary, away from the original emphasis on worker's councils. The study of the organization of the work place thus clarifies basic principles of direct democracy: unless there is work-group organization and responsibility, gaps between the decision-making process and the work *process will continue to exist. The question is not of differences in class background or function in the enterprise: a workers' council without a decision role will encounter the same problems of relating adequately to the work floor as a joint council. The problem again, basically, is one of responsibility.*

Toward Freedom in Work
James Gillespie

The heart of this essay is the idea of free work in fellowship, and it can be illustrated simply from practice.

In an electrical components factory we had trouble planning for smooth flow of components and balancing of operations. Output varied considerably from one operator to another. Monday's output was some twenty-five percent lower than output on Thursday, which was the closing day of the bonus week, and work discipline was only fair. After some study a group-bonus system was designed and the outline, meaning and purpose of this was put to the group which was then left to discuss it among its members (free group discussion). The girls agreed to have a trial and they were then invited to check the base times set per operation (group participation in method). The system was introduced with the quick result that the group members so organized themselves that the flow of work was greatly improved, discipline improved as a result of internal group controls, and output increased by about twelve percent over that previously attained under the individual piecework system. (Here the group took over the local management function of internal work progressing and, more important, that of local man-management.)

But interesting though the figures given are, the heart of the matter for me was in the group's attitude to a girl called Mary, whose output, I pointed out, was some sixteen percent lower than the group average. I was met with the antagonistic group rejoinder that Mary was a nice girl. This profoundly true evaluation by the group of the worth of qualities like kindness and goodness cuts across the motivational fabric of our modern culture, and it is a statement of values I have found in nearly all small groups who work

closely together. I knew that Mary was unwittingly the "group psychia-
trist," but were I a poet it would take an epic pen to tell that here was a
guiding candlelight in the dark wasteland of our materialist culture. In
terms of production efficiency, individual cost, and export-import balance,
Mary is a dead loss whose virtues are not entered in the commercial statisti-
cian's reports; but the Marys are the symbols of the riches of small community living in which goodness and kindness are highly rewarded, whereas
our economic culture highly rewards individualist acquisitiveness and egocentric power and status seeking. In terms of individualistic costing, based
on individualist incentive schemes, the Marys are a costly burden, but in
terms of overall group efficiency, Mary was a lubricant factor without
which the group could not, would not, have reached and maintained its
state of high productive effectiveness. This effectiveness was a result of a
situation in which the group shared work and the reward of work with
encouragement of cooperation and mutual aid, and with group acclaim of
individual material and spiritual contributions.

We use the social-psychological term "group," for our little group was
more than an economic group dominated by economic self-interest. Because the group members consciously recognized the whole worth of each
person in the group, there was a fellowship (*communis*), or, it may be said,
a fellowship group. Later it will be shown that free work and fellowship are
the twin components of individual growth towards personal maturity.

Tens of thousands of kind-hearted Marys are victims of our materialist
culture, which offers high rewards for some of the basest of human characteristics and penalizes some of the best through the stupified attachment of
both managers and managed to individualistic ratings and rewards.

> Sweet Mary your production's poor,
>   Just dry your tears and go,
> For speed and greed are rated high,
>   But love-for-others, no.
> Christ! Where's the electrician?
>   Our lamps are burning low!

The illustration given describes in simple form the group-contract system
in which the group shares work and the rewards of work, and has a share in
decision-making within the local work environment, a function which hitherto was in the sole field of management. The illustration also touches on
the free or informal group-discussion system, which has been in use during
the past fifteen years in a number of companies, and in which decision-
making is shared on a wider level than in the group-contract system.

MAN CITIZEN AND MAN WORKER

Decision-making, according to orthodox management theory, is the sole function of management; why is it, then, that the primary or non-managing worker is not a significant decision-maker in work life, but in social life is a responsible citizen who, when he votes for who shall represent him at local and national level, shares in decision-making in a cogent manner? Why is it, too, that in work life the chief dependence is on money rewards and penalties to gain behavior that conforms to the economic code of laws, whereas in social life, the large majority of laws are unwritten and depend for their operation on free consent by the citizen? True, the state limits the field citizen free choice as centralized planning increases, but it is nevertheless true that man-worker and man-citizen is split schizophrenic-wise in a manner that inevitably makes for antagonism between work life and leisure life, and degrades both. Man-worker is work conscious (class conscious?), but as work life is the important, money-earning aspect of living, man-citizen occupies a secondary position and his work-consciousness enters strongly into social life with consequent anti-social behaviour that, at root, is likely to be unconscious healthy protest against a schizophrenic role in the community.

Now, there is a school of apologist thought that suggests that responsible industrial democracy is at work when opposition takes place between trade unions and employers in collective bargaining.[1] This plausible theory has, it seems, considerable support at executive level within the trade unions, but it is really a kind of verbalism; for while free opposition is a characteristic of democracy, so also is dependence on individual citizen morale and the spread of individual decision-making at the bottom as well as at the top of the social structure. A worker who is trained to sit correctly in a chair designed to promote maximum output, to move his left arm so and his right arm thus, who is clocked in and out of the works and the lavatory while engaged in continuous, repetitive production in which there is no decision-making, is certainly not playing a responsible citizen role, even though he has big brother arguing against his employer on hours of work and wages. Dependence on big brother manager and big brother trade union executive is equally neurotic in a situation in which planning is for material advantage and not also for self-respect.

In his book *Decision-Making and Productivity,* Prof. Seymour Melman, as will later be shown, indicates factually how foolish is the management doctrine that the managers must manage.[2] But the change from centralized decision-making to shared decision-making is not easy. For the holders of power, if they are not enlightened by mature insight, tend to hold on to their power. As Lord Acton said, "Power corrupts; absolute power corrupts absolutely."

I like the philosopher Roger Bacon on the effect of power on man, (I will misquote slightly): "Man doeth like the ape, the higher he goeth the more he showeth his ass." Power is of an encroaching nature, or, as the political scientist Michels put it:

> Every human power seeks to enlarge its prerogatives. He who has acquired power will almost always endeavour to consolidate and to extend it, to multiply the ramparts which defend his position, and to withdraw himself from the control of the masses.[3]

Part of the management doctrine has to do with work, but, it should be said, the idea of work held by management is that held by the majority of people:

> (1) Work is effort applied for the material values which income from work will buy. (Economic theory.)
>
> There is a corollary to this definition of work and this comprehends the notion of economic man: A whole man can wholly be bought for money and money incentives.
>
> Many managers will rightly reject the corollary out of hand, but on the whole, judging in terms of economic techniques, the corollary expresses economic doctrine. It is true that some men will sacrifice money for status, but not willingly in the following case of the loyal forty-years service clerk who went to the boss in a woollen mill for a raise from one pound a week. In those days the top men in the woollen trade wore top hats, and the boss replied, "Ah wain't gie thee a rise Nathan, but tha has been a guid and faithful servant so on Monday tha can come ti wark in a top 'at."

If we compare other definitions of work with that given above we will find ourselves leaving the concealing smoke of economic work, and breathing a sweeter air:

> (2) Work is prayer; prayer is work. (St. Benedict)
>
> (3) I pray with the floor and the bench. (Hasidic Judaism)
>
> (4) Labor is the great reality of human life. In labor there is a truth of redemption and a truth of the constructive power of man. (Berdyaev).
>
> (5) Laying stress on the importance of work has a greater effect than any other technique of reality living. (Freud)

(6) Work and love are the two chief components in the growth of mature personality in community. (Erich Fromm)

Although our stress is on the psychological value of work, as in Freud, Fromm and others, it would be pleasing if we had more room to develop a work philosophy and to quote the poets' work visions, the fine work philosophy in the Hindu *Bhagavat Gita,* Zen Buddhism, which somewhat parallels Benedictine work practice, Chinese neo-Confucianism, which affirms the Tao or Way as that of drawing water and gathering wood, and as the marriage of the sublime and the commonplace, and the respect for the common task in *Isaiah, Deuteronomy* and *Ecclesiastes:* "There is nothing better for a man than that he should eat and drink, and that he should make his soul enjoy good in his labor."

But there is small joy in work within the work institution, for work is an enforced means to earning money; and how can the soul enjoy good in its labor when there is no soul in the places where labor is organized? But these are big, if somewhat odd thoughts, which have as yet no echo in the work institution, for to equate work with fellowship, with love, with the liberated vitality of the artist of which Morris, Ruskin, Kropotkin and others speak, is to be met with the hidden smile behind the polite hand, or with a psychiatric diagnosis. Once I attacked what is now called "work study" in one of my books[4] and quoted Plato. "What," a reviewer of the American edition asked, "has Plato to do with work?" What indeed?

Yet there is joy in work when the task is a man's own; when he is not ant-heaped in a monstrous tall flat that shrinks him to less than man-size, but has a garden in which there is the poetry of fulfillment.

Or he makes a table, or she bakes a good cake, or sews a dress, or together they raise a family—why is there fulfillment only in this work and not in the other? I have been told, "But that's different; we couldn't organize production that way." Why is it different, and who is this "we"?

What function, if any, has work in the well-being of the personality or, on the other hand, what relationship has work to life as a whole? Why is it, for example, that the capacity regularly to work is a dominant factor in individual normality from the psychiatric and the depth psychological points of view? Why too is work-therapy an essential treatment in neurotic and psychotic illnesses where there is a withdrawal from reality? It is because in free, meaningful work that calls for skill and decision-making there is at once a focusing of consciousness on the world of reality and a protection against the retreat to unconscious fantasy and infantilism.

Work in which there is free expression of the whole man is an ego-building and sustaining function of the self. The age of primitive innocence, of the participation mystique, when men were yet in the mindless state of oneness with nature, was the Golden Age spoken of in the great religious traditions. In the Hindu epic, the Mahabarata, there is a description of the Krita or Golden Age: "In that age no buying or selling went on, no efforts were made by man; the fruits of the earth were obtained by their mere wish; righteousness and abandonment of the world prevailed." The Greek peasant poet Hesiod bemoans the passing of the Golden Age in which men cared nothing for toil and lived like gods and had no sorrow of heart. But of his own, the Iron Age, Hesiod cries: "Dark is their plight. Toil and sorrow by day are theirs and by night the anguish of death."

Writing over 2,000 years ago, the Chinese philosopher Chuang-tzu described the Golden Age of Chaos, of placid tranquility in which no work was done and there was no need for knowledge. In Genesis, man lived in a paradisial Golden Age until with the expression of self-consciousness, of knowledge of good and evil, the curse of work was placed upon humanity.

Always, in the great traditions, the pain of work and the rise of self-conscious individuality are twinned, and in other language the story is repeated by modern anthropologists who have studied primitive societies and tell of their loathing of work. Primitive man obeyed the call of the ancient blood that would charm us away from the sore round of duties and obligations to a state of primitive indolence in which personality disintegrates and, as in the primitive, the wish substitutes for the act, and fantasy substitutes for directed thought. It is against this regression, so well-known to psychotherapists, that Freud warned us:

> Laying stress upon the importance of work has a greater effect than any other technique of reality living in the direction of binding the individual to reality. The daily work of earning a livelihood affords particular satisfaction when it has been selected by free choice; i.e. when through sublimation it enables use to be made of existing inclinations, of instinctual impulses that have retained their strength, or are more intense than usual for constitutional reasons.[5]

Jung has this to say: "The best liberation (from the grip of primitive and infantile fantasy) is through regular work. Work, however, is salvation only when it is a free act and has nothing in it of infantile compulsion.[6]

Work that is creative and thought-provoking is a blessing and a boon to growing personality, but work in which there is no thought and no decision-making breeds infantilism and is once accursed for those who, like repetitive psychopaths, are forced to do it, but manifold for those who enforce it and would reduce another person to the level of instinctive beast or cataleptic stone. Men do not so much dislike work as they dislike their management-dependent status. They do not dislike work as such, but mainly work that calls for small skill and for repetitive movement, the effect of which, the American sociologists Walker and Guest show, is to reduce interest in social affairs, in sport, in religion, and in out-of-work activities generally.[7] The important aspect of this is that if a man's occupation is thoughtless and skill-less, or if he has no occupation, he will introvert and so retreat from the call of social, family and economic duties.

This is the unspoken fear of the many writers on the problem of leisure: that man, drugged by comfort and distracted by mass amusements, will regress to a state of neurotic dependence on the state, the managers, the amusement caterers, and the computerizers:

> Here where brave lions roamed, the fatted sheep,
> and poppies bloom where once the golden wheat.

WORK IN FELLOWSHIP

We are ceaselessly told that the major solution to our social and economic problems is more production to keep up employment which will keep up buying power which will keep up production; and in this automation is to play a large part. The function of production and so forth, is said by orthodox economists to be the satisfaction of increasing natural wants— this is the economics of scarcity. But, as the brilliant Harvard economist John Kenneth Galbraith points out, we are no longer in an age of scarcity but in an age of affluence, and instead of production satisfying natural wants, it is also geared to the satisfaction of artificially created wants on the promotion of which millions are spent in advertising. We are caught up in a vicious circle from which, it seems, there is no escape—yet there are electronic sleeping machines, not yet marketed; so. . . .

There is no doubt that technological progress has far outstripped human progress towards personal and social maturity, and many are the valiant efforts to solve this threat. Perhaps it may be solved by large educational measures; perhaps one of history's erupting minorities may opt out of the rat race and lead us in the process of challenge and response; perhaps there will be a new Franciscanism, perhaps a nation like India may opt out in Gandhian terms. Perhaps small communities of individuals will form to do useful work by hand and with small tools on the land and in workshops.

There is as much cause for hope as for gloom, and I think that the escape from automated leisure in and through fellowship work groups is a probability.

The broken fellowship of authoritarian work life and democratic social life bespeaks the schizoid disease of our culture. But this is not seen as a root problem of community life but rather as a problem of education for leisure. We are going to become artists, handicraft men, do-it-yourself specialists and what have you, so that we shall not become a decadent society living under the compulsion of the unconscious wish to regress to that primitive indolence against which Freud and Jung warn us. This work in which we have to be educated is free work, and it is known to be a personal and social good.

But why not also have the work we do *now* as a personal and social good? The way forward for man is the way of free work in fellowship. Erich Fromm puts it thus, when writing of man as a free, spontaneous creature:

> Love is the first component of such spontaneity; not love as the dissolution of the self in another person, not love as the possession of another person, but love as the spontaneous affirmation of others on the basis of the preservation of the individual self.
>   Work is the other component—work as creation in which one becomes one with nature in the art of creation.[8]

There is a large difference between co-management meetings and free-group meetings in that a member of the management team may set the pace for the meeting by bringing forward certain problems. Over the last twenty years we have had many co-management meetings of the kind used in the electricity-supply industry, but we now attempt to interlock the foremanship function with free-group activity by suggesting the foreman attend for a group-agreed time to state local management problems. Our experience is that if the atmosphere of the meeting is not permissive, the basic we-they attitude existing in the work situation will not alter because the individuals involved in meeting should feel free to express their deep assumptions even if these are irrational. For example, many times we have had from the free groups the statement that management and especially top management is only an expensive overhead which the primary workers have to carry; to us this was an opportunity to exhibit the educational aspect of free-group discussion with excellent results.

The free-group meeting aims at reducing dependence on figures of authority who know all the answers; that is, we attempt in social-psychiatric terms to reduce leader-centeredness and to foster maturity and independence. On the other hand, my experience with psychiatric groups indicates that if the group conductor does not take the lead but, in Lao-tzu's words of 2,500 years past, seems to follow, the results will be somewhat akin to those aimed at by those who sponsor free-group meetings.

FREE GROUP THEORY

Basic in free group theory is the idea that if we want willing obedience from a man we must first obey the man: that is, we must maturely comprehend the laws of the man's nature as expressed in his material, psychic and spiritual aspirations in fellowship with other men.

That we should be able to treat a man, not as a mere means to economic or other ends, but as a self-transcending person, that we should be able to listen to what another man *is,* and not merely to what he says, is a counsel of perfection that smacks of do-goodism. But the problem of authentic relationships is my own ever-present problem, the solution to which comes only in moments, and without warning.

Now, there is no point in idealizing either the primary workers or the managing workers in the process of stating free-group theory; what is meant is that we cannot expect one hundred percent support for such a theory. Managers are involved in matters of personal status and power, and they have a fair percentage of selfish and prejudiced individuals. Primary workers have a similar percentage of selfish and prejudiced individuals, and if I dare to estimate how many will refuse to take responsibility under a free group system I would put thirty percent as a figure based on experience. About thirty percent will welcome responsibility, and the remaining forty percent will be influenced largely by local operating circumstance which, by and large, is in the domain of management and of worker-group leadership. Among those who refuse to take any responsibility are the egocentrics, the many who have a masochistic dependence on a big-brother manager, the cynics who just don't believe management is capable of sharing real power, and the ones who don't care what happens. Self-interest is a factor that cannot be ignored, and if group operation is tied to group economic reward, the groups will operate more actively than on, say, individual piecework. Such rewards as a group bonus, profit sharing for people whose activity is related directly to profit, and the development of a sense of co-operative property are all aids to free-group cooperation. I have not found that formal co-ownership has much more than a superficial effect if it is not accompanied by individual, direct involvement in the managing process. The ideal, of course, is the small, cooperative group of managers, technicians and primary workers owning (or renting) capital and justly sharing the proceeds after meeting technical and social obligations.

The free-group method requires a multi-way communication system for the method's effective operation. On the whole, a company will be as efficient as its communication system is effective quantitively and qualitatively. If the communications are not free then the company is to that extent ineffective in the long run. Orthodox management's communication theory is a limited one. Communicated information, such as is given here, may change attitudes, but attitudes change information, a fact which educators are aware of, but of which management seems largely unaware. Management seems to accept what Dr. M. L. Johnson[9] calls the jug-and-bottle theory of education, which takes the learner to be an empty vessel ready to be filled from the management bottle. Given that the bottle is uncorked (which it sometimes is not) and the neck is not too narrow (which it sometimes is), all that is necessary is that some of the contents of the jug get into the bottle, when it is taken for granted that the substance in the bottle will be similar to that poured from the jug. Alas, both the management bottle and primary-worker bottle contain powerful emotionalized assumptions and attitudes, which change the substance poured from the jug, if, indeed, any gets into the bottle at all. Most of us, it has been shown by research[10] are as unconscious of our assumptions as we are unconscious of the earth's movements. We can, however, discover that the earth moves by comparing it with other heavenly bodies, and we can study our own assumptive world by comparing it with somebody else's, and are thus in a better position to change our assumptions if they do not lead to socially effective action. The permissive atmosphere of free-group discussion makes this change possible, for in a permissive atmosphere we can expose our irrationality without feeling that we are making fools of ourselves, and the bases of our assumptions can be examined in a supportive group atmosphere. This is true of primary worker and supervisory groups.

FREE GROUP STRUCTURE AND METHOD

The free-expression of informal group method is a kind of joint consultation in depth but it may also be an integral part of an interlocking management structure, as when the local supervisor with group consent regularly attends local group meetings for such limited time as is required for him to put his local problems to the group for its consideration. Or, of the method of having a trained group conductor present is preferred (not a chairman, it is important to note), the conductor may attend for part or the whole of the meeting, according to his mature discretion and sense of the meeting. The idea of the trained group conductor has been mentioned earlier under the description of the electricity-supply industry's co-management groups; our experience shows that if the group conductor is not a permissive person, is not mature, the groups will be and do better without a conductor.

The structure of the method is roughly as follows:

(1) Each group of twelve to twenty individuals, drawn from a specific work place if possible, meets for a certain time once each month in work time, if this is feasible.

(2) The groups operate only after the matter of group meeting has been put to groups and consented to.

(3) Each group appoints a group chairman and a secretary.

(4) The secretary keeps minutes of group deliberations and these are published in the monthly communications journal along with the names of those attending the group meeting.

(5) The group chairman attends a monthly meeting of a central group, consisting of elected members who are in touch with the small groups and representatives of management.

(6) A communications journal is published, which gives minutes of small groups and of the central-group meetings so that each member of a group knows what is happening to group ideas and management's general policy response.

(7) Where there is a personnel welfare worker the final choice of this worker, after academic and other necessary qualifications have been scrutinized by management, may fittingly be left to the groups, as the practice shows. At such firms as L. G. Harris, Ltd., Aston Chain and Hook, Ltd., and Best and Lloyd, Ltd. personnel workers have been rejected or accepted by group decision.

(8) It is held by some of those interested that a profit-sharing or co-partnership scheme is an effective seal on genuine co-partnership. These schemes by themselves accomplish little in the improvement of morale, but with a participating group system at base they take on meaning. Thus L. G. Harris and Best and Lloyd have profit-sharing schemes.

(9) Management should each month put at least local problems to the groups. If the local supervisor attends the start of his local group meeting, he should be the spokesman for such problems.

(10) For groups made up of persons eighteen years old and under, it is worth considering having a management-appointed and group-agreed adult secretary to assist the young groups in their deliberations. (11) Group meetings should be about one hour in duration and should be carefully scheduled in advance by the personnel worker or a member of the management team.

(12) For best results group members should not only be engaged in jobs in close proximity, but if possible the job operations should be closely related and the bonus earnings for task performance should be a group and not an individual bonus. Or an effective profit-sharing scheme may be preferred. If individual bonus or piecework is in use, a start may be made by splitting the total bonus earned so that a percentage is paid out on the basis of individual earnings and a percentage on group effort. This combination system is usually quite acceptable.

FIFTEEN YEARS OF GROUP DISCUSSION

It is often said that primary worker groups discuss trivialities; the following analysis of subjects discussed by the groups at Best and Lloyd Ltd. over a period of ten of the fifteen years free groups have been in operation may correct this impression.

Subject Discussed	Times Discussed
Small group procedure	48
Welfare, social club and safety (largely controlled by groups)	44
Design (and saleability of designs)	42
Holiday organization	40
Capital expenditure	37
Management and Management Board	32
Planning	30
Canteen (run by the groups)	28
Co-partnership policy	28
General quality control	26
Sales and advertising	18
Estimating	17
Office-works relationships	15
Day-work pay system	14
Explanation of accounts	14
Self-discipline and the group system	14
Job of Personnel Welfare Worker	11
Wages and allied matters	11
Batch production as cost reducer	9
Personnel problems	9

Publicity for group scheme	9
Young people's training	7
Finishing processes and quality	6
Expense control	5
Price policy	5
Works rules	4
Possible suggestion scheme	3
Best and Lloyd News	2
Stock control	2

I should have liked to include whole copies of the Aston Chain and Hook Co.'s monthly *Communicator,* and especially that number in which the Tool Room Group asked the managing director for permission to reorganize the tool room, and did so with excellent results. And, at the same company, the discussions in the groups when they were involved in drawing up a new Works Rule Book. But space forbids reproduction of many group minutes. Here, however, is one from L. G. Harris Ltd.'s brush works, where there are many young women workers.

The adult groups are quite able to discuss intelligently matters of capital expenditure; this is evident in the group minutes from Aston Chain and Hook and Best and Lloyd, companies in which there is a good proportion of skilled craftsmen. Here is an excerpt from the minutes of a group discussing capital expenditure:

The members of the group would like to know if the figures stated are competitive, and if tenders have been invited. The new lathe was not considered necessary at the present time; the polishing spindle was urgently required.
Joint Brush Making and Bristle Section Group Meeting 18.3.64
Chairman: P. J. Clarke   Guest: The Managing Director
Members present: (29 names)
Business of the Meeting:
Bonus: The Bristle Dressing operators, who have to be experienced, feel that they should have more bonus especially when they find that operators on the brush making machine are receiving more bonus than they are.
Pipes: Could the air pipe be put back on the bristle dressing machine please?
Minutes: After our last meeting, which was a considerable time ago, we were asked to omit some of our minutes. This we refused to do and in consequence none of our minutes were printed, obviously because the Management did not approve of them.
Is this supposed to be free discussion?
Mr. L. G. Harris was called in to discuss various grievances and complaints which are affecting workers' outputs. The main griev-

ance was that there are insufficient tools to enable us to reach our output figures by causing considerable delays. Also the labour position (shortage of operators and misplacement of personnel) was fully discussed. Mr. Harris kindly agreed to look into these matters for us immediately.

Trays: Members asked if they could be supplied with more trays for the bristle dressing machines.

Cones: More tin cones are also required and Mr. Harris agreed to look into this also.

That concluded the business of the meeting: (Signed) P. J. Clarke.

When the free discussion group is initiated there is a release of historic criticism which, to the immature manager, may be very disturbing:

"The trouble is that we get no real understanding from management."

"The trouble with our company is that when the managing director says 'black is white' then black *is* white."

"Management is just an overhead which the workers have to carry."

"How do we know that the free-group system is not just another trick? . . . If we say what we really think we will soon be out on our necks."

"You say the managing director really believes in this free-group idea as plain commonsense management—perhaps he does, but we don't know him and we doubt if he wants to know us. We'll see."

The three companies mentioned employ no more than 500 people each, and the electricity-supply industry, mentioned earlier, employs some thousands. Each company tailors its system to its own liking; each has strong points and failings in my opinion; but all of them are alike in that they are fostering a new concept of work relationships.

From some large companies I have been met with the argument "We are too big for the free or informal group system," and while it is true that in a firm of more than, say, 500 people, the group system is apt to become a formal method, the huge electricity-supply industry, with its groups operating in fairly small management units, gives an effective answer to the "we-are-too-big" argument. Decentralization is the rule rather than the exception in very large companies, and in such companies decentralization of group structure in management units, each with its own communication journal, would be essential. A pilot unit to prove or disprove the system would be valuable.

When the free or autonomous groups were first started in 1948 at Best and Lloyd, we aimed at interlocking primary worker groups at workshop,

office and technical levels with management through primary-group representation on a management board and not, it is important to note, on a joint
council separate from, though perhaps influencing top management organization. Best and Lloyd is a very old company engaged on making high-
grade craft-work lighting fittings and metal work, and employs about 100
people. On the Management Board are three elected group members, three
management-appointed group members and a top manager as chairman. It
might be thought that the chairman would dominate the group. But the
spirit of the business is indicated by the response of the chairman to an
impasse on the question of diverting funds from employee profit sharing to
capital development:

> When you are dealing with a product such as ours, which has a
> fluctuating demand, the company is entitled to more than from a gilt-
> edge investment, to enable it to plough back a reasonable amount for
> plant, tools, future development and inflation. But having said that I
> am sure that after ten years, we are not going to fall out over a matter
> of this sort. I don't want to be grasping and neither do the co-partners,
> I know. If we cannot agree there is one way of reaching a reasonable
> decision, and that would be to find somebody impartial outside this
> business and ask him for a reasonable opinion as to what would be a
> fair distribution.

As the foreman or supervisory group, the office group, and the production worker group are represented, with management-appointed representatives on the Board, it is clear that in Best and Lloyd there is here interlocking group management, with multi-way communication through the *Best
and Lloyd News,* and appropriate spread of decision-making.

In a recent book by Prof. Rensis Lickert there is advanced the idea of
what is called "overlapping management," in which at each level from top
to bottom of an organization there is grouping with each lower group meeting attended by or run by someone from a higher level. Thus, a production
or primary group would be run by the supervisor of that group, and the
supervisor group would be run by, say, the works manager, and the executive group at works manager level may be run by the general manager, and
so on up the organization. Lickert's very readable and interesting book
proves with a wealth of research data that overlapping group management
is superior to the orthodox chain-of-command management.[11]

In the firm of L. G. Harris, some foremen attend primary group meetings
for a part *only of group meeting time with group and foreman consent,* thus
tending to interlock the lower supervisory function with primary group

operation—the consent is not the result of a managed meeting but results from primary and foremen meetings respectively, in a permissive atmosphere. The theory of foreman attendance at primary group meetings is that the foreman should be the communicating channel for local matters coming within his daily province as well as for such wider matters as are passed to him from higher up. Thus the foreman may report on such matters as work quality and output, department work load, orders, and the like.

THE FREE GROUP CONTRACT SYSTEM

Where a free or autonomous group operates to share work and the rewards of work, "the law of free work" is in command; that is, the disciplines do not emanate so much from management, but are in the work itself and the work situation. This has been called the "law of the situation," and it has been suggested that appeal to this law takes the place of the use of coercion. But in an unfree environment the law of the situation is an abstraction that operates to control the work process without consideration of the concrete situation in terms of relationships and of power distribution within that situation. The law of the situation will inevitably take its color from the existing power structure and may justify extreme poverty and wealth, or domination and submission in the same economic environment; this is a truism in political science which is put very well by, I think, Anatole France, when he says: "The law in its majestic equality forbids the poor as well as the rich to sleep under bridges, to beg, and to steal food."

The free-group contract system expresses in practice the psychological theory of work, quoted earlier, in Freud, Jung and Fromm, in that the work is freely done in and for fellowship with consequent growth towards maturity for the individual and for society. This to me is a most important aspect of the free-group system in general and the free-group contract system in particular. Freedom in work is usually supported by economic arguments and proofs about production or by vague ideological theorizing, but its chief logical support comes from psychology and sociology. With the free-group contract method in its full form within an existing work situation, man-supervision is withdrawn and transferred to the work itself, although technical guidance will be necessary.

At the other end of the scale is the group contract method in which a group undertakes certain work in return for a money reward which is shared in some just manner among the group members. But even with the latter simple system there is usually freedom to arrange internal affairs and to utilize labor where it is most needed, and we have the group imposing its own internal disciplines which spring naturally from the law of the work, and, it will be clear, the group performs one or more functions which were hitherto the function of management. In the free-group meeting system we have the same law operating in a wider field with the primary group inter-locking with management in the carrying out of the work process.

The free-group meeting system may operate without the more or less free contract system, and vice versa, but it is doubtful if the use of individual piecework or bonus is conducive to cooperative effort. True, a profit-shar-ing system may make for cooperative effort in a situation in which there are free group meetings, but the incentive of profit sharing may be too remote to have any direct effect on the work.

The vital importance of autonomy at the actual work-point in terms of the social and personal benefits to be gained from effective grouping, as well as from output, indicates that wherever possible the group-bonus system should be encouraged. My experience indicates clearly that, on the whole, primary workers resent individual bonus to the extent that, given a choice, they would prefer group bonus. There is not much research on this, but the following from a machine tool firm may be interesting:

	For	Against	Indifferent
Individual piece-rates or bonus	21%	70%	9%
Group bonus with group sharing	61%	32%	7%
Individual and group bonus with 30% of individual earnings shared	38%	55%	7%

Group bonus is to be preferred from the human standpoint to individual bonus, and its fruitful use is indicated in the following situations:

(1) Where primary worker morale is not all it should be.

(2) Where skill and experience is high and the use of refined work study and operation planning techniques is expensive with consequent increase in cost of management.

(3) Where sub-tasks within a task have job times which are so differ-ent that there is a serious problem of labor allocation within the task.

(4) Where it is possible to derive a contract time or price from the costing estimates and to use this time of price as the contract with the group, thus saving much documentation, considerable applied opera-tion timing and planning techniques.

(5) Where labor costs is low compared with material cost in a job and it is not worthwhile using expensive work-study techniques and the method of 4 above is suitable.

(6) Where the primary workers' desire is for group bonus.

(7) Where the costs of man-management are high or are increasing and/or top managers are enlightened enough to wish to gain the benefits of the spread of decision-making to the work-point. The full benefits will be gained by a group pay system with the group contracting to do the needed work under the control of the group-appointed leader but with technical foremanship as a parallel (but interlocked) procedure. This is the free-group contract system with the group leader as contract negotiator and taking responsibility for group discipline, work progressing and output.

It is understandable that many managers will be somewhat startled by these proposals, and especially that which suggests that man-management be left to a group-appointed leader.

It was while on a foundry job that I first observed primary worker selection of a foreman. The group was a tough group of fettlers (casting dressers and cleaners) and getting a foreman to stay with them was quite a problem. I suggested to management we try letting the men decide which member of the fettling team they would like for a foreman; management was extremely doubtful and seemed sure the team would pick firebrand X, whereas Y was obviously the best man. The group picked Y by secret ballot, whereupon Y called a meeting and told the team what a lot of shirkers they were, etc., etc., to the team's great delight. I have only one other experience of this kind, but the experiments indicated that a group of adults will pick the man best suited to the situation; as was undoubtedly true when our small free groups made the final selection of personnel managers in three separate instances.

My experience of the simple group contract system is considerable, but of the free-group contract system in which the group takes over considerable man-management, it is much less. Dubreil, in his classic book *A Chance for Everybody,*[12] tells of a group of engineers who with management consent worked out job rates for each job and successfully took on the whole group task on contract with group responsibility for results: this was some thirty years past.

Some years ago I was called upon to help reorganize a fifty-man foundry engaged on craft-work production of intricate castings. The moulders themselves controlled sand-fetching and mixing, mould-box selection, moulding method, metal pouring, and mould opening. Based on the manager's experience, my checking, and discussion with the moulders, who on heavy work were in gangs or groups, we set a rate per ton for a number of different classes of work, but without any detailed work study, which would have been very expensive indeed. There were no full-time foremen and only very general control by the foundry manager. The moulders took on group replacements where necessary, and had control of group internal labor movement and allocation. My experience of foundry work told me that these moulders were performing equal to or better than other moulders operating under orthodox management organization and control, in terms of cost-per-ton and quality.

In passing, one skilled group of moulders left the firm to go to a car factory where wages were much higher, but came back after a few days with the comment that "A man isn't a man in that blurry place, but only a blurry machine."

One of the comic aspects of "scientific" individual bonus schemes is that the working group may remain on group bonus in spite of the applications of orthodox planning and work study techniques—this among skilled men usually, but prevalent throughout the work situation. When I served a short apprenticeship in a Glasgow car works we were on individual bonus but our internal work code was such that we limited earnings on any job to a group-agreed maximum. In Yorkshire, I found the same "group bonus system" operative in an engineering factory that was supposed to be on individual bonus. This kind of thing is irrational economically, but if we take it deep enough we may find that the irrational is the real, and the healthy.

On the other hand, where there is no underlying fellowship in an aggregate of workers on individualized piecework, it is painful sometimes to watch the struggle for money. In one clothing factory there was an almost animal struggle for bundles of work during the slack season. As was said earlier, our economic culture rewards some of the worst of human characteristics and penalizes some of the best, in the running of the economic rat-race.

THE DURHAM MINERS' FREE GROUP PROJECT

There are two weighty reports on this project by psychologists, experts on human relationships.[13] Peculiarly enough, these experts in their reports retreat behind a technico-socio-mathematico-psychologese which is at once a character armor and an omnipotential barrier to a meaningful relationship between the specialist and the ordinary reader. Names take the place of people, and the gracious mystery of human relationship is wrapped from sight in the papered concealment of statistical tabulations. Were the miners merely a group pursuing economic interests? Or were they a fellowship in which the whole worth of each person was consciously recognized and re- warded? The latter is the truer, as is shown in their sharing of group pay on the basis of equality.

In short, in earlier days before the onset of mechanization, specialization of labor, and the development of modern management theories of control and individual incentives, small groups of miners working at the coal face shared group earnings and took responsibility for local regulation and con- trol of the actual coal-getting at the work-point. The newer management outlook and method dealt with the mechanized practice which required larger groups of forty to fifty men in much the same way as modern man- agement does with the application of time-and-motion study, sub-operation regulation and control through process planning, and individualistic incentives. This did not work either in terms of profitability or of human satisfaction in work. So, the miners themselves in a number of pits, de- signed and worked out a method which was a return on a higher level to the old group method, with equal sharing of the rewards of effort. They proved that the alternative to "scientific" and hierarchical management is group effort with group bonus and appropriate spread of decision-making within an organization.

The miners concerned were already a group, and as pointed out earlier, they behaved like any normal group of adult primary workers by organizing and regulating the local work situation by allocating effort, skill, and expe- rience where it was most needed on the job, and sharing the proceeds of the work among the group members. This, to those used to the operation of work groups is not at all surprising, but what is surprising is that the new group method was a *spontaneous growth* among the miners themselves. Nor is it surprising that output per man-hour increased and cost per ton was reduced, but what is surprising is that the authors of the reports do not stress, as Melman does, that the change brought about by the miners was a fundamental change in orthodox management theory and practice and that such a change, through sharing of group earning and spread of the decision- making process (or sharing of power) is appropriate to any organized pro- duction process with consequent increase in primary worker significance and self-respect in the otherwise authoritarian work situations.

The elite among the miners and among the managers can pilot this in- formative free-group process to higher and more satisfactory levels. At this moment it is a candlelight in the depths of the earth, a promise. But through the extension of the free-group contract system by the initiation of interlocking labor foremanship (group leadership) and technical foremanship, and the meeting of these (and higher functions) in free groups, the guild system which many miners dreamed that nationalization would bring, might develop, and each man in a mine might play a whole man's part in the conduct of his mine's affairs.

The linking of mines by districts already exists, as does a central board, and the communication structure of joint consultation needs modification and extension in depth to create out of what is a formalized institution an organic industry with each organ serving the whole. A first step has been taken and it will be a long way to the realization of the guild concept of a "parliament of work" which by its very nature will dignify work, and the structure of which will interlock all industries.

The guild system has much thoughtful support in sociological, political and religious thinking. The guild system is already in seed in work in both private and public industry, and it is for thoughtful workers to bring it to flower. For many of us it will be the revivication of past dreams, for others a newfound upward path with a far view, not of economic man, or of organization man, or of role-playing man, but of cooperative man, be he laborer, craftsman, manager, technician, or administrator, working in and for the fellowship.

THE WIDER ISSUES

We have taken more than the usual worm's eye view of work and its organization, and of the relationship of increasingly automated work to the use and abuse of leisure. The problem of leisure and its effects on the individual and the social group is becoming of increasing urgency—

> If Satan idle hands as tools created,
> are idle brains his factories, automated?

Behind this often stated problem of leisure is hidden the problem of worker and work significance and of the schizoid relationship between work life and social life; and yet deeper is the problem of the strongly individualistic and acquisitive motives that largely activate our culture. It is at this root fault in economic life that this essay is directed, for to reiterate: our economic culture highly rewards some of the basest of human characteristics and penalizes some of the best. There are larger problems than those which have been stated here, but narrow though the level of our approach is, I am unaware of any major social problem the solution of which would not be aided by the fostering of free groups in both work and social life, in the authoritarian work situation and in mass democracy. To conclude with the opinions of two social scientists: George C. Homans writes that

> At the level of the small group society has always been able to cohere. We infer therefore, that if civilization is to stand, it must maintain, in the relations which make up society and the central direction of sanity, some of the features of the small group itself.[14]

And Wilhelm Aarek has this to say, after writing of the frustrations of mass society composed of huge institutions:

> The small groups will be able, through fellowship, to make amends to people, to give them something of a feeling that the social and international forces can be coped with after all. For it is just this spirit of fellowship in the many small groups which must, in the long run, give life and content to the large social and international groups.[15]

NOTES

[1] H. Clegg, *A New Approach to Industrial Democracy* (Blackwell, 1960).

[2] Seymour Melman, *Decision-Making and Productivity* (Blackwell, 1958).

[3] Robert Michels, *Political Parties* (New York: Dover, 1959 [1915]).

[4] James J. Gillespie, *Dynamic Motion and Time Study* (New York: Tudor, 1951).

[5] Sigmund Freud, *Civilization and Its Discontents* (New York: Norton, 1962).

[6] Carl Jung, *Psychology of the Unconscious* (New York: Dodd, 1963).

[7] Walker and Guest, *The Man on the Assembly Line* (Cambridge, Mass.: Harvard, 1952).

[8] Erich Fromm, *Escape from Freedom* (New York: Holt, 1941).

[9] M. L. Johnson, *Group Discussion* (London: Central Council for Health Education, 1954).

[10] *Ibid.*

[11] Rensis Likert, *New Patterns of Management* (New York: McGraw-Hill, 1961).

[12] Dubreuil, *A Chance for Everybody* (London: Chatto and Windus, 1939).

[13] P. G. Herbst, *Autonomous Groups Functioning* (Tavistock Publications, 1962); see also E. L. Trist, *et al., Organizational Choice* (Tavistock Publications, 1963).

[14] George C. Homans, *The Human Group* (New York: Harcourt, Brace, & Co., 1950).

[15] Wilhelm Aarek, *Loneliness and Fellowship* (Society of Friends, 1959).

By now it should be evident that a participatory democracy cannot be organized on a mass scale. The value of Murray Bookchin's discussion of a liberatory technology is that it shows that technology can be used to regain this smallness of scale. A liberatory technology, as Bookchin shows, is a decentralized technology, ecologically in balance, using local resources. This kind of technology is essential if those who are affected by it are to control it. When technology is organized, as it is today, into huge centralized complexes for a particular commodity—Detroit for cars, Pittsburgh for steel, New York for banking and advertising—the economic decisions that affect society as a whole are out of reach of the people.

Whether one relies on Pittsburgh for one's steel or on the kind of small-scale steel mill that Bookchin describes, one still needs a given quantity of steel; but to have control over a significant part of one's resources is a value in itself. Big utility companies run roughshod over the small consumer; they will happily run power and gas lines to large factories, but often leave the isolated household to fend for itself. By contrast, rural electric cooperatives have served the consumer much more responsibly. In short, there is no substitute for local control, if one is seeking local accountability. Decentralized technology is thus crucial not simply to regain control of technology itself: since control of technology brings with it the power to make key political and economic decisions regarding where people will work, what will be produced, whether there will be roads or public transportation, a decentralized technology can affect these, too. When communities can control their own technology they can control their shape, their growth, where and how their residents work.

At present, a mythology of free choice is encouraged through consumerism: one is free to select among competing (and almost identical) brands. But with technology under community control, free choice would be much more real. Communities could develop autonomy and individuality in life styles centering around the kind of rural-urban mixes that Bookchin speaks of, around unique adaptations to particular natural environments. Regional and local economies would give communities specific identities: towns in forest areas could produce lumber, but also furniture for their surrounding region; local styles in dress, housing material and design, home furnishings, could become prevalent.

There are also problems attendant on decentralizing the technology; in Yugoslavia, there is a tug of war between the economically well-off northern provinces and the poorer southern provinces. This kind of discrepancy is more quickly overcome in a centralized economy. On the local level, the problem posed by the desire for autonomy on the part of productive enterprises is not settled. But when technology is centralized dependency is always created; large, centralized bureaucratic organizations possess an inherent insensitivity to individual and local needs. They prefer to deal with other large bureaucracies, and, thus, the world comes to be divided between big organizations dealing with each other. The little man gets the crumbs. Moreover, for the little man to get anything at all, whether it be welfare or automobiles, he must fit the standardized requirements of the big organization. Thus, the values of decentralization extend beyond the economic to the psychosocial.

Toward a
Liberatory Technology
Murray Bookchin

Not since the days of the industrial revolution have popular attitudes toward technology fluctuated as sharply as in the past few decades. During most of the twenties and even well into the thirties, public opinion generally welcomed technological innovation and identified man's welfare with the industrial advances of the time. This was a period when Soviet apologists could justify Stalin's most brutal methods and worst crimes merely by describing him as the "industrializer" of modern Russia. It was also a period when the most effective critique of capitalist society could rest on the brute facts of economic and technological stagnation in the United States and Western Europe. To many people, there seemed to be a direct, one-to-one relationship between technological advances and social progress—a fetishizing of the word "industrialization" that excused the most abusive of economic plans and programs.

Today, we would regard these attitudes as naive. Except perhaps for the technicians and scientists who design the "hardware," the feeling of most people toward technological innovation could be described as schizoid, divided by a gnawing fear of nuclear extinction on the one hand, and by a yearning for material abundance, leisure, and security on the other. Technology, too, seems to be at odds with itself: the bomb is pitted against the power reactor, the intercontinental missile against the communications satellite. The same technological discipline tends to appear as much a foe as a friend of humanity, and even traditionally man-oriented sciences, such as medicine, occupy an ambivalent position, as witness the promise opened by recent advances in chemotherapy and the threat created by recent research in biological warfare.

It should not be surprising, then, to find that this tension between promise and threat is increasingly resolved in favor of threat, by a blanket rejection of technology and the technological spirit. To an ever-growing extent, we find that technology is viewed as a demon, imbued with a sinister life of its own, that is likely to mechanize man if it fails to exterminate him. The deep pessimism this view tends to produce is often as simplistic as the optimism that prevailed in earlier decades. There is a very real danger, today, that we will lose our perspective toward technology, neglect its liberatory tendencies, and worse, fatalistically submit to its use for destructive ends.

If we are not to be paralyzed by this new form of social fatalism, a balance must be struck. The purpose of this essay is to explore three questions: What is the liberatory *potential* of modern technology, both materially and spiritually? What tendencies, if any, are reshaping the machine for use in an organic, man-oriented society? And finally, how can the new technology and resources be used in an ecological manner, that is, to promote the balance of nature, the full, lasting development of natural regions, and the creation of organic, humanistic communities?

The emphasis in the above remarks should be placed on the word "potential." I make no claim that technology is necessarily liberatory or consistently beneficial to man's development. But I surely do not believe that man is destined to be enslaved by technology and technological modes of thought, as Juenger and Elul seem to imply in their books on the subject.[1] To the contrary, I shall try to show that an organic mode of life, deprived of its inorganic, technological components (be they a plentitude of raw materials or machines), would be as non-functional as a man deprived of his skeleton. Technology, I submit, must be conceived as the basic structural support of a society, the indispensable frame on which hang all the living institutions of a dynamic social organism.

TECHNOLOGY AND FREEDOM

The year 1848 stands out as a turning point in the history of modern revolutions—the year when Marxism made its debut as a distinct ideology in the
pages of *The Communist Manifesto* and when the proletariat, represented
by the Parisian workers, made its debut as a distinct political force on the
barricades of June. It could also be said that 1848, a year close to the half-
way mark of the nineteenth century, represents the culmination of the
traditional steam-powered technology initiated by the Newcomen engine a
century and half earlier.

What strikes us about the convergence in a single year of these ideological, political, and technological milestones is the extent to which the revolutionary goals in *The Communist Manifesto* and the socialist ideals that permeated the thinking of the Parisian workers were in advance of the
industrial possibilities of the time. In the 1840's, the Industrial Revolution
was limited primarily to three areas of the economy: textile production, iron-
making, and transportation. The invention of Arkwright's spinning machine, Watt's steam engine, and Cartwright's power loom, had brought the
factory system to the textile industry, and a number of striking innovations
in iron-making technology assured the high-quality, inexpensive metals
needed to sustain the expansion of the factories and of a newly discovered
means of transportation, the railways. But these innovations, important as
they were, were not accompanied by commensurable changes in other areas
of technology. For one thing, the common run of steam engines used at the
time rarely yielded more than fifteen horse-power, compared with the enormously powerful steam turbines in use today, and the best blast furnaces
provided little more than 100 tons of iron a week, a mere fraction of the
two to three thousand tons produced daily by modern furnaces. More important still, the remaining areas of the economy had barely been affected
by technological innovation. The mining techniques underpinning the new
metals technology, for example, had changed very little since the days of
the Renaissance. The miner still worked the ore face with a hand-pick and
crowbar, and drainage pumps, ventilation systems, and hauling techniques
were not greatly improved over the descriptions we find in Agricola's classic
on mining, written three centuries earlier. Agriculture was only first emerging from its centuries-old sleep. Although a great deal of land had been
cleared for food cultivation, soil studies were still a novelty, and so heavy
was the weight of tradition and conservatism that most harvesting was still
done by hand, despite the fact that a mechanical reaper had been perfected

as early as 1822. Buildings, despite their massiveness and ornateness, were erected primarily by sheer muscle power—the hand-crane and windlass still occupying the mechanical center of the construction site. Steel was a relatively rare metal. As late as 1850, it was priced at $250 a ton and, until the discovery of the Bessemer converter, steel-making techniques had stagnated for centuries. Finally, although precision tools had made great forward strides, it is worth noting, after all, that Charles Babbage's efforts to build a mechanical computer were completely thwarted by the inadequate machining techniques of the time.

I have reviewed these technological developments because both their promise and limitations exercised a profound influence on nineteenth-century revolutionary concepts of freedom. The innovations in textile and iron-making technology provided a new sense of promise, indeed a qualitatively unique stimulus to socialist and utopian thought. To the revolutionary theorist, it seemed that for the first time in history, he could anchor his dream of a liberatory society in the visible prospect of material abundance and increased leisure for the mass of humanity. Socialism, he argued, could be based on the self-interest of man rather than on his dubious nobility of mind and spirit. Technological innovation had transmuted the socialist ideal from a vague, humanitarian hope into a practical program, superior in its realism to all prevailing modes of bourgeois thought.

By the same token, this new sense of realism compelled many socialist theorists, particularly Marx and Engels, to deal with the technological limitations of their time. They were faced with a strategic issue: in all previous revolutions, technology had not developed to a level where men could be freed from material want, from toil, and from the struggle over the necessities of life. However glowing and lofty were the revolutionary ideals of the past, the vast majority of the people, burdened by material want, had to depart from the stage of history, return to work, and deliver the management of society to a new, leisured class of exploiters. Indeed, any attempt to equalize the wealth of society at a low level of technological development would not have eliminated want, but would have merely made it into a general, overall feature of society as a whole, thereby recreating all the conditions for a new struggle over the material things of life, new forms of property, and eventually, a new system of class domination. "A development of the productive forces is the absolutely necessary practical premise [of Communism]," wrote Marx in 1846, "because without it want is generalized, and with want the struggle for necessities begins again, and that means that all the old shit must revive."

And the truth is that virtually all the utopias, theories, and revolutionary programs of the early nineteenth century turned on the problematical axis of necessity—on the two poles of want and toil. The problem of necessity— the formulation of theories that would answer to the need to allocate labor and equitably distribute material goods at a relatively low level of technological development—permeated revolutionary thought with an intensity comparable only to the problem of original sin in Christian theology. The fact that men would have to devote a substantial portion of their time to toil, for which they would get scant returns, formed a major premise of all socialist ideology, be it authoritarian or libertarian utopian or scientific, Marxist or anarchist. Implicit in the Marxist notion of a planned economy is the fact, incontestably clear in Marx's day, that socialism would still be burdened by relatively scarce resources. Men would have to plan—in effect, restrict—the distribution of goods and rationalize—in effect, intensify—the use of labor. Toil, under socialism, would be regarded as a duty, a responsibility that every able-bodied individual had to undertake. Even the great libertarian Proudhon advanced the same view when he wrote: "Yes life is a struggle. But this struggle is not between man and man—it is between man and Nature; and it is each one's duty to share it." This austere, almost Biblical emphasis on struggle and duty reflects the harsh quality of socialist thought during the Industrial Revolution.

The problem of dealing with want and work—an age-old problem perpetuated by the early Industrial Revolution—produced the great divergence in revolutionary ideas between socialism and anarchism. Freedom would still be circumscribed by necessity in the event of a revolution. How was this world of necessity to be "administered"? How would the allocation of goods and duties be decided? Marx left this decision to a state power, a transitional, "proletarian" state power, to be sure, but nevertheless a coercive body, established above and beyond society. According to Engels, the state would "wither away" as technology developed and enlarged the domain of freedom, granting humanity material plenty and the leisure to control its affairs directly. This strange calculus of necessity and freedom, mediated of all things by the state, differs very little politically from the common run of radical bourgeois-democratic opinion in the last century. The anarchist hope for an immediate abolition of the state rested largely on a belief in the viability of man's social instincts. In Bakunin's mind, to be sure, custom would compel anti-social individuals to abide by collectivist values and needs without obliging society to use coercion. But Kropotkin, who exercised more influence among anarchists in this area of speculation, invoked man's propensity for mutual aid—essentially a social instinct—as the guarantor of solidarity in an anarchist community, a concept that he hard-headedly derived from his study of animal and social evolution.

The fact remains, however, that in both cases—the Marxist and anarchist—the answer to the problem of want and work is shot through with ambiguity. The realm of necessity was brutally present; it could not be conjured away by mere theory and speculation. The Marxists could hope to administer it by means of a state; the anarchists, to digest it through free communities. But given the limited technological development of the last century, both schools depended in the last analysis on an act of faith to cope with the problem of want and work. Anarchists could argue that any transitional state-power, however revolutionary its rhetoric and democratic its structure, would be self-perpetuating; it would tend to become an end in itself, to preserve the very material and social conditions it had been created to remove. For such a state-power to "wither away," that is, to promote its own dissolution, would require that its leaders and bureaucracy be people of superhuman moral qualities. The Marxists, in turn, could invoke history as evidence that custom and mutualistic propensities were never effective barriers to the pressures of material need, to the onslaught of property, and finally, to the development of exploitation and class domination. Accordingly, they dismissed anarchism as an ethical doctrine, reviving the mystique of the natural man and his inborn social virtues. The problem of want and work—the realm of necessity—was never satisfactorily resolved by either body of doctrine in the last century. It is to the lasting credit of anarchism that it uncompromisingly retained its high ideal of freedom—the ideal of spontaneous organization, community, and the abolition of all authority —although this amounts to saying that it remained an ideology of man's future, of the time when technology could eliminate the realm of necessity entirely. Marxism increasingly compromised its ideal of freedom, painfully qualifying it with transitional stages and political expediencies, until today it is an ideology of naked power, pragmatic efficiency, and social centralization, almost indistinguishable from ideologies of modern-day state capitalism.[2]

In retrospect, it is astonishing to consider how long the problem of want and work lingered at the core of revolutionary theory. In a span of only nine decades—the years between 1850 and 1940—Western society created, passed through, and evolved beyond two major epochs of technological history—the paeotechnic age based on coal and steel, and the neotechnic age based on electric power, synthetic chemicals, electricity, and internal combustion engines. Ironically, both ages of technology seemed to enhance the importance of toil in society. As the number of industrial workers increased in proportion to other social classes, labor—more precisely, toil—acquired an increasingly high status in revolutionary thought. During this period, the propaganda of the socialists often sounded like a paean to toil; the workers were extolled as the only useful individuals in the social fabric. They were imparted with a superior instinctive ability that rendered them into the arbiters of philosophy, art, and social organization. This curious emphasis on toil, this puritanical ethic of the left, instead of diminishing with the passage of time, acquired a new sense of urgency by the 1930's. Mass unemployment made the job and the social organization of labor *the* central theme of socialist propaganda. Instead of focusing their message on the emancipation of man from toil, socialists tended to depict socialism as a beehive of industrial activity, humming with work for all. The Communists incessantly pointed to Russia as a model of a socialist land, where every able-bodied individual was employed, indeed, where labor was continually in demand. Surprising as it may seem today, the fact is that little more than a generation ago, socialism was equated with a work-oriented society and liberty with the material security provided by full employment. The world of necessity, in effect, had subtly invaded and corrupted the ideal of freedom.

If the socialist notions of the last generation now seem to be anachronisms, this is not due to any superior insights that prevail today. The last three decades, particularly the years of the late 1950's, mark a turning-point in technological development—a technological revolution that negates all the values, political schemes, and social perspectives held by mankind throughout all previous recorded history. After thousands of years of torturous development, the countries of the Western world, and potentially all of humanity, are confronted by the possibility of an affluent, workless era—an epoch in which all the means and luxuries of life can be provided almost entirely by machines. As we shall see in the following section, a new technology has been developed that could replace the realm of necessity by the realm of freedom. So obvious is this fact to millions of people in the United States and Europe, that it no longer requires elaborate explanations or theoretical exegesis. This technological revolution and the prospects it holds for society as a whole form the premises of radically new life-styles among many young people, a generation no longer burdened by the values and age-old, work-oriented traditions of their elders. Even demands for a guaranteed annual income irrespective of whether the recipient is engaged in work or not, sound like faint echoes of a new reality that currently permeates the thinking of young people today. Owing to the development of a cybernated technology, the notion of a toilless mode of life became an article of faith to an increasing number of young people in the 1960's.

In fact, the real issue we face today is not whether this new technology can provide us with the means of life in a workless society, but whether it can *humanize* society, whether it can contribute to the creation of new relationships between man and man. The demand for a guaranteed annual income is still anchored in the *quantitative* promise of a cybernated technology—the possibility of satisfying essential material needs without toil. I submit that this quantitative type of solution, if such it can be called, is already lagging behind technological developments that carry a new, *qualitative* promise—the promise of decentralized, communitarian life-styles, or what I prefer to call ecological forms of human association.[3]

What I am asking, in effect, is a question that differs from what is ordinarily posed with respect to modern technology: is this technology staking out a new dimension in human freedom, in the liberation of man? Can it lead man not only to freedom from want and work, but aid directly in shaping a harmonious, balanced human community—a community that would provide man with the soil for the unrestricted development of his potentialities? Can it not only eliminate the age-old struggle for existence, but nourish the desire for creation, both communally and individually?

THE POTENTIALITIES OF MODERN TECHNOLOGY

Let me try to answer these questions by pointing to a decisive feature of modern technology: for the first time in history, technology has reached an open end. What I mean by an "open end" is that the potential for technological development, for providing machines as substitutes for labor is essentially unlimited. Technology has finally passed from the realm of *invention* into that of *design,* from fortuitous discoveries into systematic innovations.

The meaning of this qualitative advance has been stated in a rather free-wheeling way by Dr. Vannevar Bush, the former director of the U.S. Office of Scientific Research and Development:

> Suppose, fifty years ago, that someone had proposed making a device which would cause an automobile to follow a white line down the middle of the road, automatically and even if the driver fell asleep. . . . He would have been laughed at, and his idea would have been called preposterous. So it would have been then. But suppose someone called

for such a device today, and was willing to pay for it, leaving aside the question of whether it would actually be of any genuine use whatever. Any number of concerns would stand ready to contract and build it. No real invention would be required. There are thousands of young men in the country to whom the design of such a device would be a pleasure. They would simply take off the shelf some photocells, thermionic tubes, servo-mechanisms, relays and, if urged, they would build what they call a breadboard model, and it would work. The point is that the presence of a host of versatile, cheap, reliable gadgets, and the presence of men who understand fully all their queer ways, has rendered the building of automatic devices almost straightforward and routine. It is no longer a question of whether they can be built, it is rather a question of whether they are worth building.

Bush focuses here on the two most important features of the new, so-called "second industrial revolution": the potentialities of modern technology and the cost-oriented, non-human limitations imposed upon them. I shall not belabor the fact that the cost factor—the profit motive, to state it bluntly—inhibits the use of technological innovations as well as promoting their application in many industries. It is fairly well established that in many areas of the economy it is often cheaper to use labor than machines. Instead, I would like to review several developments that have brought us to an open-end in technology and deal with a number of practical applications that have profoundly affected the role of labor in industry and agriculture.

Perhaps the most obvious development leading to the new technology has been the increasing interpenetration of a scientific abstraction, mathematics, and analytic methods with the concrete, pragmatic, and rather mundane tasks of industry. This new order of relationships is relatively new. Traditionally, speculation, generalization, and rational activity had been sharply divorced from technology—a chasm created by the sharp split between the leisured and working classes of ancient and medieval society. Although a number of bridges had been created between the two domains, these structures were largely the inspired but episodic works of a few rare men, the pioneers of early applied science. Actually, applied science did not come into its own until the Renaissance and it began really to flourish in the nineteenth century, when scientific knowledge—the growing corpus of man's generalizations about the physical world—fertilized the mundane world of technology. The authentic personification of this new interplay between scientific generalization and technology is not the inventor, the James Watt or Thomas Edison, but the systematic investigator with catholic interests, the Michael Faraday, who almost simultaneously adds both to man's knowledge of scientific principles and to engineering. In our own day the synthesis embodied by the work of a single, inspired genius now reposes in the anonymous team of specialists—the co-operative activity of physicists, biologists, engineers, and technicians—with its clear-cut advantages, to be sure, but also with the resulting lack of vision, imagination and inspiration so characteristic of bureaucratic modes of organization.

A second development, often less obvious, is the impact produced by industrial growth itself. This development is not always technological in the sense that a machine replaces labor. One of the most effective means of increasing output, in fact, has been the continual reorganization of the labor process, the extension and sophistication of the division of labor. Ironically, by an inner dialect of its own, the steady breakdown of tasks to an ever-more-inhuman dimension, to an intolerably minute, fragmented series of operations, to a cruel simplification of the work process, suggests the machine that will recombine all the separate tasks of many workers into a single mechanized operation. Historically, it would be difficult to understand how mechanized mass manufacture emerged, how the machine increasingly displaced labor, without tracing its development from craftsmanship, where an independent, highly skilled worker engaged in many diverse operations on a single commodity, through the purgatory of the factory, where these diverse tasks were parceled out among a multitude of unskilled or semi-skilled employees, to the highly mechanized mill, where the tasks of many were largely taken over by machines, manipulated by a few operatives, and finally the automated and cybernated plant, where operatives are now replaced by supervisory technicians and highly skilled maintenance men.

Looking further into the matter, we find still another development—the evolution of the machine from an extension of human muscles into an extension of the human nervous system. In the past, both tools and machines enhanced man's muscular power over raw materials and natural forces. The mechanical devices and engines developed during the eighteenth and nineteenth centuries did not replace human biceps but rather extended their effectiveness. Although the machines increased output enormously, the worker's muscles and brain were still required to operate them, even for fairly routine tasks. The calculus of technological advance could be formulated in the strict terms of labor productivity: One man, using a given machine, produced as many commodities as five, ten, fifty, or a hundred before the machine was employed. Nasmyth's steam hammer, exhibited in 1851, for example, could shape iron beams with only a few blows, an effort that would have required many man-hours of labor. But the hammer required the muscles and judgment of a half-dozen able-bodied men to pull, hold, and remove the casting. In time, much of this work was diminished by the invention of handling devices, but the labor and judgment involved in operating the machines formed an indispensable part of the productive process.

To develop fully automatic machines for complex mass-manufacturing operations requires the successful application of at least three technological principles: a built-in ability of the machine to correct its own errors; sensory devices for replacing the visual, auditory, and tactile senses of the worker; and finally, devices that provide an approximation of the worker's mental faculties—judgment, skill, and memory. The effective use of these three principles, to be sure, presupposes that we have also developed the technological means, the effectors, if you will, for applying the sensory, control and mind-like devices to everyday industrial operations; that we can adapt existing machines or develop new ones for handling, shaping, assembling, packaging, and transporting semi-finished and finished products.

The use of automatic, self-correcting control devices in industrial operations is not new. James Watt's flyball governor, invented in 1788, provides an early mechanical example of how steam engines were self-regulated. Attached by metal arms to the engine valve, the governor essentially consists of a thin, rotating rod supporting two freely mounted metal balls. If the engine begins to operate too rapidly, the increased rotation of the rod impels the balls outward by centrifugal force, closing the valve; conversely, if the valve does not admit sufficient steam to operate the engine at the desired rate, the balls collapse inwardly, opening the valve further. A similar principle is involved in the operation of thermostatically controlled heating equipment. The thermostat, manually preset by a dial to a desired temperature level, automatically starts up heating equipment when the temperature falls and turns off the equipment when it rises.

Both control devices illustrate what is now called the "feedback principle." In modern electronic equipment, the deviation of a machine from a desired level of operation produces electrical signals, which are then used by the control device to correct the deviation or error. The electrical signals induced by the error are amplified and fed back by the control system to other devices, which adjust the machine. A control system in which a departure from a norm is actually used to adjust a machine is called a *closed* system. This may be contrasted with an *open* system—say, a manually operated wall switch or the arms that automatically rotate an electric fan—in which the control operates without regard to the function of the device. Thus, if the wall switch is flicked, electric lights go on or off quite aside from whether it is night or day; similarly, the electric fan will rotate at the same speed whether a room is very warm or relatively cool. The fan may be automatic in the popular sense of the term, but it is not self-regulating in terms of its function.

Obviously, an important step toward developing self-regulating control mechanisms is the discovery of sensory devices. Today, these consist of themocouples, photo-electric cells, x-ray machines, television cameras, and radar transmitters. Together or singly, they provide machines with an amazing degree of autonomy. Even without computers, these sensory devices make it possible for man to engage in extremely hazardous operations by remote control, placing a great deal of distance between the worker and the job. They can also be used to turn many traditional open systems into closed ones, thereby expanding the scope of automatic operations. For example, an electric light controlled by a clock represents a fairly simple open system; its effectiveness depends entirely upon mechanical factors. Regulated by a photo-electric cell that turns it off when daylight approaches, the light becomes a highly sophisticated and flexible device that responds to daily variations in sunrise and sunset. It is now meshed directly with its function.

With the advent of the computer, we enter into an entirely new dimension of industrial control systems. The computer is capable of performing all the routine tasks that ordinarily burdened the mind of the worker a generation or so ago. Basically, the modern digital computer is an electronic calculator, capable of performing arithmetical operations enormously faster than the human brain.[4] This element of speed is a crucial fact: the enormous rapidity of computer operations—a quantitative superiority of computer over human calculations—has a profound qualitative significance. By virtue of its speed, the computer can perform advanced, highly sophisticated mathematical and logical operations. Supported by memory units that store millions of bits of information, and using binary arithmetic (the substitution of the digits 0 and 1 for the digits 0 through 9), a properly programmed digital computer can perform operations that approximate many highly developed logical activities of the mind. It is arguable whether computer "intelligence" is, or ever will be, creative or innovative, although every few years brings sweeping, often revolutionary changes in computer technology and programming. But there is no doubt that the digital computer is capable of taking over all the onerous and distinctly uncreative mental tasks of man in industry, science, engineering, information retrieval, record-keeping, and transportation. Modern man, in effect, has produced an electronic "mind" for co-ordinating, guiding, and evaluating most of his routine industrial operations. Properly used within the sphere of competence for which they are designed, computers are faster and more efficient than man himself.

Taken as a whole, what is the concrete significance of this new industrial revolution? What are its immediate and foreseeable implications for work? Let us trace the impact of the new technology on the work process by examining its application to the manufacture of automobile engines at the Ford plant in Cleveland. This single instance of technological sophistication in about a decade of development will help us assess the liberatory potential of the new technology in all manufacturing industries.

Until the advent of cybernation in the automobile industry, the Ford plant required about 300 workers, using a large variety of tools and machines, to turn an engine block into an engine. The process from foundry casting to a fully machined and complete engine took more than three weeks. With the development of what we commonly call an "automated" machine system, the time required to transform the casting into an engine was reduced from three weeks to less than 15 minutes.

Aside from a few monitors to watch the automatic control panels, the original 300-man labor force was entirely eliminated. Later a computer was added to the machining system, turning it into a truly closed, cybernated system. The computer regulates the entire machining process, operating on an electronic pulse that cycles at a rate of three-tenths of a millionth of a second.

But even this system is obsolete. "The next generation of computing machines operates a thousand times as fast—at a pulse rate of one in every three-tenths of a billionth of a second," observes Alice Mary Hilton. "Speeds of millionths and billionths of a second are not really intelligible to our finite minds. But we can certainly understand that the advance has been a thousand-fold—within a year or two. A thousand times as much information can be handled or the same amount of information can be handled a thousand times as fast. A job that takes more than 16 hours can be done in one minute! And without any human intervention! Such a system does not control merely an assembly line but a complete manufacturing and industrial process!"

There is no reason why the basic technological principles involved in cybernating the manufacture of automobile engines cannot be applied to every area of mass manufacture—from the metallurgical industry to the food processing industry, from the electronics industry to the toy-making industry, from the manufacture of prefabricated bridges to the manufacture of prefabricated houses. Many phases of steel production, of tool- and die-making, of electronic equipment manufacture, of industrial chemical production—the list, in fact, is nearly endless—are now partly or wholly automated. What tends to delay the advance of complete automation to every phase of modern industry is largely the enormous cost involved in replacing existing industrial facilities by new, more sophisticated ones and, partly, the innate conservatism of many major corporations. Finally, as I mentioned before, it is still cheaper to use labor instead of machines in many industries.

Every industry, to be sure, has its own peculiar problems and the application of a workless technology to a specific plant would doubtless reveal a multitude of kinks that would require careful, painstaking solution. It would be necessary in many industries to alter the shape of a product and the layout of a plant so that the manufacturing process lends itself to automated techniques. But to argue from these problems that the application of a fully automated technology to a specific industry is impossible would be as preposterous as to have argued, years ago, that flight was impossible because the propeller of an experimental airplane did not revolve fast enough or the frame was too fragile to withstand buffeting by the wind. There is no industry that cannot be fully automated if we are willing to redesign the product, the plant, the manufacturing procedures, and the handling methods. In fact, any difficulty in describing how, where, or when a given industry will be automated arises not from the unique problems we can expect to encounter, but rather from the enormous leaps that occur every few years in modern technology. Almost every account of applied automation, today, must be regarded as provisional, for no sooner do we commit a description of an automated industry to paper but that we learn of remarkable advances that render our description obsolete.

There is one area of the economy, however, in which any form of technological advance is worth describing—the area of work that is most brutalizing and degrading for man. If it is true, as radical thinkers have argued, that the moral level of a society can be gauged by the way it treats women, its sensitivity to human suffering can be gauged by the working conditions it provides for people in raw materials industries, specifically in mines and quarries. In the ancient world, mining was often a form of penal servitude, reserved primarily for the most hardened criminals, the most intractable slaves, and the most hated prisoners of war. The mine is the day-to-day actualization of man's image of hell—dismal to the eye, stunting the body and spirit, a deadened inorganic world, a treacherous cavern that demands pure mindless toil. "Field and forest and stream and ocean are the environment of life: the mine is the environment alone of ores, minerals, metals," writes Lewis Mumford.

> . . . In hacking and digging the contents of the earth, the miner has no eye for the forms of things: what he sees is sheer matter, and until he gets to his vein it is only an obstacle which he breaks through stubbornly and sends up to the surface. If the miner sees shapes on the walls of his cavern, as the candle flickers, they are only the monstrous distortions of his pick or his arm: shapes of fear. Day has been abolished and the rhythm of nature broken: continuous day-and-night production first came into existence here. The miner must work by artificial light even though the sun be shining outside; still further down in the seams, he must work by artificial ventilation, too: a triumph of the "manufactured environment."

The abolition of mining as a sphere of human activity would represent, in its own way, the token of a libertory technology. That we can point to this achievement already, even in a single case at this writing, presages the freedom from toil implicit in the technology of our time. The first major step in this direction, at least so far as the coal industry is concerned, was taken by the continuous miner, a giant cutting machine with 9-foot blades that slices up eight tons of coal a minute from the coal face. It was this machine, together with mobile loading machines, power drills, and roof bolting that reduced mine employment in areas like West Virginia to about a third of the 1948 employment levels—at the same time nearly doubling individual output. The coal mine still required miners to place and operate the machines. The most recent technological advances, however, replace the operators by radar sensing-devices and eliminate the miner completely.

By adding sensing devices to automatic machinery we could easily remove the worker not only from the large, productive mines needed by the economy, but also from forms of agricultural activity patterned on modern industry. Although the wisdom of industrializing and mechanizing agriculture is highly questionable (I shall return to this subject at a later point), the fact remains that if society so chooses, it can easily automate large areas of modern agriculture, from cotton-picking to rice harvesting. We could operate almost any machine, be it a giant shovel in an open-strip mine or a grain harvester in the Great Plains, either by cybernated sensing devices or by remote control with television cameras. The amount of work needed to operate these devices and machines at a safe distance, in comfortable quarters, would be minimal, assuming that a human operator were required at all. It is easy to foresee a time, by no means remote, when a rationally organized economy could automatically manufacture small "packaged" factories without human labor; when parts could be produced with so little effort that most maintenance tasks would be reduced to the simple act of removing a defective unit from a machine and replacing it by another, a job no more difficult than pulling out and putting in a tray; when machines, in short, would make and repair most of the machines required to maintain a highly industrialized economy. Such a technology, oriented entirely toward human needs and freed from all considerations of profit and loss, would provide humanity with an abundance of goods unprecedented even by modern Western standards of material affluence. The machines at man's disposal would eliminate the *ponos* of want and toil, the penalty inflicted in the form of denial, suffering, and inhumanity exacted by a society based on scarcity and labor.

In these circumstances, the issues raised by a cybernated technology would be transformed from the satiation of man's material needs to the reintegration of society. It would be our responsibility, now, to determine how the machine, the factory, and the mine could be used to foster human solidarity, a balanced relationship with nature, and a truly organic community. Would our new technology be employed on a large scale, based on a national economy, and vested in giant industrial enterprises? This type of industrial organization—an extension, in effect, of the Industrial Revolution—would require a centralized system of national planning, the delegation of authority to economic and political representatives with strategic, decision-making powers—powers strengthened by the control they exercise over a large, socialized industrial plant, national in scope and anonymous in character. Large-scale industry by its very nature is the breeding ground of bureaucratic modes of administration, be it privately owned or under "workers' control." To the degree that it is socialized in the regressive sense that it transcends the human scale, it becomes the strongest material support for the centralized, authoritarian state.

Or does the new technology lend itself to small-scale production, based on a regional economy and physically structured on a human scale? This type of industrial organization tends to place all strategic economic decisions in the hands of the local community, with its popular assemblies and with its technical boards clearly within the purview of the individual communitarian. To the degree that material production is decentralized and localized, to that degree is the primacy of the community asserted over national institutions, assuming that any develop to a significant extent. Primary authority belongs to the popular assembly of the community, convened in a face-to-face democracy; the authority of the assembly is qualitatively strengthened by the fact that it has exclusive command over all the material resources of society.

The question, in effect, is whether society would be organized around technology or whether technology would be organized around society. Our answer can be obtained only by examining the new technology itself with a view toward determining if it can be scaled to human dimensions.

THE NEW TECHNOLOGY AND THE HUMAN SCALE

In 1945, J. Presper Eckert, Jr., and John W. Mauchly of the University of Pennsylvania unveiled ENIAC, the first digital computer to be designed entirely along electronic principles. Commissioned for use in solving ballistic problems, ENIAC required nearly three years of work to design and build. The computer was enormous. It occupied 1,500 square feet of floor space and weighed more than thirty tons; it contained 18,800 vacuum tubes with 500,000 connections (these connections took Eckert and Mauchly two and a half years to solder), a vast network of resistors, and miles of wiring. The computer required a large air-conditioning unit to cool its electronic components and it broke down often or behaved erratically, entailing time-consuming repairs. Yet by all previous standards of computer development, ENIAC was an electronic marvel. It could perform 5,000 computations a second, generating electrical pulse signals that cycled at 100,000 a second. None of the mechanical or electro-mechanical computers in use at the time could approach this rate of computational speed.

Some twenty years later, the Computer Control Company of Framingham, Massachusetts, offered the DDP-124 for public sale. The DDP-124 is a small, compact computer that closely resembles a bedside AM-FM radio receiver; together with a typewriter and memory unit, the entire ensemble comfortably occupies a typical office desk. The DDP-124 performs over 285,000 computations a second. It has a true stored program memory that can be expanded to retain nearly 33,000 words (the "memory" of ENIAC, by contrast, progressed according to preset plug wires and lacked anything near the flexibility of present-day computers); its pulses cycle at 1.75 billion per second. The DDP-124 does not require any air-conditioning unit, it is completely reliable, and it creates very few maintenance problems. It can be built at a minute fraction of the cost required to construct ENIAC.

The difference between ENIAC and the DDP-124 is basically one of degree rather than kind. If we leave aside their memory units, both digital computers operate according to the same basic electronic principles. ENIAC, however, was composed primarily of traditional electronic components (vacuum tubes, resistors, etc.) and thousands of feet of wire; the DDP-124, on the other hand, relies primarily on microcircuits. These microcircuits are generally very small electronic units—squares a mere fraction of an inch in size—that pack the equivalent of many of ENIAC's key electronic components.

Paralleling the miniaturization of computer components is the remarkable sophistication of traditional forms of technology—a degree of sophistication that yields ever-smaller machines of all types. To cite one example: a fascinating breakthrough has already been achieved in reducing the size of continuous hot-strip steel rolling-mills. A typical mill of this kind is one of the largest and costliest facilities in modern industry. It may be regarded as a single machine, nearly a half mile in length, capable of reducing a ten-ton slab of steel about six inches thick and fifty inches wide to a thin strip of sheet metal, a tenth or a twelfth of an inch thick. A hot-strip mill runs the steel slab through scale-breaker stands, roughing stands with huge vertical rollers, and a series of finishing stands. The entire installation, including heating furnaces, coilers, long roller tables, and buildings, may cost in excess of fifty million dollars and occupy fifty acres. It produces 300 tons of steel sheet an hour. To be used efficiently a continuous hot-strip mill must be operated together with large batteries of coke ovens, open-hearth furnaces, blooming mills, etc. These facilities, in conjunction with hot and cold rolling mills, may cover several square miles. It is a modern steel complex, geared to a national division of labor, to highly concentrated sources of raw materials (located at a great distance from the complex), and geared toward large national and international markets. Even if totally automated, its operating needs and management far transcend the capabilities of a small, decentralized community. The type of administration it requires is essentially national in scope. Its economic weight, in effect, is thrown in support of centralistic institutions.

Fortunately, we now have a number of alternatives—in many respects, more efficient alternatives—to the modern steel complex. We can replace blast and open-hearth furnaces with electric furnaces. These are generally quite small and produce excellent pig iron and steel; they operate not only with coke as a reducing agent, but also with anthracite coal, charcoal, and even lignite. Or we can choose the HyL process, a batch process in which high-grade ores or concentrates are reduced to sponge iron by means of natural gas. Or we can turn to the Wiberg process in which reduction is achieved by the use of carbon monoxide and a little hydrogen. In any case, we can eliminate the need for coke ovens, blast furnaces, open hearth furnaces, and possibly even solid reducing agents.

But the most important step in the direction of scaling down the size of the steel complex to community dimensions is the development of the planetary mill by T. Sendzimir. The planetary mill reduces the typical continuous hot-strip mill to a single planetary stand and a light finishing stand. Hot steel slabs, two and one-fourth inches thick, pass through two small pairs of heated feed rolls and a set of work rolls, mounted in two circular cages, which also contain two back-up rolls. By operating the cages and back-up rolls at different rotational speeds, the work rolls are made to turn in two directions. This gives the steel slab a terrific mauling and reduces it to a thickness of only one-tenth of an inch. Sendzimir's technique can be regarded as a stroke of engineering genius; the small work rolls, turning on the two circular cages, are given a force that can only be achieved by four huge roughing stands and six finishing stands in a continuous hot-strip mill.

What this means is that the rolling of hot steel slabs requires a much smaller operational area than that occupied by a continuous hot-strip mill. With continuous casting, moreover, we can produce steel slabs without the need for large, costly slabbing mills. Taken altogether: several electric furnaces, the use of continuous casting, a planetary mill, and a small, continuous cold-reducing mill, occupying little more than an acre or two, would be fully capable of meeting the steel needs of a moderate-sized community. This small, highly sophisticated complex would produce an extremely high grade of steel and involve substantially lower heat costs and scale losses. Without automation, it would still require fewer men to operate, even if we account for its lower output level, than a conventional steel complex. It could reduce lower grade ores more efficiently and with less difficulty. And finally, since the planetary mill produces a shiny and clean strip for cold rolling merely with high-pressure water, it eliminates acid-pickling and the need to dispose of waste-pickling liquor—a major source of stream pollution caused by conventional steel plants.

The complex I have described is not designed to meet the needs of a national market of the kind that exists in the United States today. It is suited for meeting the steel requirements of small- or moderate-sized communities and industrially undeveloped countries. Most electric furnaces produce about 100 to 250 tons of molten iron a day, compared with new large blast furnaces that produce 3,000 tons daily. A planetary mill can roll only a hundred tons of steel strip an hour, roughly a third of the output of a continuous hot-strip mill. Yet the very productive scale of our hypothetical steel complex constitutes one of its most desirable features. Owing to the more durable steel produced by our complex, the community's need to replenish its steel products continually is appreciably reduced. Since the complex requires ore, fuel, and reducing agents in only small batches, many communities can rely on local resources for their raw materials, conserving the more concentrated resources of centrally located sources of supply, strengthening the independence of the community itself *vis-à-vis* the traditional centralized economy, and reducing the expense of transportation. What may seem to be a costly, inefficient duplication of effort that could be solved by a few centralized steel complexes would prove, in the long run, to be more efficient as well as socially more desirable.

The new technology has produced not only miniaturized electronic components and strategic alternatives to centralized forms of production, but also highly versatile, multi-purpose machines. For more than a century, the trend in a machine design moved increasingly toward technological specialization and single-purpose devices, reflecting the intensive division of labor that tightened its grip around industry. The operation was subordinated to the product. In time, this narrow pragmatic approach "led industry far from the rational line of development in production machinery," observe Eric W. Leaver and John J. Brown. "It has led to increasingly uneconomic specialization. . . . Specialization of machines in terms of end product requires that the machine be thrown away when the product is no longer needed. Yet the work the production machine does can be reduced to a set of basic functions—forming, holding, cutting, and so on—and these functions, if correctly analyzed, can be packaged and applied to operate on a part as needed."

Ideally, a Leaver and Brown drilling machine would be able to produce a hole small enough to hold a thin wire or large enough to admit a pipe. Machines with this operational range were once regarded as economically prohibitive. By the mid-1950's, however, a number of these machines were actually designed and put to use. In 1954, for example, a horizontal boring mill was built in Switzerland for the Ford Motor Company's River Rouge Plant in Dearborn, Michigan. The boring mill would qualify beautifully as a

Leaver and Brown machine. Equipped with five optical microscopic-type illuminated control-gauges, it drills holes smaller than a needle's or larger than a man's fist. The holes are accurate to one ten-thousandth of an inch.

The importance of machines with this kind of operational range can hardly be overestimated. They make it possible to produce a dazzling variety of products in a single plant. A small- or moderate-sized community using multipurpose machines could satisfy many of its needs for a limited number of goods without burdening itself with underused industrial facilities. There would be less loss in scrapping tools for the older single-purpose machines and less of a need for single-purpose plants. The economy of the community, in effect, would become more compact and versatile, more rounded and autarchical than anything we find today in industrially advanced countries. The effort that goes into retooling machines for new products would be enormously reduced. Retooling would generally involve changes in dimensioning rather than in the design and type of machine required for the job. This might merely mean changing the drill in a boring machine or the cutting tool in a lathe. Finally, multipurpose machines with a wide operational range are relatively easy to automate. The changes required to use these machines in a cybernated industrial facility would generally involve changes in circuitry and programming rather than in machine form and structure.

Single-purpose machines, of course, would continue to exist and they would be used for much the same function they have today: the mass manufacture of widely used non-durable goods. At the present time we have striking examples of highly automatic, single-purpose machines, often small installations, that can be employed with very little modification by decentralized communities. Bottling and canning machines, for example, are compact, automatic, and highly rationalized installations. We could expect to see smaller automatic textile, chemical processing, and food processing machines after decentralized communities are established. A major shift from conventional automobiles, buses, and trucks, to electric vehicles would undoubtedly lead to industrial facilities much smaller in size than existing automotive plants. Many remaining centralized facilities could be effectively decentralized by making them as small as possible and sharing their use among several communities.

I do not profess to claim that all of man's economic activities can be completely decentralized, but the majority surely can be scaled to human and communitarian dimensions. *It is enough to say that we can shift the overwhelming weight of the economy from national to communitarian bodies, from centralized bureaucratic forms to local, popular assemblies in order to secure the sovereignty of the free community on solid industrial foundations.* This shift would comprise a historic change of qualitative proportions, a revolutionary social change of vast proportions, unprecedented in man's technological and social development.

THE ECOLOGICAL USE OF TECHNOLOGY

I have tried, thus far, to deal with a number of tangible, clearly objective issues: the possibility of eliminating toil, material insecurity, and centralized economic control. In the present section, I would like to deal with a problem that may seem somewhat subjective, but one that is nonetheless of compelling importance: the need to make man's dependence upon the natural world a visible and living part of his culture.

The problem is unique to our highly urbanized and industrialized society. In nearly all pre-industrial cultures, man's relationship to his natural environment required very little clarification; the relationship was well-defined, viable, and sanctified by the full weight of tradition and myth. Changes in season, variations in rainfall, the life cycles of the plants and animals on which humans depended for food and clothing, the distinctive features of the area occupied by the community—all were familiar, comprehensible, and evoked in men a sense of religious awe, of oneness with nature, and more pragmatically, a sense of respectful dependence. Looking back to the earliest civilizations of the Western world, we rarely encounter a system of social tyranny so overbearing and ruthless that it ignored this relationship. Barbarian invasions and, more insidiously, the development of commercial civilizations may have destroyed the gains achieved by established agrarian cultures, but the normal development of agricultural systems, however exploitative they were of men, rarely led to the destruction of the soil and terrain. During the most oppressive periods in the history of ancient Egypt and Mesopotamia, the ruling classes tried to keep the irrigation dikes in good repair and promote rational methods of food cultivation. Even the ancient Greeks, heirs to a thin, mountainous forest soil that suffered heavily from erosion, shrewdly reclaimed much of their arable land by turning to orchardry and viticulture. Throughout the Middle Ages the heavy soils of Europe were slowly and superbly reworked for agricultural purposes. Generally, it was not until commercial agricultural systems and highly urbanized societies developed that the natural environment was unsparingly exploited. Some of the worst cases of soil destruction in the ancient world were provided by the giant, slave-worked commercial farms of North Africa and the Italian peninsula.

In our own time, the development of technology and the growth of cities has brought man's alienation from nature to a breaking point. Western man finds himself confined to a largely synthetic urban environment, far removed physically from the land, his relationship to the natural world mediated by machines. Not only does he lack familiarity with how most of his goods are produced, but his foods bear only the faintest resemblance to the animals and plants from which they were derived. Boxed into a sanitized urban milieu (almost institutional in form and appearance), modern man is denied even a spectatorial role in the agricultural and industrial systems that satisfy his material needs. He is a pure consumer, an insensate receptacle. It would be cruel to say that he is disrespectful toward his natural environment; the fact is that he scarcely knows what ecology means or what his environment requires to remain in balance.

The balance must be restored—not only in nature but between man and nature. Elsewhere, I tried to show that unless we establish some kind of equilibrium between man and the natural world, the viability of the human species will be placed in grave jeopardy.[5] Here, I shall try to show how the new technology can be used ecologically to crystalize man's sense of dependence upon the environment; how, by reintroducing the natural world into the human experience, we can contribute to the achievement of human wholeness.

The classical utopians fully realized that the first step in this direction must be to remove the contradiction between town and country. "It is impossible," wrote Fourier nearly a century and a half ago, "to organize a regular and well-balanced association without bringing into play the labors of the field, or at least gardens, orchards, flocks and herds, poultry yards, and a great variety of species, animal and vegetable." Shocked by the social effects of the Industrial Revolution, Fourier added: "They are ignorant of this principle in England, where they experiment with artisans, with manufacturing labor alone, which cannot by itself suffice to sustain social union."

To argue that the modern urban dweller should once again enjoy "the labors of the field" might well seem like gallows humor. A restoration of the peasant agriculture prevalent in Fourier's day is neither possible nor desirable. Charles Gide was surely correct when he observed that agricultural labor "is not necessarily more attractive than industrial labor; to till the earth has always been regarded . . . as the type of painful toil, of toil which is done with 'the sweat of one's brow.' " Fourier does not remove this objection by suggesting that his Phalansteries will mainly cultivate fruits and vegetables instead of grains. If our vision were to extend no further than prevailing techniques of land management, the only alternative to peasant agriculture would seem to be a highly specialized and centralized form of farming, its techniques paralleling the methods used in present-day industry. In fact, far from achieving a balance between town and country, we would be faced with a synthetic environment that had totally assimilated the natural one.

If we grant that the land and the community must be reintegrated physically, that the community must exist in an agricultural matrix that renders man's dependence upon nature explicit, the problem we face is how to achieve this transformation without imposing "painful toil" on the community. How, in short, can husbandry, ecological forms of food cultivation, and farming on a human scale be practiced without sacrificing mechanization? Some of the most promising technological advances in agriculture made since World War II are as suitable for small-scale, ecological forms of land management as they are for the immense, industrial-type commercial units that have become prevalent over the past few decades. Let us consider a few examples.

The augermatic-feeding of livestock illustrates a cardinal principle of rational farm mechanization—the deployment of conventional machines and devices in a way that virtually eliminates arduous farm labor. By linking a battery of silos with augers, for instance, different nutrients are mixed and transported to feed pens by merely pushing some buttons and pulling a few switches. A job that may have required the labor of five or six men, working a half day with pitchforks and buckets, can now be performed in a few minutes. This type of mechanization is intrinsically neutral: it can be used to feed immense herds or just a few hundred head of cattle; the silos may contain natural feed or synthetic, hormonized nutrients; the feeder can be employed on relatively small farms with mixed livestock or on large beef-raising ranches, or on dairy farms of all sizes. In short, augermatic-feeding can be placed in the service of the most abusive kind of commercial exploitation or the most sensitive applications of ecological principles.

This holds true for most of the farm machines that have been designed (in many cases, simply redesigned to achieve greater versatility) in recent years. The modern tractor, for example, is a work of superb mechanical ingenuity. Garden-type models can be used with extraordinary flexibility for a large variety of tasks; light and extremely manageable, they can follow the contour of the most exacting terrain without damaging the land. Large tractors, especially those used in hot climates, are likely to have air-conditioned cabs; in addition to pulling equipment, they may have attachments for digging post-holes, for doing the work of forklift trucks, or even providing power units for grain elevators. Plows have been developed to meet every contingency in tillage. Advanced models are even regulated hydraulically to rise and fall with the lay of the land. Mechanical planters are available for virtually every kind of crop. On this score, "minimum tillage" is achieved by planters which apply seed, fertilizer, and pesticides (of course!) simultaneously, a technique that telescopes several different operations into a single one and reduces the soil compaction often produced by the recurrent use of heavy machines.

The variety of mechanical harvesters has reached dazzling proportions. Harvesters have been developed for many different kinds of orchards, berries, vine and field crops, and of course, grains. Barns, feed pens, and storage units have been totally revolutionized by augers, conveyor belts, air-tight silos, automatic manure removers, climate-control devices, *ad infinitum*. Crops are mechanically shelled, washed, counted, preserved by freezing or canning, packaged, and crated. The construction of concrete-lined irrigation ditches is reduced to a simple mechanical operation that can be performed by one or two excavating machines. Terrain with poor drainage or subsoil can be improved by earth-moving equipment and by tillage devices that penetrate well beyond the true soil.

Although a great deal of agricultural research is devoted to the development of harmful chemical agents and nutritionally dubious crops, there have been extraordinary advances in the genetic improvement of food plants. Many new grain and vegetable varieties are resistant to insect predators, plant diseases, and cold weather. In many cases, these varieties are a definite improvement over natural ancestral types and they have been used to open large areas of intractable land to food cultivation. The tree shelter program, feebly initiated during the 1920's, is slowly transforming the Great Plains from a harsh, agriculturally precarious region into one that is ecologically more balanced and agriculturally more secure. The trees act as windbreaks in the winter and as refuges for birds and small mammals in warm weather. They promote soil and water conservation, help control insects, and prevent wind damage to crops in summer months. Programs of this type could be used to make sweeping improvements in the natural ecology of a region. So far as America is concerned, the tree shelter program (much of which has been carried out without any state aid) represents a rare case where man, mindful of the unfulfilled potentialities of a region, has vastly improved a natural environment.

Let us pause, at this point, to envision how our free community is integrated with its natural environment. We suppose the community has been established after careful study has been made of its natural ecology—its air and water resources, its climate, its geological formations, its raw materials, its soils, and its natural flora and fauna. The population of the community is consciously limited to the ecological carrying capacity of the region. Land management is guided entirely by ecological principles so that an equilibrium is maintained between the environment and its human inhabitants. Industrially rounded, the community forms a distinct unit within a natural matrix, socially and artistically in balance with the area it occupies.

Agriculture is highly mechanized but as mixed as possible with respect to crops, livestock, and timber. Floral and faunal variety is promoted as a means of controlling pest infestations and enhancing scenic beauty. Large-scale farming is permitted only where it does not conflict with the ecology of the region. Owing to the generally mixed character of food cultivation, agriculture is pursued by small farming units, each demarcated from the other by tree belts, shrubs, and where possible, by pastures and meadows. In rolling, hilly or mountainous country, land with sharp gradients is covered by timber to prevent erosion and conserve water. The soil on each acre is studied carefully and committed only to those crops for which it is most suited.

Every effort is made to blend town and country without sacrificing the distinctive contribution that each has to offer to the human experience. The ecological region forms the living social, cultural, and biotic boundaries of the community or of the several communities that share its resources. Each community contains many vegetable and flower gardens, attractive arbors, park land, even streams and ponds which support fish and aquatic birds. The countryside, from which food and raw materials are acquired, not only constitutes the immediate environs of the community, accessible to all by foot, but also invades the community. Although town and country retain their identity and the uniqueness of each is highly prized and fostered, nature appears everywhere in the town, and the town seems to have caressed and left a gentle, human imprint on nature.

I believe that a free community will regard agriculture as husbandry, an activity as expressive and enjoyable as crafts. Relieved of toil by agricultural machines, communitarians will approach food cultivation with the same playful and creative attitude that men so often bring to gardening. Agriculture will become a living part of human society, a source of pleasant physical activity and, by virtue of its ecological demands, an intellectual, scientific, and artistic challenge. Communitarians will blend with the world of life around them as organically as the community blends with its region. They will regain the sense of oneness with nature that existed in humans from primordial times. Nature and the organic modes of thought it always fosters will become an integral part of human culture; it will reappear with a fresh spirit in man's paintings, literature, philosophy, dances, architecture, domestic furnishings, and in his very gestures and day-to-day activities. Culture and the human psyche will be thoroughly suffused by a new animism.

The region will never be exploited but it will be used as fully as possible. This is vitally important in order to firmly root the dependence of the community on its environment, to restore in man a deep, abiding respect for the needs of the natural world—a respect identified with human survival and well-being. Every attempt will be made to satisfy the community's requirements locally—to use the region's energy resources, minerals, timber, soil, water, animals, and plants as rationally and humanistically as possible, and without violating ecological principles. In this connection, we can foresee that the community will employ new techniques that are being developed today, many of which lend themselves superbly to a regionally based economy. I refer, here, to methods for extracting trace and diluted resources from the earth, water, and air; solar, wind, hydro-electric, and geothermal energy; the use of heat pumps, vegetable fuels, solar ponds, thermo-electric convertors, and eventually controlled thermo-nuclear reactions.

There is a kind of industrial archeology that reveals in many areas the evidence of a once-burgeoning economic activity long abandoned by our predecessors. From the Hudson Valley to the Rhine, from the Appalachians to the Pyrenees, we find the relics of mines and highly developed metallurgical crafts, the fragmentary remains of local industries, and the outlines of long-deserted farms—all, vestiges of flourishing communities based on local raw materials and resources. In many cases, these communities declined because the products they once furnished were elbowed out by industries with national markets, based on mass production techniques and concentrated sources of raw materials. The old resources quite often are still available for use in the locality; "valueless" in a highly urbanized society, they are eminently suitable for decentralized communities and await the application of industrial techniques that are adapted for small-scale, quality production. If we were to take a serious inventory of the resources available in many depopulated regions of the world, the possibility for communities satisfying their material need in these areas is likely to be greater than we ordinarily think.

Technology itself, by its continual development, tends to expand these local possibilities. As an example, let us consider how seemingly inferior, highly intractable resources are made available to industry by technological advances. Throughout the late nineteenth and early twentieth centuries, the Mesabi range in Minnesota provided the American steel industry with extremely rich ores, an advantage which led to the rapid expansion of the domestic metal industry. As these fine reserves declined, the country was faced with the problem of mining taconites, a low-grade ore that contains about forty percent iron. Mining taconites by conventional methods is virtually impossible; it takes a churn drill an hour to bite through only one foot. In recent years, however, the mining of taconites became feasible when a jet-flame drill was developed, which cuts through the ore at the rate of twenty to thirty feet an hour. After holes are burned by the flame, the ore is blasted and processed for the steel industry by means of a series of newly perfected grinding, separating, and agglomerating operations.

When we reach the next technological horizon it may be possible to extract highly diffused or diluted minerals and chemicals from the earth, gaseous waste products, and the sea. Many of our most valuable metals, for example, are actually very common, but they exist in diffused or trace amounts. Hardly a patch of soil or a common rock exists that does not contain traces of gold, larger quantities of uranium, and progressively more amounts of industrially useful elements, such as magnesium, zinc, copper, and sulphur. About five percent of the earth's crust is made of iron. How to extract these resources? The problem has been solved, in principle at least, by the very analytical techniques chemists use to detect them. As the highly gifted chemist, Jacob Rosin, argues, if they can be detected in the laboratory, there is every reason to hope that eventually they will be extracted on a sufficiently large scale to be used by decentralized communities.

For more than half a century, already, most of the world's commercial nitrogen has been extracted from the atmosphere; magnesium, chlorine, bromine, and caustic soda are acquired from sea water; sulphur from calcium sulphate and industrial wastes. Large amounts of industrially useful hydrogen could be collected as a by-product of the electrolysis of brine, but normally it is burned or released in the air by chlorine-producing plants. Carbon could be rescued in enormous quantities from smoke and used economically (actually, the element is comparatively rare in nature), but it is dissipated together with other gaseous compounds in the atmosphere. The problem industrial chemists face in extracting valuable elements and compounds from the sea and ordinary rock, centers around sources of cheap energy. Two methods—ion exchange and chromatography—exist and, if further perfected for industrial uses, could be used to select or separate the desired resources from solutions; but the amount of energy involved to use these methods would be very costly to any society in terms of real wealth. Unless there is an unexpected breakthrough in extractive techniques, there is little likelihood that conventional sources of energy—fossil fuels such as coal and oil—will be used to solve the problem.

Actually, it is not that we lack energy *per se* to realize man's most extravagant technological visions, but we are just beginning to learn how to use the sources that are available in limitless quantity. The gross radiant energy striking the earth's surface from the sun is estimated to be 3,200 Q, more than 3,000 times the annual energy consumption of mankind today.[6] A portion of this energy is converted into wind or used in photosynthesizing land vegetation, but a staggering quantity is theoretically available for domestic and industrial purposes. The problem is how to collect it, even if only to satisfy a portion of our energy needs. If solar energy could be collected for house-heating, for example, twenty to thirty percent of the conventional energy resources we normally employ could be redirected to other purposes. If we could collect solar energy for all or most of our cooking, water heating, smelting, and power production, we would have relatively little need for fossil fuels. What is tantalizing about recent research in this area is the fact that solar devices have been designed for nearly all of these functions. We *can* heat houses, cook food, boil water, melt metals, and produce electricity with devices that use the sun's energy exclusively, but we can't do it efficiently in every latitude of the earth inhabited by man and we are still confronted with a number of technical problems that can be solved only by crash research programs.

At this writing, quite a few houses have been built that are effectively heated by solar energy. In the United States, the most well known of these are the MIT experimental buildings in Massachusetts, the Lof house in Denver, the Thomason homes in Washington, D.C., and the prize-winning solar-heated house built by the Association for Applied Solar Energy near Phoenix, Arizona. Thomason, whose fuel costs for a solar-heated house barely reach five dollars a year, seems to have developed one of the most practical systems at hand. Solar heat in a Thomason home is collected by a portion of the roof and transferred by circulating water to a storage tank in the basement. (The water, incidentally, can also be used for cooling the house and as an emergency supply for drinking purposes and fire.) Although the system is simple and fairly cheap, it is very ingeniously designed. Located in Washington near the fortieth parallel of latitude, the house stands at the edge of the "solar belt"—the latitudes from 0 to 40 degrees North and South. This belt comprises the geographic area where the sun's rays can be used most effectively for domestic and industrial energy. That Thomason requires a miniscule amount of supplemental conventional fuel to heat his Washington homes comfortably augurs well for solar-heating in all areas of the world with similar or warmer climates.

This does not mean, to be sure, that solar house-heating is useless in northern and colder latitudes. Two approaches to solar house-heating are possible in these areas: the use of more elaborate heating systems which reduce the consumption of conventional fuel to levels approximating those of the Thomason homes, or the use of simple systems which involve the consumption of conventional fuel to satisfy anywhere from ten to fifty percent of the heating needs. In either case, as Hans Thirring observes with an eye toward costs and effort:

> The decisive advantage of solar heating lies in the fact that no running costs arise, except the electricity bill for driving the fans, which is very small. Thus the one single investment for the installation pays once and for all the heating costs for the lifetime of the house. In addition, the system works automatically without smoke, soot, and fume production, and saves all trouble in stoking, refuelling, cleaning, repair, and other work. Adding solar heat to the energy system of a country helps to increase the wealth of the nation, and if all houses in areas with favorable conditions were equipped with solar heating systems, fuel saving worth millions of pounds yearly could be achieved. The work of Telkes, Hottel, Lof, Bliss, and other scientists who are paving the way for solar heating is real pioneer work, the full significance of which will emerge more clearly in the future.

It is significant that Thirring's words read like an appeal to a world strangled by considerations of profit (particularly those of industries enriched by the exploitation of conventional fuels)—indeed, that these words must seem like a justification for a shamefully neglected area of research.

The most widespread applications of solar energy devices, today, are cooking and water heating. Many thousands of solar stoves are used in underdeveloped countries, in Japan, and in the warm latitudes of the United States. A solar stove is simply an umbrella-like reflector, equipped with a

grill that can broil meat or boil a quart of water in bright sunlight in only 15 minutes. Safe, portable, and clean, it does not require fuel or matches nor does it produce any annoying smoke. A portable solar oven delivers temperatures as high as 450 degrees and is even more compact and easy to handle than a solar stove. Solar water-heaters are employed to heat water for private homes, apartment buildings, laundries, and swimming pools. Some 25,000 of these units are used in Florida and are gradually coming into vogue in California.

In terms of technical know-how, some of the most impressive advances in the use of solar energy have occurred in industry, although the majority of these applications are marginal at best and largely experimental in nature. The simplest of these devices is the solar furnace. The collector is usually a single large parabolic mirror, or, more likely, a huge array of many parabolic mirrors mounted in a large housing. A heliostat—a smaller, horizontally mounted mirror that follows the movement of the sun—reflects the rays into the collector. Several hundred of these furnaces are currently in use. One of the largest, Dr. Felix Trombe's Mont Louis furnace, develops seventy-five kilowatts of electric power and is used primarily in high-temperature research. It makes a remarkable industrial smelter. Since the sun's rays do not contain any impurities, the furnace will melt a hundred pounds of metal without the contamination produced by conventional smelting techniques. A solar furnace built by the U.S. Army Quartermaster Corps at Natick, Massachusetts, develops 5,000 degrees Centigrade—a temperature high enough to melt steel "I" beams. It looks like nothing more than a small, outdoor movie screen covered with a battery of concave mirrors.

Solar furnaces have many limitations but these are not necessarily insurmountable. Their efficiency can be appreciably reduced by haze, fog, clouds, atmospheric dust, and by heavy wind loadings which deflect equipment and interfere with the accurate focusing of the sun's rays. Attempts are being made to resolve some of these problems by sliding roofs, covering material for the mirrors, and firm, protective housings. On the other hand, solar furnaces are clean, efficient when they are in good working order, and they produce extremely high-grade metals which none of the conventional furnaces currently in use can hope to match.

An equally promising area of research are the attempts made to convert solar energy into electricity. Theoretically, an area roughly one square yard in size, placed perpendicular to the sun's rays, receives energy equivalent to one kilowatt. "Considering that in the arid zones of the world many million

millions of square meters (or yards) of desert land are free for power production," observes Thirring, "we find that by utilizing only one percent of
the available ground for solar power plants a capacity could be reached far
higher than the present installed capacity of all fuel-operated and hydro-
electric power plants in the world, which is about 200 million kilowatts." In
practice, work along the lines suggested by Thirring has been inhibited by
cost considerations, market factors (there is no large demand, today, for
electricity in those underdeveloped, hot areas of the world where the project
is most feasible), and essentially the conservatism of designers in the power
field. The greatest research emphasis in converting solar power into electricity has been placed in recent years on the development of solar batteries, a
result largely of work on the space program.

Solar batteries—devices that have been used most successfully in space
travel—make use of the thermoelectric effect. If strips of antimony and
bismuth are joined together in a loop, for example, a temperature differential, say by producing heat in one junction, yields electric power. The sophistication of solar batteries over the past decade or so has produced devices that have a power-converting efficiency as high as fifteen percent, and
twenty to twenty-five percent is quite attainable in the not too distant future. Grouped in large panels, solar batteries have been used to power electric cars, small boats, telephone lines, and singly or several in number,
radios, phonographs, clocks, sewing machines, and other appliances. Eventually, it is expected, the cost of producing solar batteries will be diminished
to a point where they will provide electric power for homes and even small
industrial facilities.

Finally, the sun's energy can be used in still another way—by collecting
heat in a body of water. For quite some time engineers have been studying
ways of acquiring electric power from temperature differences produced in
the sea by the sun's heat. If solar ponds are built to behave according to
prescribed conditions, a body of water one square kilometer in size can
yield thirty million kilowatt-hours of electricity annually, enough to match
the output of a sizeable power station, operating more than twelve hours
every day of the year. The power can be acquired without any fuel costs, or
as Henry Tabor observes, "merely by the pond lying in the sun." Heat can
be extracted from the bottom of the pond by passing the hot water over a
heat exchanger and then returning the water to the pond. In warm latitudes,
where solar ponds are likely to be most effective, 10,000 square miles committed to this method of power production might be able to provide enough
electricity to satisfy the needs of 400 million people!

The ocean's tides represent still another untapped potential to which we could turn for electric power in many coastal areas. We could trap the ocean's waters at high tide in a natural basin—say, a bay or the mouth of a river—and release them through turbines at low tide. A number of highly suitable places exist where the tides are high enough to produce large blocks of electric power. The French have already built an immense tidal-power installation near the mouth of the Rance River at St. Malo with an expected yield of 820 kilowatt-hours annually. They also plan to build another dam in the bay of Mont Saint-Michel. In England, highly suitable conditions for a tidal dam exist above the confluence of the Severn and Wye Rivers. This dam could provide the electric power produced by a million tons of coal annually. A superb locale for producing tide-generated electricity exists at Passamaquoddy Bay on the frontier between Maine and New Brunswick. Good locales exist on the Mezen Gulf, a Russian coastal area opening into the Arctic Ocean, the Kola Peninsula, and the Okhotsk Sea. Argentina has plans for building a tidal dam across the estuary of the Deseado River near Puerto Desire on the Atlantic coast. Many other coastal areas could be used to generate electricity from tidal power, but except for France, no country has seriously initiated work on this resource.

We could use the differences of temperature in the sea or in the earth to generate electric power in sizeable quantities or as sources of heat for domestic purposes. A temperature differential as high as seventeen degrees Centigrade is not uncommon in the surface layers of tropical waters; along coastal areas of Siberia, winter differences of thirty degrees exist between the water below the ice crust and the air. The interior of the earth becomes progressively warmer as we descend, providing selective temperature differentials with respect to the surface. Heat pumps could be used to avail ourselves of these differentials in order to drive steam turbines for industrial purposes or merely to heat homes. The heat pump works like a mechanical refrigerator: a circulating refrigerant draws off heat from a medium, dissipates it, and returns to repeat the process. During winter months, the pumps, circulating a refrigerant in a shallow well, could be used to absorb subsurface heat and release it in a house. In the summer, the process could be reversed; heat, withdrawn from the house, could be dissipated in the house. In a centralized society, based entirely on coal, petroleum, or atomic power, the heat pump is regarded as too costly to operate; the price of electric power needed to work the pump is prohibitively expensive. In a humanistic, decentralized society, where solar or wind power is available and where "cost" is subordinated to human needs, the pump would be an ideal device for space heating in all north temperate and subarctic latitudes. The pumps do not require costly chimneys, they do not pollute the atmosphere, and they eliminate the nuisance of stocking furnaces and carrying out ashes. If we could acquire electricity or direct heat from solar energy, wind power, or temperature differentials, the heating system of a home or factory would be completely self-sustaining; it would not drain valuable hydrocarbon resources or require external sources of supply.

I have mentioned wind power as a possible source of energy. Actually, the winds could be used on an extensive scale to provide electric power in many areas of the world. About 90 Q of the solar energy reaching the earth is converted into wind. Although much of this goes into making the jet stream, thirty to forty thousand feet above sea-level, a great deal of wind energy is available a few hundred feet above the ground. A U.N. report, using monetary terms to gauge the feasibility of wind power, finds that efficient wind plants in many areas could produce electricity at an overall cost of five mills per kilowatt, a figure that approximates the price of electric power generated by the use of conventional fuels. Several wind generators have already been established and used with a high measure of success. The famous 1,250 kilowatt generator at Grandpa's Knob, near Rutland, Vermont, successfully fed alternating current into the lines of the Central Vermont Public Service Co. until a shortage of parts during World War II made it difficult to keep the installation in good repair. Since then, larger, more efficient generators have been designed. P. H. Thomas, working for the Federal Power Commission, has designed a 7,500 kilowatt windmill that would involve an investment of $68 per kilowatt. Eugene Ayers notes that if the Thomas device were actually constructed and costs proved to be double the amount estimated by its designer, "wind turbines would seem nevertheless to compare favorably with hydro-electric installations which cost around $300 per kilowatt." The potential for generating electricity by means of wind power is probably enormous in many regions of the world. In England, for example, where a careful three-year survey was made of possible wind-power sites, it was found that the newer wind turbines could generate several million kilowatts and save from two to four million tons of coal annually.

Let there be no mistake about the extraction of trace minerals from rocks, solar and wind power, and the use of heat pumps; except for tidal power and the extraction of raw materials from the sea, these sources cannot supply man with the bulky quantity of raw materials and large blocks of energy needed to sustain densely concentrated populations and highly centralized industries. Solar devices, wind turbines, and heat pumps can be expected to produce power in relatively small quantities. Used locally and in conjunction with each other, they could amply meet all the power needs of a small community, but we cannot foresee a time when they will be able to furnish the electricity currently used by cities the size of New York, London, Paris, or similar megalopolitan areas.

This "limitation of scope," however, could well represent a profound advantage from an ecological point of view. The sun, the wind, and the earth are experiential realities to which men have responded sensuously and reverently from time immemorial. Out of these primal elements man developed his sense of dependence—and respect—for the natural environment—a dependence that kept his destructive activities in check. The Industrial Revolution and the urbanized world that followed it obscured their role in human experience—literally hiding the sun with a pall of smoke, blocking the winds with massive buildings, desecrating the earth with sprawling cities. Man's dependence on the natural world now became invisible, more precisely theoretical and intellectual in character, the subject-matter of text books, monographs, lectures, and laboratories. True, this theoretical dependence supplied us with insights (partial ones, at best) into the natural world, but its onesidedness robbed us of all sensuous dependence, all visible contact and unity with nature. In losing our sensuous, visible dependence upon nature, we lost a part of ourselves as feeling animal beings. We became alienated from nature. Our technology and environment, in short, became totally inanimate, totally synthetic—a purely inorganic physical thing that promoted the de-animization of man and his thought.

To bring the sun, wind, earth, indeed the world of life, back into technology, into the means of human survival, would represent a revolutionary renewal of man's ties to nature. To bring it back in a way that evokes a sense of regional uniqueness in the community, a sense not only of generalized dependence but of dependence on a *specific* region with distinct qualities of its own, would give this renewal a truly ecological context. And here we come to another advantage that derives from the "limitation of scope"; since it is very unlikely that solar energy alone, or wind power alone, or heat derived from the earth would suffice to meet all the energy needs of the free community, the community would have to use several of these resources in most cases, combining them in varying proportions, depending upon its latitude, prevailing wind loads, and geothermal reserves. Man's relationship to a given region would be reinforced by the ecology of his energy system.

I believe it will be a real ecological system, a delicately interlaced pattern of local resources, honored by continual study and artful modification. As a sense of regionalism grows in the community, every resource will find its place in a natural, stable balance, a truly organic unity of social, technological, and natural elements. Art will assimilate technology in the deepest sense that art can exist—as social art, the art of the community as a living process. Small or of moderate size, the free community will be able to re-scale the tempo of life, the work patterns of man, and its own architecture, systems of transportation and communication to completely human dimensions. The electric car, quiet, slow-moving, and clean, will come into its own as a form of intra-urban transportation, replacing completely the noisy, filthy, and high-speed automobile. Monorails will link community to community, replacing railroads and reducing the number of highways that scar the countryside. Crafts will regain their honored position as supplements to the factory; they will become a form of domestic, day-to-day artistry. A high standard of excellence, I believe, will replace the strictly quantitative criteria of production that prevail today; a respect for the durability of goods and the conservation of raw materials will replace the shabby, huckster-oriented criteria that result in built-in obsolescence and an insensate consumer society. The community will become a beautifully molded arena of life, a vitalizing source of culture and a deeply personal, ever-nourishing source of human solidarity.

TECHNOLOGY FOR LIFE

In a future revolution, the most pressing task assigned to technology will be to produce a surfeit of goods with a minimum of toil. The immediate purpose of this task will be to permanently open the social arena to the revolutionary people, *to keep the revolution in permanence.* Thus far, every social revolution has foundered because the peal of the tocsin could not be heard over the din of the workshop. Dreams of freedom and plenty were polluted by the mundane, workaday responsibility of producing the means of survival. Looking back at the brute facts of history, we find that as long as revolution meant continual sacrifice and denial for the people, the reins of power fell into the hands of the political "professionals," the mediocrities of Thermidor. How well the liberal Girondins of the French Convention understood this reality can be judged by the fact that they sought to reduce the revolutionary fervor of the Parisian popular assemblies—the great Sections of 1793—by decreeing that the meetings should close "at ten in the evening," or, as Carlyle tells us, "before the working people come . . ." from their jobs. The decree proved ineffective, but its aim was shrewd and unerring. Essentially, the tragedy of past revolutions has been that, sooner or later, their doors closed, "at ten in the evening." *The most critical function of modern technology must be to keep the doors of the revolution open forever!*

Nearly a half century ago, while Social Democratic and Communist theoreticians babbled about a society with "work for all," those magnificent madmen, the Dadaists, demanded unemployment for everybody. The decades have detracted nothing from this demand; to the contrary, they have given it form and content. From the moment toil is reduced to the barest possible minimum or disappears entirely, however, the problem of survival passes into the problem of life and it is certain that technology itself will pass from the servant of man's immediate needs into the partner of his creativity.

Let us look at this matter closely.

Much has been written about technology as an "extension of man." The phrase is misleading if it is meant to apply to technology as a whole. It has validity primarily for the traditional handicraft shop and, perhaps, for the early stages of machine development. The craftsman dominates the tool; his labor, artistic inclinations, and personality are the sovereign factors in the productive process. Labor is not merely an expenditure of energy but the personalized work of a man whose activities are sensuously directed toward preparing, fashioning, and finally decorating his product for human use. The craftsman guides the tool, not the tool the craftsman. Any alienation that may exist between the craftsman and his product is immediately overcome, as Friedrich Wilhelmsen emphasized, "by an artistic judgment—a judgment bearing on a thing to be made." The tool amplifies the powers of the craftsman as a *man,* as a *human;* it amplifies his power to impart his artistry, his very identity as a creative being, on raw materials.

The development of the machine tends to rupture the intimate relationship between man and the means of production. To the degree that it is a self-operating device, the machine assimilates the worker to preset industrial tasks, tasks over which he exercises no control whatever. The machine now appears as an alien force—apart from and yet wedded to the production of the means of survival. Starting out as an "extension of man," technology is transformed into a force above man, orchestrating his life according to a score contrived by an industrial bureaucracy; not *men,* I repeat, but *bureaucracies,* i.e., *social machines.* With the arrival of the fully automatic machine as the predominant means of production, man becomes an extension of the machine, not only of mechanical devices in the productive process but also of social devices in the social process. Man ceases to exist in almost any respect for his own sake. Society is ruled by the harsh maxim: production for the sake of production. The decline from craftsman to worker, from the active to the increasingly passive personality, is completed by man *qua* consumer—an economic entity whose tastes, values, thoughts, and sensibilities are engineered by bureaucratic "teams" in "think tanks." Man, standardized by machines, is finally reduced to a machine.

This is the trend. Man-the-machine is the bureaucratic ideal.[7] It is an ideal that is continually defied by the re-birth of life, by the reappearance of the young, and by the contradictions that unsettle the bureaucracy. Every generation has to be assimilated again, and each time with explosive resistance. The bureaucracy, in turn, never lives up to its own technical ideal. Congested by mediocrities, it errs continually. Its judgment lags behind new situations; insensate, it suffers from social inertia and is always buffeted by chance. Any crack that opens in the social machine is widened by the forces of life.

How can we heal the fracture that separates living men from dead machines without sacrificing either men or machines? How can we transform the technology for survival into the technology for life? To answer any of these questions with Olympian assurance would be idiotic. Liberated man may choose from a large variety of mutually exclusive or combinable alternatives, all of which may be based on unforeseeable technological innovations. As a sweeping solution, they may simply choose to step over the body of technology. They may submerge the cybernated machine in a technological underworld, divorcing it entirely from social life, the community, and creativity.

All but hidden from society, the machines would work for man. Free communities would stand, in effect, at the end of a cybernated industrial assembly line with baskets to cart the goods home. Industry, like the autonomic nervous system, would work on its own, subject to the repairs that our own bodies require in occasional bouts of illness. The fracture separating man from the machine would not be healed. It would simply be ignored.

I do not believe that this is a solution to anything. It would amount to closing off a vital human experience: the stimulus of productive activity, the stimulus of the machine. Technology can play a very important role in forming the personality of man. Every art, as Lewis Mumford has argued, has its technical side—the self-mobilization of spontaneity into expressed order, the need during the highest, most ecstatic moments of subjectivity to retain contact with the objective world, the counterposing of necessity to "disordered subjectivity" and a concreteness that responds with equal sensitivity to all stimuli—and therefore to none at all.[8]

A liberated society, I believe, will not want to negate technology—precisely because it is liberated and can strike a balance. It may well be that it will want to assimilate the machine to artistic craftsmanship. What I mean by this is that the machine will remove toil from the productive process, leaving its artistic completion to man. The machine, in effect, will participate in human creativity. "The potter's wheel, for example, increased the freedom of the potter, hampered as he had been by the primitive coil method of shaping pottery without the aid of a machine; even the lathe permitted a certain leeway to the craftsman in his fashioning of beads and bulges," observes Mumford. By the same token, there is no reason why automatic, cybernated machinery cannot be used in a way so that the finishing of products, especially those destined for personal use, is left to the community. The machine can absorb the toil involved in mining, smelting, transporting, and shaping raw materials, leaving the final stages of artistry and craftsmanship to the individual. We are reminded that most of the stones that make up a medieval cathedral were carefully squared and standardized to facilitate their laying and bonding—a thankless, repetitive, and boring task that can now be done rapidly and effortlessly by modern machines. Once the stone blocks were set in place, the craftsmen made their appearance; inhuman toil was replaced by creative, human work. In a liberated community the combination of industrial machines and the craftsman's tools could reach a degree of sophistication, of creative interdependence unparalleled by any period in human history. William Morris's vision of a return of the crafts would be freed of its nostalgic nuances. We could truly speak of a qualitatively new advance in technics—a technology for life.

Having acquired a vitalizing respect for the natural environment and its resources, the free decentralized community will give a new interpretation to the word "need." Marx's "realm of necessity," instead of expanding indefinitely, will tend to contract; needs will be humanized and scaled by a higher valuation of life and creativity. Quality and artistry will supplant the current emphasis on quantity and standardization; durability will replace the current emphasis on expendability; an economy of cherished things, sanctified by a sense of tradition and by a sense of wonder for the personality and artistry of dead generations, will replace the mindless seasonal restyling of commodities; innovations will be made with a sensitivity for the natural inclinations of man as distinguished from the engineered pollution of taste by the mass media. Conservation will replace waste in all things. Freed of bureaucratic manipulation, men will rediscover the beauty of a simpler, uncluttered material life. Clothing, diet, furnishings, and homes will become more artistic, more personalized, and more Spartan. Man will recover a sense of the things that are *for* man, as against the things that have been *imposed* upon man. The repulsive ritual of bargaining and hoarding will be replaced by the sensitive act of making and giving. Things will cease to be the crutches for an impoverished ego and the mediators between aborted personalities; they will become the product of a rounded, creative individual and the gift of an integrated, developing self.

A technology for life can play the vital role of integrating one community with another. Rescaled to a revival of crafts and to a new conception of material needs, technology can also function as the sinews of confederation. The danger of a national division of labor and of industrial centralization is that technology begins to transcend the human scale, becomes increasingly incomprehensible, and lends itself to bureaucratic manipulation. To the extent that a shift away from community control occurs in real material terms, technologically and economically, to that extent do centralized institutions acquire real power over the lives of men and threaten to become sources of coercion. A technology for life must be *based* on the community; it must be tailored to the community and regional level. On this level, however, the sharing of factories and resources can actually promote solidarity between community groups; it can serve to confederate them on the basis not only of common spiritual and cultural interests, but also common material needs. Depending upon the resources and uniqueness of regions, a rational, humanistic balance can be struck between autarchy, industrial confederation, and a national division of labor; the economic weight of society, however, must rest overwhelmingly with communities, both separately and in regional groups.

Is society so "complex" that an advanced civilization stands in contradiction to a decentralized technology for life? My answer to this question is a categoric, *no!* Much of the social "complexity" of our time has its origin in the paperwork, administration, manipulation, and constant wastefulness of capitalist enterprise. The petty bourgeois stands in awe of the bourgeois filing system—the rows of cabinets filled with invoices, accounting books, insurance records, tax forms—and the inevitable dossiers. He is spellbound by the "expertise" of industrial managers, engineers, style-mongers, manipulators of finance, and architects of market consent. He is totally mystified by the state—the police, courts, jails, federal offices, secretariats, the whole stinking, sick fat of coercion, control, and domination. Modern society is incredibly complex—complex even beyond human comprehension—if we grant that its premises consist of property, production for the sake of production, competition, capital accumulation, exploitation, finance, centralization, coercion, bureaucracy—in short, the domination of man by man. Attached to every one of these premises are the institutions that actualize them—offices, millions of "personnel," forms and staggering tons of paper, desks, typewriters, telephones, and of course, rows upon rows of filing cabinets. As in Kafka's novels, they are real but strangely dreamlike, indefinable, shadows on the social landscape. The economy has a greater reality to it and is easily mastered by the mind and senses. But it too is intricate if we grant that buttons must be styled in a thousand different forms, textiles varied endlessly in kind and pattern to create the illusion of innovation and novelty, bathrooms filled to overflowing with a dazzling variety of pharmaceuticals and lotions, kitchens cluttered with an endless number of imbecile appliances (one thinks, here, of the electric can-opener)—the list is endless.* If we single out of this odious garbage one or two goods of high quality in the more useful categories and if we eliminate the money economy, the state power, the credit system, the paperwork and policework required to hold society in an enforced state of want, insecurity, and domination, society would not only become reasonably human but also fairly simple.

I do not wish to belittle the fact that behind a single yard of high quality electric wiring lies a copper mine, the machinery needed to operate it, a plant for producing insulating material, a copper-smelting and shaping complex, a transportation system for distributing the wiring—and behind each of these complexes, other mines, plants, machine shops, and so forth. Copper mines, certainly of a kind that can be exploited by existing machinery, are not to be found everywhere, although enough copper and other useful metals can be recovered as scrap from the debris of our present society to provide future generations with all they need. But let us grant that copper will fall within a sizeable category of material that can be furnished

---

* For supplemental reading, consult the advertising pages of the *Ladies Home Journal* or *Good Housekeeping*.

only by a national division of labor. In what sense need there be a division of labor in the current sense of the term? Bluntly, there need be none at all. First, copper can be exchanged for other goods between the free, autonomous communities that mine it and those that require it. The exchange need not require the mediation of centralized bureaucratic institutions. Secondly, and perhaps more significantly, a community that lives in a region with ample copper resources will not be a mere mining community. Copper mining will be one of many economic activities in which it is engaged, a part of a larger, rounded, organic economic arena. The same will hold for communities whose climate is most suitable for growing specialized foods or whose resources are rare and uniquely valuable to society as a whole. Every community will approximate, perhaps in many cases achieve, local or regional autarchy. It will seek to achieve wholeness, not only because wholeness provides material independence (important as this may be), but also because it produces complete, rounded men who live in a symbiotic relationship with their environment. Even if a substantial portion of the economy falls within the sphere of a national division of labor, the overall economic weight of society will still rest with the community. If there is no distortion of communities, there will be no sacrifice of any portion of humanity to the interests of humanity as a whole.

A basic sense of decency, sympathy, and mutual aid lies at the core of human behavior. Even in this lousy bourgeois society, we do not find it unusual that adults will rescue children from danger although the act will imperil their lives; we do not find it strange that miners, for example, will risk death to save their fellow-workers in cave-ins, or that soldiers will crawl under heavy fire to carry a wounded comrade to safety. What tends to shock us are those occasions when aid is refused—when the cries of a girl who has been stabbed and is being murdered are ignored in a middle-class neighborhood.

Yet there is nothing in this society that would seem to warrant a molecule of solidarity. What solidarity we do find exists despite the society, against all its realities, as an unending struggle between the innate decency of man and the innate indecency of the society. Can we imagine how men would behave if this decency could find full release, if society earned the respect, even the love of the individual? We are still the offspring of a violent, blood-soaked, ignoble history—the end products of man's domination of man. We may never end this condition of domination. The future may bring us and our shoddy civilization down in a Wagnerian Gotterdammerung. How idiotic it would all be! But we may also end the domination of man by man. We may finally succeed in breaking the chain to the past and gain a humanistic, anarchist society. Would it not be the height of absurdity, indeed of impudence, to gauge the behavior of future generations by the very criteria we despise in our own time? An end to the sophomoric questions! Free men will not be greedy, one liberated community will not try to dominate another because it has a potential monopoly of copper, computer "experts" will not try to enslave grease monkeys, and sentimental novels about pining, tubercular virgins will not be written. We can ask only one thing of the free men of the future: to forgive us that it took so long and that it was such a hard pull. Like Brecht, we can ask that they try not to think of us too harshly, that they give us their sympathy and understand that we lived in the depths of a social hell.

But then they will surely know what to think without our telling them.

NOTES

¹ Both Juenger and Elul seem to believe that the debasement of man by the machine is intrinsic to the development of technology, and they conclude their works on a grim, unrelieved note of resignation. Their works reflect the social fatalism I have in mind—especially Elul, whose views are more symptomatic of the contemporary human condition. Cf. Friedrich Georg Juenger, *The Failure of Technology* (written in the pre-World War II period) and Jacques Elul, *The Technological Society* (written in the 1960's).

² It is my own belief that the development of the "workers' state" in Russia thoroughly supports the anarchist critique of Marxist statism. Indeed, modern Marxists would do well to consult Marx's own discussion of commodity fetishism in *Capital* to better understand how everything tends to become an end-in-itself under conditions of commodity exchange. On the other hand, the Marxist critique of anarchist communitarianism has been grossly oversimplified. For an excellent discussion of this problem see Buber's *Paths in Utopia* (London: Routledge; New York: Beacon Press).

³ An exclusively quantitative approach to the new technology, I may add, is not only economically archaic, but morally regressive. It partakes of the old moral principle of *justice*, as distinguished from the new moral principle of *liberation*. Historically, justice is derived from the world of material necessity and toil; it implies a domain of relatively scarce resources which are apportioned by a moral principle that is either "just" or "unjust." Justice, even "equal" justice, is a concept of *limitation*, involving the denial of goods and the sacrifice of time and energy to production. Once we transcend the concept of justice, of limitation—indeed, once we pass from the *quantitative* to the *qualitative* potentialities of modern technology—we enter the unexplored domain of liberation,

of unrestricted freedom based on spontaneous organization and unlimited access to the means of life.

⁴ There are two broad classes of computers in use today: the analogue computer and the digital. The analogue computer has a fairly limited use in industrial operations. My discussion on computers in this article will deal entirely with digital computers.

⁵ See Lewis Herber: "Ecology and Revolutionary Thought," *Anarchy,* 69 (November, 1966).

⁶ A "Q" is equal to 2.93×10^{14} kilowatt-hours.

⁷ The "ideal man" of the police bureaucracy is a being whose innermost thoughts can be invaded by lie detectors, electronic listening devices, and "truth" drugs. The "ideal man" of the political bureaucracy is a being whose innermost life can be shaped by mutagenic chemicals and socially assimilated by the mass media. The "ideal man" of the industrial bureaucracy is a being whose innermost life can be invaded by subliminal and predictively reliable advertising. The "ideal man" of the military bureaucracy is a being whose innermost life can be invaded by regimentation for genocide.

Accordingly men are graded, fingerprinted, tested, mobilized in campaigns from "charity" to war. The horrible contempt for the human personality implied by these "ideals," tests, and campaigns provides the moral climate for mass murder, acts in which the followers of Stalin and Hitler are mere pioneers.

⁸ The phrase "disordered subjectivity" is Mumford's, but I will defend it to the death, even if it is offensive to those to whom I feel the closest affinity. I refer to the radical "underground"—the artists, poets, and revolutionaries who seek ecstatic, hallucinatory experiences, partly as a means of self-discovery, partly in rebellion against the demands of a grotesquely bureaucratized and institutionalized world. "Disordered subjectivity," *as a permanent state of being and as an end in itself, can be as dehumanizing as the most bureaucratic society in existence today.* A point can be reached where there is no intrinsic difference between the two, where they are joined under the precept: hallucination for its own sake. *The system has everything to gain by the mystification of existing reality.* What is more hallucinatory than production for the sake of production, consumption for the sake of consumption, the wanton accumulation of money, the cult of authority and the State, the fear of real life that pervades the soul of the petit bourgeois? Nature produces order dialectically, through spontaneity. The existing society, by trying to extinguish spontaneity and place man under bureaucratic control, produces disorder, violence, and cruelty. Let us distinguish order from bureaucracy and call this society what it really is: not orderly but bureaucratic, not practical but shot through with the hallucinatory symbols of power and wealth, not Real and Rational in Hegel's sense, but fetishistic and logical in the murderous sense of consistency without truth. A return to Dionysius and Orpheus—yes! A return to the cloisters and the Gothic—never!

The description of self-management and direct democracy in Yugoslavia is significant from a number of perspectives. As one of the few laboratories of the principles of workers' control and community control, the successes and problems that have been encountered offer a fund of concrete information from which lessons can be learned for those interested in the practical aspects of direct democracy. One significant point here concerns the extent to which the workers' council was perceived to be inadequate as a vehicle of democratic participation and control; this experience here links with James Gillespie's discussion of free groups and workers' councils, since it shows that only group organization at the work place can guarantee an experience of full participation.

When workers' control was first instigated in Yugoslavia, there was a widespread feeling that sitting in decision-making meetings wasted time that could better be put into production. While such feelings are still found among older workers, there is strong support for the system of workers' control at present, and it has evolved continuously toward more direct control via the economic or work units.

Yugoslavia is often cited as an example of a neocapitalist system by the Western press and by the Russians in their more critical moods. Both ignore the structure of the enterprise and its relationship to the society. This paper indicates the limits placed on the market system, through price controls and the like; most important, it makes clear that the existence of the market in no way makes the Yugoslav system capitalistic. Capital and investment do not control the enterprise; it is involved in a complex network of social control, represented by the commune, the enterprise's work units and workers' council, and regional banks, which are also democratically controlled. Profits do not accrue to the few at the expense of the many, but are instead functionally controlled by those most affected by the enterprise.

The shifts that continue to occur in the Yugoslav system—from workers' councils to work units, from commune assemblies to local communities— give evidence of the flexibility and experimental strength of the system, and its continuing dedication to functional democracy. Nothing is fixed, and in this kind of a system politics changes from party sloganeering to debates about how to create structures that best embody the principles of functional and direct participation. Yugoslavia represents one significant sense of the "withering away" of the state: the withering away of a political superstructure as a separate entity above and apart from the social, economic, cultural, and educational institutions of the society.

The basis of the Yugoslav system is not so much the system of workers' self-management—even though this is essential—as it is the commune, the basic cell of the society. The thought parallels that of Martin Buber, who suggests in Paths in Utopia *that the health of a society derives not from the state but from the health of its cell or nuclear units. Here much can be learned from Yugoslavia, in particular with respect to the problems encountered by the commune system. The tension between work and the commune represents one significant area where economic and technological imperatives threaten the ecological integrity of basic social units. The problem of resource allocation and its effect on the integrity of commune decision-making is also important.*

It is easy to focus on problems and shortcomings in the Yugoslav system, since this is where debate centers. But the broad social benefits that have to do with the meaningfulness of work and life are much harder to catch, since they are difficult to quantify. Nevertheless, they represent the meaning and purpose of the Yugoslav experiment, and it is by them that the system must be judged.

The Yugoslav System of Decentralization and Self-management
Gerry Hunnius

PEOPLE AND PROBLEMS

Evaluation of the Yugoslav system presupposes some knowledge of the long history of national conflicts between the peoples of that area, and their struggle of resistance to foreign domination.[1] The Communist Party of Yugoslavia, founded in 1919 and later renamed The League of Communists of Yugoslavia (LCY) was the first truly Yugoslav party in the history of that country in the sense that it included within its ranks the many Yugoslav nationalities and minorities.

Yugoslavia today is a multi-national state of more than twenty million inhabitants. The Slav peoples, who constitute a great majority of the population, belong to five main ethnic groups: Serbs, Croats, Slovenes, Macedonians, and Montenegrins. Each of these groups has its territorial center in one of the five autonomous republics. A sixth republic, Bosnia-Herzegovina, has a population of Serbs, Croats, and Yugoslav Moslems. In addition to the six republics, two autonomous provinces have been created within Serbia. Kosovo-Metohija (Kosmet), has an Albanian majority, and Vojvodina in northern Serbia has a mixed population including a large number of Hungarians. Non-Slavic minorities in Yugoslavia make up about ten percent of the total population. Equality under the law is guaranteed to all Yugoslav citizens in article thirty-three of the Constitution. Article forty-one guarantees every citizen "the freedom to express his nationality and culture, as well as the freedom to speak his language." Incitement to national, racial, and religious hatred is unconstitutional, and as a rule this law is rigorously enforced.

When the new Yugoslavia was created at the end of the Second World War, it inherited a country devastated by war. According to Yugoslav sources, some thirty-six percent of Yugoslavia's industry was destroyed and 1,700,000 people lost their lives during the war. Another difficulty was the extremely low technological and economic base of the country. Industrial development in most of Yugoslavia had been concentrated in extractive industries, which were largely in the hands of foreigners. Only in Slovenia and Croatia did a native industry exist. All these factors have made the task of nation-building exceedingly difficult. The Yugoslav Communists, under Tito, have to be given credit for accomplishing as much as they have, given the difficulties they had inherited.

There are additional social and economic factors that must be kept in mind in any serious attempt to evaluate the Yugoslav experience of self-management. First, the level of education and industrial experience is low for a great part of the working force, including sections of the managerial personnel. The steady stream of peasants deserting the rural areas for the cities has vastly increased the number of unskilled and semi-skilled workers. While the government has done much to combat illiteracy and provide vocational training for workers, the problem is still a serious one with direct implications for the development of self-management within enterprises.

Next, there is a division between the more industrialized northern regions and the less developed southern parts of the country. While regional equalization is the official policy of government and party, progress in this respect has not been up to expectations. Resentment directed against the federal government has come from the rich as well as the poor republics. The introduction of the system of workers' control in 1950 and the economic reforms of 1965 have reduced the role and the resources of the federal government in aiding the development of the poorer regions and have shifted part of the burden on enterprises and banks. Where the principles of socialist solidarity and the maximization of profits have clashed, the former have frequently been the loser. The battle between the developed and underdeveloped republics is no longer fought out in secret. It pervades almost every political forum.

The factors raised in these few introductory paragraphs only scratch the surface. Without further precision, we can state that analysis of the new Yugoslav system must be tempered by an awareness that, in their efforts to introduce socialist democracy, the Yugoslav people and leadership are confronted with a number of formidable obstacles.[2]

THE POLITICAL FRAMEWORK

The post-war Yugoslav system was modeled on that of the Soviet Union. The end of this first period was reached in the late 1940s when the break with the Soviet Union reached its climax. From 1950 onwards, Yugoslavia moved towards increased decentralization of her economy, and somewhat later, of her political-administrative structure. The elevation of the commune to the "basic social-political community"[3] in Yugoslavia, was accompanied by a number of significant innovations. Deputies of republican assemblies and the Federal Assembly were elected (and removable) by commune assemblies. In the early 1950s, a constitutional provision was passed that delegated to the local commune responsibility over all activities not expressly reserved to the districts,[4] republics, and the Federation. A year later, a provision was passed that stipulated that local administrative agencies were responsible only to their own local assemblies and councils and no longer to higher governmental agencies.

The introduction and use of elements of direct democracy, such as the system of recall of elected members; referenda in local communities, communes, and enterprises; meetings of voters; the increasing activity by local residential communities within communes; and the system of continuous rotation of all elected deputies and political functionaries—these are all elementary and basic components of direct socialist democracy. The ultimate announced aim of these and other provisions is the "withering away of the state." As one of the architects of the 1963 Constitution has pointed out, "the experience which has been gained in socialist development indicates that the state, apart from its positive aspects, is the source of bureaucratic tendencies." [5] Bureaucracy, statism, and opposition to self-management have become targets of continuous political attacks in Yugoslavia today.

The 1963 Constitution initiated a number of structural changes in the parliamentary system. Instead of the former two chambers, the Federal Assembly was now divided into five chambers: The Federal Chamber, the Economic Chamber, the Chamber of Education and Culture, the Chamber of Social Welfare and Health, and the Organizational-Political Chamber. The former Chamber of Nationalities was incorporated into the Federal Chamber where it would sit separately on certain specified questions relating to the equality of the peoples of Yugoslavia and the rights of the republics. A subsequent amendment, passed in 1967, has greatly extended the power and independence of the Chamber of Nationalities. Recent changes in the election of these functional chambers of the Federal and republican assemblies have retained the principle of indirect voting.[6] What has changed is the composition of the electoral body, which is now composed of members of the communal assemblies and delegates of work communities in the commune (enterprises and institutions), while formerly it used to be the communal assemblies alone that elected the deputies of the functional chambers of republican assemblies and the Federal Assembly. This change has increased the influence of local work communities in policy-making on the republican and Federal level. Of particular interest is the fact that university and high school students have obtained the right to be elected to the Chamber for Education and Culture.[7]

NOTES ON THE ECONOMY

Decentralization and self-management in the economy were introduced in the 1950s and culminated with the socio-economic reforms of 1965. In July 1950, control and management of factories was turned over to the workers and their elected organs. There are four key economic components at work in the Yugoslav economy:

    (1) Workers' self-management of the publicly owned enterprises;

    (2) Social planning, which consists of an intricate network of enter-

prise plans, commune plans, and indicative planning by republican and federal agencies;

(3) The market mechanism;

(4) The mechanism of economic instruments, which regulate the business conditions and criteria for the autonomous enterprises.

The integration of the plans and activities of individual enterprises is now increasingly being transferred to autonomous associations of producers, economic chambers, and other groupings in the economy. The flow of command has been partly reversed [8] and the individual enterprise is becoming the focal point and originator of an increasing number of important decisions relating to planning, production, and investment (the latter in cooperation with banks). This transfer of former government functions to autonomous associations of producers is one of the steps taken toward the final goal of the withering away of the state.

Yugoslav enterprises are responsible for developing their own production and financial plans. Indicative planning carried out centrally should not be brushed aside as mere forecasting. These estimates frequently serve as a guide to enterprises and may thus increase the likelihood of mutually consistent and socially desirable decisions. The price system can also be used to give force to centrally desired goals and priorities. Commodities may be taxed or subsidized at different rates thus changing the pattern of expenditures.[9]

Using the definition recently made by a Canadian economist, the Yugoslav economic model approximates Oskar Lange's "market socialist model," where the individual enterprises are expected to maximize their profit but where prices are to a large extent centrally controlled.[10]

The process of decentralization, economic decision-making, and the increase in reliance on the market mechanism, culminated in the reforms of 1965 which transferred to the enterprises and banks the bulk of the remaining investment resources still in the hands of the socio-political communities.[11]

Tito, in his introductory address to the Ninth Congress of the LCY in March 1969, stated: "We certainly do not idealize the market economy, but accept it as a necessity at the present level of development. But it is our policy, now—under conditions of money-commodity relations,—to guide development towards the promotion of genuine socialist social relations and the affirmation of the role of the working man on the basis of the principle of remuneration according to work performed." [12]

The proportion of income at the disposal of the organs of self-management in enterprises has increased from a low of twenty percent in 1959-60 to approximately sixty percent in 1968. The planned ratio of distribution is seventy percent to the working organizations and thirty percent to the wider community. Enterprises have been quick to point out that this ratio of net earnings at their disposal includes monetary resources deposited in banks which in turn have a decisive influence over the disposition of these resources.[13] The growing importance of banks in the allocation of investment resources becomes evident when we compare the percentage of investment resources at their disposal in 1961 (0.9 percent) to those at their disposal in 1967 (43.8 percent).[14] The trade-union movement has recently demanded the establishment of complete equality between banks and enterprises by the end of 1970.

The most dramatic change, at least in theory, has been in the position of the individual worker in the enterprise. He now controls the management of his work place, directly in the economic unit, and indirectly through the elected organs of self-management. He no longer receives a salary, but shares in the net income of his economic unit and the enterprise. In theory, the self-interest of the individual worker and the working collective will result in increased efforts to maximize the net income of the enterprise. At the same time, the spectre of alienation will gradually be removed by the increasing direct participation of the worker in the control and management of the economic unit and the entire enterprise.

THE COMMUNE [15]

Local self-government in Yugoslavia has evolved from a network of National Liberation Committees formed during the War for Liberation (1941-45). This network of elected local organs was further consolidated in the Constitution of 1946 and subsequent laws passed in 1949 and 1952, until in 1955, the Law on the Organization of Communes and Districts came into force.[16]

Prior to the establishment of the communal system, workers' self-management was introduced in 1950. It became increasingly clear that genuine self-management in the economy was not feasible unless it was accompanied by self-government in the political system. After extensive debate and experiments, the 1955 law establishing the communal system was passed. The communal system has undergone many changes since that date and must still be regarded as being in a process of change.

As the power and jurisdiction of the commune has increased, its size has increased as well. In 1969, there were 501 communes in Yugoslavia with an average population of between 30,000 and 40,000 and an average size of close to 500 square kilometers. In practice, the tendency to increase the size of the communes has resulted in the merging of urban centers with their rural environments in the expectation of creating economically viable entities.[17]

The most important political organ in the commune is the assembly. The individual citizen is perceived to have interests and requirements, both as a citizen of the commune, and as a worker or employee in his work place. Since all these interests should be represented in the policy formulation of the communal assembly, a system of two chambers has been established: the Communal Chamber, elected by all adult citizens in the commune, and the Chamber of Working Communities, elected by the working people in enterprises and institutions, who thus exercise a double vote. The latter chamber is representative of the working people in the following basic groups of activity: economy, education and culture, social welfare and health services, and public services. One Yugoslav writer has noted that the Chamber of Working Communities, "in a sense constitutes a lengthened limb of the workers' councils and management boards of enterprises and institutions, for through the chamber of work communities, the position taken by these bodies of management is transmitted to the commune assembly and their influence is exercised on the policies of the commune." [18] As a general rule, the two chambers pass laws in joint sessions. At present, there are 40,279 councillors in communal assemblies, about equally divided between the two chambers. Some of the larger communes have begun to experiment with four functional chambers and we may expect this trend to accelerate in the future. Elements of direct democracy find their expression in meetings of voters, referenda on important communal and local issues, and decision-making by local communities, of which there are 6,335 with 79,228 elected councilors.[19]

The communal assembly is autonomous in its decision-making power within the legal framework as laid down by the Constitution and subsequent federal acts. The communal authorities are also obliged to enforce federal and republican laws, as there are ordinarily no republican and federal organs of authority on the territory of the commune. The communal organs are, however, not subordinated to republican or federal authorities.

The slow development of the communal system is largely due to the very real obstacles it has to overcome: poverty, inexperience, and low educational background of many of its citizens; division of the country into rich and poor; and the entrenched party and government bureaucrats who lack the required skills and hold on to traditional and authoritarian methods in order to keep their privileged positions.

While in theory, the communal assembly is the highest decision-making organ in the commune, real power is frequently wielded by a combination of formal and informal decision-makers. A recent survey of seventeen communes illustrates the distance between theory and practice.[20] Let us look at the actual influence in a few key decisions within the commune.

Decisions on the communal budget:

Moderate influence is exerted by the mayor, the communal assembly, the communal administration, and the communal council for finances and budget. Very little influence is exerted by voters' meetings, local communities, professional and voluntary associations, and other councils of the assembly (such as those of education, public health and urbanism). No single individual or institution exerts great influence on the formation of the communal budget. There is little *direct* influence by the citizens on decisions relating to the formation of the budget. One explanation for this, is the very complexity of the budget proposals which are put before the meetings of voters and the local communities.

Decisions on financing of education:

The largest part of communal expenditures is earmarked for education. It is an issue of concern to all groups and citizens in the commune. It is also a major headache insofar as there is a constant shortage of funds for that purpose.

The influence of sixteen groups was measured in this instance. Seven groups exerted moderate influence (the communal assembly, the mayor, the communal administration, the educational community,[21] the communal council for education and culture, the council for finances and budget, and educational and cultural workers). The other nine groups exerted little influence and nobody exerted great influence on the financing of education. Voters' meetings, representing the largest interest group, exerted little influence.

Decisions on the urban plan and the zoning plan:

Again sixteen groups were measured. The structure of influence for these two decisions was very similar. The communal council for urbanism exerted great influence; the communal assembly, the administration, the mayor, and planner, exerted moderate influence. Voters' meetings and local communities came close to exerting moderate influence, while the political organizations exerted little.[22]

Jerovsek remarked that these two decisions were the result of compromises between assembly, administration, planners, and council. If these organs had communicated intensively with the citizens, which they did not, there would have been a possibility of greater influence by citizens. Surprisingly, the influence of working organizations was small in relation to these two decisions.

Current trends seem to indicate that the following organs will increase their influence in the future: the communal assembly, the councils of the assembly (largely composed of experts), the voters' meetings, local communities, and voluntary and professional associations. These organs exert at present greater influence in developed communes than in undeveloped ones, while the reverse is the case with communal political organizations, officials, and political organizations on the republic level, and individuals holding key positions in the commune. In short, greater dispersion of power and a more democratic decision-making pattern was evidenced in developed communes. The present pattern of decision-making processes in communes, however, continues to approximate a centralized, hierarchical authority structure.[23]

It is interesting to note that when the respondents were confronted with the open-ended request to name three groups or positions which in their opinion have the most influence upon events in the commune, and three groups or positions which *should* have the greatest influence, their responses to the first question were close to the actual state of affairs in the commune, while their judgment of the way things *should* be came close to the levels of influence envisioned by the law: [24]

Groups	Influence Exerted %	Influence they should Exert %
1. Socialist Alliance of Working People	3.0	3.4
2. Voters' Meeting and Local Communities	2.3	14.8
3. Trade Unions, Veterans' Association	—	0.7
4. Mayor, Deputy Mayor and Department Heads of Communal Administration	30.2	11.7
5. Administration of Communal Assembly, Professional Services	2.0	0.7

6. Communal Assembly,
   Councils of Communal
   Assembly   37.0   56.0

7. League of Communists,
   Secretary of Communal
   Committee of LCY   4.7   4.0

8. Leaders of Political
   Organizations   3.0   1.0

9. Political Organizations   2.7   2.0

10. Working Organizations,
    General Manager of Working
    Organizations, and other
    leaders.   12.1   4.7

A few words should be said about the present system of the nomination and election process in Yugoslavia. It applies in general, not only to communal, but also to provincial, republican, and federal elections. The most recent changes have produced the following mechanism in which the Socialist Alliance of the Working People of Yugoslavia, a mass organization with a generally communist orientation and over eight million members, plays a prominent part. Because of the importance of the nominating process, and the cautious introduction of elements of direct democracy, we will attempt to outline this process in some detail.[25]

The first stage consists of meetings of voters (citizens), which discuss candidates and make preliminary nominations. The first stage is openly democratic and no serious attempts are made to obstruct the popular will. Each commune has several such meetings with an average of two thousand to three thousand voters attending each meeting. The meetings of voters then send their preliminary nominations to the commune nominating conference (the second stage in this process). The nominating conference is organized by the Socialist Alliance. The participants of this conference are delegates from all the socio-political and other citizens' organizations registered in the commune.[26]

This second stage is more complex and consists of a mixture of direct and "guided" democracy. The Socialist Alliance, apart from organizing the nominating conference, fulfills two political functions at this stage:

(1) It makes sure that those candidates favored by the Alliance are nominated (the practice today is to nominate at least two "approved" candidates), if they have not already been nominated at the voters' meetings.

(2) In cooperation with delegates from other like-minded organizations, it "filters out" those candidates nominated at the voters' meetings who are considered to be undesirable.

The choices of the nominating conference go back to the meetings of voters for final approval. At this third stage, deletions and additions are possible but difficult to achieve in practice. It takes either one-third of the voters' meetings in a given commune or at least ten percent of all voters of all the meetings of voters, to effect a change. Difficult as it is to re-introduce candidates deleted at the second stage, or to delete candidates nominated by the nominating conference, such events did happen during the last 1969 elections.[27]

The nominating process is thus of greater importance than the actual election. It is, in a sense, a typical example of direct democracy tempered at present by elements of guided democracy.

SELF-MANAGEMENT IN THE ENTERPRISE

The Organizational Framework of Workers' Self-management

Yugoslav industrial enterprises operate within a framework of workers' self-management. The supreme authority within each enterprise is the workers' collective, which consists of all members of the enterprise. In all but the smallest enterprises, the workers elect a workers' council, which meets approximately once a month and is charged with making decisions on all major functions of the enterprise (prices on its products whenever these are not centrally controlled, production and financial plans of the enterprise, the statutes of the enterprise, allocation of net income, budget, etc.). The workers' council elects a management board, in practice largely from its own ranks, which acts as an executive agent of the former. At least three-fourths of the members of the management board must be production workers. This board meets more frequently and works in close cooperation with the director who is also elected by the workers' council and who is an ex-officio member of the management board. The workers' council is elected for a period of two years, half of its members being elected every year. Its composition is supposed to approximate the ratio between production workers and employees in the enterprise. Meetings of the workers' council are usually open and every member of the working collective is entitled to attend. Decisions are taken by majority vote and the members of the council, individually or as a group, can be recalled by the electors. No one can be elected twice in succession to the workers' council, and more than twice in succession to the management board. The management board is elected for a period of one year and is answerable for its work to the workers' council, which may recall individual members or the whole board at any time. Service on management boards and workers' councils is honorary and members do not receive any payment for their work. The director is the actual manager of the enterprise. All day-to-day operations are entrusted to him and he represents the enterprise in any external negotiations. In theory, but rarely in practice, he can be removed by the workers' council, which also decides on his term of office.

The most recent innovation in the organizational structure of the enterprise is the emergence of the working (or economic) unit.[28] The working unit may represent a department, or in large enterprises, an entire plant. The establishment of the working units is an organizational innovation introducing significant additional elements of direct industrial democracy into the system of self-management. The working units have moved from the discussion and recommendation stage to their present level where they are given increased decision-making powers. The current controversy about their role centers largely on their degree of authority in relation to the distribution of the income of the enterprise as well as the distribution of personal income to the members of the working units. Increasingly, entire enterprises are divided into working units, including the managerial staff, the accounting service, and the production departments. Relations between these units are conducted on the basis of contracts and payments for services rendered. Disputes arising between working units are dealt with by an arbitration commission appointed by the central worker's council.[29]

Small working units are managed directly by the entire membership. Decisions are taken at meetings, usually called "the conference of the working unit." The introduction of direct decision-making is the main feature distinguishing the smaller working units from the enterprise as a whole. In the latter, direct decision-making is largely limited to occasional referenda and voters' meetings prior to elections.[30] In larger working units the conference elects a council which it can recall at any time. The conference also appoints a manager, after announcing an open competition for his post.[31]

The Yugoslav system of self-management implies two hierarchies within each enterprise. One, concerned with self-management, includes the working units, the workers' council, the managing board and the manager. The second hierarchy approximates the conventional chain of command with workers on one end, followed by supervisors, heads of working units and managers at the other end.[32] The system is designed to achieve ideological and practical objectives. "Ideologically, the system attempts to realize a form of democratic participative management. Practically, the system is designed to minimize (if not eliminate) conflicts, increase confidence and trust between all members, improve inter-personal communication, enhance members' involvement, improve their motivation, and maintain their support for the organization and its objectives." [33]

Another way of looking at the actual functioning of the self-management system within the enterprise is to see it in terms of two levels of authority: the professional, dominated by skilled, highly skilled, and lower managerial personnel, and a second level, which bases its judgments on the social and political values of the wider community.[34] The protagonists of this second approach are the socio-political organizations represented within the enterprise. This is, again, a typically Yugoslav solution insofar as the heavy hand of the central government has been replaced by non-governmental organizations which base their influence largely on persuasion. It would be fair to say that in the initial period of the self-management system, the socio-political organizations did little else but act as transmission belts of the central authority of party and government. The situation, however, has changed, and today the decisions reached by these organizations within the enterprise are the result of a variety of influences and pressures, including that of their own central organs in Belgrade, their communal and republican organs, and many others which have not hitherto played a significant role.

Composition of the Organs of Self-management in Enterprises

It is important to remember that the workers' council is not a homogeneous group. It consists of semi-skilled and skilled workers, white collar employees and management personnel, communists and non-communists, trade union members and workers not connected with any socio-political organizations.

Important changes have taken place in the composition of the workers' council and the management board between 1964 and 1968. The numbers of women and young people have dropped. In workers' councils, persons with a background of university education (or schools of higher learning) accounted for five percent in 1964 and eight percent in 1968, while the share of skilled and highly skilled workers remained constant. The changes in the composition of the management board were even more pronounced. The share of skilled and highly skilled workers dropped by thirteen percent in the same period, while that of persons with university or higher education increased by five percent.[35] Skilled and highly skilled workers, however, still constitute the largest single group within workers' councils and management boards. In 1966 they constituted approximately fifty percent.[36]

Dr. Kratina of the Institute of Social Sciences in Belgrade recently undertook a survey of workers' opinion in the Crvena Zastava Automobile Works of Kragujevac in central Serbia. One of the questions related to the opinion of workers on the desired composition of their workers' council. The results shown in the table indicate the important influence of skilled workers.

The Opinion of Workers concerning the groups of Producers that should have more Representatives in the Workers' Council of the Enterprise[37]

Groups of Producers	Opinions of all participants in the enquiry	Opinions of unskilled & semi-skilled workers	Opinions of skilled & highly skilled workers	Opinions of workers with primary school education	Opinions of workers with secondary, schools of higher learning or university education
	%	%	%	%	%
1. Skilled Workers	60	61	67	50	41
2. Highly skilled Workers	51	35	69	38	48
3. Foremen	46	31	56	52	58
4. Engineers and Technicians	34	28	31	24	55
5. Unskilled Workers	29	49	17	29	11
6. Economic and Financial Experts	29	20	25	48	58
7. Semi-skilled Workers	26	45	18	24	3
8. Administrative and Office Staff	8	9	5	21	8
9. Leading officials in other than production units	5	8	2	2	6

The growing number of experts, particularly on the managing board, has caused some concern among many Yugoslavs. Their importance is well recognized; in fact, the socio-political organizations are constantly pressing for a more effective use of experts. There are, however, indications to the effect that serious proposals might be made soon to separate the experts, who are now finding their way into the workers' councils and managing boards, from the decision-making process in the organs of self-management and to group them instead entirely within separate consultative organs.

Perceived and Desired Powers of the Organs of Self-management

Tannenbaum and Zupanov, in their study of fifty-six workers attending a two-year course at the Workers' University in Zagreb,[38] have analyzed the perceived and ideal (desired) control curves within enterprises as seen by the respondents. The results refer to the two hierarchies within enterprises: one, including the workers as producers at one end, followed by supervisors, heads of economic units and the manager at the other; the second including the workers' council at one end, followed by the managing board and the manager at the other. The two curves are represented below without further comments as they are self-explanatory.[39]

ACTUAL AND IDEAL CONTROL CURVES

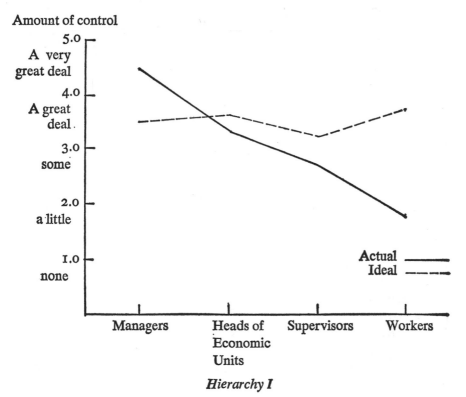

Hierarchy I

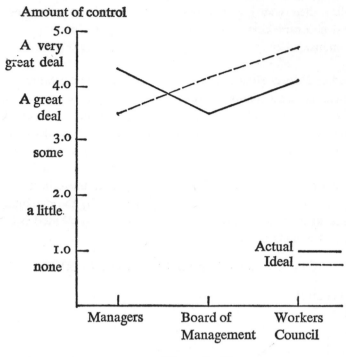

Hierarchy II

   The authors of this study comment on the large discrepancy between the actual and ideal degree of control for the workers as a group. Since the workers' council is elected by the workers and is composed in a large part of workers, this discrepancy seems to suggest that the workers' council as a representative of the workers does not give the workers a sense of control in their enterprise.[40] One possible explanation is indicated by the results of another study published in 1961, which found the workers' council oriented towards management and official views.[41] There is also evidence to the effect that management, including the managerial staff, the director and frequently members of the management board, are the most active participants in the meetings of the workers' council. The complexity of many of the issues under discussion and the control over relevant information in the hands of management, gives the latter a powerful advantage if they wish to use it, in having their proposals accepted by the workers' council.[42]
   The establishment of economic units and the increasing delegation of greater authority to these organs, has been one attempt to reduce the discre-

pancy between actual and desired control. This introduction of direct democracy is one of the more significant political innovations in recent years. Zupanov and Tannenbaum suggest that the discrepancy between the ideal and the actuality can be attributed in part to the rather high ideals expressed by the respondents. They point out that discrepancies are smaller in American industrial organizations studied, "not because the actual curves are more positive, but because the ideals are more negative." [43] The high ideals held by respondents in this sample and others which have in the main supported these findings, are one of the hopeful signs in the development of industrial democracy in Yugoslavia. This is particularly relevant given the official proclamations of the LCY and the government in general support of the aspirations held by the respondents.

The Director: Problems and Contradictions

The director and the managerial group surrounding him exert the greatest influence in enterprises; there are problems and contradictions inherent in this influence. During the administrative period prior to the introduction of workers' self-management in 1950, the director functioned as an agent of the state with almost complete power within the enterprise. His responsibilities were narrow, however, since all important decisions came from Belgrade. The typical director of this period was a man whose main qualification was his political reliability and the contacts he had in party and government circles. With the introduction of workers' self-management, his role and function changed. His responsibility now was real, but at the same time it was divided. As the chief executive officer of the enterprise, he was directly responsible to the workers' council. At the same time he was expected to act on behalf of the wider community. He retained a veto power over those decisions of the workers' council which, in his view, violated the law.[44] The commune, at this stage, had considerable influence over the appointment and dismissal of the director. The hundreds of pages of detailed instructions which the director used to receive from Belgrade every week prior to 1950, were now replaced by a network of paragraphs circumscribing his functions and his responsibilities. One Yugoslav writer has stated that the functions of a director are "circumscribed by more than 500 paragraphs in law," [45] not counting the statute of the enterprise. Many of these demands made on him may be contradictory.

Due to the scarcity of trained and experienced personnel, the desire on the part of the party leadership to retain some control over the newly created organs of self-management, and the very real problem of the large number of politically reliable but inexperienced managers who could not be pensioned off, most directors of the pre-1950 period retained their positions after the introduction of workers' self-management. The many pressures exerted on the director—for economic efficiency, adherence to national guidelines, responsibility to the organs of workers' self-management—made it increasingly difficult to attract qualified individuals for the position of director. This difficulty has yet to be entirely resolved. Added to the difficulty of attracting new directors was the reluctance of the existing directors to relinquish their positions. The director and managerial staff wield power beyond that envisaged by legislation, and the tightness of the local power structures enabled them to withstand internal and outside pressures for their removal. In the mid-1960s, when a large number of directors were up for re-selection, the number of new qualified applicants was so small that a real crisis developed.[46]

The unresolved status of the directors frequently leads to their reliance on informal groups, called by many Yugoslavs "informal management" or "cliques." These groups usually have their connections with leading groups in the commune which further consolidates their illegitimate authority. The situation today is, however, more complex than it appears. No longer does one power group dominate the commune or the enterprise. Clashes of opinion and compromises between contending groups are a frequent occurrence today. According to a study of cliques in enterprises, published in 1965, the key figures in such cliques are usually the director and other senior staff members of the enterprise. Frequent transfer of "troublesome workers" to inferior positions is one of the techniques used by cliques to subdue potential opposition.[47]

The existence of informal groups of decision-makers within enterprises today is similar in principle to the, now condemned, system of "parallelism," which refers to situations in which the League of Communists or the trade unions duplicate the work of the organs of self-management and, in effect, act as the real decision-makers in the enterprise.

As unqualified managerial personnel is gradually being replaced by younger professionals and as an ever greater number of workers gain experience and confidence in the self-management system, such distortions are slowly decreasing in frequency. The discrepancy between the actual power of the director and the officially proclaimed supremacy of the workers' council which also corresponds to the desired ideal of most workers, however, continues to be the rule rather than the exception.

Attitude of Workers on Price Control and Closure of Factories

The recently introduced and still controversial socio-economic reforms of 1965, which were to strengthen the income principle, raise the quality and efficiency of production, and prepare Yugoslavia's entry into the international economy, have resulted in a greater reliance on the market mechanism as an internal discipline for the economy. Increased unemployment and closing of unprofitable enterprises were two of the problems that confronted the organs of workers' self-management with increased force. The position of enterprises is very delicate. The reform has underlined the autonomy of enterprises and has stressed their responsibility to bear the results and risks inherent in their autonomy. At the same time, enterprises still lack sufficient resources and authority to overcome inherited difficulties and make the changes necessary for a more intensive and efficient economic operation. Government regulations still inhibit the activity of enterprises and the market mechanism works in very narrow limits. Restricted credit policies have further limited the independence of enterprises.[48]

A recent study undertaken by Professor Josip Zupanov has given some interesting results as to the opinions of workers on some of the problems now confronting the enterprise.[49] Interviews conducted in ten Croatian factories in 1966 (one year after the introduction of the reforms) showed that the majority of workers favored the continuation of price control. Only in the managerial group did the survey, taken at a time when over seventy percent of prices were centrally controlled, find a majority in favor of the elimination of price controls and even in this group, one-third wanted the contols to continue.

In response to the question as to what to do with an unprofitable enterprise (keep it going with government support and try to improve it or to close it down), the majority of workers were against the closing of unprofitable enterprises. White-collar employees and supervisors were approximately evenly divided in their opinion while the majority of managers and staff were in favor of closing down unprofitable enterprises.[50]

The income principle of remuneration according to work performed is supported by the government and all socio-political organizations in Yugoslavia and yet it has encountered serious opposition from workers as well as from intellectuals. The main problem, as seen by the critics, is the existence of unequal operating conditions. Personal income is thus dependent on a number of external factors beyond the immediate control of the individual worker and the enterprise as a whole. The size and technological nature of the means of production, the possible monopolistic position of an enterprise, and the availability of resources are just a few of the external factors that have a direct bearing on the net income of the enterprise and thus the personal income of the workers.

The whole question of the autonomy of enterprises is unclear at present. There are tendencies within the country in the direction of greater autonomy. For instance, regulations on depreciation have been liberalized and enterprises can now more or less set depreciation rates themselves. At the same time, there are tendencies in the opposite direction, e.g., the wage fund may be subjected to a progressive tax if it exceeds a certain stipulated level.

Recent Trends

The most recent constitutional changes in the system of workers' self-management are based on Amendment 15 to the Yugoslav Constitution which came into force in April, 1969 at the time all Yugoslav enterprises were holding their elections for workers' councils. Amendment 15 has abolished the obligation to elect any other organ of self-management in enterprises than the workers' council.

The implications of this pronouncement are far-reaching. Until the forthcoming revision of the legislation on working organizations is passed, it is essentially up to the workers' collective and its workers' council to experiment with new forms of self-management in enterprises. At the moment, attention centers around the managing board and the possibility to replace this organ with a new one. A frequently mentioned substitute to the management board is a "business board," which in essence, if not in name, already exists in a number of large enterprises in the form of a "technical collegium" of senior specialists appointed by the director. While lacking formal power, its influence has been considerable. There has been considerable opposition to this trend, including that of the trade unions. Critics of the introduction of the technical collegium fear that the business boards will in effect become a legalized form of the technical collegium and thus introduce a basically undemocratic element into the system of self-management.

The discussion of the revision of the legislation on working organizations has now reached the stage where a series of theses have been published, which do not, however, have a binding character. Solutions proposed in those theses include the following:

(1) The director should cease to be an organ of management and should be made the executive organ of the workers' council. He would still be appointed by the workers' council.

(2) Specialists from outside of the enterprise could be recruited to various committees and commissions appointed by the workers' council.

(3) Members of the organs of self-management would be given an increase in their income in recognition of their extra work and responsibility.

(4) The scope and power of the working units would be decided by the workers' council of each enterprise, thus avoiding a uniform formula applicable to the entire country.[51]

ASPECTS OF DIRECT DEMOCRACY

A number of important elements have been built into the system of self-management and self-government to increase the direct decision-making of large numbers of citizens and to prevent the emergence of bureaucracies and informal power groups in enterprises and socio-political communities. Some of these measures, such as the provision that, with few exceptions, no one can be elected twice in succession to the same organ of self-government, are also meant to provide the largest possible number of Yugoslavs with the opportunity of gaining experience in self-government.

Figures compiled for me by the Center for Self-Management in Belgrade show that a total of close to 700,000 individuals were serving in various elected organs during 1967/68. Here are the details: [52]

Economic Working Organizations (1968)

Economic working organizations with more than 30 workers:

Members of workers' councils	145,488	
Members of management boards	49,145	
		194,633

Economic working organizations with fewer than 30 workers:

Number of workers in collectives[53]	46,216	
Members of management boards	10,016	
		56,232

Working units which elect a council:

Members of councils	124,625	

Working units where all workers participate in decision-making:

Number of workers	178,703	
		303,328

Institutions (1968):

Members in organs of self-government	72,367	
Members of managerial councils[54]	15,668	
		88,035

Socio-Political Communities (1967):

Members of commune assemblies	40,279
Members of regional assemblies	
(two autonomous provinces)	620
Members of republican assemblies	2,260
Members of Federal Assembly	670

	43,829
Grand Total	686,057

These figures include a certain number of duplications but they exclude the elected representatives in socio-political organizations, such as the League of Communists, the Socialist Alliance, the Trade Unions and many others. The claim made by one Yugoslav observer that nearly one million individuals (five percent of the total population of Yugoslavia) participate annually in decision-making processes within organs of self-government is probably a reasonable approximation.

Referenda in enterprises have only been used infrequently in the past and the overwhelming majority have been on questions relating to the merger or the separation of enterprises. In 1967, in enterprises with 250 to 1000 workers, 203 referenda were held of which 133 dealt with mergers or separations.[55] The results of a referendum are binding on the workers' council.

Referenda in local communities have, however, increased in the last few years. Their use in local communities and communes is usually connected with efforts of self-help by the citizens. Examples of this are funding of additional schools and kindergartens for which sufficient funds are not available through the regular channels. Initiatives for such referenda may come from the commune itself or from meetings of voters or teachers. Proposals for voluntary self-help are almost always passed.[56] The cost of administering such schemes is such that referenda are only held if a favorable response by citizens can be expected with some certainty. In a recent survey undertaken in Slovenia, about one-half of the top administrative personnel in communes favored an extension of the scope of referenda to include additional political and economic issues of importance, which are presently decided by the commune assembly. About one-half of the deputies of the republican assembly in Slovenia wanted to see referenda introduced on republic-wide issues.[57]

Very little can be said at this stage about the recall of elected deputies by the electorate, since it has not been used frequently. There are a number of explanations for the infrequent use of the recall. Responsibility on the part of elected deputies to the voters has not yet reached the level hoped for, and voters as a rule do not yet constitute a political force. Implicit in the infrequent use of the recall is the reluctance of the socio-political organizations to make its more frequent application an item of priority in their educational propaganda work. Figures on the frequency of recalls are not easy to come by, but information available for 1956 shows the following: 998 members of workers' councils (0.8 percent) and 476 members of boards of management (1.2 percent) were recalled in enterprises with thirty or more workers. Of this total of 1,474 recalls, 254 were initiated by a government department or agency, 181 by the director of the enterprise, 542 by an organ of self-management, 372 by the entire collective of the enterprise and 124 by socio-political organizations. We should note that in 1956, the system of self-management in industry was only just beginning to be put into practice.[58]

Rotation of elected government and political functionaries has not yet achieved its democratic potential. One gets the impression that rotation is reduced to a game of musical chairs. Each time a new recruit enters the inner circle, a shift occurs in the positions of a number of functionaries who then move from a position of influence in one organization or organ to a similar one in another. Occasionally a functionary is encouraged to retire to give room for a younger newcomer.

The same problem exists with elected deputies of assemblies. No one, for instance, can be elected more than twice in succession to the Federal Assembly. This provision has been introduced for the same basic reason as that requiring the rotation of political functionaries: to check political "professionalism" and to prevent the formation of informal power groups. However, the provision does not preclude a deputy of the Federal Assembly being elected to a republican assembly, and then again to the Federal Assembly, or vice versa.[59]

We have already referred to the influence of local communities within communes. While their present influence appears to be small to moderate, it is conceivable that, with official encouragement, it may increase. As elements of participatory democracy, local communities have an inherent advantage over voters' meetings. The former have an organizational structure which is lacking in the meetings of voters. It is thus much more likely that continuous grass-roots pressure will result in increased authority being given to the local communities rather than to the meetings of voters (assuming the sincerity of the Yugoslav leadership in moving in the direction of direct socialist democracy).

CONCLUDING COMMENTS

The commune is seen by Yugoslav theoreticians as the fundamental cell of a future socialist society. The commune is the political expression of groups of local communities, which implies a social and political structure of self-government that has been removed from centralized state control. In practice, the commune is a community of self-managing and largely autonomous subjects (economic organizations and institutions) and its fundamental socio-economic function consists of reconciling general and individual interests.

In the field of economic policy, the commune enforces a range of regulatory and coordinating functions, ranging from investment (it frequently acts, in cooperation with existing enterprises, as founder of new enterprises), to taxation (within the rather narrow limits set by republican and federal authorities). It may place enterprises under receivership in certain stipulated instances, it determines the sites of new projects, it passes an annual social plan that covers all activity within its territorial limits, and it makes recommendations to enterprises that the latter are obliged to consider. The commune also manages the "reserve fund for intervention in the economy," for the purpose of assisting collectives that find themselves in financial difficulties.

In the educational and cultural sphere, it is the commune that establishes the "educational community," which has its own assembly made up of representatives from educational institutions as well as from working organizations and citizens. In the field of public health, the commune establishes medical institutions and related services. One Yugoslav writer has defined the commune as a "state in miniature," with its own statute (constitution) and legislation, "performing almost the entire range of functions of a state with the exception of foreign policy." [60]

The role of the commune, particularly its economic function, has changed repeatedly. Prior to the introduction of the communal system in 1955, it managed and administered the enterprises on its territory. During the second phase after 1955, when the commune became the basic socio-economic unit in the country, its organs were concerned to a large extent with economic problems. The economic power and influence of the commune was probably greatest during the second phase. With the 1965 reform, the commune entered its third phase of development. It lost some of its material base, which began to shift in favor of enterprises and banks. Working organizations are now becoming more and more the "bearers of expanded reproduction." [61] The commune is now in a state of crisis and transformation despite the fact that its total economic assets are continually increasing. The real change with the earlier period consists in the fact that these increased assets are largely controlled by enterprises and banks and not by the elected organs of the commune.[62] With the recently passed "Resolution on the Socio-Economic and Political Position of the Opstina [commune] and the Further Development of Self-Management Relations in the Opstina," the commune is now entering its fourth phase. This resolution, which we will discuss later, was passed by the Federal Assembly on December 24, 1968.

There are a number of problems with the official, somewhat idealized, definition of the commune, its functions and resources, one of them being the inadequate level of the resources under the autonomous control of the commune. The basic distribution of resources is in essence still regulated by republican and federal organs and the commune is subjected to numerous regulations in determining its budget. Republican and federal regulations place limits on the two most important sources of commune revenue, the retail-trade turnover tax and the tax on enterprise funds earmarked for personal income.[63]

The institutional allocation of investment resources has also undergone drastic changes. The governmental share (federal, republican and communal) has been reduced while that of enterprises and banks has risen sharply.

Institutional Allocation of Investment Resources[64]

	1961	*1964*	*1966*	*1967 (first half)*
1. Governments	61.7%	36.5%	15.7%	18.4%
2. Enterprises	29.5	25.9	39.8	33.4
3. Banks	0.9	31.4	37.3	43.8
4. Others	7.9	6.2	7.2	4.4

There has been a shift since 1967, giving the communes and banks increased resources at the expense of enterprises. There is, however, considerable controversy about this recent shift. In the distribution of receipts within the governmental sector, the Federal Government still took about one-half of all receipts in 1966 while the communes received a little less than one-third. The part received by the communes dropped sharply in 1967 to a little over one-quarter, due to the establishment of the educational communities, which are financed autonomously. The withdrawal of funds earmarked for education from the communal budget has produced the misleading impression of a reduction in the income of the commune. In fact, the communes received a larger share in every other field of expenditure in 1967.[65]

One of the greatest sources of frustration for the communal assembly is the continuous transfer of functions from the republican and federal level to that of the communes, without a transfer of the necessary resources for the performance of these new tasks. At times, such transfers are even introduced without prior consultation with the communes.[66] This entire practice is in direct contradiction with the principles of the 1963 Constitution and the declarations of the LCY. To put it bluntly, the constitutional aim of making the commune the basic self-governing community of citizens in Yugoslavia is being violated by the very organs that established this principle. In practice, the commune still resembles a decentralized but dependent unit of federal and republican authority. One Yugoslav critic makes the following two points in relation to this:

(1) Since the commune assembly acts to a large extent as a dependent state organ, it does not feel a real political need to consult citizens about the formulation of policies because it does not have the ability to meet their numerous demands.

(2) Working organizations and other autonomous and self-financing services lose faith in the ability and effectiveness of the commune in satisfying the general needs of the community. Loss of interest in the work of the commune assembly is a natural consequence of this situation.[67]

The criticism contained in the 1968 Federal Resolution on the opstina (commune) is in essence very similar. It comes to the conclusion that these shortcomings are the reason, "why certain forms of self-organization [local and other communities], direct decision-making and expression of citizens [referenda, meetings of citizens, meetings of working people, meetings of electors, meetings of insured persons and users of services, etc.] have not been adequately developed nor become effective, and opportunities for the development of long-term interopstina cooperation have been restricted." [68]

A brief mention should be made of enterprise "particularism" and commune "localism." This behavior describes an attitude of excessive self-interest at the expense of the wider community. The multitude of organizations and checks operating on the level of communes and enterprises are expected to curb and correct such tendencies, but this problem has nevertheless not been entirely eliminated.[69] So-called group entrepreneurship or group capitalism, based on self-managing enterprises, falls into this category. The charge is usually made by opponents of the creation of a capital market in Yugoslavia. Apart from presenting an ideological dilemma to socialists, its introduction could easily lead, in the opinion of its critics, to a system where the collectives of a profitable enterprise would grow rich on the unearned income derived from trade investment.[70]

Increasingly, as the central government has moved away from direction and control of enterprises, the latter have become involved in a complex network of internal and external checks and controls. It would go beyond the scope of this paper to discuss these integrative elements in detail, except to outline briefly the major categories involved in this process. The diagram below gives an indication of the complexity of this network as it applies to enterprises.

All of the external influences on the enterprise operating within the commune have formal or informal links with counterparts on the republican or federal level. Many of these units have been operating within enterprises long before the withdrawal of direct governmental controls, such as the socio-political organizations. Others, such as the economic chambers and the associations of enterprises, have been specifically introduced to act as integrative non-governmental elements replacing to a degree the former function of the central government. The economic chamber, membership in which is compulsory, is probably the most important element of social integration in the economy. Economic chambers are formed on a territorial basis, in communes and republics, culminating in the Federal Economic Chamber. According to law, they cannot limit in any way the self-management and independence of enterprises, and their resolutions have the character of recommendations. It is no secret, however, that they are used at times to enforce federal "recommendations" on the enterprises. Representatives of the government have been members of the economic chambers since 1958, together with representatives of enterprises (usually directors or their appointees). In theory, the economic chambers are a typically Yugoslav innovation. They delegate a former government function to an autonomous institution. Initial government interference in the activity of such an autonomous institution to safeguard national interests is gradually eliminated as the emerging socialist consciousness results in the expected blend of individual self-interest and concern for the wider community.[71]

One Western observer has pointed out that the reality of local autonomy seems to operate toward nation-wide integration. The devolution of decision-making powers to the level of the commune, he argues, has provided avenues for "cross-republican activities beyond the control of the state superstructure." [72]

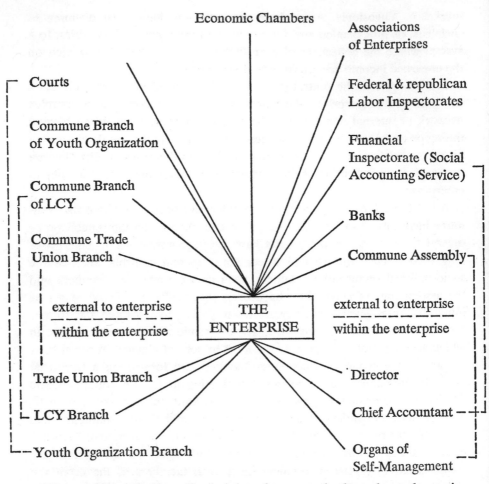

The gradual reduction of administrative controls throughout the socio-economic system has also placed added responsibility on the shoulders of the socio-political organizations who are themselves undergoing a process of decentralization and democratization. The entire system of social controls on the enterprise is highly complex, not only because of the large number of organizations and services involved, but also because the relations of many of these organizations to the enterprise are not clearly defined and their influence is based on a constantly changing mix of persuasion and informal authority. This is particularly true of the socio-political organizations operating within the enterprise. The influence of the same organizations in the commune operates according to much the same pattern. There is also a substantial overlapping of membership between organs in the commune and the enterprise, notably in the composition of the communal assembly. The second chamber of the communal assembly (the council of work communities) consists of delegates from enterprises and institutions. This element of overlapping membership is expected to assist in reconciling the individual interests of enterprises and institutions with the general interest of the wider community.

The dividing line between the autonomy of the enterprise and the commune's power of social control continues to be a subject of controversy. Recently, the courts have begun to hear cases of disputes between communes and enterprises, but until the division of authority has been more clearly defined and enforced, the controversy is likely to continue. The goal of making the commune assembly the forum where, by agreement of the self-governing units within the commune, the joint policies affecting all aspects of communal life are determined, has not yet been realized.

The growing financial autonomy of enterprises has created a number of problems which the commune, as presently constituted, has not been able to resolve. Just to mention three of the more important ones gives an illustration of the potential seriousness of the situation:

(1) How can those enterprises that enjoy a monopolistic position be persuaded not to exploit this position for their own self-interest at the expense of the interest of the community?

(2) What assurance is there that those self-governing institutions, which are of special concern to society, will in fact operate in a manner favorable to their customers?

(3) How can the enterprises be persuaded to use part of their resources for the goals of the commune? [73]

It is argued by some Yugoslavs that the Constitution lacks clarity on the vital question as to whether the commune and the enterprise are two different forms of self-management cooperating and co-existing with each other, or whether the commune is the basic socio-political collective which unites all other forms of self-governing units within its territory. While the Constitution speaks of the commune as "the basic socio-political community" through which the citizens shall, "coordinate individual and common interests with the general interests" (article 96), it treats separately the self-management of enterprises and that of the commune. Nowhere does it specifically treat the mutual relations of these two forms of self-government, nor does it stress their uniformity. Practice in the past supports the view that there are two separate forms of self-government in the commune, each with a distinct existence of its own.

There would seem to be two theoretical approaches to the solution of these contradictions. A large number of Yugoslav observers view the clash of interests as a necessary and dynamic part of a growing socialist society. Remedies are not to be found by replacing the system producing these conflicts but rather by adaptations and a continuous process of education and persuasion. The experience gained by hundreds of thousands of citizens who serve on the various organs of self-government in enterprises, communes, institutions and other bodies, is felt to be one of the best ways to create an attitude that will harmonize personal and group interests with those of the wider community.

Another view sees the solution in the formation of a uniform system of communal self-government that would respect the autonomy of the enterprises and institutions as to their internal self-management, but would subordinate them to the commune in all questions of commune-wide importance.

The 1968 Federal Resolution on the opstina recognizes inadequacies of the present situation in the commune and makes a number of far-reaching recommendations.[74] Two of the most significant recommendations deal with the financial and political independence of the commune and the need to further the application of methods of direct democracy in the decision-making processes at the local level. The resolution specifically calls for "consistent realization of the constitutional principle under which opstinas independently establish their revenue within the framework of sources and types established by law, and independently handle those revenues." The relinquishment of the budgetary method of financing, whereby funds are in practice distributed to the communes by republican and federal authorities, and the introduction of self-financing of social needs, is seen as an absolutely essential, but long-term process which must depend on the actual income of citizens in the commune. The resolution recommends that where these needs cannot at present be met by opstina resources, the republics shall establish a minimum level and shall provide the necessary resources to meet it.

Throughout this document, references are made to the negative implications of the low level of citizens' participation in the decision-making processes in the commune. The resolution explicitly calls for a greater application of direct socialist democracy within the commune and makes a number of specific recommendations in this respect.

In themselves, these recommendations are not startling. Similar ones have been made before without essentially changing the existing pattern.

What gives rise to the expectation that these recommendations will be acted upon is the fact that they are more detailed and have resulted in specific proposals made to specific governmental and political authorities.

The whole Yugoslav experiment raises the important question as to whether a system of decentralization, based in theory, and increasingly in practice, on self-management and direct democracy, can be reconciled with the objective needs of an industrialized society. The answer to this question is clearly of relevance beyond the borders of Yugoslavia.

After having passed through one revolutionary phase, which resulted in the abolition of private property,[75] the Yugoslavs see themselves now entering the second revolutionary phase, moving from state ownership of the means of production to social ownership and from centralized political and economic decision-making to a new system of socialist democracy. This new system, according to the Yugoslavs, will contain elements of both direct and indirect democracy. This system should be based, as Lenin has said, on "the conjunction of parliamentarianism and direct democracy." [76]

NOTES

[1] An excellent, if somewhat dated, general introduction to the Yugoslav system, is *Yugoslavia and the New Communism,* by Hoffman and Neal; New York: Twentieth Century Fund, 1962.

[2] The most recent and most complete study of the nationality question in Yugoslavia is *Communism and the Yugoslav National Question,* by Paul Shoup; New York: Columbia University Press, 1968.

[3] The term socio-political communities refers to communes, republics and the Federation. Socio-political organizations include the League of Communists, the Socialist Alliance, the trade unions, and so forth.

[4] Districts have now been abolished. The governmental structure now consists of communes, republics, and the Federal Government, except for the two autonomous provinces within the territory of the Serbian Republic.

[5] Jovan Djordjevic, "Preface," *Constitution of the Socialist Federal Republic of Yugoslavia,* Belgrade: Institute of Comparative Law, Collection of Yugoslav Laws, Vol. VIII, 1963, p. vii.

[6] The official designation of these functional chambers is: "Chambers of work communities." In Croatia, direct voting by the citizens has been introduced in the election of the functional chambers.

[7] "An Assessment of the Elections," in *Socialist Thought and Practice,* No. 34 (April–June 1969), p. 59.

[8] After the Second World War, the flow of command in the economy originated with the central agencies of Federal Government and proceeded, via

the Economic Ministries and the Directorates (one Directorate for a specified number of enterprises) to the individual enterprise. With the introduction of the new system in the 1950s, the administrative ties were cut to give more freedom to the periphery. Gradually, the flow was reversed. Initiatives now originate to a large extent, in the periphery.

9 T. Wilson and G. R. Denton, "Plans and Markets in Yugoslavia" in *Economic Reform in Yugoslavia,* London, PEP, Planning, Vol. XXXIV, No. 502, 1968, p. 233.

10 George Lermer, "Market Socialism and the Allocation of Resources," in *Co-Existence,* Vol. 6, No. 2 (1969), p. 127.

Approximately fifty percent of all prices are presently controlled centrally.

11 The LCY, in one of the Resolutions passed at its Ninth Congress, demanded that, "the entire process of reproduction should be under the control of the working collectives which earned, accumulated, and pooled their resources. The producer must wield a greater and more direct influence on the policies of the banks and on their business activities, and the banks must together with them shoulder economic responsibility for the results and development policies of the self-managing organizations."

Resolution on, "Socialist Development in Yugoslavia on the Basis of Self-Management and the Tasks of the League of Communists," Ninth Congress of the LCY, in *Socialist Thought and Practice,* No. 33 (January–March, 1969), p. 47.

12 J. B. Tito, "Introductory Address to the Ninth Congress of the LCY," in *Socialist Thought and Practice,* No. 33 (January–March, 1969), p. 32.

13 As participants in the founding of banks, enterprises now have some influence over their activities.

14 *The OECD Observer,* No. 31 (December, 1967), p. 43.

15 For a brief introduction to the Commune, as seen by Yugoslav officials, consult:
Dragoljub Milivojevic, *The Yugoslav Commune,* Belgrade: Medunarodna Politika, Studies No. 8, 1965.
Zivorad Kovacevic, *The Yugoslav Commune,* Belgrade, 1965.
Martin Kosir, *The Kranj Commune,* Belgrade, Medunarodna Politika, Studies, No. 11, 1966.

16 We will not discuss the period prior to 1955 when the local organs had relatively few independent powers and instead functioned largely as executors of republican and federal agencies.

17 There are, however, rural communes with as few as 3,000 inhabitants and twenty urban communes have a population of over 100,000 each. The territory of the commune is determined by republican laws.

18 Dragoljub Milivojevic, p. 14.

19 The statistical data used in this section has been taken from the 1968 edition of the Statistical Yearbook of the Socialist Federal Republic of Yugoslavia.

Statisticki Godisnjak Jugoslavije. Belgrade: Federal Institute of Statistics, 1968.

[20] The following data, unless indicated otherwise, is taken from: Janez Jerovsek, "Structure of Influence in Selected Decisions," Llubljana (mimeographed), April 1969. This paper is part of a larger study conducted by the Institute for Urban Planning in the S.R. of Slovenia, the Institute of Sociology and Philosophy and the School of Sociology, Political Science and Journalism, all of Llubljana. Eighteen leaders were interviewed in each of the seventeen communes, which were arranged into underdeveloped and developed groups. Because of lack of space, I can only present generalized conclusions of this study. Research done elsewhere in Yugoslavia largely confirms the conclusions reached by Jerovsek.

[21] The educational community is an autonomous association of all those institutions and individuals engaged in educational activities. Since 1967, it collects, controls, and distributes the funds earmarked for educational purposes.

[22] The only decision studied in which the political organizations exerted con-considerable influence was the selection of the candidate for mayor.

[23] See also, Eugen Pusic, "Territorial and Functional Administration in Yugoslavia," in *Administrative Science Quarterly*, Vol. 14, No. 1 (1969), p. 68.

[24] Jerovsek, p. 29.

[25] I am grateful to Muhamed Kesetovic, member of the Executive Council of the Federal Conference of the Socialist Alliance for the factual information relating to the nominating process. (Interview in Belgrade, April 16, 1969.) The political comments made in this connection are solely my responsibility.

[26] Delegates from several commune nominating conferences create a federal nominating conference (one for each federal electoral unit). The same process applies essentially to the election of all those assembly chambers which are elected directly by citizens.

[27] There are, of course, other ways to persuade an "undesirable candidate" to withdraw. If he happens to be a member of the League of Communists pressure can be put on him by the League. If he holds an elective position, such as mayor of a commune, it can be made clear to him that he would lose the support of the socio-political organizations in any future attempt to run for public office.

[28] For a part of a working organization to be able to become a working unit, the following prerequisites are necessary:
"—That there exists an integrated technological and operational process on a specified area, plus the necessary means of production;
"—That tasks can be determined, within the plan of the working organization as a whole, for such a narrower framework of a working organization within the latter's plan as a whole;
"—That it is practicable to observe the execution of the planned tasks for such a narrower organizational part of a working organization as well as to ascertain

separately its economic results, viz., as a quantity demarcated from the working and operating results of the rest of the working organization;

"—That a material base can be established for such a narrower organizational part of a working organization, to provide the foundation for the transfer of a series of self-management functions from the central—indirect—bodies of the working community to a narrower organizational part; and

"—That it is economically justified to establish a working unit." Vojislav Vlajic, *The Working Units,* Belgrade, The Central Council of the Confederation of Trade Unions of Yugoslavia, 1967, pp. 20–21.

[29] There is really no adequate treatment in the English language on this important innovation. The best available soruce on the working unit is: *Stellung und Aufgaben der ökonomischen Einheiten in den jugoslawischen Unternehmungen,* by Gudrun Lemân, Berlin: Verlag Duncker & Humblot, 1967.

[30] The holding of a referendum is compulsory for certain important questions such as the decision to merge with another enterprise. The results of a referendum are binding on the workers' council. If an issue is defeated in a referendum, it cannot be raised again for six months.

[31] The appointment of the manager requires a two-thirds majority of all members of the working unit, as well as the approval of the management board of the enterprise. His removal takes place by the same procedure. The manager's term of office is four years.

[32] B. Kavcic, V. Rus, A. S. Tannenbaum, *Control, Participation and Effectiveness in Four Yugoslav Industrial Organizations* (mimeographed), Llubljana (March 1969), p. 1.

[33] *Ibid.,* pp. 1–2.

[34] This view has been supported by Dr. Branko Horvat at a seminar given at The American University, Washington, D.C., November 25, 1968.

[35] *Jugoslavija Izmedu VIII i IX Kongresa SKJ, 1964–1968* (Yugoslavia between the VIII and IX Congress of the League of Communists of Yugoslavia), Belgrade: Savezni zarod za statistiku, 1969, p. 19.

[36] Of a total of 150,389 members of workers' councils, 81,504 were highly skilled and skilled workers. Of a total of 50,422 members of the boards of management, skilled and highly skilled workers amounted to 25,100.

Statisticki Godisnjak Jugoslavije (Statistical Yearbook of Yugoslavia) Savezni Zarod Za Statistiku, 1968, p. 65.

[37] Husein Kratina, *Samoupravna i Druge Organizacije u Preduzecu* (Self-Managing and Organizational Structure of Enterprises), Belgrade: Institute of Social Sciences, 1968, Table 8, p. 53.

[38] These respondents comprise a very special group, which includes a relatively high proportion of formally educated, highly skilled and aspiring workers. Approximately eighty-nine percent are members of the LCY (as compared to 10.6 percent of workers in the district of Zagreb). Thirty-nine percent are first line supervisors. The respondents spent part of their time at the university while working four hours a day in Zagreb industries.

[39] Josip Zupanov and Arnold S. Tannenbaum, "The Distribution of Control in Some Yugoslav Industrial Organizations as Perceived by Members," in Arnold Tannenbaum, *Control in Organizations,* New York: McGraw-Hill Book Company, 1968, p. 98.

[40] *Ibid.,* pp. 97–98.

[41] David S. Ridell, "Social self-government: the background of theory and practice in Yugoslav socialism," *British Journal of Sociology* (March, 1968), p. 66.

[42] See e.g. Jiri Kolaja, *Workers' Councils: The Yugoslav Experience,* New York: Frederick A. Praeger, 1966, pp. 19–20 and 23.

[43] Zupanov and Tannenbaum, p. 109.

[44] As one Yugoslav critic has pointed out, the director is supposed to simultaneously play a statist and a self-managing role. *Yugoslav Trade Unions,* Belgrade: (February, 1968), p. 8.

[45] Jovo Brekic, "Model of the Function of a Director under the Conditions of Development of Self-Management," *Ekonomiski Pregled* (Zagreb), No. 1–2 (1968) (JPRS:45,794, p. 76).

[46] See f.i. Veljko Ivosevic, "What Kind of a Director is Needed by the Economy Today?", in *Opstina,* Belgrade (June 1969) (JPRS:46,040, pp. 140–143).

[47] Veljko Rus, "Cliques in Yugoslavian Labor Organizations Characterized" in *Gledista,* Belgrade, No. 8–9 (August–September, 1966) (JPRS:38,737). A survey undertaken in 1964/65 shows that over one-half of the leading positions within enterprises were occupied by individuals with insufficient professional training. Ibid. p. 33.

[48] See a report by a team of economists of the Zagreb Economic Institute and the Research Center, Faculty of Economics, University of Zagreb, "Topical Problems of Economic Development and Policy in Yugoslavia," in *Economic Reform in Yugoslavia,* London, *PEP,* 1968, p. 243.

[49] The results of this study have been published in *Ekonomist,* No. 3, 1967.

[50] Interview with J. Zupanov, Zagreb, April 23, 1969.

[51] *Yugoslav Trade Unions,* Vol. 10 (June 1969), pp. 3–4.

[52] Interview with Momcilo Radosavljevic, Director of the Center for Self-Management, Belgrade, April 15, 1969. There are duplications in these figures, such as the frequently overlapping membership in workers' councils and management boards. Some figures apply to 1967 while others apply to 1968.

[53] All members of the collective assume the function of the workers' council.

[54] Managerial councils in institutions are equivalent to management boards in enterprises. Their membership includes individuals of the wider community.

[55] *Jugoslavia Izmedu VIII i IX Kongresa SKJ: 1964–1968,* Table 11, p. 22.

[56] Voluntary self-help may take the form of an agreed-upon additional tax for a specified purpose and over a specified period of time. It can usually also be honored by supplying materials or one's own working time in place of a finan-

cial contribution. As a rule, at least fifty percent of citizens polled must approve the proposed project before it can be put into practice.

⁵⁷ Interview with Dr. Drago Zajc, Center of Research in Public Opinion, Llubljana, April 21, 1969.

⁵⁸ *Workers' Management in Yugoslavia*, Geneva, International Labor Office, 1962, p. 91n.

⁵⁹ See "An Assessment of the Election," *Socialist Thought and Practice*, No. 34, (April-June, 1969) p. 60.

⁶⁰ Dusan Bilandzic, *Some Aspects of the Yugoslav System of Self-Government and Worker Management*, Belgrade: Medunarodna Politika, Studies No. 28, 1968, p. 61. Much of the above summary of the functions of the commune has been taken from this source.

⁶¹ Expanded reproduction refers to investment for replacement and to new investment, while simple reproduction refers to investment for replacment only.

⁶² Milan Popovic, "The Opstina and the Economic Organization" in *Radna i drustvena zajednica* (Working and Cooperative Community), Belgrade, Vol. XIV, No. 8–9 (1966) (JPRS: 38,241, p. 48).

⁶³ The commune not only collects its own taxes but also functions as a collection agency for taxes and contributions earmarked for the republican and federal budgets.

⁶⁴ Organization for Economic Co-operation and Development, *Socialist Federal Republic of Yugoslavia*, Economic Surveys, Paris: OECD, 1967, table 11, p. 29. This is a summarized version.

⁶⁵ *Statisticki Godisnjak Jugoslavije 1968*, table 117.2, p. 248

⁶⁶ Unsigned, "The Material Basis of the Opstina and the Methods for its Self-Financing," in *Komuna*, Vol. 14, No. 11, (1967) (JPRS: 44, 315, p. 43).

⁶⁷ *Ibid.*, pp. 44–45

⁶⁸ *Resolution by the Federal Assembly on the Socio-Economic and Political Position of the Opstina and the Further Development of Self-Management Relations in the Opstina*, Belgrade: Sluzbeni List SFRJ, December 24, 1968, pp. 1136–1141.

⁶⁹ The above-mentioned 1968 Federal Resolution on the opstina also draws attention to this phenomenon and urges the elimination of the causes which produce such behavior.

⁷⁰ See f.i. *PEP*, pp. 215–216.

⁷¹ While the scope of activities of the economic chanbers is practically unlimited, their main tasks can be summarized as follows: studies of new ways to expand production, encouraging integrational processes in the economy, expert assistance to Yugoslav enterprises in the establishment of business ties with overseas companies, studies of production layouts, setting up centers for professional training and taking part in economic legislation.

Llubo Veljkovic (ed.) *Economic Development in Yugoslavia*, Belgrade, Medunarodna Stampa-Interpress, Studies, No. 25, 1968, p. 14.

There is a trend in Yugoslavia today to make the Economic Chambers de facto self-governing organs of the economy. Their present function is largely one of transmission belts between the state and the economy.

See f.i. Unsigned, "Chambers—A Form and Expression of the Self-Organization of the Economy" in *Privredni Pregled,* Belgrade, Dec. 9, 1967 and Dec. 12, 1967 (JPRS: 44007, p. 26).

[72] Solomon J. Rawin, "Social Values and the Formation of Managerial Elites: The Case of Yugoslavia and Poland," paper presented at the Annual Meeting of the Canadian Sociology and Anthropology Association, York University, Toronto, June 5–7, 1969, p. 29.

Rawin mentions that the cross-republican activities are particularly evident in such areas as transportation, distribution network, and production expansion. He also points out that the functional significance of communal autonomy is quite different from that of the territorial autonomy of the republics; the latter being "primarily a concession exacted by the centrifugal nationality forces," its main function being the preservation of the "ethnic integrity of the minority nationalities against the traditional Serbian ascendance." (pp. 28–29).

[73] This does not mean that all enterprises and institutions exhibit self-interest to the point of neglect of the wider community, but the fact that the problem is raised so frequently in Yugoslavia indicates its existence and its potential seriousness.

[74] While the resolution endorses the view that there are two distinct forms of self-government operating within the commune, it nevertheless proposes at one point, "the pooling of the resources of working and other self-managing organizations and communities." Unless this statement is defined more clearly, it is likely to inflame the controversy instead of settling it.

[75] The significant exception is the agricultural sector, which is still partly privately owned. There is also a small but growing privately owned service sector.

[76] Jovan Djordjevic and Najdan Pasic, "The Communal Self-Government System in Yugoslavia," in *International Social Science Journal,* Vol. XIII, No. 3 (1961), p. 405.

While the language and concepts that surround cybernetics are difficult, the approach provides both a new basis for understanding group organization and a critique of traditional organizational theory. The basic idea in McEwan's article is that organization must be designed functionally. As the nature of the task changes, so must the makeup of the group and its leadership. This he calls the principle of redundancy of potential command. As the conditions of the environment change, a group must be capable of change and, also, growth. Rather than being a closed system, incapable of adaptation, an organization must be open and self-organizing, capable of changing its structure to conform with a changing environment.

Modern management literature has suggested that the form of the industrial organization of the future will be characterized by shifting task forces, made up of people with the requisite skills for an immediate task, which dissolves when the task is done. This vision by itself is inadequate, for it ignores the structure of overall control and the relationship of such task forces to capital and financing, and these are crucial in shaping overall goals. Where control is vested in capital through stock ownership, organizational goals are limited to those that can be subjected to monetary cost accounting. Broader objectives that resist reckoning by cost cannot be recognized except in a very subsidiary fashion; in this case, therefore, the structure of the organization prevents evaluations of effectiveness in broad areas involving social purpose.

This problem can be seen as a problem in the evaluation of feedback: how can one devise methods of social cost accounting that will allow organizations to evaluate their subtle and long-term effects—pollution, relocation of workers, consumption of scarce resources, and so forth? With such methods, organizations could develop intelligent decision criteria. This problem applies equally to private firms, state-owned firms, and cooperatively owned firms. As new technologies develop, the problem of evaluating their benefits and costs requires that a new calculus be developed to provide accurate decision criteria related clearly to social goals. It is already clear that present levels of air pollution, ecological disturbance, and unplanned proliferation of products are intolerable. So, also, are basic working conditions, uncertainties of employment, and current definitions of efficiency. Currently, however, these poisonous effects cannot even be considered by the accounting process. Hence, the challenge is to develop organizations so structured as to take social goals into account.

It would seem that self-organizing systems should also be self-controlling. If this is defined functionally, then control should be vested in all those involved in some major way with the activities of the organization—workers, members of the immediate environment, or clients. The cooperative seems to be the form that best meets the requirement that an organization be self-organizing and self-controlling. The cooperative is controlled from within rather than by private capital from without. Organizations controlled by outside capital are closed systems, in which basic goals are dictated by the nature of the control. They can neither grow nor organize themselves on a continuing basis, and are therefore unacceptable in a participatory democracy.

The Cybernetics of Self-organizing Systems

John D. McEwan

The purpose of this essay is to suggest that some of the concepts used by cyberneticians studying "evolving self-organizing systems" are relevant to participatory democracy, and that some of the conclusions drawn from their study tend to favor libertarian models of social organization.[1]

The simplest definition of a self-organizing system is "a system in which order increases as time passes." Let us make this definition more clear. An outside observer of a system is likely to be unable to predict its behavior in a given situation; the number of different responses to the situation (*variety*) is a measure of the system's complexity. A system is said to exhibit varied behavior when a large number of responses seem equally likely; as time passes, a self-organizing system will behave less erratically, with fewer and fewer responses possible or probable: the ratio of *variety exhibited* in a given situation to the *maximum possible variety* will decrease over time.

This definition is a good beginning, but it is somewhat restrictive, and must be modified. The best such a primitive self-organizing system can do is, over time, reach some sort of optimum state, and there remain. There is no provision for growth. Moreover, in the "real world" the environment in which a system operates *also* changes with the passage of time; a primitive self-organizing system, if it is a "control system" trying to maintain stability in a fluctuating environment, will be limited (by its fixed maximum possible variety) in the number of environmental disturbances with which it can deal. Unpredictable disturbances are liable to prove too much for it.

We should therefore incorporate in our definition the concept that maximum possible variety can also fluctuate over time. Thus, Gordon Pask restricts the term "self-organizing systems" to systems whose history can be represented as a series S^0, S^1, . . . S^n, in which each term represents the system in a given period of time, with a temporarily fixed maximum possible variety and self-organizing in the sense that order increases during the period of time. This definition enables us to analyze control systems of the type found in living organisms, the clearest example of self-organizing systems. (Indeed, with a few limited exceptions, biological and social organization are the only fields in which such control systems have so far been found. Some exceptions—artificially constructed systems, for instance—despite their crude and elementary nature in comparison with living organisms, do exhibit remarkably advanced behavior in comparison with control systems that are not self-organizing.)

In order to illustrate how our expanded definition works, let us consider a human being learning to solve certain types of problems, as his behavior appears to an observer. When a baby first starts to crawl, he is likely to do it badly; but as time passes, he will become increasingly proficient—a self-organizing system. When he begins walking, however, the maximum possible variety in this system will suddenly increase; he will walk awkwardly at first, then more proficiently as he masters the art, as the system reorganizes itself. Similarly, when he first runs, he will do it badly, but improve as time passes. In more theoretical terms: when the learner develops a new concept or method (walking as opposed to crawling), there will be a break in the development of his behavior (he will walk awkwardly), after which his behavior will again be self-organizing (he will walk proficiently). This sequence—self-organization, break, self-organization—will continue, each time becoming more complex, as the learner continues to adapt to changing conditions or increasing skills.

In many discussions of control situations the concept of *hierarchy* appears very quickly. The term should not make us recoil, since its usage is a technical one and does not coincide with its usage in anarchist critiques of socio-political organization.

The cybernetician distinguishes between two types of hierarchy, which Pask calls *anatomical* and *functional*. The former is exemplified in part by hierarchical social organization in the normal sense—the chain-of-command structure of industry, for example. In this case, there are at least two distinct levels, two entities involved. Functional hierarchy, on the other hand, refers to a case in which there may be only one entity, but two or more levels of information structure operating in the system, as, for example, in certain types of neuron networks. Seymour Melman's concept of "disalienated decision procedure" is comparable. Even in the anatomical sense, the term need have none of the connotations of coercive sanctions in a ruler-ruled relationship which are common in other usages. The term only means that different parts of the system deal with different levels of decision-making and learning: for example, some parts may deal directly with the environment, while others relate to the activity of these first parts; some may learn about individual occurrences, while others learn about sequences of occurrences, and still others about classes of sequences.

In self-organizing systems, the interaction between information flowing in the system and the structure of the system is an important phenomenon. In a complex system, in which information and structure interact frequently, this interaction leads to *redundancy of potential command*—a term applied when one cannot determine the critical decision-making element, because it changes from time to time and depends on the information in the system. It will be evident that in such a system the idea of a hierarchy can have only limited application.

Having, I hope, made clear the concepts of self-organizing systems and hierarchy, I shall sketch briefly one partly artificial self-organizing system involving interaction between human beings and machines—a group teaching machine developed by Gordon Pask.[2] This helps illustrate the concepts introduced and, I feel, suggests some important general characteristics of self-organizing systems—characteristics that may sound familiar to libertarians.

Prior to developing the group teaching machine, Pask had created individual teaching machines that were important advances in the growth of applied cybernetics.[3] When he considered the problem of teaching a group, he did not simply combine individual machines. The important insight he had was that a group of individuals in a learning situation is itself an evolutionary system, which suggested that the machine be used as a catalyst to modify the communication channels in the group, thus producing different group structures.

When he experimented with individual teaching machines, Pask had employed situations in which the pupil dominated the machine. The degree to which the pupil was helped by the machine was related to his success in problem-solving. The more successful he was, the less the machine helped him. For experiments with the group machine, Pask introduced "money," a quantity of which was allocated to each member of the group. By using his "money," a pupil was able to buy for himself control over the communication structure of the group, by controlling the machine's partial specification of the solution to the problem it posed (that is, the pupil who had "purchased" the machine had exclusive access to its help). In the group machine, the allocation of money was coupled to two conditions—increasing success and increasing variety in the group structure. This second condition is the key to the novelty of the system. This system, then, has changing dominance and exhibits redundancy of potential command.

In practice, each pupil sits in a little cubicle provided with buttons and indicators for communication. A computer is used for control, to calculate the various measures of success for each student, and so forth. The operator is provided with some way of seeing what is going on, and can deliberately make things difficult for the group. He may, for instance, introduce false information into the channels to see how the group copes with it.

(The role of the computer in Pask's system is not analogous to that of an authoritarian "guiding hand." This is an artificial exercise; the operator sets a problem for the group to solve, and the computer merely determines and feeds back success/failure information. The other important role of the machine, as a catalyst in the learning process, is one we have already discussed. There is a rough analogy here with the role of "influence leader" in the Hausers' sense,[4] rather than with any authoritarian overseer.)

The problem that Pask formulated for the group to solve had to do with conveying information about the position of a point in space, with noise in the communication channels. Groups were asked to imagine that they were air traffic controllers, and were given co-ordinates specifying the position of aircraft at a certain time.

In such a situation, there are two kinds of decision-making activity: (1) formulating policy (which of several planes has priority to land, what the others should do, and so forth) on the basis of agreed-upon facts, and (2) formulating policy when the facts are in dispute or incomplete (when the machine deliberately provides erroneous information, for instance). Pask discovered, interestingly, that the problems of agreeing on a choice of policy are in principle the same in both cases. In the second instance, obviously, the group would not be able to formulate a policy for bringing the planes in to land; but the problem to which it did address itself—ascertaining the facts—was resolved in an essentially similar manner. In each case the group may be regarded as decision-maker.

It should be noted that the state of the system when in equilibrium *is* the solution to the problem, and that this solution (and hence the equilibrium) changes with time. This is also true in the case of an improvisational jazz band—the first example from purely human organization that occurred to me.

Although, as Pask emphasized, he had insufficient data to make far-reaching and well substantiated generalizations from his experiments, the results he did obtain were interesting and, I believe, provide considerable insight into the characteristics of self-organizing systems and their advantages over other decision-making systems.

Some groups, after gaining familiarity with the machine, assigned specific roles to their members and introduced standard procedures. This led to a drop in efficiency and an inability to handle new factors introduced by spurious information and other complications. The learning curve rises, flattens, then drops sharply whenever some new element is introduced. The system, no longer self-organizing, no longer works as well. In order for a group to be a self-organizing system, Pask suggests it must avoid fixed role-assignments and stereotyped procedures. This, of course, is tied up with redundancy of potential command. We might sum up "fixed role assignment and stereotyped procedures" in one word—institutionalization.

At least the following characteristics are necessary for effective, self-organizing action: the group must first of all constitute a system in a meaningful sense; second, there must be communication between the members—a sufficient structure of information channels and feedback loops; third, it must avoid an inflexible structure. Pask suggests that, in decision-making, this is perhaps the only way in which "two heads are better than one"—if the "two heads" constitute a self-organizing system. The clue as to why a number of heads—committees are notorious examples—often turn out to be much worse than one, is, he suggests, to be found in this business of role assignment and stereotyped procedure.

Pask has not, however, suggested reasons why institutionalization should arise. By drawing on our knowledge of behavior of a self-organizing nature exhibited in other groups (such as informal shop-floor organizations, the adaptability and efficiency exhibited in instances of collective contract working, and similar phenomena),[5] we can perhaps offer some hints as to how institutionalization arises in certain circumstances.

Imagine a workshop of reasonable size, in which a number of inter-related processes are going on, and where one must take account of some variation in the factors affecting the work. There is considerable evidence that the workers in such a shop, working as a cooperating group, are able to organize themselves without outside interference, in such a way as to cope efficiently with the job, and show remarkable facility in coping with unforeseeable difficulties and disruptions of normal procedure. The workers in such a situation have two levels of task:

(1) The complex of actual production tasks;
(2) The task of solving the problem of how the group should be organized to perform these "first-level" tasks, and how information about them should be dealt with by the group.

In situations of the kind I am imagining, the organization of the group is largely determined by the needs of the job, which are fairly obvious to all concerned, since all the workers are more-or-less familiar with the job. There is a continual feedback of information from the job to the group. Any unusual occurrence will force itself on its notice and will be dealt with according to its resources at that time.

By contrast, let us now consider the situation of the same type of shop, only this time assuming that it is organized by a committee outside the shop-floor. The situation in which the committee finds itself is completely different from that of the work group. For the committee, there are three levels of problem:

(1) The complex of actual production tasks;
(2) The problem of organization of the work group;
(3) The problem of organizing the committee in such a way that it can effectively organize the work group and supervise production.

In both cases, success or failure is determined on the shop-floor, that is, by the net result of the solution of first-level problems. But it will be obvious that the committee operates under severe handicaps. The committee is denied the continuous feedback that the group had. While working on its solution to the second level problem, it will have little information about the success of alternatives, outside of previous findings, coded, probably, in an inadequate way; the degree of success will be observable only after a trial period. Unusual circumstances can only be dealt with as *types* of occurrence, since the committee, in its directives, cannot enumerate all possibilities. This is important in determining the relative efficiency of the two methods of organization, but is of less importance in our immediate problem.

The work group on the shop-floor solved its second-level problem on the basis of its familiarity with the first-level problem: knowing the job to be done, it knew how to organize to do the job. The committee, however, cannot solve its third problem by a method analogous to that used by the original work group in solving the second-level problem; while working on the second-level problem the committee has no comparable information available to determine the solution of the third-level problem. But it must adopt some procedure, some organization at a given time. How then is it to be determined?

In theory, such a controller could still remain a self-organizing system, learning the structure to adopt in particular circumstances over a longer period of time, though it would still suffer from imperfect information, and from the time lag.

In practice, however, the committee promptly convenes a meeting, assigns specific functions to its members, and decides on standard procedures. The information on which it bases its organization is probably a mixture of personality factors (including externally derived status) and the existing ideas on organization theory (including local precedent) possessed by the members. Once decided, they will shelve the third-level problem unless disaster, or a new superior, strikes, when a similar but more cumbersome procedure will be necessary to reorganize the committee along the same general lines.

In other words, within the closed system of the committee and work group, there is virtually no coupling between the success of the actual undertaking (the production job) and the decision-making procedure used to solve the third-level problem. Worse, the factors influencing the solution of this problem, far from increasing the possible variety of the committee, lead to rigidity and low variety. Owing to its structure, it will generally prove less efficient than a single imaginative person, and much less efficient than a self-organizing system.

We can suggest, then, that a committee's isolation from the very process that defines its success—which is generally typical of a committee situation—leads it generally to fail to exhibit self-organizing characteristics, and frequently causes it to fail as a decision-maker.

Let us reconsider the first case, the case of the self-organizing work group. Here the *job itself* is the analogue of Pask's machine, insofar as feedback of success/failure information is concerned. Also, it has frequently been pointed out that in a face-to-face group in a situation where the need for collective action is fairly obvious, and where some common criteria of success exist, group leadership tends to be granted to the member or members best suited (from the point of view of the group) to the particular circumstances obtaining, and to change as these circumstances change. In other words, in this case we have changing dominance, determined by the needs of the situation; the job, acting through the psychology of the face-to-face group, performs a function analogous to Pask's machine, allocating temporary dominance in accordance with success.

I now wish to turn from small group organization to larger systems, and consider some criticisms of conventional industrial organization developed, in particular, by Stafford Beer. He maintains that conventional ideas of control in complex situations, such as an industrial company or the economy of a country, are miserably inadequate. "The fact is," he says, "that our whole concept of control is naive, primitive, and ridden with an almost retributive idea of causality. Control to most people (and what a reflection this is upon a sophisticated society!) is a crude process of coercion." [6]

In his lectures, Beer developed the thesis that truly efficient control of a complex undertaking is impossible if one uses the rigid hierarchical organization with which we are familiar. Such systems have managed to survive and work in some sort of manner, obviously. Beer suggested that they do because they are not entirely what they are supposed to be. In the organization, there are unofficial self-organizing systems and tendencies, which are essential to its survival.

Beer is unusually perceptive and frank in emphasizing the prevalence and importance of unofficial initiatives at all levels (of shop-floor workers for example). "They arrange things which would horrify management, if they ever found out. If *they* did not talk things over and come to mutual agreements, the whole business would collapse."

The theoretical keystones of Beer's argument are Ashby's *principle of requisite variety* (from the theory of homeostats), and requirements for adequate channel capacity in a multi-level system (from information theory). I shall explain these formidable-sounding terms.

The principle of requisite variety states: if stability is to be attained, the variety of the controlling system must be at least as great as the variety of the system it controls. We have already seen what happens when this principle is not met, for this was really the trouble with our hypothetical committee: due to its rigid structure and the need to issue instructions in terms of standard procedures, it could not possibly be efficient in a situation of any complexity. If we made the further assumption that there was no organization of the work group other than that imposed by the committee, chaos would be unavoidable in non-routine circumstances. Approximations to this occur in "working to rule." In normal working, the initiatives of the shop-floor workers serve as an additional source of variety, enabling the principle of requisite variety to be satisfied, at least as far as normal variations in the factors affecting the production situation are concerned.

The requirements for channel capacity are relevant because information available at the top of the hierarchy is inherently inadequate (in practice, the channel capacity could never be made adequate in the sort of pyramidical structures we have) and because of the inadequacy of formal channels between the subsystems (departments and such) that co-ordinate their activities.

Conventional managerial ideas of organization are drastically far from satisfying the principle of requisite variety. So far, that if an uninitiated visitor came to any large manufacturing concern (in Beer's illustration the visitor was, as he usually is, a Martian) and studied only the activities at the lower level of the concern, the intelligence of the workers on the shop-floor, and the organizational chart purporting to show how the undertaking is controlled, he would leave his studies with a grossly exaggerated estimate of the brains of the men at the top. Quite simply, in a large corporation, management cannot manage—although it tries.

When an inadequate control system attempts to control a system of greater variety, it is likely to accumulate vast amounts of unassimilable information, as control vainly struggles to keep track of the situation. A comparable converse phenomenon, which illustrates the complexity of the control situation in social organization, was pointed out by Proudhon in 1851, in what must rank as one of the most prophetic statements about the development of social organization ever written: "[The government] must make as many laws as it finds interests, and, as interests are innumerable, relations arising from one another multiply to infinity, and antagonism is endless, lawmaking must go on without stopping. Laws, decrees, ordinances, resolutions, will fall like hail upon the unfortunate people. After a time the political ground will be covered by a layer of paper, which the geologists will put down among the vicissitudes of the earth as the *papyraceous formation*." [7]

The need to combine cohesion with wide-open channels of communication raises the issue of centralization versus decentralization in industry. Beer puts the problem thus:

> Centralize: insufficient channel capacity, etc.—cannot work efficiently
> Decentralize: completely autonomous units—no cohesion, probably ceases to be a system at all

Neither alternative corresponds to what we find in really efficient self-organizing systems, such as complex living organisms. Instead we find a number of different, interlocking control systems. Beer also draws attention to the prevalence, and importance, of redundancy of potential command in self-organizing systems, and points out that it is completely alien to the sort of theory of organization found in industry and similar undertakings.

The type of organization at which we should aim is, he suggests, an organic one, involving interlocking control systems, intermeshing at all levels, utilizing the principle of evolving self-organizing systems, with the channel capacity and flow of information kept as high as possible.[8] He mentioned in this connection an American businessman who claimed that his business was organized along somewhat similar lines and seemed to work very well. The idea was that anybody at all, no matter how "junior," could call a conference at short notice to discuss anything he wanted, whether connected with his work or not. Such a meeting could call in the president of the company himself, or anyone he thought was needed.

Let us begin to draw some political conclusions, by contrasting two models of decision-making and control. First we have the model current among management theorists in industry, with its counterpart in conventional thinking about government in society as a whole. This is the model of a rigid pyramidal hierarchy, with lines of "communication and command" running from the top to the bottom of the pyramid. There is fixed delineation of responsibility—each element has a specified role; the procedures to be followed at any level are determined within fairly narrow limits, and can be changed only by decisions of people higher in the hierarchy. The role of the top group of the hierarchy is sometimes called the "brain" of the system.

The other model is from the cybernetics of evolving self-organizing systems. Here we have a system of large variety, sufficient to cope with a complex, unpredictable environment. It is characterized by a changing structure that modifies itself under continual feedback from the environment, exhibits redundancy of potential command, and involves complex interlocking control structures. Learning and decision-making—the "brain"

—are distributed throughout the system, denser perhaps in some areas than in others.

The second model may sound familiar to students of participatory democracy. Peter Kropotkin spoke of a society that "seeks the fullest development of free association in all its aspects, in all possible degrees, for all conceivable purposes: an ever-changing association bearing in itself the elements of its own duration, and taking on the forms which at any moment best correspond to the manifold endeavours of all . . . a society to which pre-established forms crystallized by law, are repugnant, which looks for harmony in an ever-changing and fugitive equilibrium between a multitude of varied forces and influences of every kind, following their own course." The language is perhaps somewhat vague and ambiguous, but as a brief, non-technical description of a society conceived as a complex, evolving, self-organizing system, it can hardly be bettered.

The tragedy of so-called progressive thinkers today is not that they dismiss anarchist ideas of society and social organization as inadequate; this is excusable, and indicates the anarchists' failure to develop and spread their ideas. The tragedy is that liberals think the other model *is* adequate, and that they are incapable of thinking in any other terms.

Hence such thinkers are surprised when they cannot find the great efficient decision-makers they expect in control of our institutions. The "solutions" they propose to the muddle they find would require supermen to make them work—even if the supermen could obtain adequate information to determine their decisions. This, from the nature of the structure, they can never do.

Again, when existing systems break down, as in industrial disputes, leaders on both sides usually attempt to remedy the situation by measures that increase the inadequacy of the system. That is, they attempt, by reorganization and contractual measures, to increase the rigidity of the system by defining roles and responsibilities more closely, and try to confine the activities of human beings, who are themselves evolving self-organizing systems, within a predetermined contractual framework.

To return to the conventional picture of government and the supposed control by the governed in democratic theory:

First, does what I have said about the inefficiency and crudity of the governmental model as a control mechanism conflict with Grey Walter's analysis in his article "The Development and Significance of Cybernetics" in *Anarchy* 25, in which he claimed that Western democratic systems were remarkably sophisticated from the cybernetic point of view? I do not think so. The point is that Western democratic systems are inadequate for controlling the economy, say, or providing the greatest compatible satisfactions for the governed, as Proudhon pointed out. They are inadequate mechanisms for maintaining order in society, unless society is conceived of as largely self-regulating without governmental institutions. I do not deny that the government-electorate system has proved an efficient machine for maintaining itself, although I might be inclined to give a little more importance to unofficial, informal elements in the system in this context than Mr. Walter does in his article.

If the model of effective control by the government is inadequate, the naive democratic theory of control of government by the people is much more so. This theory puts great stress on the importance of elections as the means by which the governed control their rulers, and defining the results of the elections as expressions of "the will of the people." However, the individual, in a two-party system, is allowed one binary choice every four years or so, in which to reflect all the complex and dimly understood effects of government actions, intended and unintended. The model seems to allow of no structured subsystem to be identified as "the people"—there is only an aggregate of individual choices.

It seems to me significant that this theory of self-government of the people, by the people, for the people, through the universal or at least wide suffrage, developed in the eighteenth and nineteenth centuries along with the growth of the "rabble hypothesis" of society, which saw society as an unstructured aggregate of individual social atoms, pursuing their own egocentric interests, held together only by authority and coercion. Sociologists and social psychologists now find this picture of society completely inadequate.[10]

This is not to deny the genius of some of the thinkers who worked within the limitations of this model of democracy, for they were able to see the difficulties of electoral politics in practice, and devised most complicated systems of checks and balances to render their systems practicable (the architects of the American Constitution for example). However, they could not be expected to overcome the fundamental inadequacies of their model of government no matter how successful they were in developing the skeletons of viable self-perpetuating systems, because of the inadequacies of the "rabble hypothesis" on which they based their work.

In contrast to the "rabble hypothesis," we find that libertarian socialist thought, especially in Kropotkin and Landauer, showed an early grasp of the complex group structure of society. They saw society as a complex network of changing relationships, involving many structures of correlated activity and mutual aid, independent of authoritarian coercion; it was against this background that they developed their theories of social organization.

Neither am I convinced by the more sophisticated pressure-group theory of democracy, introduced in an attempt to avoid the obvious inadequacy of the naive theory. As a descriptive theory of the socio-political situation, pluralism does seem reasonably adequate, but as a means by which the individual obtains a voice in decisions affecting him, it is just as inadequate as the naive theory. This in fact is generally admitted by its adherents, who have largely dropped the idea of democracy as self-government.[11]

When a group of a self-organizing type freely organizes itself to tackle a problem, the structure they adopt might be taken as exhibiting "the will of the group." However, since self-organizing groups are usually capable of genuine group decisions, such an expression—with its connotation of naive democratic theory—is a rather dangerous shorthand. In practice, a genuine group decision can be made only by fairly small groups, since, beyond a certain size, an unstructured aggregate of human beings is unable to act as a group, because there is too much information to be handled. The channel capacity is probably inadequate, and, even if the individual member could be presented with sufficient information, he would be unable to deal with it, and unable, therefore, to make a full and understanding contribution to a multilateral decision.

In certain work situations, the job effectively constrains the system, and only part of the behavior needs to be correlated: in such a case we might expect larger aggregates to be capable of true group behavior. This is borne out by experience. In a situation where complex activity has to be correlated and there are few prior constraints (such as collective improvisation in a jazz band, most research groups, and discussion groups), a maximum of the order of ten seems to be imposed; in manual jobs of certain types, and in the groups of the gang system at Coventry, much larger aggregates are capable of coherent behavior—groups of the order of a hundred or even a thousand members are possible. Some of the very large groups, for example in the motor industry, may, however, be examples of more complex organization.

We have said that only small aggregates of human beings, if regarded initially as unstructured, can exhibit genuine group behavior. There is no reason, however, why large aggregates, *if sufficiently structured,* should not maintain coherent behavior, while retaining genuine self-organizing characteristics enabling them to deal with unpredictable disturbances in their environment without developing a hierarchic structure in the authoritarian sense.

This is not to say that there will be no hierarchy in the *logical* sense. There will certainly be functional hierarchy (multi-level information flow, that is, problem-solving at the level of group environment, internal activity of subgroup, relations between subgroups, and so on). We have seen that this need not necessarily mean different isolatable physical parts handling the different levels. In a situation of great complexity, however, we would expect to find anatomical hierarchies, in as far as there would be identifiable subgroups of varying degrees of permanence of form and constitution, dealing with different levels of activity.

The essential points are that a system with redundancy of potential command and changing dominance cannot be analyzed in terms of a hierarchic model except with extreme caution, and that, where an anatomical hierarchy is distinguishable, the higher levels need not control the lower by coercive sanctions; their influence would entail feeding information to bias the autonomous activity of the other subgroup. Clearly, this is a very different sort of hierarchy from that of managerial theory of the system. There certainly need be no isolated "control unit" dominating the rest of the system.

I am using "structured" here in a sense comparable to Martin Buber's use of the term (possessing a structure of connected groups or subgroups of a functional nature), but I would place relatively less emphasis on formal federation of subgroups, even in multiple federation, than Buber,[12] emphasizing instead more complex forms of connection. Also, I am, in my analysis, including both localized and more diffuse structures, formal and informal. One important form of connection between structures occurs when members of diffuse substructures "penetrate" into more localized ones; for example, certain members of a particular subgrouping are likely to be members of some more widespread grouping—and thus serve as a means by which information about special forms of activity can pass between the widespread and the local structures, and play a part in determining the subsequent behavior of both.

I hope I have shown that ideas derived from cybernetics and information theory are suggestive and fruitful lines of approach in considering social organization, especially in a participatory democracy built on the libertarian/anarchist model. I would not, however, expect too much in the way of rigorous direct application of cybernetic technique to social situations, for two reasons. First, it is difficult to specify adequate and generally accept-able models of complex social situations, where the bias of the observer is notoriously effective in determining the picture he adopts. Secondly, infor-mation theory's concept of "information" is an abstract one that empha-sizes only the selective characteristic of information. There are situations in which concept is not entirely adequate.

This, however, is no reason to remain bound by a primitive and inade-quate model of decision-making and control procedures. The basic premise of the governmentalist—namely, that any society must incorporate some mechanism for overall control—is certainly true, if we use "control" in the sense of maintaining a large number of critical variables within limits of toleration. Indeed, the statement is virtually a tautology, since if such a situation did not exist, the aggregate would not possess sufficient stability to merit the designation "society."

The error of the governmentalist is to think that "incorporate some mechanism for control" is always equivalent to "include a fixed isolatable control unit to which the rest, *i.e.* the majority, of the system is subservi-ent." This may be an adequate interpretation in the case of a model railway system, but not for a human society.

The alternative model is complex, and changing in its search for stability in the face of unpredictable disturbances—and much less easy to describe. Indeed, we are perhaps just beginning to develop an adequate language to describe such situations, despite the prophetic insights of a few men in the past.

A quotation from Proudhon makes a fitting conclusion—and starting point: "People like simple ideas and are right to like them. Unfortunately, the simplicity they seek is only to be found in elementary things; and the world, society, and man are made up of insoluble problems, contrary prin-ciples, and conflicting forces. Organism means complication, and multiplic-ity means contradiction, opposition, independence." [13]

NOTES

[1] See Seymour Melman, *Decision-Making and Productivity* (Blackwell, 1958).

[2] Gordon Pask, "Interaction between a Group of Subjects and an Adaptive Automaton to produce a Self-Organising System for Decision-Making" in *Self-Organising Systems, 1962,* a symposium ed. by Jovits, Jacobi and Goldstein (Spartan Books).

[3] See Stafford Beer, *Cybernetics and Management* (Science Editions, 1964), pp. 123–127, and Gordon Pask, *An Approach to Cybernetics* (Hutchinson, 1961).

[4] See Richard and Hephzibah Hauser, *The Fraternal Society* (Bodley Head, 1962).

[5] See, for example, the paper by Trist on collective contract working in the Durham coalfield, quoted by H. Clegg in *A New Approach to Industrial Democracy* (Blackwell, 1960), and the discussion of this book by Geoffrey Ostergaard in *Anarchy 2*. Note the appearance of new elements of job rotation.

Despite his emphasis on the formal aspects of worker organization, Melman's analysis (see Note 1) of the worker-decision process brings out many of the characteristics of a self-organizing system: the evolving nature of the process; the difficulty of determining where a particular decision was made; changing dominance; the way in which the cumulative experience of the group changes the frame of reference against which subsequent problems are set for solution. A better idea of the gang system from which this derives can, however, be obtained from Reg Wright's articles in *Anarchy 2 & 8*.

[6] Beer, *op. cit.,* p. 21.

[7] P.-J. Proudhon: *The General Idea of the Revolution in the Nineteenth Century* (Freedom Press, 1923). (Proudhon's italics.)

[8] Compare also the concluding section of Pask's *An Approach to Cybernetics*, in particular the discussion of a "biologically organized" factory.

[9] Peter Kropotkin, *Anarchism, its Philosophy and Ideal* (Freedom Press, 1895).

[10] See, for example J. A. C. Brown, *The Social Psychology of Industry* (Penguin, 1954), ch. 2.

[11] See Clegg, *A New Approach to Industrial Democracy* and G. Ostergaard's discussion in *Anarchy 2*.

[12] See Martin Buber, *Paths in Utopia* (Boston: Beacon, 1958).

[13] P.-J. Proudhon, *The Theory of Taxation* (1861) quoted in Buber, *op. cit.*

The systematic theoretical austerity of much of Marxist theory means, unfortunately, that an attempt to confront it a key points must share some of its dryness. The tradition of Marxist theory presents us with extraordinary tools for social analysis, and the essay that follows by no means attempts to discard it altogether. Indeed, it employs a number of key Marxist concepts—such as the dialectical conception social reality, although it sees the operation of the dialectic in somewhat different terms. In addition, it identifies the motive force for social change as the interaction between technologically-induced changes and the structures that embody them.

But there are departures. Where Marxists hold that the dialectic of changing means of production and their impact on relations of production is final and historically determined, Benello leaves open the outcome of this interaction. He sees the result in terms of an area of essentially free human response to technological and organizational demands that can and must be resisted, despite their power. Implicit in this approach is a refusal to equate progress with technological advance, as both Marxism and liberal progressivism have done. In Benello's view technological advance is progressive only when it increases the overall area and scope of human freedom. But when it serves as an incentive for subtle and rationalized forms of organizational enslavement, technological advance is social regression.

The ideal of free association is basic to the traditions of Utopian Socialism, and of communally-minded anarchists such as Kropotkin. It is also, as de Tocqueville demonstrated, part of the genius of democracy, and for him, its saving grace; the third sector of society, made up of all manner of voluntary organizations between the private sector and the public sector, was for him the guarantor of the health of the society. It was the training ground for citizenship, the bulwark against the fascist potential implicit in the abdication from power inherent in representative as opposed to direct or participatory democracy.

Free association requires participation. According to the analysis presented in this article, when organizations are not structured to provide for extensive participation, they will always polarize around two groups, the governors and the governed. This sets up the dynamic of class conflict, which comes to pervade the social system at a certain stage. Benello also suggests that, with the further fragmentation of social purpose within society, organizations can come to dominate their members in such a fashion that the ruler and the ruled are both subjected to the imperatives of the organization.

Even class conflict, which presupposes internal class cohesion, is eroded by the ongoing process of fragmentation that characterizes an advanced industrial society. As a result, groups that do maintain their cohesion in the face of growing fragmentation are not so much the classically exploited classes as the groups whose very affluence gives them the opportunity to be more socially aware. An exception, however, are black groups, which have retained a degree of cohesion through racial solidarity, which permits sustained and systematic resistance to the society.

Only when class solidarity exists can social conflict rise above individual acts of rebellion and lawlessness to the stature of organized resistance. But the modern unifying factors are not the classical Marxist ones. Thus social conflict continues as groups that are both aware and cohesive reject the prevailing assumptions. But, the article points out, within the system of ruling organizations, conflict in its traditional Marxist sense has become muted and co-opted. Hence resistance in its current form increasingly constitutes rejection of the whole organizational apparatus of advanced industrial society, as the 1968 events in France showed. The demand for voluntarism and free association were crucial there; and the black flag of freedom was raised alongside the red flag of revolution. To the extent that this article illuminates the nature of that juxtaposition, it can serve as a guide to the building of the future.

Organization, Conflict, and Free Association

C. George Benello

"The intent of a sociological theory of conflict is to overcome the predominantly arbitrary nature of unexplained historical events by deriving these events from elements of their social structure."

Ralf Dahrendorf

More adequately than any other system of social thought, Marxism has confronted the phenomenon of conflict within social systems. The tool with which it has done so is class analysis, focused mainly on economic relations and ascribing primary importance to relations among the means of production. Other analysts have seen society in more general terms—dominator and dominated—or in terms of a general description of a power-oriented society. One can look at the phenomenon of classes and class-conflict from still another perspective, and when one does so the dynamics revealed offer new and fundamental implications for a strategy of change. Classical Marxist analysis is grounded in a universal dialectic of history. Its historical orientation has proved most helpful in understanding the development of Western societies, but has diminished its importance in planning for social change. To deny the inevitability of class conflict and turn instead to the Marxist vision of a classless society, it is necessary to seek a greater analytical understanding of both the conditions that give rise to class conflict and the conditions that would end it. If, instead of considering class conflict inevitable, one attempts to understand it in microcosm—by discovering those structural conditions that cause conflict and those that harmonize interests, within the same basic organizational units—two major problems at once arise. First, inherent structural contradictions within an organization are often obscured by administrative facades that mystify and pacify. These must be penetrated if we are to expose the sources of conflict. Second, in order to demonstrate that conflict is arbitrarily determined by the structure of an organization, models must be created for the harmonization of conflict. This problem becomes specific when one confronts the existing system of advanced technology. If stratification and consequently, conflict are necessary for the organized use of advanced technology, then even though the structure of conflict is revealed, changing it becomes a utopian venture.

Thus the focus here is on the structure of organizations in an advanced industrial society, and, specifically, on the nature of those organizations most closely involved in the application of advanced technology. This essay analyzes the structures as they exist in the present, and reinforces this with an historical description of the way these organizational structures evolved into their present form. To do this in detail would be an immense project; this essay merely sketches the outlines in order to reveal the possibilities for an effective strategy of change.

Organizations have power in more than the usual sense. They have power as ordinarily understood, because only through them can major social projects and purposes be realized. But they also have the power in their effects on the members of the organization. The participants in organizations are socialized to the purposes of the organization, simply because organizations that can achieve important social purposes are at a premium within the social order. This fact tends to be obscured because such organizations develop an aura of legitimacy through law, myth, or tradition, even though they are inequitable and dehumanizing to their members. Organizations, thus, mask the distinction between the social purposes they serve and the techniques and organizational modes with which they carry out these purposes. What is involved is a kind of organizational totalitarianism, which arises because the tangible and immediate benefits of the organization are perceived far more readily than the subtler, long-term effects of a particular organizational style and structure. There has been much confusion on this point because a number of thinkers have identified centralism, bureaucracy, and resulting dehumanization with efficiency. To question this, however, it is necessary to bring into question not simply the organizational structure of the typical productive enterprise, but the structure of work organization as well. The specialization of the limited skills involved in machine tending on the assembly line perfectly mirrors the specialization of the administrative apparatus. Hence, the myth of efficiency arises out of the smooth intermeshing of both organizational orders.

It is easy to see this state of affairs as dictated by the technological imperative. But the human elements enter in at all levels, and several studies prove that alienated labor contains too many social costs to be efficient in the long run. It might seem that letting machines dictate the organization of the work place would be most efficient, and this would be so in a cybernated work place. But, when human labor is involved, efficiency is achieved by forms of organization that meet the needs of men, rather than machines. However, since human demands are subtler and less understood, the machine tends to dominate.

Beyond what is falsely seen as the technological imperative are several ecological and sociological factors that can falsely give rise to what then is perceived as an organizational imperative. The organizational imperative involves the overwhelming of the individual by the organization. The family enterprise depended on the affective relationships within it, basd on face-to-face contact. But as enterprises grew, lured on by the prospect of increasing productivity and profits, their *gemeinschaft* quality was abandoned as strangers were introduced. The human effort involved in integrating each new person into the organization was abandoned in favor of rational job definition and a specialization that is not simply of job, but of human role as well. Modern management, recognizing the human factor in enterprise, has modified the trend toward depersonalization by reintroducing small group organization. But this has been done in order to make the existing system more efficient; therefore, the focus has been on affective relations, but not on participation in decision-making and involvement with the goals of the organization. Seen from this perspective, the problem posed by the organizational imperative is how to organize large social systems involving advanced technology while maintaining wholeness of human relations, including genuine participation.

As studies indicate, the algebra of scale means that the effect of increases in group size is not continuous. In a group of fifteen everybody can communicate with everybody else. In a group of thirty this is no longer possible. Thus group structure changes discontinuously, and the experience available in small groups differs qualitatively from the experience in large groups. Small groups enable their members to be truly involved and participate as equals. Also, they require that members perform a variety of roles. The demands of large groups are for specialization, competitiveness for the few status positions, and for passive support roles elsewhere. When primary group relationships are lost, the classical attributes of bureaucracy develop as necessary substitutes. The alternative is personal leadership; however, in large organizational structures with an adequate system of rewards there is no need to rely on the vagaries of personal leadership. Monetary reward is substituted for involvement in the guiding of the organization and for whole human relationships.

Whole human relationships are in fact discouraged in hierarchies, since too much contact breeds intimacy, and distance is required for the higher echelon to govern the lower. Once the affirmation of wholeness in human relationships is abandoned, impersonal and manipulative relations become the rule.

The psychic void that results is filled by a search for status within the organization, achieved by climbing the status ladders of the hierarchy. Hence, the very notion of organization becomes identified with compulsion, since the play of individual motives and personality have no place; the goals of the organization are no longer integrated with personal goals. Thus, through the repression and frustration of human personality, and the substitution of compulsive status-seeking as the motive force for the individual, the organization exerts a powerful form of social control over its members. Where the free interplay of individual purposes is capable of shaping and reshaping organizational activity and goals, such social control would be unnecessary. But where the goals and activity have been dictated from on high, an artificial system of motivation must operate to ensure performance. The result is dehumanizing and stultifying.

Thus, where participation and freedom are denied, hierarchy and status determine organizational form and motives. The system requires, moreover, that the scarce values of prestige and power cluster disproportionately at the top. While monetary reward may be effective in ensuring conformity, real involvement requires a deeper personal commitment, and this is achieved through organizational identification. Moreover, since the goals of the organization are often trivial, as in the case of enterprises producing for profit, commitment comes from identification with organizational position, not with its goals. The trappings of power become all-important.

Basically, then, such organizations are vertical in their structure, involving military-style chains of command. But this hierarchy is not altogether linear; it also embodies a dyadic power relationship between the dominator and the dominated. Organizations that involve hierarchies of status, with middle levels responsible to those above and ruling those below, are also dyadic. There are the troops or workers, and there are the officers or managers. The distinction derives from the need to isolate a ruling group, which is rewarded with disproportionate prestige and power, so that it can be trusted to identify with the objectives of the organization, even though the majority of members of the organization do not so identify.

It is important to recognize, however, that within the managerial caste, the organizational relationships are still coercive. They are imbued with the organizational ideology, co-opted so as to ensure they identify with the values and beliefs of their peers, and bribed by exorbitant rewards. But above all, theirs is the exclusive prerogative to exercise power within the organization, and through this they are corrupted to its purposes. The power, however, is not a free power capable of serving humane and universal ends; it is power to seek the preestablished ends of the organization, and from this derives the paradox that the rulers of such organizations have great power but little freedom.

The analysis can be summed up briefly: when the purposes of the organization are no longer integrated with those of its members and it cannot enlist people as whole human beings to serve its purposes freely, then it develops the status ladders, prestige positions, and schisms between the rulers and the ruled that characterize most large organizations. Such organizations are antithetical to free association. Free association involves a voluntary enlistment of members who freely identify with the goals of the organization. For this to happen they must identify themselves as part of the organization, voluntarily committed to its goals, personally involved with its members. When such identification exists, there is no need for status hierarchies and inordinate prestige for leadership. In the *kibbutzim,* where everybody is involved, and community exists, people qualified for management must be sought out and asked to take the job, since no special status goes with the position.

It is possible to understand more clearly how the present coercive form of productive enterprise arose by considering its genesis. The invention of steam power and the coming of the factory opened a new field of productive possibilities. Society placed a premium on successful productivity, and, consequently, every effort was made to reward those who organized productive enterprises, and to free them from any form of legal or social control. The development of the joint stock company removed the penalty for failure, and the entrepreneur was conveniently left to concern himself with profits at the expense of the ecological environment and of those who labored within his establishment. The depredations of early industrial development now tend to be forgotten, but their impact on man and his environment was comparable to the effects of a war. Subsequently, the organization of labor and consequent legislation mitigated some of the grosser effects of industrialization on workers, while leaving the subtler psycho-social ailments to flourish.

At the outset of the industrial age, class division based on institutions of domination already existed and was deeply embedded in Western society in its feudal form. When an essentially new entrepreneurial class arose with the industrial age, it followed existing patterns and exacerbated class divisions. Two levels of skills are involved in the development of an industrial enterprise. Initially a high level of entrepreneurial skills is needed for capital accumulation, industrial planning, and human organizing. Subsequently the enterprise can be operated by workers with machine tending and operating skills. When industrial enterprises were being formed, entrepreneurial skills were well rewarded and entrenched in power, while the workers had to organize and fight for their rewards. In the process, coercive, power-based organization developed to its present sophisticated form, where the carrot of pay and the stick of job loss and poverty serve to institutionalize domination under the guise of a labor market.

In the period of primitive capital accumulation, it was possible to see the individual entrepreneur as the enemy, but even this perspective neglects the extent to which the grant of unfettered power to the entrepreneur was a product of acquiescence by the whole social order. In the United States, the framers of the Constitution refused to recognize the corporation, either fearing or unaware of the power it could attain. When the States took over the job of chartering corporations, they initially required the organizations to conform to minimum conditions of social purpose. Even these were abandoned in the face of burgeoning industrialization, and the process of chartering became a mere formality. What followed was a history of sordid attempts to justify and rationalize the ensuing state of chaos, first by appeals to Social Darwinism, as with the early apologias put out by the National Association of Manufacturers, and then on the basis of doctrines of pluralism and countervailing power. In the present period, there is hardly an individual entrepreneur worthy of attack—no J. P. Morgan, John D. Rockefeller, or Andrew Carnegie. Instead, power is held by corporate and financial groupings, united in complex and often hidden ways to the owners of corporate wealth. The process of institutionalization and bureaucratization of the free enterprise system, and with it much of the political system, has run full course, hiding the individual from confrontation with the implications of his acts in a system of organized irresponsibility, just as it hides the harsh facts of domination from the dominated.

What has been described are the structural causes of class conflict that lie rooted in the present organizational system. It is a story of a society bedazzled by the possibilities of industrialization and technological advance, supporting a system of subtle and concealed coercion. The analysis also indicates that the responsibility for the system must be shared and the guilt is general. The system could not have arisen without the premium placed on its results. In the United States and England, where it has a broad popular base, government has been unable to legislate even weak forms of control. In developing nations today the process is seen condensed, and clarified. The effects of rapid industrialization and the creation of moneyed elites are approved, at least passively, because people believe that the positive results —overcoming "backwardness," higher standards of living, greater national prestige—far outweigh such depredations as destruction of tribal life and community tradition. Moreover, if the organizations that arise in both the public and private sectors to carry out the process of development exert powerful and coercive forms of social control over their members, it is a control that dominates both those at the top and those at the bottom, even if in subtler ways.

Contrary to the popular myths, the divorce of power from function, which is at the heart of coercive organizations, reduces efficiency. Where worker's control operates, for example, on the work floor, floor management is taken over by workers, and management overhead is, thus, significantly reduced. In general, free associations, such as free universities, free radio, off-off Broadway theater, do a better job for their members and for society than the commercial enterprises, and do it more cheaply. People are motivated by the job itself, not by extrinsic considerations such as status and prestige, and energy is directed to the task at hand. The difficulties that face such free associations result from having to function in a society structured to favor conventional profit-oriented organizations.

Thus, it is the path of least resistance, not efficiency, that dictates the organizational forms that dominate mass industrial society. A system of quantitative and monetary reward substitutes for modes of organization that could achieve complete and free association of people in their tasks. Work is thus degraded, and the free play of human spontaneity, ingenuity, and imagination is denied. The costs to the society are enormous but difficult to quantify: there are no hard data to reveal the psychic deprivation, repression of impulse life, consequent symptomatic disturbances, outbursts of violence and destructiveness, and loss of sense of worth that result from the existing system. No area of society escapes the impact. Those sectors that are traditionally organized by free association are impoverished, since they are not functionally related to the institutions in which primary social power is exercised. Moreover, they take on the coloration of the dominant institutions of the society, primarily the corporation. Thus, education is corporatized, and the university, originally oriented to scholarship and learning for its own sake, becomes a feeder establishment for industry. Moreover, in both structure and purpose the university patterns itself on the corporation, processing its students in the same depersonalized way that industry uses on its labor force. In place of monetary reward, education hands out grades and thereby conditions its students to accept the same system of extrinsic reward that they will find in their future jobs. They learn that, while free association may be relevant for birdwatching clubs, the important purposes of society are carried out in different fashion. As power becomes increasingly centralized, politics becomes a process of voting for Tweedledum or Tweedledee, while representative legislatures become increasingly subordinate to entrenched administrative bureaucracies that are closely tied to the corporate order.

Success breeds success. This holds for the organizational structure even more than for the technology of production, for the latter may evolve with breakthroughs in technology while basic organizational forms remain constant. Those changes that do take place—the individually owned enterprise giving way to the mature corporation, which in turn gives way to the conglomerate—do not affect the basic social forms. They merely follow the laws of rationalization and stabilization of the enterprise. In the meantime, what has arisen is an ideology of organization based on a glorification of bigness and an appeal to a mythical efficiency, enshrined and codified by law and custom. To organize a productive enterprise rooted in free association thus involves courting the enmity of organized labor, creating forms unrecognized by existing civil law, raising funds outside established channels, dealing with a suspicious if not inimical corporate environment, and flying in the face of accepted beliefs.

It is apparent that class conflict creates the need for power-ridden and coercive organizations, which produce a controlling group that identifies primarily with organizational objectives. Yet this does not explain fully the impact of such organizations on their members. As the enterprise evolves from one-man rule to government by managers on behalf of ownership groups that often remain uninvolved, even management takes on many of the characteristics of hired hands. Ultimately the objectives of the enterprise—a stable market, steady growth, an adequate return to the investor—do not derive from any controlling group at all, but rather from the general socio-economic environment of which the enterprise is a part. This environment dictates the general objectives of the enterprise and is, in turn, shaped by these objectives. The salient fact is, thus, that at no level, even the top, is the full play of human purpose given scope. Those who rule the vast industrial baronies are not free to turn their productive powers to objectives that extend beyond the criteria imposed by cost accounting. Hence, basic social needs go begging, since their fulfillment is insufficiently profitable, while what is produced is often socially useless or even destructive, and can be sold only through the artificial stimulation of demand.

Those involved at all levels accept the system as it is, since its success in meeting the more obvious aspects of socio-economic needs assures it of high payoffs, and its ideology comes to dominate the scene. Moreover, no alternatives exist on a scale capable of challenging the basic assumptions of the system. The socialist alternative seems to be trivial, since class divisions and conflict arise equally in enterprises controlled by the state. The failure, here, is to understand that property ownership is not the basic question, since ownership can be analyzed as a specific and limited form of control. The capacity for overall planning is greater within a socialist system, but the decision-making capacity within the enterprise is much the same. Thus the impact of the enterprise on its environment may be controlled more rationally, but the organizational forms that give rise to class divisions and to conflict are perpetuated under a new name. Only in Yugoslavia have significant structural alternatives to the present organizational forms been developed, but by debating with the Soviet forms of bureaucratic centralism in Marxist terms, they seem to have overlooked the fundamental theoretical distinctions. Instead, the debate has tended to take the shape of wrangles about the dominance of a market system versus planning.

The problem is that Marxist analysis sees conflict as revolving around the question of classes distinguished according to their relations to the means of production. But in both the Eastern and Western variants of bureaucratic centralism, ownership can be distinguished from the concrete and ongoing system of control, and it is the system of control that generates conflict, which extends well beyond class divisions. Who owns has an impact on the fundamental style of control. But ownership by the people is as much a myth as ownership by all the shareholders in an enterprise, since in both cases managerial control is vested in a few, who themselves are subservient to rigid purposes determined by the socio-economic environment.

In fact, conflict is related mainly to the coercive form of organizations whose members are motivated primarily by money and status. Where artificial incentives dominate, the scarce psychic and material benefits at the top of such organizations dictate a highly competitive and conflict-filled state as people struggle to climb the status ladders. In the case of workers, who are the ruled, vertical mobility is slight, and competition tends to give way to anomie. Since the worker is not involved in status-seeking within the enterprise, he can be organized in unions, usually with little more involvement than exists for him within the enterprise. But there is little basis for extensive conflict along class lines in such a system; conflict, instead, tends to be within classes. Class conflict is blunted, indeed, by the very process of bureaucratization, and its close concomitants of extrinsic reward and motivation.

Here we have a key perspective on the rationalization of administrative apparatus that is a central feature of bureaucracy. Where power is disseminated according to job categories and defined by rules, there is a final refuge from the possibility of organized pressure from below or from outside. For, in such a case, the person is subservient to the position in which he serves, and can deflect pressure by arguing that he is just doing his job. Hence, we see revealed another systemic reinforcement in the structure of coercive organization: where organizational categories dominate and define the role of the individual, he is freed from the need to confront attacks upon his authority directly. Final responsibility finds no locus in such a system and attacks are blunted: lower management points to higher management; higher management points to the directors; the directors, already one step removed from the process of daily governance, point to the shareholder, who is totally removed and faceless. Thus the system is one of carefully organized irresponsibility.

When face-to-face relationships predominate, as in the family or other small enterprises, people are free, but they are also responsible. The nature of such relationships precludes impersonal manipulation, the treatment of people as items in a labor market, or the domination of people by organizational imperatives. Hence, a system that seeks to manipulate people in the interests of the organizational objectives must be run either by a powerful tyrant, who makes a tempting target for attack, or, more cunningly, must be run by no one. When organizations come to dominate even their top managers, that domination serves a purpose: it blunts and obfuscates resistance to the organization, allowing it to survive and flourish in spite of personal costs to its members that, otherwise, would cause is instantaneous downfall.

The impact of such an organization on members is to socialize them to the pattern of the authoritarian personality. Such people suppress feelings, project resentments that result from their alienation onto out-groups, value tough-mindedness, and are basically manipulative. They toady to those above them and take out resentment on those below. This adds up to a socialized incapacity, a compulsive driven-ness that destroys the possibility of joy and freedom in work, and reinforces the importance of extrinsic and power-centered motivations. As popular mythology suggests, such a system is much less a battleground made up of warring classes than it is a rat race. While the fundamental power orientation divides members of such groups into dominator and dominated, the relationship between the two classes is more symbiotic than conflicting. The authoritarianism is depersonalized and internalized, and becomes a means of social control and perpetuation of the system, rather than a basis for attack on it.

Psychic deprivation also acts as a powerful binding force for the maintenance of the status quo. The deprivation derives from the impossibility of being involved either with others or with organizational goals; it is reinforced by unnecessary specialization and routinization of work (unnecessary in terms of technological considerations *per se*). Men respond by suppressing the urge toward greater fulfillment in work, and by tailoring their personality to their job. Conformity becomes compulsive, and people refuse to consider the possibility that work could actually be intrinsically rewarding. This psychic deprivation paralyzes and atomizes those in the lower echelons who make up the passive authoritarians of the dominated class. Workers pass through the day in a semi-dreaming state, making up in fantasy for the impoverishment of reality. Among unskilled blue collar workers, a study has shown that mental illness extends to the level of ninety percent.

When his psychic energy is not entirely throttled or channeled into fantasy, the individual may see the solution to his state of deprivation in terms of moving up the status ladder. This solution is open mainly to those in the more mobile positions of management and is therefore unacceptable. Here the existing state of deprivation produces a powerful incentive to play the game in order to get ahead, to rise to those areas where more power is exercised, and where psychic plenty is perceived as existing. This system of incentives hastens the accommodation of people to the system, and reinforces social control. Thus, people generally play the game and suppress awareness of its psychic costs. Since the organizations that so successfully alienate those who work for them also spend vast sums to convince them that the way to happiness is through material plenty, the circle of psychic deprivation is made complete—the consumer consumes compulsively to fill the psychic void created by the method of production.

To summarize, then, the prevailing organizational style and structure rationalizes conflict by depriving it of an object; instead, individual competition within a system of psychic scarcity takes its place, and this is reinforced by an overall authoritarianism which binds dominator and dominated into a symbiosis based on an internalization of the power orientation. The resulting system binds its members to it by use of artificial organizational incentives in the place of natural and direct ones.

It is now possible to suggest some of the implications of this analysis as it applies to a strategy of change. The analysis has been basically in the anarchist tradition, and has sought to elucidate, from that perspective, the basis of class division and conflict as it appears within organizations. Thus anarchism can serve not only as a libertarian ideal, but as a mode of analysis applicable to the structure and dynamics of all organizations. The analysis is fundamentally psycho-social, revealing that organizational structure forms itself *from the interplay of psychological dynamics meeting technological imperatives.* It is now necessary to suggest what organizational models embodying free association would look like. This in turn will make it clear that the root problem to which a strategy of change must address itself is how to organize in a participatory and humanized fashion while effectively maintaining the existing technology.

The basis of free association is respect for the primordial links that relate people to each other in wholeness. When these are maintained in their integrity it is unnecessary to develop the elaborate system of artificial incentives, which separate people from each other and alienate them from their work. Work assumes its innately social and functional character as people join together to accomplish tasks that inherently require collaboration. This holds true whether the setting be the local community or work enterprise. Both cases require extensive investment in social organization. People today learn to rejoin each other in encounter groups, T-groups, and other forms of therapeutic association, having become aware in some fashion of the extent to which they have become alienated from each other. As they try to restore solidarity, they must consider how this solidarity can be maintained in the face of the technological demands of an industrial society. T-groups must become task groups, in which men encounter not simply each other but technology.

The structure of organizations that seek to be participatory must be such as to be capable of safeguarding the wholeness of relationships which constitute the basis of free association. Such whole relationships take more time to form and require more continued sustenance and care than do the mechanical relationships that characterize existing bureaucracies. Implicit is a different value system, personal and communitarian, that refuses to allow the integrity of human relationships to be bent and warped by organizational imperatives. For such a value system to develop, the many potential sources of change would have to come together in a counterculture to form a cultural revolution. The group-encounter movement forms one prong of such a potential coalition. The growth of intentional communities and communes forms another. The anarchist and communitarian wing of the New Left forms still another. The drop-out culture forms yet another.

Within the present fragmented counterculture, however, the vision of liberation and the restoration of authenticity in human relationships remain dim. Because the experience of structure has been one of authoritarianism without legitimacy, from family to school to work place, the present counterculture is distrustful of any structures. And in the process of attacking existing institutions, the counterculture manifests its own, still unfree, involvement in those institutions. The present counterculture can only be useful if it develops sufficient solidarity to stand as a cultural reality in its own right, capable of enveloping its members in the same complete fashion that the present culture manages.

It is from the dialectic of class conflict that Marxist analysis generates the contradictions that will bring down capitalism. But it has been suggested here that such class divisions occur in socialist bureaucracies and that modern bureaucratic organizations have ways of pacifying the conflict by so structuring organizations that there is general subservience to the organizational imperative. This suggests that bureaucratic centralism has achieved a stage of seamless unity which is capable of rationalizing all but perhaps the long term economic contradictions within itself. If the exploitation of the worker takes place within a context where all relationships to work organizations are characterized by exploitation inherent in the style and structure of the organizations, then contradictions and conflict disappear behind the seamless facade of rationalized administration.

However, the answer, in terms of strategy, is not to accept some form of gradualist revisionism. All that means is that manipulation within the organization is made a little smoother and workers are involved more closely in the exploitive process. For free association to arise, a clear break with the existing system must be made; only when this is done will the real contradictions of the existing system become apparent. As we have seen, a prime feature of the existing system is that it conditions people to accept it by virtue of its seeming rationality and consistency. Hence, its psychic costs remain concealed, and people accept them as necessary by products of technology. This myth can be shattered, not by theory, but by the creation of organizations embodying freedom in work and so proving that the whole structure based on external incentives and coerced association is unnecessary to the carrying out of the projects of the society. In the present system, the real contradiction that exists is between the people and the organizations they are in. While the authoritarianism of organizations is recognized, there is no general theoretical overview that can explain both the systemic nature of the present condition and how it came about. Thus, strategies for change still deal primarily in terms of class divisions, even though these constitute only a partial explanation of the nature of the present social reality.

Neo-Marxist theoreticians generally seek new refinements of class analysis; but, while admitting that the classic proleteriat is no longer the prime agency for change, they still seek a constituency definable by its relations to the means of production. However, the evolution of bureaucratic centralism defies such explanation. Domination by an entrepreneurial class has receded with the bureaucratization and rationalization of the corporation, while state-controlled enterprises have come to resemble closely the internal structure of the modern corporation. The subordination of people to ends dictated not by their organization but by centralized bodies either allied with or directly controlled by the state, has proceeded apace in both the East and the West. The rationalization of administration has meant that there is no point where significant power is embodied in a single person or group of persons. Thus the system appears both faceless and seamless, since one cannot point to any single elite that is not so located that its power and responsibilities are not linked to other groupings.

Certain groups benefit disproportionately from this system: the Party functionaries and intellectuals in the Soviet Union, the managerial elites in the United States. But, while it is with their consent that the system continues, they neither control it nor perpetuate it. In the corporate system, if the managerial elites do not manage rightly, they are replaced. The sort of decisions that could most significantly improve the the social environment are not within their purview, and escape the system of quantitative cost accounting that determines action. Thus a strategy of change must confront basic features of the social environment that do not lend themselves to class analysis. Class solidarity requires an identifiable sense of common interest. But it was precisely the primordial links on which common interest could be grounded that were broken down with the increasing erosion of communal existence that came about by industrialization.

Present social existence in the West is urbanized and anomic. In the United States more than seventy percent of the people live in cities, largely because the industrial system has sucked them in from rural areas. The system has made the urban centers into megalopolitan jungles. It has broken down the integrity of communities and has created ecological problems that defy solution. The possibility of class solidarity based on communal experience is replaced by the narrowest sort of common interest—material concern which provides the basis for only bread-and-butter unionism, not ideologically based militancy. Class conflict presupposes class solidarity. But with the loss of solidarity, conflict, as indicated earlier, atomizes into individual competition, which is nicely provided for by the status ladders of the organizations.

Despite these ravages, however, a constant remains, even though it is not that of classes in conflict; rather, it is the unchanging human need for concrete and sensuous freedom expressed through solidarity and meaningful activity. To speak to such a need requires that the existing organizational style and structure be totally replaced by organizations embodying the principles of free association. But as we have seen, the corporate sector of society has become institutionalized in law, in authoritarian attitudes which affect behavior, and in the structure of such supporting institutions as family, schools, universities, foundations, and governments. In the process, a systemic environment has been created into which authoritarian organizations fit perfectly, while other kinds of organizations are marginal, lack support and the capacity to endure. We have evolved to an ecosystem in which institutions, once thought to be independent of each other, actually provide the environment for each other. This ecosystem envelops both elites and masses, socializing them to a symbiotic acceptance of the system. Hence, conformity to the system comes, not out of threat or coercion, which in the long run is dangerous and inefficient, but from socialization of the most effective sort, namely mindless acquiescence to existing values which are then internalized to the point where no alternative to the system is conceivable.

To counter the existing system, space must be created for a counter system—an ecological environment of free institutions, serving mutually as the environment for each other, capable of providing the major cultural reality for individuals in them. The major activities of living must be incorporated—work, communal existence, education, culture, civic life. We can envisage a town or city, or a region within a city as embodying free association within a coordinated and linked set of institutions. Such a unit would provide the concrete basis for the exposure of the myths of the existing system. As it developed, it could seek both to expand itself and to practice a politics of confrontation and exposure.

The developing countersystem will require a dialectical linkage with the existing system. Just as it is useless to confront the existing system when an alternative does not exist, so it is useless to build a countersytem which has no bridges to the existing system. If such linkages do not exist, the countersystem will be utopian and irrelevant, developing exotically according to the whims of people who are out of touch with the broader realities that surround them. The countersystem must show itself capable of both humanizing the existing technology and evolving libertarian forms of social structure. As we have seen, the existing system represents the path of least resistance, and restoring the basic links of affectivity and function makes the organization more complex. Hence, building workable alternatives is an essential task. Such alternatives can then seriously challenge the existing system with varieties of confrontation and interaction and can be a significant force for change. It is tempting for revolutionaries to substitute rhetoric for the harder job of restructuring the basic organizational units of the society. Yet such restructuring represents the only route to lasting change.

It is the argument here that liberation must come through reconstruction around the principles of free association and solidarity. This requires a politics of participation that seeks to restructure the institutional units and, from there, work outward to the broader socio-political spheres. Only such a politics can confront directly the problem of control, which is also the problem of how power is exercised. Only such a politics can address adequately the social question. The egalitarianism demanded by the socialist vision can only be brought about by solving the problem of participation. When participation is lacking, psychic and material resources cluster in such a fashion that reinforces the organizational imperative, whether the context be state capitalism or corporate capitalism. A politics of participation requires a respect for the primordial links of solidarity between man and man, which we may define as community. Community in turn thrives only in the context of free and voluntary association.

When men sacrifice the vital links of freedom and solidarity in the interests of organizational performance, placing performance ahead of the person, the resulting enslavement, though seemingly impersonal, is as real as its grosser form of explicit domination. The carrot which motivates men to enslave themselves has been the huge material product resulting from the mastery of the technology of production.

Whereas coercive organization has been present throughout history, it has taken the lure of extensive industrialization and an economy of plenty to create a situation in which enslavement has become internalized and justified by the promise of plenty. In the days of the pharaohs, the pyramids were built by gangs of slaves, chained in quite literal fashion to the stones out of which the pyramids were built. The enslavement was explicit and personal. But today the enslavement of man to his machine is brought about by objectives which are generalized and rationalized, characteristics of the social system as a whole. The chains that enslave are chains of social custom and social structure, socializing men to a way of life that is powerfully dehumanizing and unfree. Those who would break the chains must create countersystems which use technology in a context of genuine freedom and solidarity. Such models will subvert the old totalitarianism by providing the living and concrete image of a way of life that affirms the primacy of the person.

Chickering's study of the relationship of scale to participation derives from the findings of a science in the making, behavioral ecology. It could have revolutionary implications for the shaping of communities and organizations.

When a group gets too large, some of its members are no longer necessary. They are redundant. One might see redundancy, as a product of overpopulation, but further thought should make it clear that the problem of numbers can be overcome by organization. A large population is not inherently unmanageable, except with the current style of organization. The style is one of mass organization, based on the model of the mass-producing machine, which can be seen quite clearly in the educational system. Pupils are processed like sheets of steel; they are monitored, lectured at, herded from classroom to classroom, and, generally, prepared for jobs that continue the process.

Our technological culture is much to blame for this ideology of bigness. Again and again the researchers in the Barker and Gump study that Chickering refers to were impressed with the large gymnasia and shining lab equipment of large high schools. But when they studied the situation in terms of behavioral settings, they found that small, poorly equipped schools were in fact richer: in the small schools experience, seen in terms of the number and kinds of behavioral settings per student, was found to be far more extensive. Since the culture teaches us to value the gymnasia, the lab equipment, and the more professional football teams turned out by large schools, education and experience continue to be impoverished.

More generally, the style of mass society is a spectator style. People are removed from the possibility of learning and growing from direct experience. Redundancy thus implies vicarious experience; people sit glued to their televisions, spectators to other people's drama and achievement, their desire for meaningful engagement temporarily salved by the imagination. It is much easier this way, since real engagement would require the creation of real settings. Mass organization is much simpler, too.

Behavioral ecology raises the question of human scale—a question almost totally neglected in mass society. It shows how, through size alone, organizations that are out of touch with human scale can come to dominate those within them, forcing them into personality roles that dehumanize them into caricatures of themselves. Moreover, a scarcity of settings—the other side of redundancy—creates hierarchies, role specialization, formalization of rules, and other bureaucratic characteristics. Moreover, the com-

petitive pressures we find in mass society can be understood as a product of the scarcity of settings for significant experience.

For a society to be participatory, behavioral settings must exist in sufficient quantity to involve all the people. As indicated in the Calhoun article, this requires that a society have a healthy nuclear structure, consisting of face to face groups, the settings wherein psychological development can take place. Participation on the political level cannot be dissociated from the task of creating a group structure that can instill an experience of the nature of social purpose.

How Many
Make Too Many?*
Arthur W. Chickering

Harold Taylor postulated the law that people tend to disappear when huddled together in large numbers. A corollary—put more elegantly but less clearly—is that self-fulfillment and self-development varies inversely with redundancy. The basic point is that the more a person is superfluous in a given situation the less he is apt to find it satisfying and fulfilling and the less he is apt to be affected by it.

What does "redundancy" or "superfluous" mean? Redundancy is five persons for a game of bridge or ten persons for a baseball team. It's three persons to carry a suitcase, six to carry a trunk, or twelve to move a piano. It's twenty persons on a trout stream, two thousand on a beach, twenty thousand in a city block. It's a senior-class play that calls for twenty with a class of eighty, an athletic program with places for eighty in a school for eight hundred, recreational facilities for eight hundred in a community of eighty thousand. To put it generally, redundancy occurs when increases in the number of persons in a given setting leads to decreasing opportunities

* This paper amplifies a version originally published under the title *How Big Should a College Be?*, published in *Liberal Education*, October, 1966, Vol. LII, No. 3. It was prepared in the context of the Project on Student Development in Small Colleges which is supported by NIMH grant #MH14780–04.

for participation and satisfaction for each individual, when available man-power exceeds the number required for the job.

The consequences of shifting ratios of persons to settings are illustrated by my own experiences with baseball. I first grew up in a neighborhood where there were five other boys about my age and we all liked to play baseball. Fortunately for us there were three younger brothers and two younger sisters among these six families, and in addition there were two fathers and one mother who were energetic, if not athletic. Out of this pool of fourteen persons we used to construct baseball games. This baseball setting had several salient characteristics:

(1) We were all in action most of the time. Each usually had a lot of territory to cover and it came your turn to hit often. Sometimes a teammate would have to come out on base and run for you so you could go to bat.

(2) We seldom played the same position in two consecutive games, or even within the same game. Different persons pitched, caught, or played right field, depending upon who was available. If another player came home from his piano lesson, positions shifted to accommodate his particular capabilities.

(3) We judged players on what they could do and how well. Assignments were made and accepted accordingly.

(4) We boys would press into service whoever was available and willing. Visiting peers and adults were vigorously enjoined to play, and no small child was spared.

(5) We played by rules never heard of in the majors, and seldom by the same ones twice. Where one could hit the ball, whether a team "caught for itself," which team covered home plate—these and other regulations were modified freely in order that our purposes were best met. Even within an inning the rules might change; the pitcher would have to move up half way and throw underhand to the younger brother.

At age eleven I moved downtown. In this new neighborhood of about twenty-five boys there were usually enough players "for a good game." This setting differed strikingly from the other:

(1) In the field or at bat, we stood or sat around a lot.

(2) Specialists developed. A couple of good pitchers did little else. One boy loved to catch and always did. First base and shortstop were usually nailed down.

(3) A hierarchy of leadership developed.

(4) The rules were standard.

(5) Younger brothers and inept parents were never included; some peers with marginal skills were consistent spectators when "we had enough." And some were punished severely even when they were able to play. I can still feel the tension that developed as there were two places to be filled and four or five persons left. Not to be chosen was painful, to be chosen last frequently was not much better.

After a while I entered a college along with about three hundred others, and played some baseball there. The college baseball setting had four salient characteristics:

(1) Competition was severe. Most persons didn't get to play at all and coaching was reserved for those already highly skilled. Evaluation was comparative and choices were made on the basis of fine distinctions.

(2) A good hitter could always play. Exceptional skills in some other area sometimes could counterbalance mediocre hitting but no hit, no play.

(3) Players seldom moved from one position to another. Each developed to a high degree the skills associated with his position.

(4) There was both formal leadership, a captain and co-captain, and an informal structure of prestige and power.

The differences in these three situations, differences which result from the increased numbers of persons per setting, suggest several propositions. A cautious scientist would call them hypotheses. For clarity they are stated baldly. As the number of persons increases in relation to a given task or setting, six things occur:

(1) A smaller proportion of the total persons participate actively.

(2) The activities and responsibilities of those who do participate become less varied and more specialized.

(3) Persons with marginal ability are left out, deprived of chances to develop the skills they lack.

(4) Evaluation shifts from how well a person's abilities fit the requirements of a given position, to how good one person is compared to another, with distinctions being made on an increasingly fine basis.

(5) Hierarchies of prestige and power develop.

(6) Rules and behavioral expectations become formalized and rigid.

These propositions seem to hold true for other situations in which the ratio between the number of persons and the number of settings changes. They are most clearly documented by the work of Roger Barker and his associates, who have studied the ratios of persons to settings in high schools and communities of varying size. A "setting" is pretty much what common sense suggests. The behavior and objects within a setting are organized in a non-random fashion and the boundary of the setting is usually apparent. The persons who inhabit a setting are to a considerable extent interchangeable; there may be a continuing stream of persons but the setting remains fairly constant. A living room, for example, is a behavior setting. The behavior and objects within this setting are organized so that it is easily distinguished from the kitchen or the bedroom; living room behavior across many different kinds of families is more similar than living room and kitchen behavior within the same family. Similarly, a college is a behavior setting. It differs from a living room in the number of sub-settings it contains and it belongs to a different variety of settings, but both are places where behavior is patterned in recognizable ways and through which different persons move without effecting serious change.

Barker found that as schools increased in size, the number of persons increased much faster than either the number of settings or the varieties of settings. In the smallest school there were about two *settings* for each person while in the largest there were more than four *persons* for each setting. And while the largest school has only half again as many varieties of settings, it has sixty times as many students.

What were the consequences of these differences for the students? Here are some of the findings:

(1) Students in small schools (enrollments eighty-five to one hundred fifty) held seven times as many responsible positions per student (members of play casts, officers of organizations, members of musical groups, members of athletic teams) as those in large (enrollments about two thousand).

(2) Students in small schools held twice as many different *kinds* of responsible positions as those in large.

(3) Students in small schools received twice as many pressures to participate, or to meet the expectations of the school, as those in large.

(4) Academically marginal students in small schools received almost five times the pressures to participate as those in large.

(5) Self-evaluations of students in small schools were based on the adequacy of their contributions and on their level of competence in relation to jobs undertaken; self-evaluations of students in large schools were based on comparison with others.

(6) Students in large schools exceeded those in the small in satisfy-

ing experiences related to vicarious enjoyment of others' activities. (7) Students in small schools exceeded those in large schools in satisfying experiences related to the development of competence, to being challenged, and to engaging in important activities.

(8) Students in small schools tended to achieve relatively limited development in a wide variety of areas while those in large tended to achieve greater development in more narrow or specialized areas.

These differences in school experiences were reinforced by differences that appeared as a function of community size. Four towns with populations ranging from 450 to 1150, comprising "Midwest" county with a total population of 2,888, were compared with two cities with 23,296 and 101,155 inhabitants. In the towns adolescents constituted twenty-eight percent of the working force, in the cities, fifteen percent. And adolescents in professional and business settings were 187 percent more frequent in towns than in the smaller city. The small town adolescents also more frequently participated in church activities and other out-of-school organizations than did the city boys and girls.

Reporting an earlier study of a single rural town of 721 people, Barker and Wright say:

> The community behavior settings of Midwest were not neutral behavior areas, but demanded in different degrees the participation of Midwest citizens. . . . The 585 behavior settings had the "use" of only 721 people; the average Midwesterner was, therefore, under pressure to participate in a number of settings. In fact, during 1951/52, he participated in positions of trust and responsibility in 7 community settings . . . [indicating that] most citizens participated responsibly in a wide variety of the behavior patterns of the town. This was true not only for adults; it was also true for children . . . . Because they were under pressure to take part in so many diverse activities, Midwest children were able to attain in few of them the maximal levels of which they were capable. For this same reason Midwest children were valued for general competence, versatility, and willingness to assume responsibilities as much as for outstanding achievement. Midwest's functioning was so dependent upon the cooperation of a relatively large proportion of the eligible population that Midwest value systems could not give highest status to the specialist who restricted his range of activities. . . .
>
> Midwest children had to tolerate a wide range of individual differences . . . and they had to develop skill in making diverse people fit into the same behavior patterns. The need for participants was so great in relation to the number of inhabitants that selection on the basis of sex, age, social group, intelligence, personality, political be-

liefs, or wealth was virtually impossible. . . . The children of Midwest were not a luxury in the community; they performed essential
functions. The meaning of this . . . was that their achievements were
not relegated to unimportant settings; children had the opportunity
to achieve power and status in behavior settings which were generally
prestigious. . . .

"The public behavior areas of Midwest were safe and secure places
for the children of the town. Because almost all of the town was
familiar, because almost all people (with their idiosyncrasies) were
known, because there were few sudden transitions to new positions,
because children were not without power in many settings, and because responsible adults were present in all settings, children (and their
parents) saw Midwest as a generally safe place."

These findings of Barker and his associates ring with relevance for
"urban problems," "inner city youth," the "multiversity," "school decentralization," "participatory democracy," "alienation." And the results are
consistent with the findings of others who have studied size differences in
factories, public agencies, discussion groups, and other task groups. All suggest negative relationships between size, and individual participation, involvement, and satisfaction.

The dynamics that underlie these findings have been postulated by Edwin
Willems, but he should not be held responsible for the paraphrasing and
elaboration that follows.

Behavior settings offer a variety of satisfactions and opportunities that
individuals find attractive. When the number of persons is low there are
more opportunities to participate per person, and thus each experiences the
attractions with greater force. In task-oriented settings there are functions
and purposes to be carried out that impose obligations on the participants.
When manpower is low, each participant has to assume more responsibilities and each becomes the focus for more obligations. Under such conditions individuals perceive more clearly the importance of their own
participation, and of the participation of others. Thus, feelings of loyalty or
responsibility are added to the intrinsic satisfactions that attracted the
individuals initially.

In addition to these internal or personal forces, if the setting has importance as part of a larger context, external pressures increasingly will be
brought to bear as manpower diminishes. There will be more invitations or
demands and the social rewards for contribution will increase. At the same
time, requirements for admission or for certain kinds of positions will become more liberal. Thus, persons who usually might only be spectators will

be pressed into service, and reticent followers more often will find themselves in leadership roles. In this way those who under circumstances of overpopulation might seem unsuitable find themselves in demand under conditions of limited manpower.

Anyone who has been a member of a small town PTA has seen all these principles in operation. In our town, the last two presidents had lived in the community and in the state for less than two years, and in Vermont, that's about as marginal as you can get. And it was difficult to find members who were not on at least one committee, and who didn't help in other ways during the year.

What are some of the likely effects of size, or more accurately, of redundancy, on human development? To the best of my knowledge, there has been virtually no research that has attempted to study relationships between personal development and size. So it should be emphasized that the following comments about the effects of size on development rest solely on theory and personal observation. Thus, I can only hypothesize that redundancy has implications for the development of competence, the development of identity, the freeing of inter-personal relationships, and the development of a personal-value system.

Competence is a three-tined pitchfork. One tine is intellectual competence, another is manual skill, and the third is social and interpersonal competence. Most important of course is the handle of the pitchfork; without a handle you can't pitch much hay even if the tines are sound. The handle is what R. W. White calls "sense of competence." The whole pitchfork is affected when redundancy sets in, that is, when the number of persons per setting, and variety of settings, hold positions of leadership and responsibility less frequently, play active roles less frequently, and participate in a less varied constellation of settings.

Under conditions of redundancy less development of intellectual competence will occur. Because of fewer opportunities to deal with problems of significance, and because fewer challenges are encountered, intellectual skills and working knowledge will be less fully developed among most persons. Some persons who are particularly talented, or who capture a responsible position, may develop to a high degree in a particular area. But for most, development will be less than it would be if they were less superfluous.

The development of interpersonal competence is more limited also. Because of increased selectivity of participants there is less need to find ways of working with persons of diverse abilities and attitudes. Deviants are screened out and one doesn't have to discover productive ways of working with them.

Most importantly, because of fewer opportunities to hold positions of leadership and responsibility, and because of fewer opportunities for active mastery and successful coping with a wide range of tasks, a sense of competence develops less fully, rests on a more limited sphere.

The shift in the basis of self-evaluation may have even more significance for sense of competence than the limited opportunities for significant achievement. As self-evaluation comes to be based primarily upon comparisons with others, it is difficult to see oneself as very competent. Those who are better in the areas to which one aspires are highly visible; there seem to be so many of them up there in front. Those less skilled are quite invisible and their presence carries little force. Because by definition only a few can be "on top," the rest struggle along, frequently using as much energy to cope with feelings of inadequacy as to cope with the tasks at hand. But when the emphasis is on who can do the job and who is willing to undertake it, and where esteem and respect derive from the successful completion of significant tasks rather than from relative standing, there is a more accessible and solid basis for learning where competence lies and how far it extends.

In general, I would hypothesize that under conditions of redundancy, less development of competence occurs, except for a minority of talented individuals in whom special abilities and knowledge may develop to an unusually high degree.

The development of identity is like learning to drive. Progress occurs in fits and starts and there is much wandering from one side of the road to another. But with experience and practice change occurs. The driver and vehicle become acquainted. Peculiar requirements for operation become known. The driver comes to know his own limits and those imposed by certain conditions. In time, snow, heavy traffic, occasional skids, and mechanical failures are encountered with assurance and with some ease. Finally driving becomes a pleasure, not a chore, and other things can be attended to while doing it.

The implications of redundancy for this vector of development seem clear. If opportunities for active participation and involvement are limited, and particularly, if the variety of environments and activities are limited, then so are the opportunities for the kinds of self-discovery through which a full and rich sense of identity may come about. If only rarely can one get behind a wheel, and if one can only drive then on a country lane in sunshine with an automatic transmission, not much development occurs and one feels uncomfortable if other conditions must be faced. Of course, a similar result occurs if one only drives through snow and mud with smooth tires in a car without a heater.

The response to the combination of limited opportunities and competitive pressure is often observed. In high schools there is the too frequent settling on either beauty, brains, or athletic prowess as the center of one's self-esteem, as the core of one's being. In college it takes more particular forms: the beats, the grinds, the party boys and others. In communities, the country club, bridge club, bowling team, church group, professional or vocational associations, lodge or fraternal organizations become more mutually exclusive; individuals less frequently participate in several. However, when opportunities are many and varied, and when competitive pressures are lessened, one can range more widely, and those roles found satisfying can be held more tenuously. The increased range of vicarious experiences available to the person in the over-populated setting may somewhat compensate for the decreased opportunities for more active participation, but they do not provide the experience of self-testing on which a sense of identity ultimately is built.

According to R. W. White the "natural growth of personality moves in the direction of human relationships that are less anxious, less defensive, less burdened by inappropriate past reaction, more friendly, more spontaneous, more warm, and more respectful." Thus the "freeing of interpersonal relationships" involves developing a tolerance for a wider range of persons; tolerance not only in the sense of being able to "put up with," but also in the sense of being no longer upset by dosages that earlier caused distress. Ideally this tolerance develops not through increased resistance and immunization, but through an increasing capacity to respond to persons in their own right rather than with particular conventions and stereotypes. Under conditions of redundancy development of this kind is less likely to occur.

Instead, in-groups and out-groups develop and assume greater force. Relationships become more hierarchical. Increased competition for entry into attractive settings may generate personal animosities. Those who are congruent with one's own peculiar ideas and behaviors are more numerous, and thus those who are incongruent are more easily done without. As a consequence, stereotypes and biases carried to college from earlier years more frequently remain untested and the cooperative working contexts in which such attitudes might be examined and modified are not experienced. This narrowing of the range of contacts, which probably occurs with increasing overpopulation, may be primarily responsible for the large number of students who go through college relatively untouched. For it is basically the significant personal relationships which have an effect, whether they be with students or with faculty members. And when these relationships become highly self-selective then it is less likely that change, liberalization, or enrichment, will occur.

The development of a personal value system involves three stages that are sequential and that also substantially overlap. They are (a) the humanization of values, (b) the internalization of values, and (c) the achievement of congruent behavior.

Humanization of values refers to the change whereby literal belief in the absoluteness of rules gives way to a more relative view in which connections are made between rules and the purposes they are meant to serve. Thus, for example, it becomes acceptable to change the rules for a baseball game to accommodate limited numbers of players and other unusual conditions. Similarly, rules concerning honesty or sexual or aggressive behavior may become relative to circumstances and situation so that the welfare of all is best served. For some, values do not rest on a humanistic base and are never relative to external circumstance. But even then this process still operates in many significant areas, though some may be excluded.

Absolute relativity leaves one suspended in mid-air, a condition leading to considerable anxiety. Consequently, work soon begins on a supporting structure. With testing and with frequent redesigning a more stable and comprehensive basis for judgments about actions, policies, and personality characteristics develops.

The final stage in the development of values is the achievement of congruence between values verbally asserted, and behavior. One may believe in honesty and openness but be unable to refrain from the use of hidden agenda, or from the anticipation of it in others; one may believe in chastity but be unable to resist sexual temptation. When congruence is achieved there is a consistency of belief and behavior, of word and deed. At this point internal argument is minimized. Once the implications of a situation are understood and the consequences of various alternatives seem to be clear, the response is highly determined; it is made with conviction and with little debate or equivocation.

Humanizing of values is fostered when one must make choices that influence the lives of others and where the effects of those choices are observable. Value choices reside wherever decisions must be made regarding the living conditions in the community; in under-populated settings the opportunity for each individual to confront problems and to think through alternatives occurs more frequently. Similarly, where there are few individuals, the impact on the whole of the behavior of each is significant and observable. A person working with a group of five or ten others, or living in a small community, sees quickly and clearly the consequences of his choices for the lives of others.

The small community carries particular force for the development of congruence. When much behavior is visible to many others, when he works and plays, sits on committees and in general meetings, with other community members, it is difficult to talk one kind of life and to live another. Thus the development of congruence is significantly related to institutional size and organization.

There is empirical evidence relevant to this. A recent study of William Bowers found that the proportion of schools with high levels of cheating, increased with the size of the school. Bowers observed, "At small schools, students tend to know most of their peers, whereas at large schools they get to know only a fraction of the student body. Therefore, the student at the large schools is apt to feel relatively anonymous vis-a-vis the student body as a whole. The larger schools may provide a setting that facilitates the formation of deviant subgroups in which cheating is approved or at least tolerated."

Redundancy has implications for other aspects of human development but these four areas—competence, identity, interpersonal relationships, and integrity—are the most crucial to participatory democracy. As social problems become increasingly complex, higher levels of intellectual competence are required to identify problems accurately, to assimilate information from diverse sources, to weigh evidence, and to generate a reasoned response. And most democratic action involves working with others whose views and orientation differ. To work effectively and to help those with diverse viewpoints pull together requires substantial interpersonal competence.

It also requires a solid sense of identity. Pluralistic democracy is sustained by continual compromise. Meaningful mutual concessions are possible only with confidence in who one is, what one stands for, and where one is going. When these are shaky, ambivalent, or conflicting, defensiveness, irrational hostility, and unpredictability run high. Agreement, consequently, is reached only with difficulty and at considerable cost in time, effort, and emotional stress—and the agreements themselves lack stability.

Interpersonal competence and sense of identity are both amplified as interpersonal relationships become freer. For then others can be perceived for what they are. As stereotypes erode, persons become individuals in their own right, less often totalistic representatives of threatening power groups and more often concerned humans like ourselves, seeking the conditions for existence required by their particular backgrounds and beliefs. Points of common need and agreement are perceived, points of difference gain perspective, mutually satisfying solutions are more readily discovered.

Integrity is the cement for the whole system. Without it nothing holds together under the stress of changing forces and altered circumstances. Erik Erikson puts it this way: "Although aware of the relativity of all the various life styles which have given meaning to human striving, the possessor of integrity is ready to defend the dignity of his own life style against all physical and economic threats. For he knows that an individual life is the accidental coincidence of but one life cycle with but one segment of history; and that for him all human integrity stands or falls with the one style of integrity of which he partakes." The capacity to remain congruent, to assert the validity of one's own style while granting others the validity of theirs, is the inexpendable ingredient of participatory democracy. It must be sustained even while concessions are made to serve the needs of others, and it must be supported in others even as they concede to our needs. For only thus can the values of diversity be realized. When integrity is absent, compromise based on mutual respect and concern is impossible. Enter arbitration by outside forces, or violent confrontations more damaging than productive.

But redundancy need not inevitably accompany increased population. Two concomitant responses can be made. First, large units can be broken into smaller components. Some large established universities are developing small units—colleges with enrollments ranging from three hundred to a thousand, each with its own students, faculty, facilities, and substantial autonomy. Some industries are slicing production horizontally instead of vertically. Individual workers make entire components and units. Separate small departments turn out complete products, take responsibility for defects, and provide maintenance service for the units they produce. Mayor Lindsay is exploring small "City Halls" to serve New York communities. So structural reorganization is the first and principal response to increasing redundancy. The second response is to make more frequent participation possible.

If democracy is to survive rapid increases in the size of political units, and if a pluralistic society is to provide satisfying conditions for all its members, then such responses must be made. For as redundancy increases, the activities and responsibilities of those who do participate become more specialized and those with marginal qualifications are more quickly and more completely left out. Hierarchies of prestige and power become established. In-groups and out-groups develop as rules and standards for conduct become more formalized and rigid.

Under such conditions the opportunities to cope with significant problems become more limited and challenges to existing skills and knowledge less frequently encountered. Experience becomes less varied and self-testing more restricted. The range of different persons to be dealt with in matters important to one's own life decreases. Questions of value are less frequently provoked and the consequences of one's own behavior less frequently revealed. Thus, development of competence is more limited except for those with special talents and special opportunities; the development of identity, the freeing of interpersonal relationships, and the development of integrity is hampered.

Ultimately, that social organization which enables continued growth and development for all its members will survive, and that which does not will perish. Redundancy, therefore, has become a principal threat as population increases geometrically while social forms remain static. In answer, both structural reorganization and increasingly frequent opportunities for participation must occur throughout our social and economic institutions.

WORKS CITED

Barker, R. G. & Gump, P. V., eds. *Big School, Small School*. Stanford, Calif.: Stanford University Press, 1964.

Barker, R. G. & Wright, H. F. *Midwest and Its Children*. New York: Row Peterson & Co., 1954.

Bowers, W. *Student Dishonesty and Its Control in College*. Bureau of Applied Social Research, 1964.

Erikson, E. H. *Childhood and Society*. New York: W. W. Norton & Co., 1963.

Erikson, E. H. "Identity and the Life Cycle," *Psychological Issues,* 1959, vol. I, no. I New York, International University Press.

Murphy, G. *Human Potentialities*. New York: Basic Books, 1958.

Taylor, H. Excerpt from an address given at the College of Education, Wayne State University, April 23, 1964.

White, R. W. *Lives in Progress*. New York: Dryden Press, 1952.

White, R. W. "Competence and the Psychosexual Stages of Development." In M. R. Jones (Ed.) *Nebraska Symposium on Motivation.* University of Nebraska Press, 1960.

Willems, E. P. "Forces Toward Participation in Behavior Settings." In Barker & Gump, *Big School, Small School,* pp. 115–135.

With this essay Bookchin makes it clear that every political relationship has a social aspect and that every social relationship has a deeply personal dimension to it. In our society these two facts and their mutual relationship are obscured. The advent of freedom is a profoundly social act, which, consequently, raises the question of what social forms are needed to sustain it.

Bookchin disagrees with the Marxist definition of class and, therefore, with the concept of workers' councils, because this form must have a relationship to the productive process. Since he believes that we are quickly entering a post-scarcity society, that the productive process is changing very rapidly, and that labor as such will soon be abolished, a class analysis is hardly useful. He lists the dangers of workers' councils, in particular their isolation from the community and the probability that they will evolve into arms of authoritarianism.

A case could be made, however, for organizations similar to the Confederacion Nacional del Trabajo in Spain, which would form a transition between council and revolutionary assembly. Similarly, Yugoslavia's forms of direct democracy and regionally based assemblies, which include chambers of delegates from various professions, seem to have worked effectively.

Bookchin finds his sources of hope in the Athenian Ecclesia and the Paris sections of 1792–1793; both represent successful applications of the assembly principle. But to ascribe their breakdown to class antagonisms arising out of conditions of scarcity, as he does, raises serious questions. Are all pre-industrial societies scarcity economies, inevitably subject to class antagonisms? What of primitive societies? Has the development of a potential post-scarcity economy in any way lessened class antagonisms? Or are class antagonisms a product of psychosocial deprivation and, hence, scarcity of another kind? Whatever the answers here, the debate between those who would organize direct democracy around the work place and those who would make work an organic part of the community as a whole is a continuing theme in the history of direct democracy.

The Forms of Freedom
Murray Bookchin

Freedom has its forms. However personalized or Dadaesque may be the attack upon prevailing institutions, a liberatory revolution always poses the question of what social forms will replace existing ones. At one point or another, men must deal with how they will manage the land and the factories from which they acquire the means of life. They must deal with the manner in which they will arrive at decisions that affect the community as a whole. If revolutionary thought is to be taken at all seriously, it must speak directly to the problems and forms of social management. It must, at the very least, open to public discussion the problems that are involved in a creative development of liberatory social forms. Although there is no theory that can presume to replace the demands of real experience, there is sufficient historical experience and a sufficient theoretical formulation of the issues involved to indicate what social forms are consistent with the fullest realization of personal and social freedom.

The problem of what social forms will replace existing ones is basically a problem of the relations free men will establish between themselves. Every personal relationship has a social dimension; every social relationship has a deeply personal aspect to it. Ordinarily, these two aspects and their relationship to each other are mystified and difficult to see clearly. The institutions, especially the state institutions, created by propertied society produce the illusion that social relations exist in a universe of their own, in specialized institutional compartments, be they political or bureaucratic. In reality, there exists no strictly "impersonal" political or social dimension; underlying and basic to all the social institutions of the past and present are the relations between men in daily life, especially in those aspects of daily life which determine their survival: the production and distribution of the means of life, the rearing of the young, the maintenance and reproduction of life. The liberation of man, not in some vague historic, moral, or philosophical sense, but in the intimate details of day-to-day life, this conquest of the immediate conditions of existence by the individual, turns out to be a profoundly social act and raises the problem of social forms as a mode of relations between individuals.

The relationship between the social and the individual requires emphasis especially in our own time, for never before have personal relations become so impersonal and never before have social relations become so asocial. Bourgeois society has brought all relations between men to the highest point of abstraction by divesting them of *human* content and anchoring them in *objects,* in commodities. The object—the commodity—takes on roles that formerly belonged to the community; exchange relationships (actualized, in most cases, as money relationships) supplant nearly all other modes of human relationships. In this respect, the bourgeois commodity system becomes the historical culmination of all societies, precapitalist as well as capitalist, in which human relationships are *mediated,* or interposed, by alien factors rather than directly established on a face-to-face basis.

THE MEDIATION OF SOCIAL RELATIONS

To place this development in clearer perspective, let us briefly look back for a moment in time and establish what the mediation of social relations has come to mean.

The earliest social specialists, the priests and tribal chieftains who interposed themselves between men and mediated their relations, established the formal conditions for hierarchy and exploitation. These formal conditions were consolidated and deepened by technological advances—advances which provided only enough material surpluses for the few to live at the expense of the many. The tribal assembly, in which all members of the community had decided and directly managed their common affairs, dissolved into the tribal council, in which the elect or the elected few began to manage the affairs of all. In time, the council finally dissolved into the chieftainship and the community into social classes.

Despite the increasing investiture of social control in a handful of men and even one man, the fact remains that *men* in precapitalist societies mediated the relations of other men—council supplanting assembly, chieftainship supplanting council, class supplanting community. In bourgeois society, on the other hand, the mediation of social relations by men is replaced by the mediation of social relations by *things,* by commodities. The point is that commodity society turns the mediation of social relations from a problem into an absurdity. It focuses attention on mediation as such; it brings into question all forms of social organization based on indirect representation, on the management of public affairs by the few, on the distinctive existence of concepts and practices such as "election," "legislation," "administration."

The most striking evidence of this social refocusing is the demand, voiced almost intuitively by increasing numbers of American youth, for tribalism, participatory democracy, and community. These demands are regressive only in the sense that they go back temporally to *pre*-propertied forms of freedom. They are profoundly progressive in the sense that they go forward structurally to *non*-propertied forms of freedom.

By contrast, the traditional revolutionary demand for council modes of organization remain within the historical terrain of propertied, class-structured society. Workers' councils are indeed class councils. Within this context, the demand for self-management centers around workers' control of production, an arena in which man is still primarily an economic entity and the "self" still one-sided, instead of focusing on the community, where the human condition can become all-rounded and the "self" all-sided. Even the labor process remains untouched by this demand; it is merely attenuated quantitatively, as though the question of freedom is determined exclusively by the amount of working time versus free time. The transformation of time into life, like the transformation of space into community, is either ignored, dismissed as "utopianism," or acknowledged rhetorically. Finally, and most significant here, the demand for council organization takes its point of departure from mediated relations in social organization, from social structures based on interposed relations and not on directly posed ones. What the council mode of social organization demands is not the elimination of mediated relations at the basis of society, but only the elimination of the existing system of mediation—this at a time when social mediation tends, because of the centralism of the modern economy, to turn into bureaucratic state capitalism.

THE COUNCIL IN PRACTICE

Characteristically, the adherents of council organization evoke as precursors the so-called proletarian revolutions of the last hundred years: the Paris Commune of 1871, the Russian soviets of 1905 (formations inseparably linked to those of 1917), the revolutionary syndicates of Spain in the 1930s, and the Hungarian councils of 1956. These organizations have little in common, other than their limitations as mediated forms. The Paris Commune may be taken either as a highly confused revolution, which lasted less than three months, or as a popular municipal council. As a council it was more democratic and more plebeian than other highly democratic bodies of the same kind, but it was structured primarily along parliamentary lines— elected by "citizens" grouped according to geographic constituencies, structured on an indirect system of popular representation—and its widely touted commissions hardly combined legislation with administration more organically than other democratic municipal bodies in the United States today.

Fortunately, revolutionary Paris largely ignored the Commune after it was installed. The insurrection, the actual management of the city's affairs, and finally the fighting against the Versaillaise, was undertaken in great part by the popular clubs, neighborhood vigilance committees, and the battalions of the National Guard. Had the Paris Commune (the Municipal Council) survived, it is extremely doubtful that it could have avoided a confrontation and conflict with these loosely formed street and militia formations. Indeed, by the end of April, some six weeks after the insurrection that created it, the Commune constituted an all-powerful Committee of Public Safety, a body redolent with memories of the Jacobin dictatorship and terror, which had consumed left as well as right a century earlier. Thereafter, history left the Commune a mere three weeks of life, two of which were consumed in the death throes of barricade fighting against Thiers and the Versaillaise.

It does not malign the Paris Commune to divest it of historical burdens it never carried. First and foremost, the Commune was a festival of the streets; its partisans, primarily handicraftsmen, itinerant intellectuals, the lumpen, belonged to dissolving or dissolved precapitalist classes. The industrial proletariat, so dearly beloved by Marx and the Marxists, constituted a minority of the Communards.[1] One must pull the dry tit of ideology with a frenzy to describe the Commune's social conquests—the right to recall members of the Commune, the limitation of their salaries, the improvement of working conditions, the separations of church and state, the confiscation of abandoned workshops, the unity of legislation with administration, the substitution of a standing army by militia—as especially revolutionary, much less as socialistic. More hortatory than real in its claim to be a "social republic," the Commune was the last great rebellion of the French *sans culottes,* a class that had lingered on in Paris for a century after the Great Revolution. Ultimately, this highly mixed stratum was destroyed not only by the guns of the Versaillaise, but by the advance of industrialism.

The Paris Commune of 1871 was largely a city council, evoked by the need to coordinate municipal administration under conditions of revolutionary unrest. The Russian soviets of 1905 were largely fighting organizations, established to coordinate near-insurrectionary strikes. These councils were based almost entirely on factories and trade unions: a delegate for every 500 workers (where individual factories and shops contained a smaller number, they were grouped together for voting purposes) and, additionally, delegates from trade unions and political parties. The soviet mode of organization took on its clearest and most stable form in St. Petersburg, where it contained about 400 delegates at its high point, including representatives from newly organized professional unions. Arising directly from the need to coordinate the Petersburg general strike of October 1905, this soviet rapidly developed from a large strike committee into a "parliament" of all oppressed classes, broadening its representation, demands, and responsibilities. Delegates were admitted from cities outside St. Petersburg; political demands began to dominate economic ones; links were established with peasant organizations and their delegates admitted into the deliberations of the body. Inspired by St. Petersburg, soviets sprang up in all the major cities and towns of Russia and developed into an incipient revolutionary power, counterposed against all the governmental institutions of the autocracy.

The St. Petersburg soviet lasted less than two months. Most of its members were arrested in December, 1905. To a large extent, the soviet was deserted by the St. Petersburg proletariat, which in fact never rose in armed insurrection and whose strikes diminished in size and militancy as trade revived in the late autumn. Ironically, the last stratum to advance beyond the early militancy of the soviet were the Moscow students, who rose in insurrection on December 22, and, for five days of brilliantly conceived urban guerilla warfare, virtually reduced local police and military forces to impotence. They received no aid from the mass of workers in the city. Their street battles might have continued indefinitely even in the face of massive proletarian apathy, had the Czar's guard not been transported to Moscow by the railway workers on one of the operating lines to the city.

The soviets of 1917 were the true heirs of the ones developed in 1905, and to distinguish the two from each other is spurious. Like their predecessors, they were based largely on factories, trade unions, and party organizations, but they were expanded to include delegates from army groups and a sizable number of stray radical intellectuals. The soviets of 1917 reveal all the limitations of sovietism as such. Invaluable as local fighting organizations, they proved to be increasingly unrepresentative as congresses, that is, on a national scale. Structurally, the congresses were organized on an extremely hierarchical basis. Ordinarily, local soviets in cities, towns, and villages elected delegates to district and regional bodies; these, in turn, elected delegates to the actual nationwide congresses. In larger cities, representation to the congresses was less indirect, but it was indirect nonetheless: from the voter in a large city to the municipal soviet and from the municipal soviet to the congress. In either case (and both approaches were used simultaneously), the congress was always separated from the mass of voters by one or more representative levels.

The soviet congresses were scheduled to meet every three months. This permitted far too large a span of time to exist between sessions under revolutionary circumstances, still less under ordinary ones. The first congress, held in June, 1917, contained some 800 delegates; later congresses were even larger, numbering a thousand or more. To "expedite" the work of the congresses and provide continuity of function between the tri-monthly sessions, the congresses elected an Executive Committee, fixed at not more than 200 in 1918 and later expanded to a maximum of 300 in 1920. This body was to remain more or less in permanent session, but it too was regarded as unwieldy and most of its responsibilities after the October revolution were turned over to a small Council of People's Commissars. Having once acquired control of the Second Congress of Soviets (October, 1917), the Bolsheviks found it quite easy to pin-point soviet power in the Council of Peoples' Commissars and later in the Political Bureau of the Communist Party. Opposition groups in the soviets either left the Second Congress or were later expelled from all soviet organs. The tri-monthly meetings of the congresses were "permitted" to lapse; the completely Bolshevik Executive Committee and Council of Peoples' Commissars simply did not summon them. Finally, they were held only once a year. Similarly, the intervals between the meetings of district and regional soviets grew increasingly longer and finally even the meetings of the Executive Committee, created by the congresses as a body in permanent session, became increasingly infrequent until they were held only three times a year. The power of the local soviets had passed into the hands of the Executive Committee; the power of the Executive Committee had passed into the hands of the Council of Peoples' Commissars; and finally, the power of the Council of Peoples' Commissars had passed into the hands of the Political Bureau of the Communist Party.

That the Russian soviets were incapable of providing the anatomy for a truly autonomous democracy is to be ascribed not only to their hierarchical structure, but to their limited social roots. The insurgent military battalions,

from which the soviets drew their original striking power, were highly un-
stable, especially after the final collapse of the Czarist armies. The newly
formed Red Army was recruited, disciplined, centralized, and tightly controlled by the Bolsheviks. Except for partisan bands and the navy, soviet
military bodies remained inert as independent political forces throughout
the civil war. The peasant villages were turned inward toward their individual concerns, which is to say that they were apathetic about national problems. This left the factories as the most important political stimuli within
the soviets. And here we encounter a basic contradiction in *class* concepts
of revolutionary power: proletarian socialism, precisely because it empha-
sizes that power must derive from the factory rather than the community,
creates within itself the conditions for a centralized, hierarchical political
structure.

The factory is not an autonomous social organism, however much it is
refurbished by the trappings of "self-management." Whatever self-management a factory can enjoy is superficial at the very best; in reality, it is highly
dependent for its operation and very existence upon other factories and raw
materials' enterprises. The factory may be an integral part of a community,
a region, often even fitting into an elaborate division of labor. The soviets,
by rooting themselves primarily in factory and isolating the factory from its
local environment, shifted power from the community and region to the
nation, from the base of society to its summit. Not only did the soviet system consist of an elaborate skein of mediated social relationships, but it
knitted these relationships along nationwide class lines.

If the issue of social management is to be viewed in terms of class concepts, it is fair to add that the Spanish anarcho-syndicalists were the only
traditional workers' and peasants' movement that sought to limit the tendency toward centralization. They did this consciously, mindful of its dangers to the revolution. The CNT (Confederacion Nacional del Trabajo),
the mass anarcho-syndicalist movement in Spain, created a dual organization: an elected committee system for local activities and a counterbalancing assembly system for checking local bodies and national congresses.
Local assemblies of workers in specific trades invariably exercised complete
control over the committees and nationwide bodies. They formulated all
policies, countermanded any undesirable administrative actions taken by
the committees, strictly mandated and circumscribed the activities of delegates to the committees and national congresses, and finally, they were free
to take any action on their own that differed with the decisions of "higher"
bodies. In effect, there were no higher bodies in the CNT, merely coordinat-

ing bodies. Let there be no mistake about the effectiveness of this organization: it imparted to each member of the CNT a weighty sense of responsibility, a sense of direct, immediate, and personal influence in the activities and policies of the union. This responsibility was exercised with a high-mindedness that made the CNT the largest and most militant revolutionary movement in Europe during the interwar decades.

The Spanish Revolution of 1936 put this system to a practical test, and it worked admirably. In Barcelona, CNT workers seized the factories, transportation facilities, and utilities, and managed them along anarcho-syndicalist lines. It remains a matter of record by visitors of almost every political persuasion that the city's economy operated with remarkable success and efficiency—this in the face of systematic sabotage practiced by the bourgeois Republican government and the Spanish Communist Party. The experiment was reduced to a shambles when the central government's assault troops occupied Barcelona in May 1937, following an uprising of the proletariat. Despite their enormous influence, the Spanish anarchists had virtually no roots outside certain sections of the working class and peasantry. As a large minority movement, limited primarily to industrial Catalonia, the coastal Mediterranean areas, rural Aragon and Andalusia, anarchism was dependent upon the political and economic aid of alien, even hostile, social strata. What essentially destroyed the experiment was its isolation within Spain itself: the incompleteness of the revolution and the overwhelming forces, Republican as well as fascist, Stalinist as well as bourgeois, that were mobilized against it.[2]

It would be fruitless to examine the council modes of organization that emerged elsewhere (Germany to 1918, the Asturias in 1934, Hungary in 1956). These councils, in all cases, were either quickly destroyed by counterrevolution or, in the case of Germany, irretrievably perverted. There is absolutely no reason to believe that, had they developed further, they would have avoided the fate of the Russian soviets. History was to clearly show that it was not the Bolsheviks alone, with their conspiratorial techniques and centralized organization, who were capable of distorting the council mode of organization. In 1918, the so-called "majority" Social Democrats, a faction-ridden, reformist movement, succeeded in gaining control of the newly formed workers' and soldiers' councils in Germany and in using them not only for non-revolutionary but counterrevolutionary ends. Even in anarcho-syndicalist Spain there is evidence that, by 1937, the committee system of the CNT was beginning to clash with the assembly system, but the outcome was left unresolved by the assault against Barcelona from without.

The fact remains that the council mode of organization—be it the municipal council of Paris in 1871 or the soviets of 1905 and 1917—has been highly vulnerable to centralization, manipulation, and finally to perversion. Councils belong to particularistic, one-sided, and mediated forms of social management. Whatever may be their revolutionary origins, experience shows that statism is built into their structure and nourished by their class roots.

ASSEMBLY AND COMMUNITY

We must turn, now, to an alternative mode of organization, the popular assembly, which provides a remarkable insight into unmediated forms of social relations. The assembly was the structural basis of early clan and tribal society, until its functions were pre-empted by the council and tribal chieftianship. It later reappeared as the Ecclesia in classical Athens; in a mixed and often perverted form in the medieval and Renaissance towns of Europe; and as an insurgent body in Paris, under the name of "sections," during the Great Revolution. The Ecclesia and the Parisian sections deserve the greatest amount of attention. They developed in the most complex cities of their time and they assumed a highly sophisticated form, often welding individuals of different social origins into a remarkable community of interests. It does not minimize their limitations to say that they developed methods of functioning so successfully libertarian in character that even the most imaginative utopias have failed to match in speculation what they achieved in practice.

The Athenian Ecclesia probably has its origins in the early assemblies of the Greek tribes. With the development of property and social classes, the assemblies had disappeared except, perhaps, as a memory and were replaced by a feudal oligarchy. For a time, it appeared that Athenian society was on a course toward internal decay. A vast, heavily mortgaged class of peasants, a growing number of sharecroppers reduced to a serf-like status, and a large body of urban laborers and slaves, had polarized against a small number of powerful land magnates and a parvenu commercial middle class. By the sixth century, B.C., all the conditions in Athens and in Attica, the surrounding agricultural region, had ripened for a devastating social war.

The structural basis of this polis was the Ecclesia. Shortly after sunrise at each prytany (tenth of a year), thousands of Athenian male citizens from all over Attica began to gather on the Pynx, a hill directly outside Athens, for a meeting of the assembly. Here, in the open air, they leisurely disported themselves among groups of friends, chatting, composing letters, or simply dozing, until the solemn intonation of prayers announced the opening of the meeting. The agenda, arranged under the headings of sacred, profane, and foreign affairs, had been distributed days earlier with the announcement of the assembly meeting. Although the Ecclesia could not add or bring forward anything that the agenda did not contain, its subject matter could be rearranged at the will of the assembly. No quorum was necessary, except for proposed decrees affecting individual citizens.

The Ecclesia enjoyed complete sovereignty over all institutions and offices in Athenian society. It decided questions of war and peace, elected and removed generals, reviewed military campaigns, debated and voted upon domestic and foreign policy, redressed grievances, examined and passed upon the operations of administrative boards, banished undesirable citizens, etc. Roughly one man out of six in the citizen body was occupied at any given time in regular daily activity for the community. Some 1500, chosen mainly by lot, staffed the boards responsible for the collection of taxes, the management of shipping, food supply, and public facilities, and the preparation of plans for public construction. The army, composed entirely of conscripts from each of the ten tribes of Attica, was led by elected officers; the policing of Athens fell to citizen-bowmen and Scythian state slaves.

The agenda of the Ecclesia was prepared by the Council of five hundred. Lest the Council gain any authority over the Ecclesia, the Athenians carefully circumscribed its composition and functions. Chosen by lot from rosters of citizens who, in turn, were elected annually by the tribes, the Council was divided into ten subcommittees, each of which was on duty for a tenth of the year. Every day a president was selected by lot from among the fifty members of the subcommittee on duty to the polis. During his twenty-four hours of office, the Council's president held the state seal, the keys to the citadel and public archives, and functioned for his day as the acting head of the country. Once he had been chosen, however, he could not reoccupy the position again.

Each of the ten tribes annually elected 600 citizens to serve as "judges" —more precisely, what we would call jurymen—in the Athenian courts. Every morning, they trudged up to the temple of Theseus, where lots were drawn for the trials of the day. Each court consisted of at least 201 jurymen and the trials were remarkably fair by any historical standard of juridicial practice. Run almost entirely by amateurs, the Athenian polis had reduced the formulation and administration of public policy to a public affair. "Here is no privileged class, no class of skilled politicians, no bureaucracy; no body of men, like the Roman Senate, who alone understood the secrets of State, and were looked up to and trusted as the gathered wisdom of the whole community," writes W. Warde Fowler. "At Athens there was no disposition, and in fact no need, to trust the experience of anyone; each man entered intelligently into the details of his own temporary duties, and discharged them, as far as we can tell, with industry and integrity."

Overdrawn as Fowler's view may be for a society that required slaves, denied women any role in the polis, and slipped repeatedly into bitter class conflicts, it is essentially accurate. Indeed, the greatness of the achievement lies in the fact that Athens, despite the slave, patriarchical, and class features it shared with all of classical society, developed into a working democracy in the literal sense of the term. No less significant and consoling for our own time is the fact that this achievement occurred when it seemed that the polis had charted a headlong course toward social decay.

In its treatment of slaves, Athenian democracy greatly modified the more abusive and inhuman features of ancient society. The burdens of slavery were greatly diminished, except when slaves were employed in capitalist-type enterprises. Judging from inscriptions on ancient family tombstones, a warm, intimate, and at times even endearing relationship existed between the Athenian farmer and his one or two enslaved co-workers. Generally, slaves were allowed to accumulate their own funds; on the yeoman farmsteads of Attica, they normally worked under the same conditions and shared the same food as their masters; in Athens, they were indistinguishable in dress, manner, and bearing from citizens—a source of ironical comment by foreign visitors. In many crafts, slaves not only worked side by side with freemen, but occupied supervisory positions over slaves and free workers alike.

Greek women, in turn, were treated with enormous respect and rare consideration by their men. Lacking political equality, they usually reigned supreme in their homes and in the management of domestic affairs.

Nor was the class question critical in Athenian democracy. Athens produced relatively few men of great overbearing wealth. Property and class distinctions surely existed and produced serious crises. But even more important than the class differences that developed in this society were the commercial ties—the commodity relations—that slowly undermined all pre-existing community bonds and eventually catapulted Athens into an imperialist course. It is the growth of commerce, more than any other development, that irrevocably undermined the polis.

In balance, the image of Athens as a groaning slavocracy which built its civilization and generous humanistic outlook on the backs of human chattels is false—"false in its interpretation of the past and in its confident pessimism as to the future, willfully false, above all, in its cynical estimate of human nature," observes Edward Zimmerman. "Societies, like men, cannot live in compartments. They cannot hope to achieve greatness by making amends in their use of leisure for the lives they have brutalized in acquiring it. Art, literature, philosophy, and all other great products of a nation's genius, are no mere delicate growths of a sequestered hothouse culture; they must be sturdily rooted, and find continual nourishment, in the broad common soil of national life. That, if we are looking for lessons, is one we might learn from ancient Greece."

In Athens, the popular assembly emerged as the end product of a sweeping social transition. In Paris, more than two millenia later, it emerged as the lever of social transition itself, as a revolutionary form and insurrectionary force. The Parisian sections of the early 1790s played the same role as the soviets of 1905 and 1917, with the decisive difference that relations within the sections were not mediated by a hierarchical structure. Sovereignty rested with the revolutionary assemblies themselves, not above them.

The Parisian sections emerged directly from the voting system established for elections to the Estate Generale. The monarchy in 1789 had divided the capital into sixty electoral districts, each of which formed an assembly of the so-called active or taxpaying citizens, the eligible voters of the city. These primary assemblies were expected to elect a body of electors which, in turn, was to choose the sixty representatives of the capital. The districts were expected to disappear after performing their electoral function, but they remained behind and constituted themselves into permanent municipal bodies. By degrees, they turned into neighborhood assemblies of all "active" citizens, varying in form, scope, and power from one district to another.

The municipal law of May, 1790, reorganized the sixty districts into forty-eight sections. The law was intended to circumscribe the popular assemblies and centralize sovereignty in the National Assembly, but the sections simply ignored it. They continued to broaden their base and extend their control over Paris. On July 30, 1792, the Theatre-Francais Section swept aside the distinction between "active" and "passive" citizens, inviting the poorest and most destitute of the *sans culottes* to share in "the exercise of the portion of sovereignty which belongs to the sections." Other sections followed the Theatre Francais, and from this period the sections became authentic popular assemblies—the very soul of the Great Revolution. It was they who constituted the new revolutionary Commune of August 10th, which organized the attack on the Tuileries and finally eliminated the Bourbon monarchy; it was they who decisively blocked the efforts of the Girondins to rouse the provinces against revolutionary Paris; it was they who, by ceaseless prodding, by their unending delegations and by armed demonstrations, provided the revolution with its remarkable leftward momentum after 1791.

The sections, however, were not merely fighting organizations; they represented genuine forms of self-management. At the highpoint of their development, they undertook the administration of the entire city. Individual sections policed their own neighborhoods, elected their own judges, were responsible for the distribution of foodstuffs, provided public aid to the poor, and contributed to the maintenance of the National Guard. With the declaration of war in April 1792, the sections took on the added tasks of enrolling volunteers for the revolutionary army and caring for their families, collecting donations for the war effort, and equipping and provisioning entire battalions. During the period of the "maximum," when controls were established over prices and wages to prevent a runaway inflation, the sections essentially saw to it that the government-fixed prices were maintained. In provisioning Paris, the sections sent their representatives to the countryside, buying and transporting food and seeing to its distribution at fair prices.

It must be borne in mind that this complex of extremely important activities was undertaken not by professional bureaucrats, but for the most part by ordinary shopkeepers and craftsmen. And the bulk of sectional responsibilities were discharged after working hours, during the leisure time of the section members. The popular assemblies of the sections usually met during the evenings in neighborhood churches. Assemblies were ordinarily open to all the adults of the neighborhood. In periods of emergency, assembly meetings were held daily and normally they could be called at the request of fifty members. Most administrative responsibilities were discharged by committees, but the popular assemblies established all the policies of the sections, reviewed and passed upon the work of all the committees, and replaced section officers at will.

The forty-eight sections were coordinated through the Paris Commune,

the municipal council of the capital. Whenever emergencies arose, various
sections tended to cooperate with each other by means of ad hoc delegates.
This form of cooperation-from-below never crystalized into a permanent
relationship. It is almost meaningless, on the other hand, to deal with the
Paris Commune of the Great Revolution as a fixed institution; this body
was changed during almost every important political emergency and its stability, form and functions depended largely upon the wishes of the sections.
In the days preceding the uprising of August 10th, 1792, for example, the
sections simply suspended the old municipal council, confined Petion, the
mayor of Paris, and, in the person of its insurrectionary commissioners,
took over all the authority of the Commune and the command of the National Guard. Almost the same procedure was followed nine months later,
when the Girondin deputies were expelled from the Convention, with the
difference that the Commune and Pache, the mayor of Paris, gave their
consent (after some persuasive gestures) to the uprising of the radical sections.

Having relied on the sections to strengthen their hold on the Convention,
the Jacobins began to rely on the Convention to destroy the sections. In
September 1793, the Convention limited sectional public assemblies to two
a week; three months later, they were deprived of the right to elect justices
of the peace and divested of their role in organizing relief work. The sweeping centralization of France, which the Jacobins undertook in 1793–94,
completed the destruction of the sections. The Convention eliminated their
control over the police and placed their administrative responsibilities in the
hands of salaried bureaucrats. By January 1794, the vitality of the sections
had been thoroughly sapped. As Michelet observes: "The general assemblies of the sections were dead, and all their power had passed to their
revolutionary committees, which, themselves being no longer elected
bodies, but simply groups of officials nominated by the authorities, had not
much life in them either." When the time came for Robespierre, Saint-Just,
and Lebas to appeal to the sections against the Convention, the majority
did virtually nothing in their behalf. Indeed, the revolutionary Gravilliers
section—the men who had so earnestly supported Jacques Roux and the
Enrages in 1793—vindictively placed their arms at the service of the Ther-
midorians and marched against Robespierrists, the very men who, a few
months earlier, had driven Roux to suicide and guillotined the leaders of
the left.

FROM HERE TO THERE

The factors which undermined the assemblies of classical Athens and revolutionary Paris require very little discussion; they can be inferred from the most elementary histories of the periods involved. In both cases, the assembly mode of organization was broken up not only from without, but also from within, by the exacerbation and development of class antagonisms. There are no social forms, however cleverly contrived, that can overcome the actual content of a given society. Lacking the material means, the technology, and the level of economic development to overcome class antagonisms as such, Athens and Paris could achieve the forms of freedom only temporarily—and these, essentially as measures designed to deal with the more serious threat of complete social decay. Athens held on to the Ecclesia for several centuries, mainly because it still retained a living contact with tribal forms of organization; Paris developed its sectional mode of organization for a period of several years, largely because the *sans culottes* had been precipitously swept to the head of the revolution by a rare combination of fortunate circumstances. Both the Ecclesia and sections were undermined by the very conditions they were intended to hold in check—property, class antagonisms, exploitation—but which they could not eliminate. What is remarkable about them is that they worked at all, considering the enormous problems they faced and the formidable obstacles they had to overcome.

It must be borne in mind that Athens and Paris were not peasant villages but large cities, indeed complex, highly sophisticated urban centers by the standards of their time. Athens supported a population of more than a quarter of a million; Paris, over 700,000. Both cities were engaged in worldwide trade; both were burdened by complex logistical problems; both had a multitude of needs that could be satisfied only by a fairly elaborate system of public administration. Although they had only a fraction of the population of present day New York or London, their advantages on this score were more than cancelled out by their extremely crude systems of communication and transportation, and by the need, in Paris at least, for members of the assembly to devote the greater part of the day to brute toil. Yet Paris, no less than Athens, was administered by amateurs, by men who, for several years and in their spare time, saw to the administration of a city in a state of extraordinary revolutionary ferment. The principal means by which they made and sustained their revolution was the neighborhood public assembly. There is no evidence that these assemblies and the committees they produced were inefficient or technically incompetent. To the contrary: they awakened a popular initiative, a resoluteness in action, and a sense of revolutionary purpose that no professional bureaucracy, however radical its pretensions, could ever hope to achieve. Indeed, it is worth emphasizing that if Athens literally founded philosophy, mathematics, drama, historiography, and art, revolutionary Paris contributed more than its due to the culture of the time and, above all, to the political thought of the Western world. The arena for these achievements was not the traditional state, structured around a bureaucratic apparatus, but a system of unmediated political relations, of direct, face-to-face democracy organized into public assemblies.

The sections provide us with a rough model of assembly organizations in a large city during a period of revolutionary transition from a centralized political state to a potentially decentralized society. The Ecclesia provides us with a rough model of assembly organization in a completely decentralized society. The word "model" is used, here, advisedly. The Ecclesia and sections represent lived experience. But precisely because of this, they validate in practice many anarchic theoretical speculations that have often been dismissed as "visionary" and "unrealistic."

The goal of dissolving propertied society, class rule, centralization, and the state is as old as the emergence of property, classes and states. In the beginning, the rebels could look backward to clans, tribes, and federations; it was still a time when the past was closer at hand than the future. Then the past receded completely from man's vision and memory, except perhaps as a lingering dream of *"the* Golden Age," *"the* Garden of Eden." [3] At this point, the very notion of liberation became speculative or theoretical, and like all strictly theoretical visions, its content became permeated with the social material of the present. Hence the fact that even utopia, from More to Bellamy, is a heightened image not merely of a hypothetical future, but of a present drawn to the logical conclusion of rationality—or absurdity. It has slaves, kings, princes, oligarchs, technocrats, elites, scientist-godheads, suburbanites, and substantial petty bourgeois. Even on the left, it became customary to define the goal of a property-less, stateless society as a series of approximations, of stages in which the end in view was attained by a slow reworking of the institutions at hand. This approach did not exclude revolution. Marx relegated the end of the centralized state to a distant future. Concealed beneath Marx's demand that the proletariat must destroy the bourgeois state and replace it with one of its own was a demand, not for institutional dissolution, but for institutional appropriation. The revolutionists of 1917, by and large, followed this course—with disastrous results. Mediated power was preserved; worse, it was strengthened to the point where the state today is not merely the "executive committee" of a specific class, but a ubiquitous human condition. Life itself has become bureaucratized. Man has become a commodity—the product of a society reduced entirely to the status of a factory, a business office, a marketplace. Daily life has become a function of exchange value.

In envisioning the complete dissolution of the existing society, we cannot get away from the question of power—be it power over our own lives, the seizure of power, the dissolution of power. In going from the present to the future, from "here" to "there," we must ask: what is power? Under what conditions is it dissolved? And what, precisely, does its dissolution mean? In short: how do the forms of freedom, the unmediated relations of social life—assembly and community—emerge from a statist society.

We begin with the historical fact that nearly all the great revolutions started out spontaneously: the three days of disorder that preceded the takeover of the Bastille in July 1789, the defense of the artillery in Montmarte that led to the Paris Commune of 1871, the famous five days of February 1917 in Petrograd, the uprising of Barcelona in July 1936, the takeover of Budapest and expulsion of the Russian army in 1956.[4] "Revolution does not fall from the sky," declared a Trotskyist leader last December at a public debate, obviously meaning that it must be engineered presumably by his own party. This sort of pomposity ignores the fact that nearly all the great revolutions come from *below,* from the molecular movement of the masses, their progressive individuation, their explosion—an explosion which invariably takes the authoritarian "revolutionist" completely by surprise. Where popular ferment is denied its initiative and deprived of its own free movement toward self-administration revolution is debased into the Bolshevik-type *coup d'etat:* the "revolution" legislated by the Central Committee and decreed by the Politbureau. The old game of the past half-century is repeated. To rephrase the words of William Morris: Men fight and win the battle, and when their victory "turns out to be not what they mean . . . , other men have to fight for what they meant under another name."

The bitter experiences of the past half century have made it axiomatic that there can be no separation of the revolutionary process from the revolutionary goal. *A society based on self-administration must be achieved by means of self-administration.* This implies the forging of a self in the revolutionary process and a mode of administration which the self can possess.[5] If we define "power" as the domination of man over man, power can only be destroyed by the very process in which man acquires power over his own life and in which he not only discovers himself but, more meaningfully, formulates his selfhood in all its social dimensions.

Freedom, so conceived, cannot be delivered to the individual as the end-product of a "revolution" orchestrated by social philistines hypnotized by the trappings of authority and power. This means that the assembly and community cannot be legislated or decreed into existence. A revolutionary group can, purposively and consciously, seek to promote the creation of these forms; but if assembly and community are not allowed to emerge organically, if their growth is not only cultivated by revolutionists, but instigated, developed, and matured by the social processes at work, they will not emerge at all. Assembly and community, then, must arise from within the revolutionary process itself; indeed, the revolutionary process must *be* the formation of assembly and community and, with it, the destruction of power. Assembly and community must become "fighting words," not panaceas! They must be created as modes of struggle with the existing society, not bucolic retreats and refuges!

It is hardly possible to stress this point strongly enough. The future assembly of people in the block, the neighborhood, the district—the revolutionary sections to come—will stand on a higher social level than all the present-day committees, syndicates, parties and clubs adorned by the most resounding revolutionary titles. They will be the living nucleus of utopia in the decomposing body of bourgeois society. Meeting in auditoriums, theaters, courtyards, halls, parks and—like their forerunners, the sections of '93—in churches, they will be the popular assembly that the revolutionary process has demassified, the very *essence* of the revolutionary process, a people finally acting as individuals.

At this point, the assembly may be faced not only with the power of the bourgeois state but with the danger of the incipient state. Like the Parisian sections, it will have to fight against the ever-lasting committees which will surround it and proliferate like cancer cells. The assembly must become the universal solvent of institutions, cleansing away all the social flyshit—bureaus, councils, agencies, committees, directorates, boards, and above all, political parties—that impairs its initiative.[6] This is not to say that committees, councils, and boards are unnecessary as such, but whenever they are functionally soluble, they must be dissolved. They must be rooted completely in the assembly; they must be answerable at every point to the assembly; they and their work must be under continual review by the assembly; their members must be chosen, rotated, and replaced by the assembly (preferably, where possible, by lot); their meetings must be open to the assembly; their members must be subject to recall by the assembly. The specific gravity of society, in short, must be shifted to its base: *the armed people in permanent assembly!* [7]

As long as the arena of the assembly is the modern bourgeois city, to be sure, the revolution is located in a recalcitrant environment—one difficult to assimilate to an assembly-community. The bourgeois city, by its very nature and structure, fosters centralization, massification, and manipulation. Inorganic, gargantuan, organized by commercial forces as a grid of streets and avenues (rather than ecologically as an ecosystem), the city inhibits and obstructs organic, rounded community growth. In its role as the universal solvent, the assembly must now dissolve the city itself.

We can envision young people—society's germplasm, as it were—renewing social life as it renews the human species. Leaving the city, they begin to found the nuclear ecological communities to which increasingly older people repair. Large pools of resources are mobilized for their use; careful ecological surveys, guidelines, and suggestions are placed at their disposal by the most competent, talented, and imaginative people available. The modern city begins to shrivel, to contract, and to disappear, as did its ancient progenitors millenia earlier. In the new, rounded ecological community, the assembly finds its authentic environment and true shelter. Form and content now correspond completely. The journey from "here" to "there," from sections to Ecclesia, from cities to communities, is completed, certainly as far as men can see today. The revolutionary urban assemblies are essentially communities in their own right, but based on ecological communities, they become more rounded organisms. No longer is the factory a particularized phenomenon, but an organic part of the community. In this sense, it is no longer a factory. The dissolution of the factory into the community completes the dissolution of the last vestiges of propertied class, and above all, of mediated society into the new polis. And now the real drama of human life can unfold, in all its beauty, harmony, joy, creativity, and tragedy.

NOTES

[1] To class the bulk of the Communards as "proletarians," indeed to describe any social stratum as "proletarian" simply because it has no control over the conditions of its life, is to lump all oppressed classes—slaves, serfs, peasants, large sections of the middle class—under a single rubric. To do so and then to create sweeping antitheses between this so-called proletariat and bourgeoisie is to artificially eliminate all the determinations that characterize the various repressed classes as specific, socially limited strata. This giddy approach to social analysis divests the industrial proletariat and the bourgeoisie of all the historically unique features and contradictions which Marx believed he had discovered (a theoretical project that proved inadequate, although by no means false); it slithers away from the responsibilities of a serious critique of Marxism.

[2] This is not to ignore the disastrous political errors made by many Spanish anarchists—entry into the Republican government, concessions to the defunct Catalan state (the Generality) and to the Popular Front parties, and finally opposition to the May uprising in Barcelona. Although it must also be added that the anarchists were faced with the alternative of establishing a dictatorship in Catalonia, which they were not prepared to do (and rightly so!), this was no excuse for practicing opportunistic tactics all along the way. Ultimately, however, the fate of Barcelona and other areas committed to anarcho-syndicalism depended upon the ability of the CNT to rally all of Republican Spain behind its social demands. This the organization proved incapable of doing owing to the incompleteness of the social development in Spain itself.

[3] It was not until the 1860s, with the work of Bachofen and Morgan, that man rediscovered his communal past; but by that time the discovery had lost its reconstructive value and had become a purely critical weapon directed against the bourgeois family, property, etc.

[4] He might have also added that "money doesn't grow on trees." And when a young Digger burned several dollar bills before his nose as a repudiation of the commodity nexus, nearly all the Trotskyists in the audience, being "practical" men, were duly horrified; after all, it could have been used to print more election posters, election buttons, election stickers, or perhaps, keep the office going. There is nothing more repellant than a Poor Richard turned Bolshevik.

[5] For discussion of "selfhood" and revolution, see "Desire and Need" in ANARCHOS 1. What Wilhelm Reich and, later, Herbert Marcuse in *Eros and Civilization* have made clear is that "selfhood" is not only a domestic, a personal dimension but a social one. The self that finds expression in assembly and community is, literally, the assembly and community that has found self-expression—the complete congruence of form and content.

[6] Together with disseminating ideas, the most important job for anarchists will be to defend the spontaneity of the popular movement by continually engaging the authoritarians in a theoretical and organization duel.

[7] The use of rotating committees, councils, and boards provides us with guidelines for integrating the technical work of the assemblies, and later, of the future recentralized communities. There is no danger that unmediated relations will be replaced by mediated ones if such bodies are limited strictly to technical or advisory functions, if they are rotated as often as possible, rigorously mandated and circumscribed in their activities by the assemblies, open to thorough-going public scrutiny and to a regular accounting of their work, and above all, divested of all prerogatives in formulating policy. Rooted entirely locally in the assemblies (which alone formulate policy and administrative guidelines) and subject at any time to immediate recall, the committees, councils and boards can be used to work out practical details of regional and interregional coordination between assemblies and decentralized communities—details which, as in the Parisian sections, can be examined, approved, or modified by the assemblies.

Christian Bay's essay has important consequences for a full conception of participatory democracy. His thesis is that psychological freedom—the freedom to realize oneself as a human being—and social freedom—the freedom not to be coerced by others—are both essential if a society is to be truly free. He then illustrates how Western democracy's emphasis on social freedom to the exclusion of psychological freedom has resulted in an uncoerced, yet unfree society.

Psychological freedom requires a consensus on the nature of goals and values in terms of what is growth-promoting. But in an instrumentally oriented society, this consensus does not exist, so people are free to manipulate and be manipulated in a system whose goals are masked. In highly ideological and totalistic systems, which claim to know the truth about man, people are forced to be free and the coerciveness is clear. But the oppression of a one-sided emphasis on social freedom is more subtle, and it is this facet of our society that Bay explores.

It is just one more step to show that a system of participatory democracy can effectively combine the requirements of social and psychological freedom. Social involvement and commitment requires a sacrifice of what may be called individual freedom in the interests of an ultimately greater freedom. Psychological growth does not take place in a vacuum, but requires that people be able to unite in meaningful activity, out of which comes growth in the accomplishment of common tasks that are impossible for the isolated individual. The principle of social freedom recognizes the variety of social purposes that can result from such a coming together, but it remains abstract and empty when it fails to consider the ways by which people can manipulate and oppress each other without explicit coercion. For it to become concrete the conditions of psychological growth, which define psychological freedom, must also be present.

Participatory democracy makes social freedom concrete not in terms of an ideology that prescribes the outlines of human nature once and for all, but in terms of a process view. Democratic participation is the process whereby growth-promoting social purposes are continuously created, modified to meet new conditions, and renewed. In a fundamental way this kind of participatory process accords with human nature. The growth psychology developed by people like Abraham Maslow, Gordon Allport, and others has shown that growth occurs in a series of stages, each with its own set of goals. One-time ends become means as further ends come into view. Thus, rather than pre-defining the direction of growth, which is impossible, a free society defines structures that can assure the process. Participatory democracy, by seeking to create structures that involve people in decisions that affect their lives, can do that.

Freedom as a Tool of Oppression
Christian Bay

I

In his youthful essay on the "Origin of Inequality," Jean-Jacques Rousseau claimed that organized society is based on fraud and force, and he painted a rosy picture of the "noble savage." [1] By the time he wrote his *Social Contract,* however, he had come to believe that ultimately man would stand to gain from the bargain of exchanging the "natural freedom" of preliterates with the "civil freedom" of the state. But not until the General Will came to assert itself more forcefully, and prevail over the selfish and greedy particular wills which tend to predominate in any class-ridden society. Just how this transition was to be brought about, however, he left quite obscure.

Sometimes lack of clarity can be an advantage. Rousseau's vagueness on the nature of legitimate alternate forms of political organization and action, coupled with his humanistic eloquence, has inspired revolutionaries of many different kinds, and Rousseau must be given a share of the credit not only for the great French Revolution, but indirectly also for the great Marxist revolutions that followed much later.

Rousseau saw potential nobility in man, if and when he could be "forced to be free," as clearly as he saw man's actual corruptibility or even depravity when oppressed by need, fear, and anxiety. "Man is born free; and everywhere he is in chains," reads the first sentence of Chapter I of *The Social Contract.* I would paraphrase as follows: man has the potentials for becoming humane, but oppressive institutions and organizations keep him dehumanized, almost everywhere, almost all the time. For most of us, freedom remains the promise; oppression remains the fact.

Just how can we work effectively toward relieving institutional and organizational oppression? This was Rousseau's crucial concern; he posed the question but left it open. He inspired emotions and will more effectively than he stimulated hard thinking; there was in his work hardly any careful socio-psychological analysis. Of course, the conceptual tools and empirical findings of twentieth-century sociology and psychology were not available to him. Today we no longer have that excuse, and it is time to go back to the same basic questions: why is man everywhere in chains? Moreover, why does he serve his oppressors so willingly? [2]

The work of both Karl Marx and Sigmund Freud may be interpreted as theories of explanation of this existential predicament of man in chains, theories replacing the Christian theory about the curse of sin as the source of human misery. Marx saw the scarcity of resources as the basic problem, and the economic necessity of capitalist exploitation as the curse of his time, but looked forward to the liberation and humanization of man once capitalism had created enough industry to make itself obsolete. Freud saw our burdens of anxiety and guilt and resulting neuroses as the basic problem, with each spiritually crippled generation passing on its neurotic infirmities to the next one. Freud saw little hope of ultimate delivery from this chain of guilt, but many neo-Freudians are hopeful about the prospects for a more humane man, now that man has been delivered from sin, and can look to progress in psychological knowledge as a road to salvation from neurotic miseries.

I shall limit the explicit scope of this paper to a consideration of the uses of the term "freedom" as a means of political control. In the last part of my argument I attempt to assess the significance of this analysis in terms of the general perspective of the problem of man's oppressing man—himself and others—and of man's dream of delivery from oppression.

II

In *The Structure of Freedom*[3] I have at some length discussed three main conceptions of freedom, and have argued that these should be considered essential dimensions of freedom, in the sense that individual freedom should be considered deficient to the extent that there are deficienciss along any one of these three dimensions of freedom. For present purposes it will suffice to discuss two of these three conceptions, termed *psychological* and *social* freedom, respectively; the third (*potential* freedom) is not in common use and *ipso facto* has not been used as a means of social control. Only

toward the end of this paper will it be appropriate to introduce the third
conception as well.

Very briefly, I equate freedom in the total sense with self-expression.
"Psychological freedom" refers to the individual's capacity to recognize and
act upon (if appropriate,—but that is a different issue unless he compulsively is driven to act) his full range of basic motives. "Social freedom"
refers to the individual's opportunity to act or refrain from acting as he
desires.

Note that "psychological freedom" focuses on the nature of individual's
self; indeed "freedom" in this sense becomes entirely an intra-personal
concept. Psychological freedom is by definition impaired to the extent that
realistic self-insight is impaired; the common impediment is loosely termed
neurosis, or in more extreme cases psychosis.[4]

Empirically, the basis for attaining our individual levels of psychological
freedom is probably largely established in our early childhood. Theoretical
and practical psychologists from Freud to Benjamin Spock have alerted us
to the need for plenty of love and security if our children are to avoid
permanent impairments or scars of repressed anxieties, guilt, and hatreds,
which would keep them moving around in circles of self-defeating defensiveness and destructiveness as adults.

Social freedom does not raise the issue of the nature of the self, for the
term refers to the presence or absence of perceived obstacles to desired
individual action (or inaction). Animals as well as humans can be free or
unfree, to varying extents or degrees, in this sense, as long as it is observable what the individual animal or man wants to do. Obstacles can be physical as well as social, so long as the will persists and obstacles are perceived
as obstacles rather than seen as legitimate or necessary. Dr. Spock is psychologically but not socially free when and if he is put in jail for supporting
young men who refuse to fight in a war of aggression; the ex-Marine having
returned from Vietnam is socially but not psychologically free, if he must
glorify the military and hate pacifists all his life in order to live with his guilt
for having killed Vietnamese without any good moral justification.

Both conceptions of freedom make sense, empirically speaking. Yet most
thinkers have opted for either the one or the other conception of freedom;
either they have taken it for granted that "freedom" refers to something like
self-mastery or to something like opportunity of choice; or they have at best
attributed primary importance to the one and only secondary importance to
the other of these two most common approaches to freedom.

Plato exemplifies the one approach: "In the human soul there is a better and also a worse principle; and when the better has the worse under control, then a man is said to be master of himself; and this is a term of praise: but when, owing to evil education or association, the better principle is also the smaller, is overwhelmed by the greater mass of the worse—in this case he is blamed and is called the slave of self and unprincipled." [5]

Thomas Hobbes exemplifies the other approach: "Liberty, or Freedome, signifieth (properly) the absence of Opposition; (by Opposition, I mean external Impediments of motion;) A FREE-MAN is he, that in those things, which by his strength and wit he is able to do, is not hindered to do what he has a will to." [6]

The disinclination of modern writers, even students of concepts of freedom, to dissociate themselves from the usual tendency of choosing one approach or the other, is well illustrated in Isaiah Berlin's elegant essay "Two Concepts of Liberty." [7] Sir Isaiah discusses representative examples of "positive" and "negative" concepts of liberty—"positive liberty" corresponding to "psychological freedom" and "negative liberty" corresponding to "social freedom"—and concludes that the latter conception yields "a truer and more humane ideal" and must be preferred over the former. His chief argument against "positive liberty" (or psychological freedom) as an ideal, or against making its prevalence a criterion of the good society, is that self-mastery or self-realization in his view presupposes some authoritative standards to lay down which aspects of the self ought to prevail over other aspects, or by which criteria degrees of achievements in self-realization were to be judged; if we believe in the necessity of authoritative standards or criteria of liberty achieved, then we open the door for totalitarianism: "To preserve our absolute categories or ideals at the expense of human lives offends equally against the principles of science and of history; it is an attitude found in equal measure on the right and left wings in our days, and is not reconcilable with the principles of those who respect the facts." [8]

Readiness to resort to violence characterizes extremists at both ends of the political spectrum, Sir Isaiah believes, and the problem with many extremists is their belief in "absolute categories or ideals" by which they judge and set criteria for human behavior, instead of being willing to "respect the facts" and derive standards pragmatically from the ways people in fact behave. "To demand more than [the ideal of freedom to live as one wishes] is perhaps a deep and incurable need," he concludes; "but to allow it to guide one's practice is a symptom of an equally deep, and far more dangerous, moral and political immaturity." [9]

What Sir Isaiah fails to see that by extolling negative liberty (or social freedom) alone he in fact condemns revolutionary (and reactionary) violence while accepting the violence of the status quo. If "freedom to live as one wishes" is to take precedence over freedom to realize our humane potentialities then to serve the convenience of the privileged is just as legitimate as to serve the desperate need of the least privileged; and if Madison Avenue's techniques can make people wish to live like imbecile automatons or vegetables, so be it, in the name of liberty! "The triumph of despotism is to force the slaves to declare themselves free," Sir Isaiah quotes from somewhere; if instead of "force" the source had said "manipulate," would we not have a pretty good perspective on the average young American conscript on his way to defend "freedom" in far-away lands?[10]

Sir Isaiah's conception of liberty represents the end of the empiricist line; it fits a pragmatist pluralist credo, which condemns violence selectively: the trouble with absolute ideals is that they can make men ruthless is their desire to change things. So let's not have any absolute ideals, which could motivate men to interfere violently with the freedom to be left alone, he is in effect saying; and let's not face the fact that our established order rests on immense amounts of cruel, suppressive violence, by which the strong maintain and enlarge their privileges, at the expense of the elementary means of subsistence and dignity for the poor. Those who proclaim their commitment to social freedom and are unconcerned with psychological fulfillment are in fact, whether intentionally or not, supporters of the established order; concerns of social justice are at best a second-priority consideration; since no ideals can be absolute, presumably even the destruction of human lives is only a relative disadvantage.

On the other hand, it must also be said that those who are unconcerned with social freedom and perceive of "freedom" exclusively in terms of self-realization and the like—and here I agree with Sir Isaiah—are essentially totalitarians without respect for men such as they are, and without the capacity or inclination to doubt their own ideological analysis and forecasts; they are neither open to facts nor to humane sympathies that might come in the way of ideologically derived expectations. To pluralist liberals and conservatives, then, "freedom" enshrines the established liberties to do as one wishes, whether rich or poor, snob or slob, benevolent or malevolent, responsible or irresponsible and so on. To the doctrinaire utopians, on the other hand—i.e. those who have accepted uncritically the whole cloth of ideologies explaining social evils and how to do away with them—"freedom" enshrines a hypothetical future state, and the will to bring it about, while tending to reject whatever humane and civilized achievements even a sick society may have accumulated.

At this point I hope to have established (1) that there are at least two sharply different, both influential approaches to defining "freedom"; (2) that the choice of either one of these two conceptions of freedom to the exclusion of the other one has important political implications; and (3) that those political implications in both cases are destructive, in that a commitment exclusively to social freedom tends to enshrine the status quo and legitimize institutionalized violence, while a commitment exclusively to something akin to psychological freedom tends to enshrine a hypothetical ideal society of the future, and to legitimize revolutionary violence which may or may not bring that ideal society nearer.

It would seem evident that some kind of combination of the two conceptions of freedom has to be attempted. I shall come to that later. But first let us consider more generally how symbolic terms like "freedom" in fact are utilized by men and groups with power, or seeking power.

III

Every stable social order has found ways to effectively inculcate most young people in values, or in respect for symbols, which affirm the legitimacy of the established order. The achievement of social stability demonstrates, at the very least, that not any great number of citizens, young or old, are committed to values or symbols sharply in conflict with assumptions rationalizing the status quo.

A stable communist-governed society, such as the Soviet Union, has induced many of its citizens to think politically, albeit within the framework of Marxist-Leninist assumptions. A stable pluralist society, such as the United States, appears to have discouraged political thinking in any universalistic sense, but has achieved a very wide acceptance of symbols associated with the etablished systems—including the Constitution, the flag, "freedom," "democracy," "God," and so on. More strictly speaking, what has been achieved is a very wide acceptance of a close association between highly attractive symbols and the established order. In this connection the term "freedom" is a symbol with political influence in the same way that the flag is.

Patriotic symbols in stable societies always serve at least two basically disparate functions: (1) they encourage loyalty and support to common interests, against potential enemies and indeed against potential dangers of any kind; and (2) they discourage criticism of the established distribution of power and privileges. Sociologically speaking, the duality exists in every social institution, even though the mix is sure to differ from one to another, and from one time to another: every institution works to some extent, perhaps infinitesimal, in the whole public's interest, and to some extent in the interest of privileged minorities. When political socialization is effective, and social stability is high, it is in part because many people have come to believe that institutions and patriotic symbols are serving their own, their group's, or the whole public's interest, rather than the interest of a few privileged groups only.

Now, every stable society is top-heavy in the sense that privileges and power are unevenly distributed. Without political society presumably the physically stronger would help themselves at the expense of the weaker, as is the rule in the animal kingdom.[11] In a political society physical prowess recedes in importance, compared to intelligence and a variety of other attributes—perhaps including ruthlessness, cunning, experience and, of course, power of parents and relatives. Every stable political society on record is stratified, with the bulk of power and privileges concentrated in relatively few families or groups; in tribal as well as modern Western societies the heads of the favored families usually have most of the power. In communist-governed societies the family has to some extent been replaced by the organizational committee as a conveyor belt for informal power, and the misery of the least privileged appears to be much less extreme than in our pluralist societies. But, for all the myths of communism or of democracy, no wide distribution of power or privilege has been achieved in any specimen of either kind of social order, up to and including the present time.

Man is the only animal equipped with a sense of justice, Aristotle wrote. And the ideal of equality appears to be natural and unextinguishable. Children appear to adopt equality as a principle of fairness quite spontaneously, at least in the Western world. After the overthrow of the feudal order based on Divine Right, except for the aberrations of right-wing dictatorships, the principle of political equality has been accepted by pluralist and socialist societies alike. In principle the people is sovereign; the state exists for their sake rather than vice versa; and only assumptions about approval by either the popular will or the majority's will can give legitimacy to government policies. Pluralist societies tend to stress immediate approval, demonstrated in elections or even in opinion-poll data, while communists in power tend to stress eventual approval by a people liberated from the mental shackles of capitalism's false consciousness; both societies accept the premises that men are equal and that the welfare of all, on the basis of justice, is the proper first-priority concern of the government. And both kinds of government have an equal stake in making most citizens believe that their governments are busily promoting freedom and justice, while in fact they are busily promoting *also,* at best (and *instead,* at worst) their own power; their power to serve the whole people, possibly, but also their power to serve their own organizational and other interests, most certainly.

It is a commonplace observation today in organizational sociology that every sizeable organization tends to develop conflicts of interest between leaders and rank-and-file. Even the most benevolent leaders have, for one thing, a vested interest in controlling the dissemination of information about their own and the organization's problems and activities. The larger the organization, the greater the built-in conflict of interest tends to become, no matter how important the interests that still unite leaders and members of each organization. But the greater the built-in conflict, the greater the incentive on the part of the leadership to distort information, raise phony issues, appeal to shared emotions, etc., for the purpose of reducing the influence of articulate critics and potential challengers.

Every state is, of course, a very large organization, and every government has particularly strong incentives to mislead the public in order to cement its power against all challengers. And every modern government has a formidable array of powerful symbols which can be used in its own defense. Normally it can mobilize the emotionally compelling symbols of nationalism and patriotism; also, it can explicitly or implicitly brand its most formidable critics with the corollary negative symbols of treason, subversion, and the like.

Moreover, the government normally has very powerful allies, in every stable society. For precisely those other elements of the citizenry who are blessed with power and privilege tend to be the most militantly conservative, since from their perspective it is indeed a worthwhile social order, worth defending against the have-nots; and they share with their government an incentive to explain poverty and other misfortunes in terms of the failings of the poor, or the poor quality of human nature (in other people), rather in terms of imperfections in the social system.

In short, every stratified political society tends to be dominated by a *de facto* alliance between the major privileged strata, one of which is composed of the men in and around the government. No matter how democratic and egalitarian and humanistic the professed objectives of governmental policies, this alliance is likely to be at work, and the empirically oriented political scientist who would understand what goes on ought to study the means by which this alliance maintains its power.

One of the many kinds of symbols utilized in defending the *status quo*—any nation's established system of privileges—is the word "freedom." Let us now focus on the political functions of this term and symbol in the modern world, and especially here in North America.

IV

A "persuasive" definition is one which gives a new conceptual meaning to a familiar word without substantially changing its emotive meaning, and which is used with the conscious or unconscious purposes of changing, by this means, the direction of people's interests.
—*Charles F. Stevenson.*[12]

The trouble with this definition of a useful term coined by Stevenson, is that it appears to imply that familiar words ordinarily have a given cognitive meaning, which is distorted when a persuader comes along and wishes to capitalize on the emotive association of certain words. Actually, most emotion-laden words serve as instruments for directing people's beliefs about their interests. Conventions about the uses of words develop informally, and periodically become recorded in dictionaries; like all other institutions, such conventions serve a duality of functions: (1) the public or group interest in facilitating clear communication, and (2) the private vested interest in producing pliable, accepting individuals. Now, many words have no political importance and hardly any emotive content, and in such cases definitions serve almost exclusively the former function. At the other extreme, however, words like "freedom" and "democracy" are normally used in ways that serve mainly the second function: they communicate emotions rather than cognitive clarity, and are commonly defined so as to convey the kinds of emotions that discourage radical criticism of established institutions. Ostensibly all definitions serve to promote clear communication; they could not be persuasive in Stevenson's sense if or to the extent that people were made aware of this purpose. In fact a great many key terms in political argument most often serve to obfuscate rather than clarify communication of cognitive content. Let us see how this applies to usages of the term "freedom," after first taking a moment to try to improve on Stevenson's definition:

"Definitions" are here called persuasive to the extent that they serve to convey emotive attitudes or commitments of one kind or another—as distinct from the purely cognitive functions of definitions.[13] Many common terms in the political dialogue are highly persuasive and of limited cognitive utility; in my view the political philosopher ought to study and evaluate the persuasive as well as the cognitive functions of these terms, and for his own purposes (that is, for the sake of improving academic dialogues about politics, and ultimately the general political dialogues) he should seek more effective ways of communicating cognitive clarity within conceptual spaces now poorly served in this respect. This can sometimes be accomplished by introducing technical terms, and at other times by seeking to rescue familiar terms for cognitive utility, at least in certain contexts.

The banner of "freedom" has been used by every kind of political cause in modern history. Ever since men ceased to be looked upon, and to look upon themselves, as mere chattels for their kings or chieftains; ever since popular opinions became politically important, rulers and rebel leaders alike have used "freedom" as a rallying cry. In the modern age of nationalism "freedom" frequently has been used to refer to deliverance from foreign rulers, but it could also be a matter of freedom from class exploitation, freedom from subversion, freedom from tyranny or from parties allegedly aiming at tyranny, and so on. Fascists and communists, Jesuits and anarchists, militarists and pacifists, chauvinists and internationalists—all have claimed to represent the cause of freedom. "Give me liberty or give me death"—ringing statements like this express noble sentiments and inspire colossal sacrifice; but if "liberty" should happen to be defined in ways to suit the selfish interests of ruling classes or cliques, who for reasons of their own have managed to induce thousands to sacrifice their lives for poorly understood aims—like liberty—then it is indeed possible that liberty at times can be a powerful instrument of oppression. Revolutionary leaders, too, can play the same game, with as few scruples.[14]

Now, Isaiah Berlin extols, as we have seen, "the ideal of freedom to live as one wishes." In most of the Western countries today, this seems only a commonsense usage of "freedom." Even to question it may at first appear absurd. Yet I shall argue that there are at least three radical flaws in this definition, which even commonsense will reveal, on closer scrutiny: (1) In an oligarchical society—and every state so far has been governed by oligarchies; in the West, the difference is that the visible political oligarchy hides the less visible and even less accountable economic oligarchy—what "one wishes" is largely determined by the interests of the oligarchies, as promoted in the schools and the other media of mass communication. (2) In the absence of any reference to the development of an independent self as the seat of freedom, "freedom" becomes a matter of wishing to accept and to adjust to established institutions; the wish to conform and to forget about justice and the plight of others becomes as valued, in the name of "freedom," as the wish to be a moral and political individual. (3) The particular aspects of "freedom" that predominate in Anglo-Saxon schools and other mass media are precisely those that suit the rich and the articulate: free enterprise and free expression in politics.

Take for a contrast Felix Greene's interpretation of the understanding of "freedom" in today's China: "A Chinese uses the word 'freedom' in a very personal, down-to-earth sense. He is not talking about abstractions, but about experience. He means that he is at last free to eat, and not to starve; he is free of the landlord and the money-lender. He is free to learn to read and write, he is free to develop skills that would otherwise have remained hidden; he is free to send his children to school, and when they are ill, there is a doctor to help make them well; he is free to look at the future with hope, not despair. For him, these are all new freedoms." [15]

To the well-socialized North American, this may well seem a perverse usage of "freedom"; while food and medical care are good things, they are not "freedom." But why not? Does it even cognitively make sense to consider a person politically "free" if he is starving, or worries all his waking hours about how to feed his family tomorrow or the next day?

Communism conquers the poor countries, writes a San Francisco journalist, "by abrogating all political and individual freedom (which means little to a starving man) and replacing it with food, housing, medical care, schools, and technical training. It strikes a bargain that the peasants and workers are only too glad to pay—for the 'freedom' they have given up is one they have never been allowed to exercise." [16]

The other side of the coin, less visible to conventional North Americans, is that the "free world"—the capitalist, pluralist ideology of "democracy"—has conquered most minds within its domain. By abrogating all the elementary freedoms (required by the body and the mind as a basis for human dignity and individuality) and replacing them with the rights to invest, to choose between Pepsi Cola and Coca Cola, to choose between political parties, newspapers, and magazines. This strikes a bargain that middle-class North Americans—indeed, poor ones, too—have come to take for granted, because by definition they are free men in a free country, no matter how debt-ridden or actually starving they may be. Worse still, such mis-

fortunes are seen as their own fault, to the extent that the prevailing North
American conception has been digested *in toto*.

The general usage of "freedom" in the sense of absence is coercion, without any reference to humane or rational ideals, is serviceable for maintaining oligarchical rule not only by way of leaving wide open the opportunity
for mass indoctrination toward the conformity of accepting established institutions and conventions; also, "freedom" in the North American idiom
almost explicitly suggests priority for (1) the freedoms preferred by the
privileged and (2) freedoms that are relatively tangential to the physical and
emotional welfare of human beings.

Free enterprise and free speech are liberties peculiarly valued, respectively, by men of wealth and by many professionals, notably including lawyers and professors. Those who are wealthy naturally tend to think that the
most important freedom is the right to protect and expand their wealth, and
their influence tends to prevail over the contrary views of the spokesmen of
the less privileged, who will argue that public-welfare aims ought to take
precedence over what suits private privileged interests. The outcome of this
unequal but perennial contest between conflicting interests is not only legislation that favors the rich; not only an all-pervasive legal and political culture that emphasizes obedience to the "rule of law" and respect for private
(and corporate) property over any conflicting dictates of morality and justice; but also a set of semantical conventions that blunt the political consciousness of the underprivileged. Leaving aside the culturally acquired
propensity of the victims of our economic system to blame themselves for
their misfortunes, steeped as they have become in the free-enterprise and
equal-opportunity ideology, they suffer the additional handicap that the
very word "freedom" is assumed to "mean" free enterprise, so that it is
difficult even for the economically desperate, as a prisoner of the accepted
semantics of "freedom," to feel morally justified in attacking the system
that stymies their lives. Who dares even to think of himself as an opponent
of "freedom"? [17]

Now, a number of North American liberals have been articulate enough
and bold enough to do just that, nevertheless; but they have established
another semantical barrier to any attack on *their* vested interest in "freedom": a free society requires a wide freedom of political speech, and any
position has an equal right to be defended by whomever has the inclination
and financial means to do so, excepting only views which by liberals are
perceived to aim at eventually limiting the freedom of speech. On this last

ground many liberals and democratic socialists have worked to restrict the freedom to defend communist views; as communists were held to harbor plans to destroy free speech for other groups, these particular libertarians thought it appropriate to emulate that expected intolerance for their own ends. Consequently they advocated, and with some success in the days of the Cold War and of McCarthyism, a freeze on communist propaganda and a ban on the employment of communists in many lines of work, including even the academic teaching profession.[18] This reduced significantly the political force of a wide range of radical ideas, and articulate but cautious liberal intellectuals were free to participate in interminable political debates which were antiseptically protected against most ideas that could have stimulated pressures for radical changes in the social order.

The men of wealth and the academically trained professionals, notably lawyers and (at least in very recent times, with the increasing awareness of the economic importance of knowledge, and of men of knowledge) professors have between them seen that "freedom" primarily has come to be associated with what they value—that is, respectively, Herbert Hoover's and John Stuart Mill's favored liberties. Thus the "freedom" message of the "free world" has tended to become roughly two thirds Hoover and one third Mill. "Freedom" in this sense is of course quite irrelevant to the human needs of Vietnamese peasants, to slum-dwellers in Rio or indeed to the underprivileged the world over. "Free world freedom" raises the spectre of liberties of practical concern mainly to the tiny upper crust of the world's population.

And even in relation to *their* lives these conceptions of freedom would be rather tangential, were it not for their anxieties or guilt about their privileges. In a highly competitive society men of wealth often become fixated on economic matters to the extent of remaining otherwise underdeveloped human beings. The more the struggle of businessmen is rationalized in terms of perceiving the world as a jungle, the greater their anxieties about the greed of others and the greater the reinforcement of their own less humane, less attractive characteristics. And life among professors and lawyers is often not much more humane and civilized; in universities, the struggle for status and promotions can be equally suppressive for the need to be human, and to enjoy life, with emphasis on creative and emotionally rewarding activities.

It would be an exaggeration to claim that free speech is tangential to the welfare of most professionals, such as we have come to view ourselves. Perhaps it would be saying too much, also, to argue that free enterprise is tangential to the welfare of businessmen, who may have lost the capacity to really involve themselves in anything but their usual work. My claim is only that other freedoms are far more basic for human well-being, in an existential sense: security in enjoying sustenance, self-esteem, affection, self-knowledge, appreciation of beauty, etc., are elements of human well-being of deeper and more lasting significance than the freedom either to invest surplus money or to choose among political parties and newspapers, or even among political ideologies perhaps. If confronted with a forced choice, after all, almost every businessman, lawyer or professor would place the well-being of his family ahead of satisfactions in his work. No doubt, many a member of either of these professions would in the abstract defend the priorities implied in the conventional usage of "freedom," but it is just possible that this kind of a stance might indicate a lack of reflective self-insight on their part, or even a trained incapacity to live as whole human beings, rather than the superior wisdom of experienced or well-trained minds.

V

My concern in this paper is not to debunk a conventional ideology that extols "freedom" in the abstract; I am not attempting to expose frauds or conspiracies; my concern is that we become more sensitive to certain sociological facts of life—above all the fact that emotively rich words like "freedom" are usually powerful political weapons. Everybody is aware of the power of such terms, when they can be conquered for use in rebellions and revolutions. But their power in cementing the oppressiveness of established institutions is far less frequently realized; indeed, to many a reader (or non-reader, perhaps more so) the title of this paper may at first seem quite paradoxical, if not a self-contradiction.

I trust a case has been made in support of the view that "freedom" is, indeed, one of the effective tools of oppression in our stable Western societies today; and perhaps in all stable societies in our time, though the argument has largely been confined to our Western world. It remains to consider what, if anything, can be done to reduce the utility of this term for oppressive purposes, and to increase its liberating potentials.

(1) Such insight as has been developed into the political uses of such terms is a prerequisite to beginning to cope with the problem. Suppose that significant numbers of people began to refuse to support, let alone fight or even kill or die for, "freedom," until it became clear whose freedom and

what kinds of liberties were involved; such a development most certainly would take much of the power to oppress out of the term.

When Mississippi Negroes cry "freedom now," quite clearly this is a cause almost totally different from the cause of "freedom" in Vietnam. In one case it is a question of bread and elementary dignities for the down-trodden; in the other it is a question of protecting American middle-class liberties for a privileged few against the demands of the downtrodden for the elementary freedoms and dignities that they crave.

(2) But what is to be said to the critic who might object that as a North American he quite naturally favors the traditional North American liber-ties, the liberties preferred by his own kind of people. One could retort that it is immoral to side with the privileged against the underprivileged, or that it is unrealistic in the sense that revolutionary bloodbaths are bound to come, sooner or later, if deepening oppression makes growing numbers in-creasingly desperate.

While I would support both lines of argument, my principal reliance would be on a third tack: only by impoverishing one's self can one come to support privileged liberties against elementary liberties. A fixation on free enterprise and the system upholding it bars one from real human contact with persons of different life experience; it makes one fear people who are different instead of becoming enriched by adding their sensitivity and knowledge to one's own. To limit one's understanding of "freedom" to free speech and other accustomed civil liberties bars one from understanding the humane concerns of communists and other radicals, and stimulates many kinds of vaguely paranoid or otherwise mentally crippling anxieties, for ex-ample anxieties about imagined evil propensities in men who ought to be considered well intentioned, whether misguided or not.

This is one aspect of the price that must be paid, in terms of human impoverishment, in any society that equals "freedom" with "the opportu-nity to do as one wishes," regardless of the individual's psychological free-dom or lack of it. It is urgent that we grasp the extent to which, in our mass-media-technology society, our wishes may reflect not our real, inner needs but the uses that the powerful wish to make of us, as consumers, producers, citizens, etc. "The range of choice open to the individual is not the decisive factor in determining human freedom," writes Herbert Marcuse, "but *what* can be chosen and what *is* chosen by the individual." [19] And Kenneth Kenis-ton has in effect argued that the success of American capitalism in building the world's most powerful industrial establishment has exacted a heavy toll in terms of psychological freedom. One chapter in one of his recent books is called "The Dictatorship of the Ego"; he shows that individual reputation and success have too often required strict suppression of impulse and emotions; and we have achieved "a society that too often discourages human wholeness and integrity, too frequently divides men from the best parts of themselves, too rarely provides objects ['objectives' might have been a better word here] worthy of commitment." [20]

In short, the freedom of the mind requires not only the absence of jail-bars and the shackles of poverty but spontaneity of impulse and sympathies, with consequent openness to the ideas and cravings of all kinds of people. We cannot indefinitely continue to constrict our Western horizon by maintaining a concept of freedom that relates to the wants and demands of a small upper crust of nations and individuals, if we want to stay in touch with the rest of the world, or indeed with our own human potentialities. We need, therefore, a radically new approach to citizenship training, which seeks to develop a breed that cares more for justice than for civil obedience.[21]

(3) In *The Structure of Freedom* I have suggested not two but three component conceptions of freedom. For the sake of more effectively challenging the usual restrictive usage, it is well to emphasize *potential* freedom as well as psychological and social freedom. A full expression of a person's self—my most general synonym for "freedom"—requires "the *capacity,* the *opportunity,* and the *incentive* to give expression to what is in him and to develop his potentialities." [22]

An enlightened approach to child-rearing, practiced by relatively non-neurotic parents, can lay the groundwork for high levels of psychological freedom in the new generation; and relative affluence with good welfare legislation and enlightened law enforcement can establish high levels of social freedom; but such achievements in liberty are not incompatible with an essentially totalitarian society in which dissent suffers ridicule and minds become conditioned to taking only one political ideology and only one style of life for granted. It is possible, in other words, to feel free while in fact being unfree in the sense that human potentialities are left systematically stymied.

Every older generation tries to limit the potential freedom of the younger one; quite naturally, we tend to want our children to behave like ourselves, or at the very least to accept the country and the social system that we believe in. Since almost every child feels indebted, consciously or unconsciously, to his parents or teachers, as well as dependent on them in many ways, chances are that they will acquire many of the values that suit their parents and the requirements of their world, and only belatedly, if at all, re-adjust their sights to the requirements of their own developing selves and of their fast-changing world.

There is no such thing, of course, as complete freedom. But, relatively speaking, freedom in the full sense requires, I conclude, not only freedom from coercion (by men, roles, traditions, organizations, or circumstances perceived as oppressive); not only freedom from crippling anxieties, fears, guilt and neurosis; but also freedom in the sense of enlightenment about oneself and one's world, about history, about competing ideas, ideals and styles of life, and so on. Enlightened child-rearing, counseling and good mental health services are required for the achievements of high levels of psychological freedom; democratic institutions and above all human rights, including economic rights as well as civil rights and liberties, are prerequisites for high levels of social freedom; and schools and universities that provide stimulating, unfettered intellectual communities are necessary for the achievement of potential freedom.

Any praise of "freedom" in a sense that implies something less than this full range of aspirations should be met with our utmost skepticism. Unless we adopt this critical attitude, chances are that we, too, are reduced to instruments of other people's exclusive liberties, at our expense, or at the expense of people less privileged than ourselves.

"Men are free to make history," writes C. Wright Mills, "but some men are much freer than others"—on account of differences in access to power or influence, for one thing. Mills believed that intellectuals, particularly students of society, have particular opportunities and therefore special responsibilities to be shapers of history rather than merely observers of events. "I am contending that if men do not make history, they tend increasingly to become the utensils of history-makers and also the mere objects of history-making." [23]

Let us in conclusion consider Rousseau's famous statement once more: "Man is born free; and everywhere he is in chains." There is no way to remove all our chains at once. But if we at least are able and willing to *see* the chains, through the fogs of obfuscation with which every social (political or economic) establishment seeks to protect its power and other privileges, it is possible to go to work on breaking some of the chains, for ourselves and for others. Living in one part of the world that is overprivileged with resources and bent on defending our privileges by military means, we could do worse as a beginning than challenge the free-world rhetoric with which North Americans have become accustomed to feel righteous about our crucial part in perpetuating a monstrously unjust world. Our massive economic power could set men free everywhere; yet in the name of our perverse concept of freedom our rulers keep men in chains, victimized by illness, starvation, and brute military oppression. Our shame and opportunity lie in the fact that the heaviest chains in our time are made in North America, and chiefly for export.

Let us use our freedom of speech, to the extent that we have the capacity and the opportunity, to fight for more basic freedoms, and first of all for the freedom to breathe and to grow up as human beings, even and indeed especially in the least privileged parts of our modern world. Let us if necessary resort to violent confrontations with the perpetrators of institutional violence. But let us never forget, in our quest for Rousseau's utopian "civil freedom," that nonviolence is the key to civility: to the humane man physical violence, institutional or deliberate, is the supreme evil. The only legitimate objective of political society—and of the bargain that Rousseau saw in exchanging "natural freedom" for an eventual "civil freedom"—is the reduction and prevention of man's oppression by man, and above all, of physical violence.

NOTES

[1] I am grateful to my friend James Sattler for his critical reading of the first draft of this essay.

[2] Oppressors may be people or circumstances, traditions or innovations. Poverty, for example, may be an oppressor; and one serves this oppressor by accepting the established order or its symbols. The oppressors, to the extent that they are people rather than circumstances, made themselves be opposed by people or by circumstances (economic, social, political and psychological).

[3] New York: Atheneum, 1965 (1958), *passim.*

[4] It is conceptually possible that the self is underdeveloped, or impoverished, but the working hypothesis should be that every self includes conscious and unconscious components, and that while the most basic common human drives may be hidden deep in the unconscious they are not entirely missing, except possibly in physically brain-damaged or otherwise seriously injured persons. It would lead too far here to discuss ways of defining "the self." For present purposes, the term refers to any stable sense of identity and will that determines, consciously and unconsciously, individual social behavior.

[5] *The Republic,* Jowett translation, Book IV 431 (New York: Modern Library, n.d.), pp. 144–45.

[6] *Leviathan* (London: Everyman's Library, 1914 [1651]), p. 110.

7 Oxford: Oxford University Press, 1958.

8 *Ibid.*, p. 56.

9 *Ibid.*, p. 57.

10 *Ibid.*, p. 50.

11 And also in certain human groups which exist on a very primitive level. Among the Sirionos of Bolivia, for example, wives would gravitate to the households of the better hunters. See Allen R. Holmberg, *Nomads of the Long Bow* (Washington: Smithsonian Institution, 1950).

12 Cf. Charles L. Stevenson, *Facts and Values* (New Haven: Yale University Press, 1964 [1963]), p. 32. See also his *Ethics and Language* (New Haven: Yale University Press, 1944).

13 A definition may be formulated explicitly, or be implied in the manner in which a word is actually used. Frequently, alas, an author will define a word in one way and then proceed to use the word in quite a different way, or ways.

14 The word "revolutionary" can of course serve the same uses: witness the many "revolutionary" parties in Latin America which in fact have been bent on upholding the interests of the rich.

15 Cf. *The Wall Has Two Sides*.

16 Sydney J. Harris, "The Levels of Freedom," *San Francisco Examiner,* April 27, 1965.

17 Thurman Arnold gives an instructive example of a sheep-rancher in the United States who during the 1930s had fallen upon hard times, to the extent that his bank kept him operating his ranch under conditions of virtual servitude; even his own grocery bills had to be supervised. His chief worry as a citizen, however, "was that the Government was tending to interfere with the liberty of individuals." Cf. his *The Symbols of Government* (New York: Harcourt, Brace & World, 1962 [1935]), pp. 255–56.

18 See especially Sidney Hook, *Heresy, Yes—Conspiracy, No* (New York: John Day, 1953); and his *Political Power and Personal Freedom* (New York: Criterion Books, 1959).

19 Cf. his *One-Dimensional Man* (Boston: Beacon Press, 1964), p. 7.

20 Cf. Keniston, *The Uncommitted: Alienated Youth in American Society* (New York: Harcourt, Brace & World, 1965), p. 424. The ideal of political pluralism "has most often meant the toleration of political faction, not the encouragement of the full diversity of human talents. . . . All too often, the 'tolerance' of Americans is a thin veneer over the discomfort created by all that is different, strange and alien to them. . . . Those who are inwardly torn, unsure of their psychic coherence and fearful of inner fragmentation, are naturally distrustful of all that is alien and strange." *Ibid.*, pp. 442–43.

21 Cf. above, note 19.

22 *Op. cit.*, p. 15.

23 Cf. his *The Sociological Imagination* (New York: Grove Press, 1961 [1959]), p. 181.

Martin Oppenheimer reminds us of the elements in the history of socialism that agitated for direct democracy and examines the ideological history out of which this trend emerged. He sees the New Left demand for participatory democracy as the latest manifestation of this trend. He also appraises the counter-arguments of those in the past who believed that bureaucratic deformation of democracy under all foreseeable circumstances was inevitable.

Oppenheimer deals, also, with those tendencies in socialism that blind its advocates into accepting all sorts of superstructural contradictions instead of extending socialism through direct democracy. Indeed, the dilemma between socialist form and socialist content has not yet been worked out. The essay points out that the faiiure of the New Left, until recently, to grapple with the theory and history of socialism threatens to destroy its ability to deal with oncoming problems with any degree of realism.

The essay traces the development of the notion of participatory democracy from its early New Left days and relates it to such experiments as Carl Rogers' and the T-group. Although he does not do so here, Oppenheimer has warned us elsewhere[1] against modern management theories of group organization and group sensitivity training, which cant praises to "participation" without reference to the economic base. Today participation is too often used as a substitute for, rather than as a means of, control in dealing with workers and with the poor. It must be understood that participatory democracy does not mean participating in power held basically by others.

For Oppenheimer, the role of participatory democracy is a limited one, since ultimately he sees all organization as oligarchic. He is right in pointing out that groups do not become democratic overnight, and that it takes time to learn democratic group process. But bureaucracy need not be the necessary form that organizations take; they too can be based on groups or variants such as task forces. And if they are, thus, able to avoid bureaucracy, it is difficult to see why they cannot avoid oligarchy as well.

[1] "The Participative Techniques of Social Integration," *Our Generation,* Vol. 6, No. 3.

The Limitations of Socialism: Some Sociological Observations on Participatory Democracy
Martin Oppenheimer

I

The history of industrialized, urbanized society is the history of man's increasing alienation from decision-making processes. As society has moved from village life to city, from closely-integrated primary groups in which one's relationship to all aspects of life was well-understood and well-regulated, to a life in which individuals are no longer the captives of tradition, freedom has become possible. Yet freedom from tradition has not become freedom to decide the course of one's life, because modern life is organized, bureaucratic, increasingly centralized. The institutions which have freed Western Man from "the idiocy of rural life" have at the same time subjected him to organizational structures farther and farther removed from his immediate control. The factory, the school, government, religion, the media and even the arts are more and more subject to bureaucratic processes, and less and less open to communication from, much less control by, those who work in them and are subject to them, except on the highest levels of the "power structure." But man's history of increasing separation from decisions over his personal destiny is accompanied by his history of struggle to become free to make his decisions; today's New Left student movement is only the latest form of that continuous struggle. Participatory democracy is therefore part of a long series of radical concepts. Some, like soviets and workers' councils, were developed consciously as part of a movement of the left; others, like client-centered therapy or student-centered teaching, were developed by bourgeois theoreticians in one way or another unconsciously faithful to the essence of radical democracy.

In this paper I want to examine the historical antecedents, nature, and problems of "participatory democracy" as a movement within the mainstream of the tradition of "socialism from below," or radical democracy. I also want to examine the challenge of participatory democracy to the tradition of those who see democracy as inevitably doomed due to something called the "iron law of oligarchy." For while mankind has persistently struggled to free itself, the limitations of such struggles must be confronted as we review the dismal defeats of socialist revolution in the Soviet Union, in the developing nations, and in other elitist societies. This paper will try to counterpose this "inevitablist" theoretical trend to that of the "alternativists," those who hold that 1984 is only one, but not the only, road to the future.

II

It seems to me that participatory democracy is the essence of socialism. It is true that various elite socialisms are dominant in the development of the left, particularly in the form of that two-headed coin called statism whether called social democracy or Stalinism. But it is the socialism-from-below of such figures as Babeuf, Marx, Luxemburg, and Debs, and of the Paris Commune and the Soviets of 1905, 1917, and 1956 that is the ideological father of the New Left. Yet no socialism-from-below has succeeded in maintaining itself in social power.

One reason for the weakness of participatory democracy, and for the failures of earlier radicalisms has been an ignorance of the forces that tend to undermine democracy, forces that many believe inhere in the very fact of organization. Above all, a simplistic either-or view of the future (either capitalism or socialism) blinded socialists to the dangers of bureaucracy as an independent force which could itself rule as a third alternative. It was the "Russian Question" that clarified this issue for many radicals, but long before 1917 a school had arisen which believed that although socialism was good on paper, these ideals could never be achieved in practice. For a variety of reasons having to do with the nature of organization as such, and involving an analysis of the relationship between leaders and followers, this school held oligarchy to be the inevitable characteristic of all political systems. The names of these "iron lawyers" are now familiar: Pareto, Mosca, Michels, and Max Weber. Even in socialist society, Mosca said, there would be those who manage the public wealth and the great mass who are managed; Michels, in his monumental work on the German social-democracy, *Political Parties,* showed how an idealistically oriented party became subverted by the very processes intended to bring it to its goal; Weber's main question in later life was this: ". . . what can we oppose to this (bureaucratic) machinery in order to keep a portion of mankind free from this parcelling-out of the soul, from this supreme mastery of the bureaucratic way of life."

It may be true that the leaders of anarchism were elitists, but I would maintain that anarchism, too, contributed to a recognition of the forces tending to undermine democracy in the society of the future. It was not organization as such which disturbed the anarchists, but government; nevertheless it was precisely that concentration of all decisions in the hands of the bureaucratic state which the iron lawyers saw as inevitable that the anarchists also feared. And in a certain sense, because participatory democracy is decentralist in its objectives, it is anarchist in its tradition.

To summarize the sociological arguments of both the iron lawyers and the anarchists, then, arguments which basically were augmented and strengthened in the debates which raged later on the "Russian Question," the following rules seem to apply:

(1) Centralization of decision-making, and in terms of both organization and personnel, tends to lead to oligarchy, regardless of the democratic intentions of the personnel.

(2) In every organization, regardless of political content, the processes by which everyday tasks are fulfilled tend to undermine democratic goals: Division of labor requires that tasks be delegated. Delegates become separated from delegates. Also, persons tend to develop specialized skills. The skilled become separated from the unskilled. Finally, fulfilling tasks becomes more important than discussing them democratically, especially in crisis periods, and discussion tends to disappear.

(3) Secondary groups—large, no longer face-to-face, Gesellschaft—tend toward impersonality. Communication becomes formal. Their communitarian aspects (essential to the therapeutic situation which is the prerequisite to truly human exchange) disappear. While small, informal groups persist, they tend to form in opposition to the formal goals of the organization. The larger the organization, the smaller the proportion of people who actually make the decisions, usually on an informal basis.

(4) Violent revolutions tend to produce organizations inside which opposition is made illegitimate or psychologically inhibited. The single-

mindedness involved in the opposition to the old regime carries over to the post-revolutionary period, so that even moderate opposition to insignificant aspects of policy tends to be perceived as subversive. Purges follow.

(5) As any revolution, movement, group develops a structure to carry out its goals, its original élan tends to deteriorate, and the routines set up by the structures tend to take over. The rank-and-file thereupon tends to lose interest, and the organization becomes a clique.[1]

Both the iron lawyers and the anarchists, then, saw the dangers of bureaucracy and statism long before they became a problem to most socialists—although, of course, the iron lawyers saw this as inevitable and the anarchists had an alternative. It was not until the "Russian Question" that modern socialism began to grapple with the issue of bureaucracy. The development of a socialist theory about Russia was foreshadowed in the work of Rosa Luxemburg, in *The Russian Revolution,* written in 1918. In it she warned of the dangers of an elite-led revolution, and urged that true socialism could only be constructed with the fullest participation of the masses. In Russia itself, the Workers' Group and the Workers' Opposition as early as 1922 challenged the concept that socialism was being constructed. In Europe, it was not until the publication in 1938 of ex-communist Anton Ciliga's *The Russian Enigma,* and in 1939 of "Bruno R.'s" *La Bureaucratisation du monde* that theoretical clarity began to develop out of the confusion sown by Trotsky's stubborn adherence to the old "either-or" concept, one which led him to defend the Soviet Union as a "degenerated workers state." And finally, it was not until the Russo-Finnish War of 1939–1940 that a new Marxist approach to statism grew out of a factional fight in the American Trotskyist movement. (James Burnham, now a conservative, and Max Shachtman, still a socialist, were allied in the fight against James P. Cannon and the leadership of the Socialist Workers Party; Trotsky himself intervened against Shachtman from Mexico.)

The common feature of all of these radical dissenters (mainly from the communist movement) was the concept made famous years later by Milovan Djilas in *The New Class*. In the pages of Dwight Macdonald's *Politics* magazine, the concept became more refined: the new class was the bureaucracy, which, because of its control of the state, effectively controlled the means of production and distribution in a society where individual owners no longer played a role. Where the state controls the means of production and distribution, one must ask who controls the state? Lacking democracy, obviously the people do not control it and hence cannot dominate. The bureaucracy, not as individuals but as a group, controls it, and constitutes a new ruling class.

As some writers saw it, the Russian system was not alone in having the bureaucracy as its dominant grouping: Fascist Germany, the American New Deal, and after 1945, England's Labor Party also were moving in the same way. For Macdonald, Keynesian economics also fitted in—a view similar to New Left views on "corporate liberalism." What politics one held relative to this kind of position was largely a function of what can be called one's "faith in the masses." As one socialist critic put it in *The Young Socialist Review* of March 1946:

> If the next stage of society is *inevitably* statist . . . then there is nothing fruitful we can do except fold our hands and wait for it to come . . . To this the revolutionary socialist replies that statism is *one* of the possibilities facing us, and that socialism is the only practical alternative to it.

But socialism could be an alternative only if appropriate organizational forms could be found, and people to fill them. The concept of workers' control came to be one of these forms, and faith in the masses' ability to determine their own destinies (the liberals' "maximum feasible participation" translated into total participation) was its underlying assumption. Another of these libertarian socialists, also writing in *The Young Socialist Review,* June 1947, foreshadowed many of the ideas of the New Left:

> If the basic problem in the struggle for socialism today is the increasing integration of potential socialist forces with the state apparatus, then the *basic* effort of socialists in this period must be directed toward restoring and developing the independence of forces . . . The moral atmosphere inside a socialist organization must try to approximate the morality of the socialist society of the future . . . The new socialist movement must be revolutionary in its perspective and practice, libertarian in its goal.

III

For fifteen years, as the Cold War imposed a frustrating and rigid atmosphere upon the North American left, discussions of socialism-from-above versus, socialism-from-below, the Russian Question, elitism, workers' control, etc., were to be found only in obscure, sectarian journals. The issues posed, while important, seemed academic except in the developing Third

World, where even European radicals were impotent to do anything much about them. Even in England, where the left of the Labor Party engaged in critical and agonizing reappraisals of what was to happen "after the welfare state," the discussion barely made an impact. It was only after the death of Stalin, the Khrushchev revelations, and the Hungarian Revolution that those Western Communists who had quit their parties began to contribute to the conversation. But even then, during the Eisenhower years of affluence and invisible poverty, it was a discussion removed from that element which was held by all to be crucial in some way: the masses. The Old Left was out of it.

Domestically, the Montgomery Bus Boycott was the first crack in the ice. The sit-ins of 1960 and 1961 followed; then poverty became visible; then the student movement emerged. The civil rights movement shifted from public accommodations for the black bourgeoisie to jobs and housing for the black masses; community organizing came on the agenda. Saul Alinsky was rediscovered. President Kennedy created the Peace Corps, then VISTA. The name of the revolutionary game became youth.

The idea of participatory democracy came about largely in response to pragmatic, in-the-field problems confronted by SNCC and SDS during various organizing campaigns. Educational problems faced by Northern white volunteers in Mississippi's Freedom Schools in the summer of 1964 helped to focus attention on the problem of students' reactions to authority figures, which reflected their life experiences. The failure of welfare agencies in the North to organize the poor through traditional agency practices made it clear that new approaches were needed. So did the failure of slum public education. So too did the increasing frustration of some college students with the mass-production nature of information-receiving, which passes for education in many colleges. All this further augmented an experimental atmosphere covering the entire range of authority-dependency relationships —everything from management-worker to bureaucrat-client, to teacher-student and even parent-adolescent. Certain of the more pioneering efforts of the government's anti-poverty programs at one point showed receptivity to some of these new ideas, although that phase seems to be passé now. The movement's response was at once a technique and a philosophy of action.

Little of theoretical interest has been written about participatory democracy. Partly this is a problem of energies being applied to other issues, and partly it is due to a basic suspicion of theory in the first place within the New Left. But a failure to grapple with theory and history of the movement can cripple efforts to deal realistically with future problems; let me therefore first attempt a definition.

Participatory democracy involves two complementary notions that people are inherently capable of understanding their problems and expressing themselves about these problems and their solutions, if given a social context in which freedom of expression is possible, that is, a situation in which one is free of personal and political hang-ups. The second is that real solutions to problems require the fullest participation of the people in these solutions, with the development of freedom from dependency on authorities and experts. The implication for community-organizing types of groups is that cultural groups which differ in their value systems from the dominant culture cannot be organized unless a context of free expression is created; for education-oriented groups, the implication is that real education (as distinct from learning information only) cannot take place for anyone unless a situation is created in which the student is able to evaluate what goes on around him critically, without being hung-up on the judgments and values of persons in an authority relationship to him. Finally, of course, participatory democracy is a way of functioning in groups so that those ideas are realized, for the purpose of helping to create a society in which everyone will participate to his fullest in decisions concerning his everyday and long-range affairs. The assumption is that the good society is one in which people will want to try to function to their fullest potential, and that, conversely, a society cannot be good unless this happens. Further, we must sow the seeds of the good society within the context of the bad, particularly within its movements for change, because the end is implied in the means, and a democratic society cannot be created by non-democratic agents of change. By the same token, the precise nature of the good society has to be determined by this same democratic process, which precludes our attempting to blueprint the future.

In practice, then, participatory democracy involves such techniques as running meetings without agendas or presiding officers (or, at worst, rotating presiding officers); allowing officers minimal decision-making powers away from the general meeting; running meetings by consensus or "sense-of-the-meeting" decision-making; refusing to limit discussion or debate; letting as many executive-administrative decisions flow from the whole body as possible, without delegation of responsibilities to agents or committees; and encouraging the body to act immediately on decisions taken, that is, dropping the artificial division between meeting and non-meeting so that in the extreme the meeting is a community and the community a virtually constant meeting. Participatory democrats, then, try to approach direct democracy as nearly as possible, and to discourage the development of a leader-follower dichotomy.

The basic approach of participatory democracy is neither new nor unique. Among other approaches which share many of the same assumptions have been these:

(1) small group sociology, which has studied the effects of democratic and non-democratic procedures on people and on getting tasks done, for a long time.

(2) the psychological tradition of learning theory and the educationalist tradition of John Dewey, with their emphases on the importance of motivation, "readiness" to learn, and learning by doing.

(3) the psychiatric tradition, especially existential and Rogerian therapy, which points up the importance of developing the freedom to make independent decisions in life;

(4) the political traditions of anarchism, libertarian socialism, and left socialism, particularly in terms of the faith that working people have the ability to make decisions about the work-place (related to the concept of soviets and workers' control), and that socialism cannot be achieved from above;

(5) Quaker and Gandhian non-violence, which assumes that all members of a group are worth hearing, that none should be overridden or beaten down, hence the practice of running meetings and other gatherings by means of a consensus rather than a parliamentary system.

In each case the literature has much to contribute to the present movement. In particular (especially for those concerned with de-alienating the educational experience, say, at the college level) attention should be drawn to the work of Carl Rogers and his colleagues in psychology. This has assumed various labels closely parallel to those used in participatory democracy: client-centered therapy, worker-centered management, student-centered teaching, and, more broadly, group-centered leadership, which is precisely what participatory democracy is. Descriptions of the 1964 Mississippi Freedom Schools, and some "free university" experiments, could be interchanged with those of Rogerian education.

Another closely-related phenomenon which can contribute significantly to practitioners of participatory democracy is the so-called "T-Group," or training group, an idea developed by the National Training Laboratories, a subsidiary of the National Education Association. The definition of a T-Group will illustrate why it is so closely related to participatory democracy:

> A T-Group is a relatively unstructured group in which individuals participate as learners. The data for learning . . . are the transactions among members, their own behavior in the group, as they struggle to create a productive and viable organization, a miniature society. . . .

So too does the description of democracy:

> Democracy stresses the potential ability of people collaboratively to define and solve the problems they encounter in trying to live and work together. It posits that common problems cannot be well solved without the participation of those affected by the solution . . . (and) assumes a procedure of consensual validation as the final arbiter of the rightness of any collective judgment or arrangement . . . The democratic principle of "consensus" assumes that group agreements can be wrong . . .[2]

The "soul sessions" of a few years ago were a related phenomenon, as is group therapy—but the emphasis of the T-Group is on the "here-and-now," on the group as it is and is becoming, rather than on the past or the unconscious. The T-Group (also called "sensitivity training"), unlike group therapy, furthermore makes no assumptions about the mental health of the participants.

In the participatory democracy group—as in the T or Rogerian group—the dynamics of the group process help the participants learn more about themselves, about others (hence helping to break down stereotyped thinking), about relationships between people, and about the wider world, by means of sharing the experiences all bring to the group, and the experiences the group confronts, say, in social action. The nature of the process creates, optimally, a situation in which many of the less verbal gain the confidence to speak out, and the more verbal learn to listen. The lack of structured leadership—involving, sometimes, the conscious refusal of an assigned leader or trainer to assume authority—forces participants to think for themselves, become more critical, engage in direct decision-making, and thus become more self-determining and less alienated. Surely this kind of communitarian decision-making and human relationship is what socialism-from-below is all about; surely it is apparent from this discussion why the elite "socialisms" of the Eastern bloc or the developing nations are so fundamentally at variance with participatory democracy that they are qualitatively different systems.

IV

Yet participatory democracy is no panacea, no perfect formula for solving the crisis of the alienated in a mass society. To act as if all circumstances were equally amenable to solution by this method, would be to throw out valuable tools which can lead to a better participatory democracy, protected against abuse and assault by those who knowingly or unknowingly undermine it. It is perhaps necessary to look at participatory democracy as a utopia, in the sense that it is not completely achievable, given various sociological and psychological limitations, but rather achievable in steps only, and certainly valuable as a tool in dealing with such problems as education, industrial democracy, organizing the poor, and giving people a strategy for self-determination.

Two broad problem areas are perhaps most critical: one involving the nature and limitations of small groups versus larger groups, and the other involving the nature and problems of all organizations, democratic or otherwise (such as the problems discussed by the "iron lawyers" mentioned above). The first is a set of problems involving interpersonal relations; the second, impersonal, structural relationships (which involve people, of course).

A number of people gathered together in one place is not necessarily a group. The development of group consciousness and morale, including a set of norms about the way things are done in a group, a climate of acceptance for the dissenter views, and for the non-verbal participant, takes *time*. The larger the number of people, the longer a time it takes because for democracy really to work we have already said we must have maximum participation, and the development of individual potential to contribute. We must maximize interaction and communication, to create what is in some ways a family, a fraternity in the true sense of that word. This cannot be done at one meeting. Furthermore, there are limits to the *number* of people that can effectively work as a democratic decision-making group. When we run over 25 to 50, there are limits to the interaction, regardless of how long the group works together. It is, therefore, clear that a one-shot mass meeting cannot develop a real spirit of participatory democracy, not even if the leader of the meeting refuses to lead and there is a lot of free discussion. In a context involving either short time or many people, one does not become free of authority hang-ups. People with reputations are listened to in a different way from people who are unknown.

Under such circumstances, when "group-ness" has not developed, the dissenter fears to speak out. If it is a consensus group, he will not like to block action and thereby risk unpopularity, especially when leaders with reputation are for an action. Or, in the attempt to maximize his own popularity and carry the decision (rather than educate a few, but lose), he will tend to become a demagogue. In this fashion a consensus procedure sometimes encourages demagogy and non-democratic actions. (In many ways, the procedural safeguards of a parliamentary system ["bourgeois democracy"] insure the rights of the dissenter, and promote the idea of speaking to educate rather than to sway much better than a sense-of-the-meeting system.)

In large groups, then, especially in the short run, hang-ups about authority are encouraged. Authoritarian types tend to dominate, because the pay-off for demagogy is higher. Real democracy is not possible in such an atmosphere. This is the critical distinction between participatory and *plebiscitory* democracy. Ten thousand people waving their rifles and shouting "yes" is not participatory democracy.

Proponents of participatory democracy thus must confront this question: in large-scale society, how much decentralization will be possible and necessary to promote real democracy? Centralization and efficiency are not necessarily linked—nor are democracy and inefficiency. Yet in a modern nation tasks must be delegated. Direct participation is not always possible. The concrete problem of where to draw the line has still to be faced.

In addition, participatory democracy groups share certain problems with all other groups that are created to carry out tasks in some organized way. As an organization comes to life, paradoxes are born which frequently abort the effort; and even when life goes on, contradictions become inherent in an organization's career. For example: say an organization is created to further democracy. It involves cooperation among members. Yet all cooperation involves, also, delegation of some tasks so that there is a distinction between initiators of tasks, and those who carry them out. The former and the latter frequently have different sets of priorities. Agents learn skills that the others do not possess, and confront situations which the others have not foreseen, but which must be dealt with. Particularly if the organization is engaged in conflict, the tendency is strong for those with skills to maintain themselves in power, so as to confront the emergency at hand.

Another paradox is that between the democratic content of a group, and the progress of the group towards a measure of power in the community. Too much discussion, and we stop moving; too little, and we are no longer what we were. To achieve a goal, we need unity, but to achieve unity it sometimes becomes necessary to compromise, to gloss over some important issues. Which shall it be?

All formal organizations, no matter how democratically conceived, develop informal patterns based on prestige, friendships, cliques, personalities, and other subjective factors such as race and sex. These are all part of the paradox: to some degree they all help to undermine the democratic processes of the organization. In democratic organizations, particularly those that are set up to help create a better society, the ends are very much involved with the means—the organizational short-cuts can be dangerous. But organizations are composed of people, and people are never as pure as the goals for which the organization was created.

To put the matter in its harshest terms, he who says organization implies oligarchy, in much the same way that he who negotiates also must compromise, hence betray. There is no way out of this; it is the socialist's equivalent of original sin, and it must be lived with, acknowledged, confronted if we are to survive as a democratic movement.

In conclusion: participatory democracy is a very positive synthesis of many earlier socialist ideas concerning the need to involve people in decisions concerning their own destinies. The revulsion on the part of many people towards growing bureaucratization of the modern world will likely lead to more experimentation, to the development of many more alternatives to alienation, of which direct decision-making is only one. The development of parallel institutions, such as the free universities, will probably involve participatory experiments, and in turn their participants will take their concern into other institutions of our society. Yet there are serious problems connected with the practice of participatory democracy, as with socialism itself. If we confront them honestly, we shall progress.

NOTES

[1] For some sociological views on this, see Merton, *Reader in Bureaucracy;* Etzioni, *Complex Organizations;* Selznick, *TVA and the Grassroots;* and *The Organizational Weapon;* Michels, *Political Parties.*

[2] Bradford, Gibb and Benne, eds., *T-Group Theory and Laboratory Method,* pp. 1, 34.

The anarchist critique of the state, which has often seemed simplistic, is here presented in one of its most sophisticated forms. Here the state is conceived of as the formalization—and rigidification—of the unused power that the social order has abdicated. In American society it takes the form of a coalition of political, military, and industrial elites, preempting space that is simply not occupied by the rest of society.

It seems simpler, always, to get things done by creating a small decision-making elite and by bribing the rest of the people to conform. But, as Ward's article and others in this collection indicate, organizing extensively so that everyone is involved is neither impossible nor costly in terms of efficiency. In fact, studies by Seymour Melman and others indicate that in the long run it is more efficient: when people participate fully their work becomes meaningful, and they put more of themselves into it. When social purposes are narrow, programmed, and static, industrialization incurs vast social costs, seen most clearly in developing nations and in government programs of urban renewal, which leave the poor far worse off than before. On the other hand, organizing so as to incorporate social purpose fully requires that purposes be broadly conceived and subjected to continuing feedback from those affected. The latter form of organizing is inevitably more complex. It asks more of its participants. Education for participation requires more than the liberation of the individual. Workers must understand the importance of participation. When workers' councils were first developed in Yugoslavia, workers were unwilling to spend time sitting around discussing how the plant should be run when they could be making money. Only slowly, through education—which mainly involved the actual process of participation—did they become enthusiastic about self-determination.

Ward believes that the state represents a kind of relationship between people which becomes formalized into a set of vested interests that operates contrary to the interests of the people—even to the point where it evaluates its means in terms of megadeaths. One could take the number of people employed directly by the state as a function of total population, the amount of state spending as a function of total spending (in socialist states this would require careful functional definition of what constituted the domain of the state as opposed to the social order) and in general compare the resource use of the two areas. One could then analyze the social order in terms of degree of participation, extensiveness of participation, key decisions involving utilization of social resources and who makes them. Studies of the correlations between state power and social participation in various countries would verify Ward's thesis: those countries that are top-heavy with state power are the countries in which social participation is weak. A more devastating critique of statism could probably not be imagined.

There is a prophetic dimension to the anarchist critique born out by the contemporary history of socialism and socialist societies. One of the principle dilemmas in socialism—whether socialism shall be imposed or achieved from the grass roots—involves some of the questions raised by Ward. The evolution of socialist societies indicates that a simple nationalization and socialization of a political economy is not enough to create a new society. We can see the problems posed by bureaucracy even in China, where this awareness was highest, and where the anarchist tradition had some influence.

Finally, the anarchist critique has proven relevant not only to the evolution of the state in the twentieth century, but to major institutions within the society. However, the anarchist alternative has usually functioned as a critical ideal, indicating the limitations of existing institutions, without the capacity to point to more than isolated and small libertarian institutions. Thus while the anarchist critique of social institutions has, at least, some basis in fact, the anarchist critique of the state, while powerful, is no more than a critique, and will remain so until a society transforms its entire social order into the libertarian ideal.

The Anarchist Contribution
Colin Ward

As long as today's problems are stated in terms of mass politics and "mass organization," it is clear that only states and mass parties can deal with them. But if the solutions that can be offered by the existing states and parties are acknowledged to be either futile or wicked, or both, then we must look not only for different "solutions" but especially for a *different way of stating the problems themselves.*

—*Andrea Caffi*

If you look at the history of socialism, reflecting on the melancholy difference between promise and performance, both in those countries where socialist parties have triumphed in the struggle for political power, and in those where they have never attained it, you are bound to ask yourself what went wrong, and when, and why. Many of us ascribe the failure to the ascendancy of the central-management design for socialism over a liberating popular-control concept. Some would see 1917 as the fatal turning point in socialism's history. Others trace the divergence back to the February revolution of 1848 in Paris as "the starting point of the two-fold development of European socialism, anarchistic and Marxist." [1] Many would locate the critical point of divergence as the congress of the International at The Hague in 1872, when the exclusion of Bakunin and the anarchists signified the victory of Marxism. In his prophetic criticism of Marx that year, Bakunin previsaged the subsequent history of Communist society:

> Marx is an authoritarian and centralizing communist. He wants what we want, the complete triumph of economic and social equality, but he wants it in the state and through the state power, through the dictatorship of a very strong and, so to say, despotic provisional government, that is, by the negation of liberty. His economic ideal is the state as sole owner of the land and of all kinds of capital, cultivating the land under the management of state engineers, and controlling all industrial and commercial associations with state capital. We want the same triumph of economic and social equality through the abolition of the state and of all that passes by the name of law (which, in our view, is the permanent negation of human rights). We want the reconstruction of society and the unification of mankind to be achieved, not from above downwards by any sort of authority, nor by socialist officials, engineers, and other accredited men of learning—but from below upwards, by the free federation of all kinds of workers' associations liberated from the yoke of the State. [2]

The home-grown English variety of socialism reached the point of divergence later. As late as 1886, an early Fabian tracts declared, "English Socialism is not yet anarchist or collectivist, not yet defined enough in point of policy to be classified. There is a mass of socialistic feeling not yet conscious of itself as socialism. But when the unconscious socialists of England discover their position, they also will probably fall into two parties: a collectivist party supporting a strong central administration and a counterbalancing anarchist party defending individual initiative against that administration." [3] The Fabians rapidly found which side of the watershed was theirs, and when a Labor Party was founded, they exercised a decisive influence on its policies. In 1919 the Labor Party finally identified itself with the unlimited increase of the state's power and activity through the giant, managerially-controlled public corporation.

And where socialist parties have achieved power they have merely created state capitalism, with a veneer of social welfare as a substitute for social justice. The large hopes of the nineteenth century have not been fulfilled; only the gloomy prophesies have come true. The criticism of the state and the structure of power and authority made by the classical anarchist thinkers, has increased in validity and urgency in the past century of total war and the total state. For the faith that the conquest of state power would bring the advent of socialism has been destroyed in every country where socialist parties have won—either by gaining a parliamentary majority or by riding the wave of a popular revolution or by entering behind tanks of the Workers' Fatherland. What has happened is exactly what the anarchist Proudhon said a hundred years ago would happen: all that has been achieved is "a compact democracy having the appearance of being founded on the dictatorship of the masses, but in which the masses have no more power than is necessary to ensure a general serfdom in accordance with the following precepts and principles borrowed from the old absolutism: indivisibility of public power, all-consuming centralization, systematic destruction of all individual, corporative and regional thought (regarded as disruptive), inquisitorial police." [4]

Kropotkin too, warned us that "the state organization, having been the force to which the minorities resorted for establishing and organizing their power over the masses, cannot be the force which will serve to destroy these privileges," and he declared that "the economic and political liberation of man will have to create new forms for its expression in life, instead of those established by the state." He thought it self-evident that "this new form will have to be more popular, more decentralized, and nearer to the folk-mote self-government than representative government can ever be." [5] He claimed that we will be compelled to find new forms of organization for the social functions which the state fulfills through the bureaucracy, and that "as long as this is not done, nothing will be done." [6]

When we look at the powerlessness of the individual and the small face-to-face group in the world today, and ask ourselves why they are powerless, we have to answer, not merely that they are weak because the state is strong, but that they are weak because they have surrendered their power to the state. It is as though every individual possessed a certain quantity of power, but that by default or negligence he had allowed someone else to pick it up, rather than use it himself for his own purposes.

Gustav Landauer, the German anarchist, made a profound and simple contribution to the analysis of the state and society in one sentence: "The state is not something which can be destroyed by a revolution, but is a condition, a certain relationship between human beings, a mode of human behavior; we destroy it by contracting other relationships, by behaving differently." It is *we* and not an abstract outside identity, Landauer implies, who behave in one way or the other, politically or socially. Landauer's friend and executor Martin Buber, begins his essay "Society and the State," with an observation of the sociologist Robert MacIver that "to identify the social with the political is to be guilty of the grossest of all confusions, which completely bars any understanding of either society or the state." The political principle, for Buber, is characterized by power, authority, hierarchy, dominion. He sees the social principle in the association of men on the basis of a common need or a common interest.

What is it, Buber asks, that gives the political principle its ascendancy? And he answers, "the fact that every people feels itself threatened by the others gives the state its definite unifying power; it depends upon the instinct of self preservation of society itself; the latent external crisis enables it to get the upper hand in internal crises. . . . All forms of government have this in common: each possesses more power than is required by the given conditions; in fact, this excess in the capacity for making dispositions is actually what we understand by political power. The measure of this excess, which cannot, of course, be computed precisely, represents the exact difference between administration and government." He calls this excess the "political surplus" and observes that "its justification derives from the external and internal instability, from the latent state of crisis between nations and within every nation. The political principle is always stronger in relation to the social principle than the given conditions require. The result is a continuous diminution in social spontaneity." [7]

The conflict between these two principles is a permanent aspect of the human condition. Or as Kropotkin put it, "Throughout the history of our civilization, two traditions, two opposed tendencies, have been in conflict: the Roman tradition and the popular tradition, the imperial tradition and the federalist tradition, the authoritarian tradition and the libertarian tradition." There is an inverse correlation between the two: the strength of one is the weakness of the other. If we want to strengthen society we must weaken the state. Totalitarians of all kinds realize this, which is why they invariably seek to destroy those social institutions which they cannot dominate. So do the dominant interest groups in the state, like the alliance characterized as the "military-industrial complex" by Eisenhower in his last address as president.

Shorn of the metaphysics with which politicians and philosophers have enveloped it, the state can be defined as a political mechanism using force, and to the sociologist it is *one* among many forms of social organization. It is however, "distinguished from all other associations by its exclusive investment with the final power of coercion." [8] And against whom is this final power applied? It is ostensibly directed at the enemy without, but it is used upon the subject society within.

This is why Buber declared that it is the maintenance of the latent external crisis that enables the state to get the upper hand in internal crises. Is this a conscious procedure? Is it simply that wicked men control the state? Could we put things right simply by voting for good men? Or is it a fundamental characteristic of the state as an institution? It was because she drew this final conclusion that Simone Weil declared, "The great error of nearly all studies of war, an error into which all socialists have fallen, has been to consider war as an episode in foreign politics, when it is especially an act of interior politics, and the most atrocious act of all." [9]

It doesn't look like this of course, if you are part of the directing apparatus, calculating what proportion of the population you can afford to lose in a nuclear war—just as the governments of all the great powers, capitalist and communist, are calculating. But it does look like this if you are part of the expendable population—unless you identify your own unimportant carcass with the state apparatus, as millions do.

In the nineteenth century, T. H. Green avowed that war is the expression of the "imperfect" state, but he was wrong. War is the state in its most perfect form; as Randolph Bourne said at the time of the first world war, "war is the health of the state." This is why the weakening of the state is a social necessity. The strengthening of other loyalties, of alternative foci of power, of different modes of human behaviour, is an essential for survival.

But where do we begin? It should be obvious that we do not begin by supporting, joining, or working to change the existing political parties from within, nor by starting new ones as rivals for political power. Our task is not to gain power but to erode it, to drain it away from the state. "One way or another, socialism must become more popular, more communalistic, and less dependent upon indirect government through elected representatives. It must become more self-governing." [10] We have to build networks instead of pyramids. All authoritarian institutions are organized as pyramids: the state, the private or public corporation, the army, the police, the church. Each has a small group of decision-makers at the top and a broad base of people whose decisions are made for them spread out below. Anarchism doesn't want different people on top; it wants to destroy the pyramid. In its place it advocates an extended network of individuals and groups, making their own decisions, controlling their own destiny.

The classical anarchist thinkers envisaged the whole social organization woven from such local groups. The commune or council would be the territorial nucleus, not as a branch of the state, but as the "free association of the members concerned, which may be either a cooperative or a corporative body, or simply a provisional union of several people united by a common need," [11] and the syndicate or workers' council as the industrial or occupational unit. These units would federate in a network of autonomous groups. Several strands of thought are linked together in anarchist social theory: the ideas of direct action, autonomy or workers' control, decentralization and federalism.

The phrase "direct action" was first given currency by the French revolutionary syndicalists of the turn of the century, and was associated with the various forms of militant industrial resistance—the strike, the slow down, encroaching control, sabotage, and the general strike. Its meaning has widened since then to take in the experience of, for example, Gandhi's civil disobedience campaign and the civil-rights struggle in the United States. Direct action has been defined by David Wieck as that "action which, in respect to a situation, realizes the end desired, so far as this lies within one's power or the power of one's group." He distinguishes this from indirect action which "realizes an irrelevant or even contradictory end. He gives this as a homely example: "If the butcher weighs one's meat with his thumb on the scale, one may complain about it and tell him he is a bandit who robs the poor, and if he persists and one does nothing else, this is *mere talk;* one may call the Department of Weights and Measures, and this is *indirect action;* or one may, talk failing, insist on weighing one's own meat, bring along a scale to check the butcher's weight, take one's business somewhere else, help open a co-operative store, and these are *direct actions.*" Wieck observes that, "proceeding with the belief that in every situation, every individual and group has the possibility of some direct action on some level of generality, we may discover much that has been unrecognized, and the importance of much that has been underrated. So politicalized is our thinking, so focused to the motions of governmental institutions, that the effects of direct efforts to modify one's environment are unexplored. The habit of direct action is, perhaps, identical with the habit of being a free man, prepared to live responsibly in a free society." [12]

The ideas of autonomy and workers' control and of decentralization are inseparable from that of direct action. In the modern state, everywhere and in every field, one group of people makes decisions, exercises control, limits choices, while the great majority have to accept and submit. The habit of direct action is the habit of wresting back the power to make decisions affecting *us,* from *them.* The autonomy of the worker at work is the most important field in which this expropriation of decision-making can apply. When workers' control is mentioned, people sadly smile and regretfully murmur that it is a pity that the scale and complexity of modern industry make it impossible to put such a beautiful ideal into practice. But they are wrong. There are no technical grounds for regarding workers' control as impossible. Evidence for this can be found in studies of the organization of work in British industry today. Seymour Melman's study of decision-making in a tractor factory showed to his satisfaction that "there are realistic alternatives to managerial rule over production," [13] and the Tavistock Institute's study of the work system used in some of the pits in the Durham coal field demonstrates "the ability of quite large primary work groups . . . to act as self-regulating, self-developing social organisms, able to maintain themselves in a steady state of high productivity." These miners are "free to evolve their own way of organizing and carrying out their task. They are not subject to any external authority in this respect, nor is there within the group itself any member who takes over a formal directive leadership function. . . . The income obtained is divided equally among team members. . . ." [14] Such examples are rare, and they operate within the limits prescribed by a capitalist economy, but they indicate that workers' control is not an impossible demand. It is simply a demand which is not made.

Similarly, decentralization is not so much a technical problem as an approach to problems of human organization. For the skeptic, you can work out a convincing case for decentralization on economic or organizational grounds, but for the anarchist there just isn't any other solution consistent with his advocacy of direct action and autonomy. It doesn't occur to him to seek centralist solutions just as it doesn't occur to the person with an authoritarian mentality to seek decentralist ones. A contemporary anarchist advocate of decentralization, Paul Goodman, remarks that

> In fact, there have always been two strands to decentralist thinking.
> Some authors, e.g., Lao-tse or Tolstoy, make a conservative-peasant

critique of centralised court and town as inorganic, verbal and ritualis-
tic. But other authors, e.g. Proudhon or Kropotkin, make a demo-
cratic-urban critique of centralized bureaucracy and power, including
feudal industrial power, as exploiting, inefficient, and discouraging initiative. In our present era of State-socialism, corporate feudalism,
regimented schooling, brainwashing mass-communications and urban
anomie, both kinds of critique make sense. We need to revive both
peasant self-reliance and the democratic power of professional and
technical guilds.

Any decentralization that could occur at present would inevitably be
post-urban and post-centralist; it could not be provincial. . . .[15]

He concludes that decentralization is "a kind of social organization; it does
not involve geographical isolation, but a particular sociological use of geography."

Precisely because we are not concerned with geographical isolation,
anarchist thinkers have devoted a great deal of thought to the principle of
federalism. Proudhon regarded it as the alpha and omega of his political
and economic thought. He was not thinking of a confederation of states or
of a world federal government, but of a principle of human organization.
He envisaged local communes and associations cooperating in regional federations. The nation would be replaced by a geographical confederation of
regions, and Europe would be a confederation of confederations. In such a
federal arrangement, the interests of even the smallest province would be
protected. Differences would be settled by arbitration. Bakunin's philosophy of federalism echoed Proudhon's and Kropotkin's too, drew on the history of the French Revolution, the Paris Commune, and, at the very end of
his life, the experience of the Russian Revolution, to illustrate the importance of the federal principle if a revolution is to retain its revolutionary
content.

Autonomous direct action, decentralized decision-making, and free federation have been the characteristics of all genuinely popular uprisings.
Staughton Lynd has remarked that "no real revolution has ever taken place
—whether in America in 1776, France in 1789, Russia in 1917, China in
1949—without ad hoc popular institutions, improvised from below, simply
beginning to administer power in place of the institutions previously recognized as legitimate." They were seen too in the Spanish Revolution of 1936
and in the Hungarian Revolution of 1956, only to be destroyed by the very
party which had ridden to power in 1917 on the essentially anarchist slogan
"all power to the soviets." In March 1920, by which time the Bolsheviks
had transformed the local soviets into organs of the central administration,

Lenin said to Emma Goldman, "Why, even your great comrade Enrico Malatesta has declared himself for the soviets." "Yes," she replied, "for the *free* soviets." Malatesta himself, defining the anarchist interpretation of revolution, wrote:

> Revolution is the destruction of all coercive ties; it is the autonomy of groups, of communes, or regions; revolution is the free federation brought about by a desire for brotherhood, by individual and collective interests, by the needs of production and defence; revolution is the constitution of innumerable free groupings based on ideas, wishes and tastes of all kinds that exist among the people; revolution is the forming and disbanding of thousands of representative, district, communal, regional, national bodies which, without having any legislative power, serve to make known and to coordinate the desires and interests of people near and far and which act through information, advice and example. Revolution is freedom proved in the crucible of facts—and lasts so long as freedom lasts, that is until others, taking advantage of the weariness that overtakes the masses, of the inevitable disappointments that follow exaggerated hopes, of the probable errors and human faults, succeed in constituting a power, which, supported by an army of mercenaries or conscripts, lays down the law, arrests the movement at the point it has reached, and then begins the reaction.[16]

His last sentence indicates that he thought reaction inevitable, and so it is, if the people are willing to surrender the power they have wrested from the former ruling elite into the hands of a new one. But a reaction to every revolution is inevitable in another sense. This is what the ebb and flow of history implies. As Landauer says, every time after the revolution is a time before the revolution for all those whose lives have not bogged down in some great moment of the past. There is no final struggle, only a series of partisan engagements on a variety of fronts.

And after a century of experience of the theory and a half century of experience of the practice of the Marxist and social-democratic varieties of socialism, after the historians had dismissed anarchism as one of the nineteenth-century also-rans, it is emerging again in the struggle for a society of participants. One thing on which most observers of the international student revolt and the events of May 1968 in France are agreed upon, is their anarchist character. Thus *Time* magazine (May 24, 1968) observed, "The black flag that flew last week above the tumultuous student disorders of Paris stood for a philosophy that the modern world has all but forgotten: anarchy. Few of the students who riot in France, Germany or Italy—or in many another country—would profess outright allegiance to anarchy, but its basic tenets inspire many of their leaders. Germany's 'Red Rudi' Dutschke and France's 'Red Danny' Cohn-Bendit openly espouse anarchy." And writing in *Encounter* (August, 1968), Theodore Draper declared, "The lineage of the new revolutionaries goes back to Bakunin rather than to Marx, and it is just as well that the term "anarchism" is coming back into vogue. For what we have been witnessing is a revival of anarchism in modern dress or masquerading as latter-day Marxism. Just as nineteenth-century Marxism matured in a struggle against anarchism, so twentieth-century Marxism may have to recreate itself in another struggle against anarchism in its latest guise." He went on to say that the anarchists did not have much staying-power in the nineteenth century, and that it is unlikely that they will have much more in this century. I don't think he was right about the old anarchists. They went down fighting, and they were their own hardest critics. Whether or not he was right about the new anarchists depends on several questions. First, have people learned *anything* from the history of the last hundred years? Second, will the many people in the East and West who seek an alternative theory of social organization to the ordinary rival political theories grasp the relevance of anarchist ideas? Last, are anarchists imaginative enough to find ways of applying their theories to today's society so as to combine immediate action with ultimate ends?

NOTES

[1] Vaclav Cerny, "The Socialistic Year 1848 and its Heritage" (Prague: *The Critical Monthly* Nos. 1 and 2, 1948).

[2] Michael Bakunin, "Letter to the Internationalists of the Romagna" 28 Jan 1872.

[3] Fabian Tract No. 4, *What Socialism Is* (London 1886).

[4] Pierre-Joseph Proudhon, *The Political Capacity of the Working Class* (1864).

[5] Peter Kropotkin, *Modern Science and Anarchism* (London 1912).

[6] The same, French edition 1913.

[7] Martin Buber, "Society and the State" (London: *World Review* May 1951).

[8] Peter Kropotkin, *Modern Science and Anarchism* (London 1912).

[9] Simone Weil, "Reflections on War" (London: *Left Review* 1938).

[10] Peter Kropotkin, *op. cit.*

[11] Camillo Berneri, *Kropotkin, His Federalist Ideas* (London 1943).

[12] David Weick, "The Habit of Direct Action" (London: *Anarchy 13* 1962).

[13] Seymour Melman, *Decision-Making and Productivity* (Oxford 1958).

[14] P. G. Herbst, *Autonomous Group Functioning* and E. L. Trist et al.: *Organisational Choice* (London 1962 and 1963).

[15] Paul Goodman, *Like a Conquered Province* (New York 1967).

[16] Vernon Richards, ed., *Malatesta: His Life and Ideas* (London 1965).

Part II

STRATEGIES FOR SOCIAL CHANGE

INTRODUCTION

The essays in Part I have focused on the theoretical problems of participatory democracy and on applications of the idea to groups, organizations, and the state. Part II deals with specific political strategies required to move toward a society of participation and popular control. The essays that follow are varied in their approaches, and taken together they mark out a broad area of strategy. But what they share is of significance, too. Social revolution is one theme that recurs in various forms in these essays. Social revolution includes not only the transfer of power from an elite class to the majority of the people, but institutional and cultural changes of the deepest kind. By institutional changes we mean a basic reorganization of society and human life (something that modern politico-economic revolutions have often promised but have not done as yet); by cultural changes we mean fundamental changes in interpersonal relations, that is, in man's view of man. This is a libertarian definition of revolution, but it does not conflict with the historic purpose of revolution—profound and egalitarian redistribution of power and the creation of a classless society—but instead adds to the wealth of this purpose with a *concrete* commitment and proposals for a structurally different society.

The classic revolutionary sees the culmination of his strategy in the overthrow of the existing power structure. But, as Lynd points out, even those who seek revolution in its classical form should consider the importance of building revolutionary institutions to gain support as they seek the overthrow of the old ones. Thus another recurrent theme in these essays is that of building during the revolutionary process itself. The revolution must embody within itself the forms it seeks to realize in the new, reorganized society; the means used by a movement for change must be closely linked to the nature of the ends.

A third shared concern, and one of extreme importance, is that change must be psychosocial as well as political and economic. Although the contributors place differing emphases on the relationship between psychosocial and institutional change, all agree that life and culture must change along with economic relationships. Clearly, Seeley's essay is at one end of the spectrum here, for it stresses the primary importance of "changing your head" as a prerequisite to changing anything else. For Seeley, this change is part of an evolving dialectic that affects increasingly larger segments of the younger generation, causing them to opt out of the present "square" culture into a counterculture. But for others—Lens, for instance—personal and psycho-social change is interrelated with institutional change, and both are necessary and congruent. It is significant that Calvert, in criticizing the Movement and SDS in particular, takes it to task for neglecting personal liberation and for failing to see how closely connected personal liberation and socio-political liberation are.

Fourth, most of the essays share the radical assumption that socialism must be an integral part of a good society. Yet they also share a belief that traditional socialist forms are inadequate. For Lynd, it is participatory socialism that is needed; for William A. Williams, it is socialism as community. But the common idea is that the problem of building a new order cannot be pushed into the future and seen as a post-revolutionary one. It must be intrinsic to the movement for change itself, and constitutes a basic part of what the movement is about.

It is here that participatory democracy comes in. If the movement for change must also be psychosocial, if it must involve "changing your head," if it must build community, then the movement must involve active and committed participation on the part of those in it, so that as individuals they can experience directly the implications of living by a different set of values. The effect of contemporary industrial society on the individual is far more than simply intellectual. It socializes people to an individualistic, privatized, exploitative code of behavior that is not outgrown even when people understand intellectually that the social order must change. To outgrow it requires the creation of living situations that are communal, collaborative, and participatory, so that people can free themselves from behavior patterns that encourage them to think first of themselves, and to see human relationships primarily in terms of bargaining instead of mutuality.

An essential organizational question in the revolutionary process involves the political form of the struggle. Up until now the organizational units used have been vanguard political parties or guerrilla groups. Both have used the organizational principle of cells. In the case of the vanguard political party, which proverbially uses the Leninist concept of "democratic centralism," the cells have some autonomy but in the end are regulated or legitimized from some central committee. In the case of guerrilla work (such as the Front du Liberation du Quebec), the cells have greater autonomy but at some point must relate to a military and political center. Both vehicles are essentially organizations for combat. The revolutionary tradition has yet to find a satisfactory form that is both ready and fit for *resistance* and which is a life/work style *alternative* to the existing order in a radical sense. Such groups, which would be highly task-force oriented with a high degree of mutual aid coupled with social relevance, are much needed. In the last few years hundreds of affinity groups, collectives, and communes, both rural and urban, have been established by a movement that refuses to be centralized. This new development is too young to allow us to speculate as to its lasting value, but in his article Roussopoulos outlines what he considers some of the imperatives in this new evolution of the resistance units.

Education is essential. There is no technical gimmick that can lead to the evolution of social or group purpose, and so a third kind of group process is necessary, the task-oriented urban commune. Here people work together to create groups that are egalitarian and democratic, wherein members learn to initiate and propose and balance group needs with individual needs. Here, in fact, is the critical kind of educational process that must go on if a society is to become participatory and, through this, egalitarian and free. Perhaps the major argument for participation is that without it the process of re-learning and re-socialization, which alone is capable of creating social purpose from the ground up, is impossible.

It is a long road that the editors and contributors to this book are mapping. The essence of a revolutionary strategy is to build new groupings that can simultaneously resist the injustices of the existing order and create an alternative to it. To understand this dialectic is, to us, to understand the basic ingredient of strategy and thus to "revolutionize revolution." From protest to resistance, and with resistance to building mutual aid groups and new institutions and new centers of people's power—these and more enrich social agitation and struggle and lend new impetus and relevance to social revolution.

The Road to
Power and Beyond
Sidney Lens

I

The New Left, though its rhetoric is delightfully fresh and its tactics highly imaginative, stands bewildered before the mammon of ideology. Is it Marxist or non-Marxist, socialist or non-socialist, violent or nonviolent, centralist or anarchist? How will it make its "revolution?" Who will be its allies? What will the revolution look like on completion? Many papers are being written on these subjects, some with great perception; yet the New Left as yet has no clear answers to these questions.

The Old Left could sink its shaft in a Marxist bedrock that had seemed firm for a century. It could tell its adherents in almost mathematical terms what was wrong with capitalism, how it would be uprooted, and what the beautiful tomorrow would look like. It was simple, pat, and plausible. Any-one with an eighth-grade education could see for himself that there was a class struggle between worker and boss. The theory of surplus value could be reduced to a single, understandable idea: the laborer received in wages only part of what he produced for his employer in commodities. The exist-ence of imperialism, waxing fat from the sweat of the colonies, was all too obvious. And the argument that imperialism was the last stage of capitalism was a consummation so devoutly to be wished that leftists accepted it as the divine word.

But none of this seems quite as cogent as it did a generation ago. The assumption that capitalism's ailment was essentially economic—that it was doomed until death to grave depressions every five or ten years—no longer fits reality; there have been no "grave depressions" in the United States for more than thirty years, and none in Western Europe for almost twenty. The assumption that the working class would lead us into the promised land seems bizarre at a time when much of the American working class is strait-jacketed in George Meany's AFL-CIO, with a leadership closer in ideology to the Central Intelligence Agency than to Eugene V. Debs. And, as for

Lenin's vision a half-century ago that capitalism was in its death throes, that the old imperialism was its last stage, it is clear that the system has been more resilient than anticipated.

On the other side of the radical equation, the "socialist countries" do not appear as glorious in life itself as many good people expected. More than half the history of the first proletarian state was a nightmare of Stalinist repression that even communists admit was something less than than idyllic; and though Stalinism is now safely interred, the Soviet Union is no longer a beacon for revolution but for moderation. The Moscow-type communists everywhere have replaced yesterday's social democracy as the apostles of reformism. While the students of Paris were shouting for revolution in May 1968, for instance, the communists were crying for a new popular front government and ten-percent wage increases, leading *The New York Times* to comment that "if the Communist Party has managed to take over the movement, then ironically, the [capitalist] institutions are safe. . . ." Moreover, within the Soviet orbit, there is one upsurge after another by youthful zealots—in Poland, Hungary, Czechoslovakia—demanding that the revolution pay off on its humanist promises.

The Marxist ideology, then, despite its high score in insights and predictions, seems to be falling behind events, outpaced both by science and history. The New Left therefore finds itself without a prefabricated pattern of ideas or an established leftist movement with which to identify. It feels a certain attraction for Castro and Guevara, both because they were Davids who fought off Goliath and because they emphasize humanism far more than the Soviet prototype. Some New Leftists also have warm feelings for Mao Tse-tung, mainly because Mao stresses moral rather than material incentives, idealism over self-interest. Neither of these radical models, however, seems to be pertinent to the United States or France or Britain or Germany or even Japan. It is difficult to visualize an America consumed by guerrilla bands, making forays from Pike's Peak or Grand Canyon or the Catskill Mountains against the American military forces. It does not seem credible that the Pentagon's legions will disintegrate like the armies of Batista or Chiang Kai-shek. And if they do not disintegrate, how will the revolution be made?

The experience of France in May and June of 1968 highlights the dilemma of the New Left. Here was the strategy of the New Left at its penultimate. Virtually all universities throughout the country were seized by students, with a good many high schools thrown in to boot. The working class responded even more dramatically, seizing more factories and engaging in more strikes than ever before in French history. The New Left had totally fulfilled its role as a catalyst, far more than in any other Western nation; it was able to completely paralyze the French economy. If ever a situation was tailor-made for revolution this was it: the decentralized power of the people challenged the centralized power of the state. Yet there was no revolution, and within a few weeks not only the leaders of labor but the laborers themselves deserted the New Left. They settled for ten to thirty-five percent wage increases, rather than forge ahead to "socialism." The role of a catalyst, it seems, was, even under the best circumstances, a limited one.

From this and similar frustrations here in the Western Hemisphere many an Old Leftist—Irving Howe and Bayard Rustin, by way of example—have concluded there is really no future for the New Left. Its failure to find an ideology, they say, is testament to its historical irrelevance. And its uncompromising attitude toward "the Establishment" is a characteristic of youthful rigidity. It is too envenomed to see some of the "good" things in American democracy, and its all-or-nothing pose dooms it to sterility.

Such criticisms have had little effect on the youth, but they must be answered, for the New Left must place itself accurately in the spectrums both of history and strategy. Otherwise it will flail at the winds for a much longer period than is necessary.

II

In the context of history, it seems to me, the New Left must compare itself not to the old one but to the new left of the first half of the nineteenth century. Like that one, it is *new* precisely because it faces a new set of historical circumstances. It lives in the backwash, on the one hand, of a Russian Revolution that failed to fulfill its hopes, and on the other, in the forefront of a second industrial revolution that offers material joy unbounded if it can be harnessed to human, rather than military, needs. That indeed was the situation of the new left in the nineteenth century. The world had just witnessed revolutions that promised "life, liberty and the pursuit of happiness " and "liberty, fraternity, equality" but had failed to make good. Moreover, the notions of individualism and liberty that philosophers had counterposed to the closed feudal society, were obviously incomplete in coping with the problems of industrialism. Industrialism made a mockery of individualism, so much so that even Jefferson, at first, vehemently rejected it and called on America to remain a nation of small but independent farmers. The producer of goods was now "free" to work where he wanted, when he wanted, but in practice he was free only to accept his employer's conditions, free to go hungry during depressions, free to have his little children work twelve and fourteen hours a day in sweatshops. In these bewildering circumstances radicals and workers either turned their backs on the Industrial Revolution or groped for new ideas and methods to humanize it.

The nineteenth-century panaceas for the beautiful tomorrow—the utopian communities, the producer cooperatives—were gropings toward a consistent philosophy of radicalism. They saw capitalism as inherently wrong and inherently greedy. But they suffered from serious defects and inadequacies. For one thing they could not explain coherently why capitalism was destined to perpetuate those evils; moderates, even while admitting that the system was no bed of roses, could made a good case, in rebuttal, that it would eventually improve. More important, the utopians were less than formidable in explaining how society would get from "here" to "there" —how, in other words, the radicals would gain power. Robert Owen, indeed, was convinced that his plan was so intellectually plausible that fellow capitalists would eagerly embrace it. The "over-wealthy" would recognize, he felt, that if they did not move toward socialism they would face destruction at the hands of the people they oppressed. Fourier's political facade was also one of class harmony—change would come as a result of an intellectual exercise in which all classes learned to understand their common destiny. And those Americans who propounded theories of producers' cooperatives were naive enough to believe they could use the present institutional structures to win their purposes. Clearly, none of these forces addressed themselves sufficiently to what in later days became known as "the road to power."

Finally, in 1848, Marx and Engels came along with answers which were not spun out of speculation but grounded in what was then known of the sciences of history and economics. For more than a century thereafter the left accepted as proven the theories of historical materialism, class struggle, and surplus value. They differed sharply over whether the class struggle could be resolved through violent revolution or evolutionary reform, through a centralized party of professional revolutionaries or a decentralized movement, and similar points. But they did not venture toward a new ideological model.

Now, a century and a quarter later, such a new model has become indispensable, and if there are those who criticize the New Left for being "fuzzy," they might well recall that it took a half century for the nineteenth-century "new left" to do the same job. Today's New Left is also going through a "Luddite" and "utopian" phase. The hippies and yippies who "resign" from this corrupt society are comparable in many ways to the Luddite machine-breakers; and most students and blacks who organize demonstrations against discrimination, poverty or the war have not yet graduated to a cohesive ideology. But that ideology—what may be called "humanistic radicalism"—is already evident in outline, and with time will fill out into a comprehensive system.

III

A radical ideology begins with an analysis of what is wrong with the present society. It must prove that that society is consumed by inner contradictions that cannot be patched up by reforms. The Old Left made its case by pointing to "surplus value." The value of a commodity, according to Marx (and many traditional economists of the time), was determined by the amount of labor that went into its production. Its price, as distinct from its value, fluctuated a little depending on supply and demand, but it fluctuated around its true value—the labor time put into its production. The amount of labor time in manufacturing a pair of $15 shoes (beginning with the slaughter of the cattle) was equivalent to the amount of labor time in mining and refining $15 worth of gold. There was one commodity, however, that was unique—"labor power." Its value too was determined by the amount of labor it took to produce it, in other words the amount of labor it took for food, clothing and shelter needed by the laborer to continue functioning. The only difference was that labor power produced more values than its own value—fabricated commodities in other words—worth much more than its own wages. This surplus—surplus value—went to the capitalist class in the form of profits, rent, and interest.

It was here that capitalism's incurable sickness began. The worker, lacking bargaining power, was always kept at the point of subsistence, immiserated. He could not buy all he produced since his wages were lower than the value of the commodities. Nor could the capitalist himself consume the surpluses, because they were too great. The only solution was to find new markets elsewhere, even if that meant conquering weaker countries and imposing colonial status on them so that they would accept the home country's surplus goods and surplus capital. Such a "solution" was only temporary, for there were just so many weaker nations to occupy and there were other capitalist powers with equally lustful appetites. A time came when the conflict between the great powers over colonies and spheres of influence spilled over to world war.

Internally, the problem of surplus goods and surplus capital transformed itself periodically (every five or ten years) into terrible depressions. Workers were hungry and in need, but the warehouses were glutted with goods that could not be sold because the workers did not have the wherewithal to buy them. The wheels of industry therefore stopped turning, millions were laid off from their jobs, and a period of readjustment took place. In that period the big capitalists swallowed smaller ones, prices fell, adjustments ran their course and finally the wheels began moving again. But the process could not go on forever because the working class was being progressively immiserated and at a certain point was bound to rise in revolution.

The phenomenon of surplus value doomed capitalism to an early death —buried by the working class which it itself had created. This was the standard Marxist gospel.

From the 1840s to the 1930s it seemed like a fair diagnosis of the capitalist malady. There was certainly no traditional economics that made any more sense, for the traditionalists insisted that the market regulated capitalism in such a way that depressions should not happen. But there were two defects to the Marxist schema. First, the trade unions, a kind of monopoly in reverse, were able to raise wages appreciably above subsistence levels, so that the working class was not being progressively immiserated. Second, the employers were able to yield concessions to their workers—bribe them, Lenin charged—from the super-profits earned in the colonies. The condition of the working class, though far from pleasant, did not become ever more wretched from year to year, nor did the worker, especially in the United States, become more revolutionary.

In addition, capitalism has stolen a march on socialist economics by adopting part of its theorem. Since Keynes it has conceded that the free market is *not* a self-regulating mechanism, and that the state must intervene to do for the economy what it cannot do for itself, namely regulate. When there is a danger of economic downturn, say the neo-Keynesians, the state must pump money into sclerotic economic veins. Through such compensatory spending it is able to revive a slothful industry and though it must finance its deficits with loans, it does not matter, for a healthy economy must be judged not on whether the budget is balanced but whether the economy is expanding. Under the New Deal, from 1933 to 1939, the Roosevelt regime doubled the national debt with its compensatory spending, and managed to put some of the unemployed back to work. Since the New Deal a trillion and a quarter dollars have been pumped into the economy as compensatory spending and the national debt is ten times what it was in 1939. Much of this spending has been for war—the Second World War, Korea, Vietnam, and the Cold War; morally we can argue against the military spending, but economically it has worked. It has staved off depression for three decades. In other nations the compensatory spending has taken different forms, less oriented on the military, but there too it has been effective in holding back steep economic downturns.

What this has meant politically and socially is all too obvious: the working class, on whom the Old Left relied to make the revolution, has improved its lot steadily and not only is non-revolutionary but has lost whatever it had of a class consciousness. This is true in Western Europe as well as the United States; the old European union leaders and the old social-democratic parties are no more radical than Hubert Humphrey.

Liberals and some ex-radicals have concluded from capitalism's recent "success story" that it has the internal strength to overcome its maladies, that its sicknesses are not terminal but temporary. The Old Left, on the other hand, clings doggedly to yesterday's dogmas or is silent on the subject. Many Old Leftists believe that a day will come, after the United States is forced to curtail its military spending, when old-style depressions will recur and the working class will again be a potential vanguard for revolution. Perhaps. But I'm inclined to believe that the capitalist disease is more complex than the theory of surplus value implies; it is also much more malignant than the liberals acknowledge.

The crisis of capitalism must be viewed not merely in economic but psycho-social terms. What makes capitalism a sick society, I think, is not merely the economic reality of surplus value, but the competitive élan which underlies it. Competition is the motif of a market economy, even of those segments of the economy which have become monopolies. Despite administered prices and cartel arrangements the monopoly competes, on the one hand against itself, trying to do more business this year than it did last year; and on the other against other industries and comparable firms in other countries for a larger share of the national and international market. Competitiveness, however, allows for a certain flexibility that the theory of surplus value neither anticipated nor predicted. At one extreme there is such a thing as "friendly competition"—two men run a 100-yard dash, the loser shakes hands with and congratulates the winner. At the other extreme, competition translates into vicious, even murderous practices—a businessman taps the telephone wires of a competitor, undersells him and drives him out of business. Or, a government based on "free enterprise" helps the Shah of Iran overthrow the government of Mossadegh because the latter has nationalized the oil industry.

Neo-Keynesianism has saved capitalism from its anarchy of production, but not from the effects of over-competitiveness. Capitalist nations, in particular the United States, can afford to "bribe" their lower classes at home with reforms and higher wages in order to achieve a tenuous class peace, but they can only afford the bribes by fiercer penetration of the so-called underdeveloped nations. American investments abroad have grown more than seven times since the end of the Second World War, from some $17 to $125 billion. And with accelerated investment (and trade) the United States has intensified its efforts to control dozens of countries—through economic and military aid that require political concessions, through machinations of the Central Intelligence Agency, and through other devices. Everywhere it tries to impose governments most favorable to its trade and investment, and where it is not possible to achieve total control, as in India, it supports the friendliest viable force, such as the Congress Party. Domination, however, is the essence of the new imperialism, just as it was of the old imperialism. If the United States does not send in its armies for occupation, as Britain used to do, it is because it can dominate through puppet armies (as in Brazil, Bolivia, etc.) or through puppet regimes. It intervenes militarily, however, in such extreme cases as in the Dominican Republic and Vietnam; and it does so even where its investments are small, as in Indo-China, in order to teach a lesson to potential backsliders among its client states.

Relative mildness in dealing with the working class at home is thus compensated for by more ruthless exploitation abroad. That is why the American steel companies, for instance, no longer seek to smash the steelworkers' union and cut their pay down to, say, sixty dollars a week. They are content to live with a union that accept their national and international goals, and helps them maintain class peace at home as well as expansion abroad. They have taken in the labor movement as junior partners in a bigger struggle than the simple one between worker and boss, and are willing to pay a price for it. But if competitiveness shifts the locus of the crisis to an extent, it does not eliminate it.

The results of such a policy are far-reaching. On the one hand there is an enormous military establishment at home which corrupts the nation's values and seeks to impose conformity on it; and on the other, intervention and small wars. The competitive spirit feeds on itself demanding more and more domination of foreign nations, more and more military domination over the home population. Unrestrained competition engenders manipulation, domination, hate, violence, exploitation, imperialism, and war. The United States, the most over-competitive society in all history, manifests all these characteristics in varying degrees in different places.

These are not, as the liberals argue, ephemeral occurrences, but fundamental to the over-competitive society. And they exacerbate the contradictions of the social system to the point where cure is impossible except through radical surgery. Liberals see but one half of the picture: the improved conditions of the workers at home, the flamboyant promises of a Great Society, the conferences for a guaranteed annual income or the negative income tax. What they don't see is the *basic* impulsion of our society toward endless Vietnams, endless foreign crises, endless military expenditures, endless distortions of the home economy, endless conflicts with the weaker of the great powers, like France. These senseless thrusts must eventually have a backlash at home, creating stagnation and instability. An inkling of the kind of backlashes we can expect in the future was evident in 1968 with the gold crisis, the threat to the dollar, and the cutback in Great Society programs—meager as they were—all due to the war in Vietnam. A symptom of the international capitalist crisis was evident in England, where the Labor Party government had to introduce austerity, and in France where tensions spilled over to a general strike.

To the credit of the New Left, it has understood instinctively what men like Howe and Rustin have forgotten: that there is something fundamentally wrong with the capitalist system, and that the liberation of man can take place only within the framework of a new institutional pattern, based on humanism and collectivism. In this respect it has lit a beacon. Its weakness is in strategy: it has not yet elaborated a road to power that flows from coherent analysis of the new capitalist economics and the new imperialism.

IV

Three new factors, it seems to me, must be included in the strategical equation:

(1) The working class apparently will not play the leading role in transforming society.

(2) The conflict with the American establishment is of a multi-class nature. Because of its competitive elan, that establishment exploits not only the worker at the point of production, but the student, the

managerial class, the non-working poor, and racial minorities, all of whom presently have greater revolutionary consciousness than the working class.

(3) The conflict is international to a far greater extent than it was a generation or two ago because this is an era of World Revolution far outstripping anything humanity has ever seen.

The road to power, as envisioned by most of the Old Left, was dramatically simple. The working class, victim of surplus value, would be activated in mine, mill and factory to fight its fate. As it struggled for immediate demands—higher wages, shorter hours, reforms—it would deepen its awareness of the evil character of capitalism. Police charging workers' picket lines during strikes would make the working class aware of the state as the instrument of the ruling class. Through such experience the working class would eventually become sufficiently class-conscious and revolutionary to organize workers' councils and workers' militia, and to seize the means of production and state power. Led by a centralized political party which knew what it was doing, the proletarians would move from immediate demands to ultimate demands, from reform, in other words, to revolution. And while other classes might help in the process, the main burden was with the workers.

The New Left has come into being precisely because this model of strategy is unrealistic, because the working class is obviously not capable of playing the leading role. It behooves the New Left therefore to find a new strategy for the road to power, one that recognizes both its prospects and its limitations. The first point to suggest itself is that the emergent radicalism of our times is centered in two areas: among students and academia (about seven million people), and among blacks (about twenty-two million). This is the New Left's most serious weakness, for, taken together and assuming all the members of these groups are radical—which they are not—the two groups constitute only fifteen percent of the population. Furthermore, neither the students nor the blacks have access to the levers of production in such a way that they can paralyze the economy. The so-called "black rebellions" each summer have burned down sections of major cities and acted as shock therapy to a racist nation, but they are basically negative and will probably be suppressed by state terror. Talk in some circles about "guerrilla warfare" by the blacks is both infantile and futile, for no guerrilla movement can succeed unless it has the support of a vast majority of the population and a black guerrilla movement would have nothing approaching such support.

On the other hand, the strength of the New Left is that it lives in an age of revolution. Never before has mankind seen anything like it—sixty-one nations with almost two billion people have wriggled from under formal colonial domination and are fighting for national independence and a viable economic life. For the United States, the most counter-revolutionary nation of our times, this creates one crisis after another. Each revolution threatens the world balance of power, and, given the present American stance, drives the United States toward greater militarization, with all of its internal and external consequences. Thus the New Left is armed with issues to mobilize a constituency. Its numbers are relatively small but growing significantly, and it also knows that it has the political wherewithal to continue on to victory.

If it sees clearly both its weakness and its strength, the New Left can formulate a realistic strategy for eventual popular power. It is obvious, for instance, that for the moment it can only act as a catalyst. Workers, peasants and students in the so-called underdeveloped nations can think in terms of an immediate or near-immediate seizure of state power. They can think in terms of gaining power all-at-once, rather than in stages, because the internal structure of their societies is rickety. But the New Left in America and most of Western Europe must think of a revolution in stages, and of itself as the catalyst to bring other forces into motion. The history of the revolutions against feudalism, from the late sixteenth century to the mid-nineteenth century, indicates that some social transformations occur over a period of time. The Danish revolution, a model of this type, took three-quarters of a century after 1784 and was accomplished nonviolently. In Germany, from the customs union to Bismarck, feudalism was also replaced in spurts and spasms over many decades.

As a catalyst, then, the twin tasks of the New Left in the United States are:

(1) To help the American people sever their allegiance to capitalism, and build pockets of power for a new order.

(2) To mobilize sufficient countervailing power to checkmate the counter-revolutionary behavior of the United States abroad, thus facilitating and aiding the revolutions in Latin America, Asia, Africa and parts of Europe.

From 1939 to approximately the mid-1950s popular identification with the present form of American society was welded stronger than ever in history. Except in the black community, "Americanism" became a phobic allegiance to the status quo. The improvement in living standards, the significant decline in unemployment, the enlargement of escapism, the bipartisan foreign policy, all contributed to create an empathy between the people and the state such as never existed before. The radical movement declined to insignificance—the Communists from 100,000 to less than 10,000, the Socialists to virtually zero and the Trotskyists to a negligible number. Unions with leftist leadership—with some as many as two million members—shed that leftist leadership so that for the first time in history there was no substantial radical minority within the labor movement. It has only been since the civil rights and peace movements began to stir the national conscience a dozen years ago that any sizeable number of people have begun to loosen their emotional ties to the state and these still number only a few disorganized millions.

If the New Left is ever to achieve its objectives, its overriding task at the moment must be to widen the sphere of disenchantment—to open the eyes of the American people to the fact that its system guarantees only permanent racism, permanent crisis, and permanent war. It is here that the New Left differs from coalitionists like Howe, Rustin, and Michael Harrington, who try to coalesce with liberals and labor people within the establishment on the thesis that it can be reformed. The New Left seeks a coalition that breaks with the establishment, that sheds its illusions about the system. The New Left understands the necessity of living with the liberals, building bridges toward them, and drawing them to the left. But where the Howe-Harrington-Rustin coalitions are ready to accept the liberal program as the vehicle for change, the New Left woos the liberals to a radical anti-establishment program. It uses partial struggles and the struggle for reform as a means of dramatizing to Americans the basic contradictions of the system.

Through demonstrations, parades, sit-ins, teach-ins, draft resistance, campaigns among soldiers, poor people's marches, formation of community unions, work in the labor movement to build left wings, and similar techniques, the New Left draws attention to the basic weaknesses of the society and begins the process, in young people in particular, of re-thinking. A man marches in a parade against the war in Vietnam and soon learns to understand that Vietnams are inherent in the "American way of life," that Vietnams are linked to the inability of this society to eradicate poverty, linked to violence in the streets, to alienation. His sights broaden, and he moves from liberalism to radicalism. He not only finds his conscience pricked but his very life and livelihood at stake. The more often this mental process takes place, the more successful is the New Left in its strategy.

Acting as a catalyst must be viewed as the first stage of a relatively long process, and in each stage the New Left must elaborate tactics which fit its purposes of broadening the radical constituency. That means that as a minority movement today it has to appeal to the majority of Americans not only on the basis of self-interest, but above all on the basis of conscience. The student about to be drafted, has a personal interest in the movement. The black man, living on relief, will understand that Vietnam war money could provide, instead, a guaranteed annual income to his family. Most of the potential New Left constituency, however, will be drawn into the movement during the present stage on the basis of conscience. That means that the New Left must prove that it is defending morality, tradition, and legality —in a word, the cause of humanity—while the government is subverting them in order to reinforce a policy of greed and privilege. Whether the New Leftist believes in nonviolence or not, therefore, most of his actions will be nonviolent if only because in most instances violence will alienate the potential constituency. The New Leftist proves by his willingness to accept personal suffering, jail, and beatings, that it is he who stands for a higher order of morality, while the state adopts the violent and repressive stand.

Moreover, the New Left treads an uneasy path between opportunism and adventurism in which it must:

(1) Seek to widen the gulf between the people and the power elite.

(2) Draw liberals and apolitical people to the left, rather than isolate them from the movement.

An example of what I would consider to be an opportunistic tactic was the decision by some New Leftists to support Eugene McCarthy or the late Robert Kennedy in the Democratic Party primaries of 1968. It was the agitation of the peace and civil rights movement which resulted in some Senators and Congressmen raising their voices against the war, though none came out for withdrawal. It was this same continued agitation, and in particular the anti-war demonstrations in April and October of 1967, which propelled McCarthy and Kennedy into the Presidential race and forced Lyndon Johnson to withdraw. In that sense the McCarthy-Kennedy campaigns were victories for the movement, reflecting its persistent activity. But joining and working within McCarthy or Kennedy political machine was not the way to widen the gulf between the people and the establishment, but to narrow it. It was no wonder that McCarthy could say "our children have come home" or that so many of the Kennedy delegates could go over to the hawk candidate, Hubert Humphrey. The focus of radical attention during the electoral campaign should have been to build independent constituencies with independent peace-and-freedom campaigns for local offices, state offices, Congress and even the Presidency.

On the other side of the spectrum there was—and is—the danger of impatience and adventurism. Young people insist that we must step up the confrontation with the establishment even if that means sustained violence or guerrilla action. The thesis is put forth by some, for instance, that a radical force can be formed by deliberately provoking repression—by what someone once called "electrifying the masses." This advice by Stokely Carmichael illustrates the point: "People won't fight; they won't fight unless you push—so you push. You create disturbances, you keep pushing the system. You keep drawing up the contradictions until they have to hit back; once your enemy hits back, then your revolution starts. If your enemy does not hit back then you do not have a revolution." What seems to be said here is that an elite can stimulate a revolution on its own, regardless of the objective circumstances, simply by creating disturbances. On the contrary, however, a revolution cannot be willed. It must spring from popular grievances and must await their tempo. Leaders can articulate those grievances and help formulate strategy, but they cannot maneuver masses of people like pawns. The New Left's concept of leadership cannot be manipulative, like that of certain segments of the Old Left. It must be based on openness, feedback, participation; and it must spring from popular disaffection rather than through manufactured synthetic disturbances. Otherwise the American conscience cannot be guided toward a break with its past.

History cannot be prodded artificially, nor can the New Left move out too far ahead of its potential legions. What will probably happen is that the movement will win basic concessions in stages, as the schisms within American society widen. By way of example, I can visualize that if the New Left can effect an end to the war in Vietnam and if the "black rebellion" accelerates, the government will be made to grant a guaranteed annual income. Around victories such as these a national Peace-and-Freedom party can cluster, demanding more concessions—changes in the electoral system, popular participation in decision-making and in the economy, and nationalization of certain basic industries.

It is impossible to chart the specific road to power by the New Left and the mass of Americans whose interests it represents, but one can outline its directions. As a catalyst the New Left will mount one campaign after another against the manifestations of imperialism and racism, splitting away one segment of the population after another which currently identifies strongly with the establishment. As it wins over these segments from the middle classes, labor, and the military, it will use its countervailing power to whittle away the present institutions, the profit motive, the competitive élan, until finally it can reconstruct a new society based on popular—participative—power.

I believe, this strategy will be generally nonviolent, if only because the enemy has a huge weapon superiority and because in a society where most grievances are not economic, reliance must be placed on appeals to conscience. In time, I think a new political party of the left will emerge, but I doubt that it will take the old "democratic centralist" form. The labor movement, as I foresee it, will also be revitalized, as the government demands more and more austerity from it, driving its most liberal wing toward the New Left—a process that has already begun.

The important things for the new radicalism to consider, I feel, are that the anticipated revolution will be multi-class, will take place in stages, and be international in scope. Those who are impatient with the slow pace of transformation in the United States must console themselves with the realization that the revolution is world-wide and developing in different tempos in different places.

V

Finally, in addition to analysis and a strategy for the road to power a new radical ideology must give us a glimpse of the beautiful tomorrow. What will the humanistic society look like? How will it function? Will it rely on material or moral incentives? Will it nationalize industry? Will it have a single-party or multi-party system?

There are no easy or ready answers. This is so in part because the New Left in the Western World is thinking of radical change in highly developed nations whereas the revolutions that have occurred so far have been in underdeveloped ones, and in part because of the experience of Stalinism in the Soviet Union, which warped the humanistic goals of the original revolution, causing wide disenchantment with the "socialist model."

There are, however, some guideposts from other philosophies and other nations that offer a clue as to the character of the humanistic society to which the New Left aspires. From Gandhi the New Left may borrow at least the concept of *psychological* nonviolence—tolerance toward friend and foe, decency in the relationship between peoples, participation in decision-making—and perhaps also an American version of *physical* nonviolence. If the New Left seeks world which eschews violence between peoples and nations and guarantees participation, the Gandhian ideal can serve as a useful model.

From Yugoslavia the New Left can appropriate certain ideas on self-management which can work far better in an advanced economy. Under the Titoist self-management principle, workers in every enterprise elect a workers' council, which in turn elects a management committee that has overall power—subject to veto by the workers' council—to determine the product, prices, management policies, social improvements, etc., including the right to fire the enterprise's supervisor. Within each department the workers plan their own production, do their own hiring and firing, and work out their own methods so that they can earn for themselves the biggest "profit" possible. The higher the profit the higher their earnings and the greater their social benefits.

Self-management can be readily applied to other sectors of daily life. For instance, the apartment-house tenants may decide what improvements to make, how to keep up the property and what rentals to charge. School boards could truly represent viable groups in the school district—teachers, students, parents, trade unions, and others. Self-management means a trend toward decentralization of the role of government ministries; and if this policy works effectively it inevitably is accompanied by relaxation of state controls over foreign travel, dissent and other popular rights—as has actually happened in Yugoslavia. You cannot depend on the people in the shops to plan production and then muzzle them by limiting their right to question and discuss.

From Cuba and, perhaps, China the New Left can borrow the concept of moral incentives, the shaping of society in such a way that people work to achieve something not only for themselves but for mankind, that they look not only to their own present but to succeeding generations, that they are ever-willing to cooperate with others for the common good. I do not believe that there is a great barrier between material incentives and the moral ones, as many radicals today insist. So long as the profit and competitive motives are held in rein, society will rely more and more on moral incentives as its living standards rise.

As to the structure of government, I believe that the New Left will take into account both the complexity of modern life and the need for the highest forms of participation possible. The first casualty of such an approach will be elections based on geography. When the American Constitution was framed, most people lived on farms or farm villages. Geographical representation was therefore also functional representation—people voted both as residents of a particular area and as farmers. But to mix up workers, farmers, professors, capitalists, and schoolteachers in one bag today, just because they live in the same neighborhood prevents each group from discussing its political problems from its own self-interest. A formula must be devised where elections are conducted on a functional level: workers in a factory electing their own delegate to some regional body, professors electing theirs, students theirs, farmers theirs, and so on. Regional bodies will then elect delegates to higher bodies, each one with not only legitislative but executive powers.

Other necessary innovations include: elected bodies of experts (say in economics) parallel to legislatures so that no law passed by the latter can be put into effect until the elected experts in that field also approve it; the principle that no man serve more than a certain number of years in any post; and the principle that earnings of government officials must be in line with that of the ordinary citizen.

Most important, society will take unto itself the control both of production and profit. This does not mean that every facet of the economy will be nationalized or that no private industry will be permitted. It does mean, however, that an economy which propels society toward racism, imperialism, poverty, militarism, and war must give way to one in which the levers for its operation will be held by the state, not individual entrepreneurs or corporations.

If this outline of the humanist society seems all too vague it is perhaps because there is no clear indication as yet how long the world revolution will take, and exactly what the stages will be for radical transformation of the American society as part of that world revolution. I offer what is said here on analysis, a strategy for the road to power, and a vision of the new social order only as tentative observations in the hope that they will be elaborated by others.

The Organizational Question and the Urban Commune

Dimitrios Roussopoulos

First, the notion of the seizure of power. Here, the old model wouldn't do any more. That, for example, in a country like the United States, under the leadership of a centralized and authoritarian party, large masses concentrate on Washington, occupy the Pentagon, and set up a new government, seems to be slightly too unrealistic and utopian a picture.

We will see that what we have to envisage is some kind of diffuse and dispersed disintegration of the system, in which interest, emphasis and activity is shifted to local and regional areas.

Now, to the organization of the New Left. I already mentioned the obsolescence of traditional forms of organization, for example, a parliamentary party. No party I can envisage today will not, within a very short time, fall victim to the general and totalitarian political corruption which characterizes the political universe. No political party, but also no revolutionary centralism and no underground—because both are all too easy victims of the intensified and streamlined apparatus of repression.

As against these forms, what seems to be shaping up is an entirely overt organisation, diffused, concentrated in small groups and around local activities, small groups which are highly flexible and autonomous. . . .

Now the strength of the New Left may well reside in precisely these small contesting and competing groups, active at many points at the same time, a kind of political guerrilla force in peace, or in so-called peace, but, and this is I think the most important point, small groups concentrated on the level of local activities, thereby foreshadowing what may, in all likelihood, be the basic organization of libertarian socialism, namely small councils of manual and intellectual workers, soviets, if one can still use the term and not think of what actually happened to the soviets, some kind of what I would like to call, and I mean it seriously, organised spontaneity.

Herbert Marcuse*

When, as radicals, we try to define the nature of our movement or its structure, we are, surely, defining the nature of the society we choose to live in

* "Radical Perspectives 1969," *Our Generation,* Vol. 6, No. 3.

and anticipate for others. As a matter of elementary political honesty we should state openly and without ambiguity or double-talk the shape of that struggle as well as the goals we should fight for. This latter point is a matter of great practical importance these days. It is necessary for the construction of a revolutionary movement and its development.

The form of urban commune that we shall discuss in this essay exists nowhere as such. What exists are many dimensions of an urban commune, and a process that makes the speculation here both the logical outcome and logical necessity of present experiments. Advanced political communes already exist in Berlin and Frankfurt, in Copenhagen and Stockholm, in Paris, London, Milan and several cities of the United States. There is growing communication among the New Left in these different countries. Uppermost in their discussions is the organizational question—the forms of survival and struggle. This paper is therefore polemical and speculative, but the area of speculation is narrow in that most of the aspects of this kind of commune already exist. What does not exist is the integration of all these aspects into a logical whole. This discussion consequently is for people who are already well advanced in their thinking on this question, and, therefore, concentrates on strategy.

Currently there are at least four main areas of debate with reference to the questions of organization: the liberal pressure group position, the cultural revolution position, the Marxist-Leninist position, and the positions that this paper tries to bring together into a whole. The first position we can discard out-of-hand. The second and third have a constituency in the radical movement and must be examined, for both positions are revolutionary in tone but conservative in substance.

CULTURAL REVOLUTION

"Change your head instead" goes the cultural position, and up to the word "instead" one can agree. This view starts with one of our generation's greatest insights, that the revolution begins at home, inside our minds, when we start being honest about our own situation—who controls us, who we are, whom we love, whom we hate.

From this approach comes a correct criticism of the "politicos" and their organizations, which rhetorically oppose the system but psychologically (or, as Marcuse puts it, "biologically") are thoroughly part of it. The ego rivalries, elitism, materialism, abstract intellectualism, and male chauvinism of the movement are not problems that can be dealt with later. They are problems that can prevent and mutilate revolution, problems that make the Left a kind of psychologically loyal opposition, hating capitalism in the abstract but unable to reject its social relationships enough to destroy it.

No genuine cultural revolution can be carried through without successful struggle against the institutions of our society. There is no choice between changing your head and struggling to change your society; one does both at the same time. The Rolling Stones owe as much to our movement as we owe to the Stones. Without successful struggle against institutions, cultural revolution will be incorporated into a subsidized and commercial form of entertainment. The only culture worth having is a culture that relates to struggle, growing from it and nurturing it in return.

The cultural revolution approach becomes even more dangerous as it naturally moves from the idea that "revolution begins with me" to the notion that "revolution is for me." People come to believe that the revolution has come because they have managed to hustle a welfare check, or set up a rural commune, or managed not to work. They no longer feel responsible for others or for a community of people. They see rebellion and revolution as an isolated act, and they dream of a very American individualized independence, rather than a collective freedom. Too many of these people are exactly like their "Easy Rider" brothers, and they are heading toward the same fate.

"MARXIST-LENINIST ORGANIZATION"

Let us now examine the Marxist-Leninist position of building a vanguard political party managed by democratic centralism. We must straightaway seek out the relationship between the movement and its constituency. If the main objective of the socialist revolution is to eliminate private property and the market in order to accelerate, through nationalization and planning, the development of production, then the mass of people has no *autonomous* and *conscious* role to play in this transformation. All steps that convert the mass of the people into an obedient and disciplined infantry under the command of "revolutionary" headquarters are seen as good and proper ones. It is enough that the classes of revolutionary change be prepared or induced to fight capitalism to the death. It is of secondary importance that the mass of people should have any creative role. The leadership knows all, and, furthermore, has a simple, direct answer for each question. The relation between party and class, then, parallels the division in capitalist society between those who direct and those who merely execute. After the revolution, management and power rests with the party, which manages society in the alleged interests of the workers. This is a concept shared by most Marxists. The reemergence of a bureaucratic class society becomes inevitable.

"POPULAR CONTROL"

Instead we must envisage a revolution whose objective is popular control. In the work sphere, this means that workers must manage production and the economy through the power of workers' councils. In the community, it means neighborhood self-management by the people who live there. The active and conscious subject of such a revolution and the whole subsequent social transformation can be none other than the people themselves. The revolution we envisage can only take place through the autonomous action of people. This immense transformation of society can take place if and only if the people find the will and consciousness for revolution in themselves. Socialism, for instance, realized that acting "on behalf of the proletariat," even by a revolutionary party, is a nonsensical conception. The revolutionary organization cannot lead the movement. The movement itself, which is the sum of all its parts, must at a point in its development consist of the majority of the population, although effective co-ordination of such a formulation will involve leadership.

The most important debates now going on in the New Left, as was the case at its birth, are over the proper relationship of the revolutionary movement to its constituency and over the movement's internal structure. Traditionally the revolutionary party is organized and functions according to certain well-proven principles of efficiency which are allegedly based on common sense, starting with a division of labor between so-called leaders and rank-and-file. Control of the former by the latter is promised but necessarily postponed, work is specialized and a rigid division of tasks is ordered. This may be common sense to some, but is sheer nonsense from a radical perspective.

The revolutionary movement should apply to itself the principles evolved by the theory and practice of participatory democracy in the course of its development into collectives, urban communes, workers' councils, neighborhood councils, and regional assemblies. These units should have the greatest autonomy given a self-regulating sense of movement unity. Direct democracy should exist wherever it can be materially applied; this means, for instance, eligibility and instant revocability of all delegates to central bodies given powers of decision-making.

The 1969 national convention of the Students for a Democratic Society erupted in ugly sectarian quarrels. The factional struggles have now begun to hit at local chapters trying to avoid the dilemmas of dogmatic quarrels. Many of these quarrels are rooted in the organizational question in its fullest dimensions. Some have maintained that the course of SDS at the national level presages an end to participatory democracy in the New Left. But it seems more likely that the national course reflects the preoccupation of many SDS members with building a mass revolutionary movement at the local level. Most New Leftists have concentrated their efforts at local organizing, with only a vague notion of how their struggles link to a national movement. Even on a regional level, their efforts are rarely coordinated. They pause from time to time in their local work to meet with each other and rap about the condition of each area. Time tables and strategies are decided on the basis of immediate needs organizers feel in their constituencies. Many excellent organizers have expressed their opposition to the national organization by indulging in the politics of absence: they avoid bothering with national organizations that are inevitably elitist, claiming that "resolutions are only paper" and that the National Office, no matter who runs it, generates dependency and authoritarianism, not leadership. So the circle has almost completed itself.

As the concept of "national organization" remains alien to much of the new left other forms of organization have begun to emerge at the local level. This localism reflects an understanding and a strategic appreciation of the progressive urbanization of North American society and the implication of this for power politics, as well as the politics of revolution. These new organizational forms have a variety of names—collectives, affinity groups, cooperatives, urban communes—and have various levels of sophistication. They add up to a rejection of such old-style concepts of organization as the liberal pressure group and the vanguard party. It is also true that some collectives are looked upon as embryos for a revolutionary party of the future, but historical developments will determine more than any theoretical contemplation whether this will come to pass. There is a clear understanding at any rate, that alternatives to the traditional organization structure are essential.

WHAT IS AN URBAN COMMUNE?

An urban commune is not a simple, temporary co-operative or a cell structure of the Old Left style. The assumption here is that the members of the commune are consciously and purposefully radical and see their commune as an agency for revolutionary social and political change.

But before we describe some of the basic essentials that make for the kind of commune we are both proposing and describing here, we will deal with its general features. It is understood that *within* the framework of both general characteristics and basic essentials there is a great deal of experimentation. The difference between the concept of an urban commune and other such experiments is that collective and individual experience during the last few years have determined these fixed general and specific essentials so that these political organisms can, not only pass the first stage of survival, but actually begin making a positive contribution to radical change. Although there is no collected body of material on these activities at collective living, a careful perusal of the underground press, conversations, and exchanged views on this subject at radical conferences suggests that answers are advancing along the lines suggested here.

Radicals interested in the organizational question agree that there are several crucial questions which have to do with internal organization as well as political orientation which must be openly discussed and understood thoroughly. To the extent this is done, to that extent the commune will be stable.

The subjective need for the creation of such revolutionary organisms is to sustain serious political work on the one hand and to protect individuals from anomie and alienation in an urban environment on the other. The development of urban communes registers support for the idea that a revolutionary organization must seek to add to its fund of consciousness without trying to manipulate that development. It also represents an effort to bring into play all the worthwhile dynamics of the small face-to-face group. Radical brothers and sisters who know each other intimately seek to combine life-styles and work-styles, make a concordance of theory and practice, thus adding to the movement's knowledge of the communal movement. Such communes are not burdened by leaders and bureaucrats from the outside or inside because they are autonomous, directly democratic, anarchic, and based on mutual aid. Urban communes should seek to seed the social environment with similar revolutionary groupings. Not only is such proliferation central to a New Left strategy, but the establishment of such a network permits the development of neighborhood councils (which we will examine later).

Whether these communes coalesce or separate at the living or work-place or on a neighborhood or industrial level depends entirely on the actual situations, not on a bureaucratic decree from some central committee. Such organisms are, it should be added superbly resistant to harassment and can respond creatively to attempts at repression. Urban communes at either the work-place or living-place are, also, ideally suited to the major metropolitan cities of North America where revolution must come as a spontaneous movement from below. Communes will clearly collaborate closely on any scale necessary by establishing wide contacts with each other and organizing common, self-disciplined activities. A rooted base for revolution logically emerges, a strong localism and autonomy provides the means for a sensitive appreciation of immediate possibilities in the particular area. In the absence of a bureaucratic apparatus, inter-commune cooperation can preserve revolutionary elan, spontaneity, and democratic instincts. Thus far communes are intensely variegated in life-styles; the communalism in some is more extensive than in others. Some are developing extensive child day-care activities, educational faculties at home, and new concepts of sexuality. Others are developing a delicate balance between privacy and collectivism. Each commune has its own resources to function completely on its own. Each seeks complete roundedness in experience, knowledge, and action by trying consciously to overcome the divisions that distort all individuals and groups in bourgeois society. Each commune continually attempts to expand its knowledge of the neighborhood and each constitutes a nucleus of consciousness, study, experience, and action, serving to reinforce and advance spontaneous revolutionary movement from below.

THE BASIC ESSENTIALS OF AN URBAN COMMUNE

More specifically an urban commune is a socio-political task force. Thus, its members should be in the same profession or vocation; e.g., social workers, teachers, sociologists, urbanists. This is important because a central strategy of this concept of the urban commune is to affect the work-place. Thus a task-force commune of, say, printers could insist upon workers' management in the plants in which they work and initiate the idea of workers' councils among their fellow workers. This process would parallel efforts by a network of communes for neighborhood control and management. In this way, the required dialectic between work-place and living-place would come into being. Such grouping sprang into existence during the May-June General Strike in France 1968. The "committee d'action" brought people together at the neighborhood level to affect both it and the places where these people worked which were on strike. Similarly in Frankfurt and Milan radicals attempt to create the idea of people of one profession or trade both to live together and to organize at their place of work. The accent on the living or working space depends on the social analysis the particular lot of radicals have. This orientation is emerging everywhere where national organizations collapse. This is the case in the U.S.A., where the SDS no longer exists as a "national" organization, in Germany where the SDS has taken a similar step, and also in France since the Mouvement 22 Mars was disbanded.

The concept of a task-force oriented commune could have another definition. A commune might well consist of a variety of professions with a common objective of, say, putting out a radical magazine or newspaper. A common political work process is what seems essential. It should be as specific as possible, for the more general it is the more complications are invited. Such a multi-vocational membership would not undercut the work-place and living-place dialectic although it definitely slows it down.

The urban commune is a brotherhood that serves as a reference group outside and inside the work-place. It breaks the barriers of isolation and creates pressures against copping out. Its self-reliance protects it from any authoritarianism from the outside. This is a departure from the old left concept of cell-organizing.

Ideally, the commune provides a forum in which people plan their political agendas and evaluate their work. An essential aspect of such a commune is the concept of mutual aid. Should a member lose his job for political work, then the commune must support him and his family until he finds a new job.

The size of the commune should be no more than six to eight adults. The communards should either live within a short walking distance of each other, preferably on the same street or within the same apartment building, although maintaining the privacy of their individual homes. The successful commune requires careful and systematic study of group dynamics by its members. There should be a weekly mutual criticism meeting at first, and perhaps bi-weekly meetings at some point in the future. Such a session could also be requested by a communard who seeks some personal advice or to deal with a complaint. Meetings should be genuine dialogue sessions.

The urban commune fully matured is a community of study in a constant effort to develop the consciousness of its members. A great deal of collective and individual study must be undertaken of the history and literature of communalism. The commune should also be a culturally enriching experience. People must be honest in admitting ignorance, must seek to remove their prejudices and, thus, learn from each other. Clearly individuals must learn to tolerate likes and dislikes of other communards, waiting for the appropriate time to challenge the assumptions held by their fellows. Our society has, after all, done a great deal to emasculate us as human beings. And since we are not utopians we must realize that the communes are always going to have problems until our society is fully transformed. It is essential that each member of the group be stronger than the commune, yet draw his ultimate strength and direction from it.

Urban communes are being developed mainly from where people live. Where there are communes with the sharpest dialectic between the living and work place we can expect the quickest growth of demands for workers' control. At the same time the constant agitation of the communes for neighborhood control will stimulate the development of neighborhood councils seeking management of their environments and the creation of cooperative economics. Such a development might also influence the development of a cooperative movement in the area of consumer buying or radicalize existing co-op institutions.

Eventually, we may expect the successes of the communes and the neighborhood and workers' councils to create confrontations between authoritarianism and direct democracy, between bureaucracy and non-violent direct action, between militarism, conformity, and civil disobedience. As revolutionary impulses are generated from below, revolutionary assemblies will be formed that will bring together, regionally, the neighborhood and workers' councils. The delegates will then hammer out broad strategies and programs, as masses of people withdraw their loyalty from the existing structures and create new ones with a new legitimacy. It is here that *community control* will come into play, facing the ecological questions of decaying environment while building the foundations for parallel government, with the urban commune as its basic building block.

Here, in summary, are the key functions of the radical urban commune:

(1) The urban commune is more than a cooperative of convience or an old left cell. It is a situation of shared and cooperative living that attempts to marry life and work styles both at the place of work and residence. The primary thrust of the commune is task-force political work of people with common professional or vocational interests, such as medical doctors, social workers, teachers, and others.

(2) The urban commune should consist of no more than six to eight adults who have known each other for some time. They should live near each other or within the same apartment building in separate

apartments. Some privacy must be maintained within the collective self-discipline. The commune helps its people define and evaluate their work; weekly meetings should describe, criticize, and evaluate what members are doing in their neighborhood and at their place of work.

(3) The commune should take on some kind of joint political activity at first to insure that participation in politics extended beyond a professional setting. Such action will also help the formation of other communes.

(4) The commune should take on the responsibility of providing certain services for the radical movement. These services should include work in political education and research. The commune should assume certain financial obligations. Some members of the commune may make large salaries. Efforts should be made to establish a common fund financed by, say, ten percent of all income over four thousand dollars per family. Such a fund would be used for a number of purposes, including aid to certain action organizations or projects or for mutual aid or protection against loss of income caused by radical activities.

(5) The commune should explore other social structures for interpersonal relations such as group or polyandrous marriage, which provide family life but may produce less children. Love, love-making, a man and a woman together, should seek, as the vehicle of mutual realization, the creation of new selves and a new world of being which could be more important than reproducing our kind.

(6) The commune should establish a collective child-care arrangement that would give responsibility for children to both men and women. This is also a practical necessity to allow all members of the commune to participate equally in political life, and other non-domestic activities. The pleasure of raising children should widen so that all need not directly reproduce to enter into this human experience. No female communard need give birth to more than one child, if any. The commune may also adopt children.

(7) The commune will seek to create more desirable alternatives to individualistic consuming patterns, for example, cooperative buying. Members would share capital goods, such as cars, washing machines, and other tools. These values will be projected into the surrounding community as others are encouraged to set up similar communes.

(8) At the work-place, communards will encourage the demand for

workers' management and control. At the same time co-workers will be encouraged to set up their own living-place communes.

It should be stressed, in conclusion, that the purpose of the commune is not to create a counter community into which radicals can retreat, or on which they can lavish their attention. Rather it is to create a communal life style that supports increased political activity at the neighborhood and work level.

These task-oriented communes would seek to get their members eventually into the same work-place while getting their fellow workers to understand the benefits of communal living with the view of forming or joining an urban commune.

A proliferation of urban communes clamoring for participatory democracy in its concrete forms of control and management in major cities can, not only revolutionize the vertical form of existing power, but also be a real alternative to the narrow revolutionary organizations of the past.

Relations between existing political communes (Columbia's communes, Berkeley's revolutionary gangs, France's committees of Action, Cleveland's groups) are slowly coming into existence. A network of communes must be created. This network or "Federation" must be characterized by structural looseness which guarantees the identity and self-determination of each group, as well as an organizational reality which allows maximum concerted actions directed toward revolution.

The urban commune in no way denies the validity of mass actions, rather, this idea increases the possibilities of those actions. The active minority is able, because it is, theoretically, more conscious and better prepared tactically, to take the initiative and make the first breakthroughs. The urban commune can play the role of a permanent fermenting agent encouraging action without claiming to take leadership. The urban commune is the source of both spontaneity and new forms of struggle.

The Movement:
A New Beginning
Staughton Lynd

What might be termed a classical period in the history of draft resistance to the Vietnam war began in April 1967, when about 150 young men burned their draft cards in Sheep's Meadow in New York. In the San Francisco area, David Harris, Dennis Sweeney, Lenny Heller and Steve Hamilton named themselves the Resistance and in its name called for the mass return of draft cards on October 16. And Muhammad Ali refused induction. The classical period ended in April 1968, when within the space of a week Lyndon Johnson withdrew from the Presidential campaign and announced a partial bombing halt, a third day of card returns brought the number of resisters to perhaps 2500, and Martin Luther King was assassinated.

During that year, April 1967 to April 1968, there was an obvious answer to the question: What is a member of the Resistance? A member of the Resistance during the classic period was one who publicly, in concert with others, resisted the Selective Service System, or who publicly advocated or aided that act.

Somehow the classic act of noncooperation with the Selective Service System has been permitted—to borrow from Karl Marx language which he borrowed from the anthropology of religion—to become a fetish to be reified, so that an action which, after all, is only one way of resisting one form of repression, has come to define our movement as a whole.

The Resistance must grow beyond its classic definition of resistance. It must find its way behind the fetish on noncooperation with the Selective Service System to the spirit which prompted that act to begin with. To move forward from an ossified form is difficult, but a spirit can grow and take new forms. We need to do whatever has to be done so that, in a manner faithful to our original spirit, we can become a mass movement of resistance to all forms of repression.

How will we respond to this challenge? What is the future of the Resistance? Probably the history books of the next century will say something like this:

> After April 1968 the Resistance began to decline. High draft calls for college students in the summer of 1968 did not materialize. The war dragged on, even in some respects escalated, but in the absence of dramatic single acts of escalation the Resistance was unable to re-capture its initial momentum. Factions crystallized into irreconcilable splinter groups. Some Resistance groups, impressed by the anti-imperialist analysis of Students for a Democratic Society, began to de-mand a multi-issue program and a coherent long-run strategy for fundamental social change. Frustrated in their efforts to induce their fellow-resisters to develop such a perspective, those who felt this way drifted away from the Resistance, often into SDS, although not with-out occasional nostalgia for the consensus decision-making, emotional openness, and decentralized structure of the Resistance community.
>
> Among those who remained in the Resistance, concerns previously secondary to the war—drugs, diet, communes, the creation of non-violence—became more and more prominent; and this in itself had a fragmenting effect, as individuals began to put their main energies into coffee houses, free schools, and other enterprises distinct from draft resistance work. When the war finally ended, the Resistance, like other groups organized around the single issue of the war, disinte-grated. Within six months of the signing of the Vietnam peace treaty, the Resistance was dead.

This, I repeat, is what the history books will probably say. Now let me project another history, not probable, but I am convinced possible. Here is how it goes:

> After April 1968 the Resistance, like the larger movement, ex-perienced the disorientation characteristic of Presidential election years. About a year later a new direction began to emerge. Despite the general confusion many Resistance groups had been patiently ex-ploring forms of resistance beyond the draft, and conducting experi-mental joint actions with high-school, GI, and women's liberation groups, as well as with some local chapters of SDS. Internal tensions, a natural result of this exploration and experimentation, were fruit-fully resolved at a national conference in Bloomington, Illinois. Work against the draft continued, of course. The draft itself continued, be-cause American imperialism required the flexible supply of manpower which the draft made available in order to fight more than one Third World insurrection simultaneously. When, in the spring of 1969, it became clear that the war in Vietnam was far from over, the Resist-ance revived. But the Selective Service System was not viewed as a

single facet of an illegitimate structure of power. Accordingly, many
members of SDS, who had hitherto dismissed the Resistance as masochistic middle-class moralism, turned toward the draft resistance
movement as a political vehicle which, in contrast to the polemical in-
fighting dominant in SDS, combined sophisticated analysis with a
humane spirit. As a result the Resistance found itself in a position to
play a key role in building the broad liberation movement which organized the revolutionary general strikes of the next decade.

I don't have a formula for bringing this to pass but I can try to help by
examining two pieces of Resistance experience. First, the year prior to
April 1967, during which we groped our way toward the act of public,
collective card return; second, the year which followed April 1968, during
which many Resistance groups revised their initial assumptions as they
sought to relate to new issues and new social classes.

I

Several groups, several strains of thinking, converged to produce the resistance actions of April 1967.

First, there was a group of pacifists for whom dissociation from the draft
expressed a more-than-political worldview. This group could trace its philosophy to A. J. Muste's essay on "holy disobedience." It included many
members of the Committee for Nonviolent Action and the Catholic Worker
community, such as Tom Rodd, David Miller and Tom Cornell. Meeting in
New York City in October 1966, adherents of this approach issued the
following "Statement of Non-cooperation with Military Conscription":

> We, the undersigned men of draft age (18–35), believe that all war
> is immoral and ultimately self-defeating. We believe that military con-
> scription is evil and unjust. Therefore, we will not cooperate in any
> way with the Selective Service System.
>
> We will not register for the draft.
>
> If we have registered, we will sever all relations with the Selective
> Service System.
>
> We will carry no draft cards or other Selective Service certificates.
>
> We will not accept any deferment, such as 2-S.
>
> We will not accept any exemption, such as 1-O or 4-D.
>
> We will refuse induction in the armed forces.
>
> We urge and advocate that other young men join us in non-coop-
> eration with the Selective Service System.
>
> We are in full knowledge that these actions are violations of the
> Selective Service laws punishable by up to 5 years imprisonment
> and/or a fine of $10,000.

Near the opposite end of the political spectrum was a tendency illustrated by David Mitchell and, after the enunciation of Black Power in mid-1966, by the Student Nonviolent Coordinating Committee. These resisters were not pacifist. Nor were they noncooperators, but they publicly refused induction. They were also explicitly anti-imperialist, in David Mitchell's case since 1961.

Between these two ideological extremes—pacifist noncooperation, and anti-imperialist induction refusal—fell the bulk of students opposed to the war. They expressed themselves in the spring of 1966 by sitting-in against the sending of class ranks to draft boards, and in the fall of 1966 by signing we-won't-go statements. It is fashionable in the Resistance to deprecate such activities, since the students involved rarely grasped the nettle of induction refusal. But for many resisters, anti-rank and we-won't-go represented a stage from which they moved on to resistance. Thus Michael Ferber, David Harris and Michael Cullen of the Milwaukee 14 signed we-won't-go statements; Kerry Berland, after taking part in an anti-ranking sit-in at Chicago, was shocked that after the sit-in many of the demonstrators took the test anyway.

I see the movement which became the Resistance emerging from certain groups of students, who, as they moved beyond a we-won't-go position, sought to combine the insights of pacifist noncooperation with those of anti-imperialist induction refusal. No doubt the most significant of these student groups was that at Stanford. Here I would like to describe two East Coast groups, at Yale and Cornell.

In July 1966 there met in New Haven a group of young men who drew up the following statement:

> We men of draft age disavow all military obligations to our government until it ceases wars against peoples seeking to determine their own destinies. On November 16 we will return our draft cards to our local boards with a notice of our refusal to cooperate until American invasions are ended. We fully realize that this action will be considered illegal and that we will be liable to five years imprisonment.
>
> We propose to develop our program August 25 and 26 prior to the SDS convention at Clear Lake, Iowa.

One of the eight men who signed that statement was a longtime worker with CNVA. A second belonged to the self-styled anarchist wing of national SDS (I recall his saying at that meeting, "SDS members have never done anything."). A third had made a detailed proposal for anti-draft activity at the SDS National Council meeting the previous spring; his proposal had been lost in rhetoric and he was ready to look elsewhere. Three of the others, as well as myself, had worked together in Mississippi in the summer of 1964. One had worked with Dennis Sweeney in McComb.

From that meeting in New Haven travellers fanned out across the country as far as the West Coast. I have a letter written from Madison on July 22, 1966 which began:

> We've made our way to Chicago and on up to Madison, Wisc. The results of our probes into Detroit and Ann Arbor have been encouraging. Seven or eight of my close co-patriots in Detroit are gravitating very strongly. Ann Arbor folks, numbering five or six, are moving as well. We've been keeping the numbers small but discussions have been intense.

This was exactly the process which Dennis Sweeney and David Harris would repeat the next summer on the West Coast. And already in mid-1966, the germs of the coming split between SDS and the Resistance were apparent. The letter went on:

> Discussion in Ann Arbor clarified another pattern of thinking; namely, that the idea and act were not political. Persons who say this attribute to this action a mere mechanical quality. For some people, like Steve Weissman and Mike Goldfield, they had to see this idea as a comprehensive political program with organization "guarantees" for its expansion into all levels of the student movement. Until that could be developed, they were unable to see it as a viable political movement. I come at the question from a different perspective. . . .

On July 30, 1966 the travellers returned to New Haven for a second meeting. A report on that meeting included the following observations on motivations for resistance:

> Since the individual commitment to go to jail is the basis of the collective strength of the movement, we talked for a while about the kinds of reasons a person would take such an action. The two basic motivations are personal and political. In the case of the former, the person sees the draft situation as his personal climax with the system—he probably would have done a similar act anyway, but decides to do it with the group because of the strength that adds to him and the group. A large majority of us, however, would not have taken this act, at least not until after [being] confronted with induction itself. We are arriving at the decision because we feel that we have a political program we can make work.

The report also laid out perspectives for organizing:

There was a very strong feeling that we have to organize by sending our field staff to places which are not normally reached by the movement, in addition to the usual centers of activity. The organizers have to really go out and *work* to build strong democratic local organizations (or anti-draft struggle committees), that have a common relationship through this and other programs. In the case of existing organizations like SDS chapters, the idea would be to strengthen the movement and deepen the particular group's commitment to change. . . . We have decided to reject the type of organizing that issues calls to do something, writes magazine articles and prints newspaper ads, and then expects people to act. . . . Only after the basic groundwork is laid over the next few months (i.e., building strong committed local groups by the field staff) will we pull out the stops of publicity. . . . Those of us who travelled west were awed by the size of the country and feel that if there is regional strength and unity this will help in the struggle that is to come.

It was generally agreed that the major program that would follow from the collective act of draft defiance would be the organizing of a broad range of forms of draft resistance. It was assumed that those who turned in their draft cards on November 16, 1966, would thereafter become organizers.

Also discussed were adult support—that was to be my province—and the alternative merits of different kinds of legal defense:

We can take a civil liberties defense (claiming that we can advocate anything and also that the government is violating our liberties by drafting us to fight their war). We can take a Nuremburg defense (the war is immoral and unjust and it is our responsibility not to fight but to resist). We can also stand mute (and declare that the court is a political tool of the system and could not possibly grant us any justice).

Finally there was discussion of womens' liberation:

It was noted that there was a vast potential for organizing young women since there was a vacuum now organizationally and programatically. Women Strike for Peace is mostly middle-aged and programatically fuzzy. SDS, despite occasional rhetoric to the contrary, remains a male-dominated organization. We agreed to raise programatic possibilities with women we know, but felt that it would be up to the women themselves to develop corollary programs to our draft resistance.

There were women's workshops at the subsequent Des Moines meeting and at the We-Won't-Go conference in Chicago in December 1966. The first women's liberation groups in the country, organized by Heather Tobis Booth, Naomi Weinstein, Sue Munaker and others, grew directly from these workshops.

The Des Moines meeting in late August 1966 decided that the projected November 16 date was premature. Individuals were urged to return to their various communities and organize solid local groups. Perhaps the most important of these was at Cornell, for it was this group which called for the mass burning of draft cards in New York the following April. The organizer of the Cornell group was Tom Bell, who had attended the July 30 meeting in New Haven and the Des Moines conference. Tom, in the characteristic Resistance manner, rather than calling a meeting sought out an individual at a time. Characteristically, too, the call for mass draft card burning was stimulated by the decision of one person, Bruce Dancis, to burn his own card.

Bruce and Tom both illustrate the attempt to synthesize ethical and political insights which I have stressed as typical of these early resistance groups. Bruce Dancis was quite active in SDS as a Cornell freshman and at the time he burned his draft card was Cornell SDS president. The other side of his background is suggested by the fact that his father had been a conscientious objector in the Second World War. He was raised in what he terms "an Ethical Culturist home," and during the summer before he went to college he met and was much influenced by David McReynolds of the War Resisters League.

On the day he registered with the Selective Service System, in May 1966, Bruce Dancis also took part in a sit-in in the university president's office against the turning over of class ranks to that same system. At this time he told his draft board that he did not want a 2-S (student) deferment, that he wanted a 1-O (conscientious objector) status, but that if granted 1-O status he might not do alternative service. By the next fall (this is still 1966),

> I began to see that CO had the same things wrong with it that 2-S had. I saw that a guy from the streets of Harlem, who couldn't get a 2-S deferment since he wasn't in college, couldn't get a CO since it is such a difficult form to fill out. I couldn't see myself having to explain to a bunch of old men why I should be exempted from killing people. . . . In December, 1966 I finally decided that I must sever my ties with Selective Service. On December 14, outside a meeting of the Cornell faculty which was discussing the university's policy towards Selective Service, I read a statement to my local board before a crowd of 300 people and then ripped up my draft card.

The Cornell anti-draft union agonized for weeks over how to respond to Bruce's action. Finally on March 2, 1967, five men—Jan Flora, Burton Weiss, Robert Nelson, Michael Rotkin, Timothy Larkin—called on others to pledge to burn their draft cards April 15 if at least 500 people acted at the same time. The language of the call combined ethical and political arguments:

> The armies of the United States have, through conscription, already oppressed or destroyed the lives and consciences of millions of Americans and Vietnamese. We have argued and demonstrated to stop this destruction. We have not succeeded. Murderers do not respond to reason. Powerful resistance is now demanded: radical, illegal, unpleasant, sustained.
>
> In Vietnam the war machine is directed against young and old, soldiers and civilians, without distinction. In our own country, the war machine is directed specifically against the young, against blacks more than against whites, but ultimately against all.
>
> Body and soul, we are oppressed in common. Body and soul, we must resist in common. The undersigned believe that we should begin this mass resistance by publicly destroying our draft cards at the Spring Mobilization.
>
> The climate of anti-war opinion is changing. In the last few months student governments, church groups, and other organizations have publicly expressed understanding and sympathy with the position of individuals who refuse to fight in Vietnam, who resist the draft. We are ready to put ourselves on the line for this position, and we expect that these people will come through with their support.
>
> We are fully aware that our action makes us liable to penalties of up to five years in prison and $10,000 in fines. We believe, however, that the more people who take part in this action the more difficult it will be for the government to prosecute.

Even after the call had been issued, Tom Bell struggled with the question of whether the decision had been right. He wrote me on March 18, 1967:

> I still have some pretty serious reservations about our action— especially as I see it at work . . . What disturbs me is that almost 50 Cornellians have pledged to burn their draft cards and I am afraid for many of them the decision comes from the emotionalism of the moment. The sessions in the [student] union are very much like revival services (even including some of the rhetoric at times). We have speeches, a collection for the anti-war office and on the spot conversions—signing pledges, plus a lot of personal witnesses. I am going to try to get all the people who have signed pledges together for some collective thinking about what we are doing and I hope that we can get

some things cleared up. There is a real agony for me in the dilemma presented by seeing this great opportunity for political organizing and action vs. the likelihood that a lot of people are going to be hurt (including myself) by the action being taken. I'm even more afraid when I think of the impersonal situation of sending out the calls. Don't really know why I am unloading all of this except that I feel caught—I don't like national actions but I do want to change America. I like a personal, deep-communication type of politics but perhaps this is not really political. I don't want to manipulate anyone but I feel that it is essential for my own struggle and for the development of all of us as human beings that people change.

On April 2, less than two weeks away from April 15, Tom wrote again: "I've begun to feel better about the draft card burning, as a political act at least, but it looks like it will not come off. We have only about 90 pledges so far and the Spring Mobilization . . . has apparently refused to let us take the action as part of the April 15 action anyway." The rest is common knowledge. On the evening of April 14 those who had signed the conditional pledge met and decided to go ahead if there were fifty persons who would burn their cards together. Just over fifty agreed. Next day three times that many acted.

What, besides nostalgia, ought we to feel in recollecting these beginnings? What struck me most as I went over the documents again was the connection between noncooperation and the 2-S deferment. Those who choose noncooperation for philosophical reasons, such as the CNVA resisters, were a minority. For most resisters noncooperation was a means whereby students protected by 2-S deferments could make themselves vulnerable to induction and so compel the government, as Steve Hamilton put it, "to deal with us." Early leaflets of the Resistance make this motivation clear. "An organization has been formed," began one, "of men preparing to jointly give up all deferments and refuse to serve." "The resistance," another stated, "is a group of men who feel we can no longer passively accept our deferments so that others can go in our place." It would seem that had there been no 2-S deferment draft resistance would have taken the form of mass induction refusal rather than mass noncooperation. And this in turn suggests that the division of the draft-resistance movement into, on the one hand, a movement of induction refusal or resistance within the armed forces, and on the other hand, a movement expressing itself by the act of noncooperation, is itself a consequence of the class character of the Selective Service System.

This conclusion, if accurate, has implications for the debate as to whether or not to give up draft card turn-ins. It suggests that noncooperation remains, as it has always been, an appropriate act of resistance for deferred college students and conscientious objectors, but that it never has been regarded as a likely form of resistance for the young man of draft age not so insulated. Therefore, the ceremony which would most precisely reflect the right relationship of noncooperation to other kinds of resistance would be one in which the noncooperator was one of several kinds of resisters each doing his thing.

II

Still another argument against the act of noncooperation must be confronted, namely, the contention that inviting imprisonment by noncooperation expresses a characteristically middle-class sentiment of would-be martyrdom. Writing in *New Left Notes* in 1967, Carl Davidson insisted that permitting oneself to be imprisoned deprives the movement of a needed organizer and actually weakens the resolve of other young men of draft age. The implication of this criticism of the Resistance is that no one should return his draft card because the act is inherently apolitical and unhealthy.

Let me begin to respond to this criticism by recalling another strand of motivation which led to the Resistance. Many of the early resisters had worked together in Mississippi. For them, myself included, draft resistance was in complex ways a means of dealing with the psychological aftermath of that experience. As of spring 1966, with the articulation of Black Power, we were irrevocably excluded from the civil rights movement. I think it was more than the escalation of the Vietnam War which caused draft resistance to begin to take form. We were looking for something white radicals could do which would have the same spirit, ask as much of us, and challenge the system as fundamentally, as had our work in Mississippi.

Dennis Sweeney felt, he remembers, that while it was wrong to build a movement on risk-taking, still risk-taking was conspicuously missing from the movement in the North. Dennis never thought that the draft was the most important of all social issues or that the Resistance could end the draft. He considered the draft a particularly clear illustration of what was wrong with the system as a whole. He also wanted a means to pull together seriously-committed white radicals for longtime work. Draft resistance seemed to Dennis a kind of net which one could pull through the campuses of the country and thus collect the people with whom one really wanted to make a movement.

What did the South, in particular Mississippi, signify in the experience of former civil rights workers. Something we wanted to get away from, something else we wanted to keep. We wanted to get away from the role of white people helping black people, the role of missionary to the oppression of others, the role of auxiliary to a radicalism the center of gravity of which was in other people's lives. In the South many of us had drifted into administrative roles, not because we wanted to be leaders, but because we were obviously better able to write press releases and answer the telephone than to approach frightened black people in remote rural communities. The objective results were that we made more decisions than we should have made, and black SNCC field secretaries had the experience of returning to their headquarters after beatings and imprisonments to find more white faces than black there. When the philosophy of control of black organizations by black people was announced our own experience made us recognize that, however painful for us personally, Black Power was right.

This time around, then, we did not want to manipulate the lives of others who ran risks which we did not share. In the words of the report of the New Haven meeting of July 30, 1966: "As organizers of draft resistance we must be the first to confront the government and to challenge its authority. We must be the first to confront the fear of long jail sentences." In the words of the call to the Sheep's Meadow: "We are ready to put ourselves on the line."

Was this a desire for martyrdom? Perhaps a politics of risk, but also a politics of guilt? Only in part. Insofar as noncooperation represented nothing more than a renunciation of a 2-S deferment it certainly resembled the impulse which sent white Northern students to the South. But noncooperation meant more than this. White radical students began to realize that the club of induction not only forced others into the army but forced themselves into a careerism and conformity which they abhorred. Hence in saying "No" to the draft one also said "No" to a gray-flannel image of one's future. In contrast to the role of the white student in the Southern civil rights movement, resistance to the draft and the war was resistance to a personal oppression.

At this point the positive memory of the South, and particularly of Mississippi, came into play. Those of us who had worked with Bob Moses saw in him a model for the democratic organizer. It was not only that, in the fall of 1961, he had put his body on the line by going alone into Amite County to begin voter registration. It was also his rejection of the conventional leadership role: sitting in the back of the room at meetings, refusing to speak, when he finally spoke standing up in place rather than coming to the front of the meeting, asking questions rather than making a speech. When I first met David Harris, I was immediately struck by the similarity between David's reasons for resigning his position as student body president at Stanford and Bob's reasons for fiercely refusing the charisma thrust upon him. In each case, the motivation was not guilt, but the desire to enable others to improvise their own militancy rather than deferring to a leader.

The emotional thrust of the resistance movement is not masochistic self-denial but self-reliance, not emasculation but manhood. Guilt is so strong a strain in our authoritarian culture that we constantly betray and caricature our best impulses. My conversation with David Harris on the genesis of West Coast Resistance, convinced me that affirmation rather than self-denial was the emotional kernel of their call for October 16. David, who spent some time in Quitman County, Mississippi, in the fall of 1964, believes the Resistance style of politics to have been a synthesis of the style developed in the South and what he terms an exploration of selfhood. Neitzsche was part of it; so was existentialism, and riding a motorcycle on the Sierras with the wind on one's face. The emotional overtones were not asceticism, discipline, suffering, but endurance, going beyond one's limits, invulnerability, adventure. Running for Stanford student-body president David's campaign buttons were "Home Rule" and "Community Not Colonialism." Their spirit anticipated the button with which SDS joined draft resistance in the spring of 1967, "Not With My Life You Don't." When David and Dennis Sweeney went up and down the West Coast in the summer of 1967 seeking noncooperators, they, like Tom Bell before them, sought out one individual at a time, spending time with him, getting to know all sides of him, playing guitar and dropping acid besides talking politics. The first leaflet of the Bay Area Committee for Draft Resistance was simply six individual statements of noncooperation. This open style of organizing, in which one man tells another why he has decided to do something, seems to me inherently life-affirming, as opposed to the style which asks others to immolate themselves in a collective, impersonal destiny.

Which brings me to an extraordinary coincidence. In February 1967, more or less at about the same time that five men at Cornell called for draft card burning in Sheep's Meadow, and that Steve Hamilton and Lenny Heller became acquainted with David Harris and Dennis Sweeney, the national secretary of SDS gave a speech at Princeton in which he described precisely that style of organizing, and that need to struggle for self-liberation, which were at the heart of the developing Resistance. Liberalism, Greg

Calvert asserted, is based on the psychology of guilt and on the program of helping others to achieve what one already has. On the other hand, radicalism stems from "the perception of oneself as unfree, as oppressed" and expresses itself in "a struggle for collective liberation of all unfree, oppressed men." And Greg opened his speech with the following vignette of what, I submit, is resistance organizing at its best:

> It is said that when Guatemalan guerillas enter a new village, they do not talk about the "anti-imperialist struggle" nor do they give lessons on dialectical materialism, neither do they distribute copies of the "Communist Manifesto" or of Chairman Mao's "On Contradiction." What they do is gather together the people of the village in the center of the village and then, one by one, the guerillas rise and talk to the villagers about their own lives: about how they see themselves and how they came to be who they are, about their deepest longings and the things they've striven for and hoped for, about the way in which their deepest longings were frustrated by the society in which they lived.
>
> Then the guerillas encourage the villagers to talk about their lives. And then a marvelous thing begins to happen. People who thought that their deepest problems and frustrations were their individual problems discover that their problems and longings are all the same—that no one man is any different than the others. That, in Sartre's phrase, "In each man there is all of man." And, finally, that out of the discovery of their common humanity comes the decision that men must unite together in the struggle to destroy the conditions of their common oppression.

That, it seems to me, is what we are about.

This speech suggests that protagonists on both sides of the debate between SDS and the Resistance should be careful not to deal in stereotypes abstracted from time and place. There was a period, roughly the years 1966–1967, when SDS and the tendencies which became the Resistance were very close to one another. One sees this not only in the speech just quoted, but in the further facts that Greg Calvert helped set up the Des Moines meeting of August 1966, that Bruce Dancis was an SDS chapter president and Tom Bell an SDS traveller, that Jeff Segal of SDS and later of Stop-the-Draft Week spoke at the Chicago We-Won't-Go Conference of December 1966, that in that same month the SDS National Council not only endorsed draft resistance, but condemned all military conscription, and finally, that at the 1967 SDS convention a resolution was passed supporting military desertion.

This was a period when draft resistance was a cutting-edge or growing-point for the radical movement as a whole. It developed for the most part outside SDS, but this was partly because of the size and heterogeneity of SDS; many people within SDS welcomed it.

What caused this happy state of things to deteriorate? It seems to me that the period when SDS and draft resistance were closest was also a period when white radicals, responding to their repudiation by SNCC, were asking how their own lives needed to be changed and whether it was possible to build a radical majority in white America. For white radicals it was a time of a politics of affirmation rather than a politics of guilt. With this in mind, perhaps one should turn the SDS critique of the Resistance inside out, and argue that SDS has been reverting to the very politics of middle-class self-flagellation which it charges to the Resistance. Since its National Council meeting in the spring of 1968, SDS has asked white people again to play the role of auxiliaries to others peoples' radicalism.

To reject guilt as a motivating force for the radical movement is not to deny that white radicalism in American history has been infected by racism, nor that the liberation front required to change America may have more black than white leaders. But the best way white radicals can contribute to that eventual coalition is by building a strong white radical movement. This movement must be free of racism; yet agitation against racism is not the best way to build it. For white radicals to make freeing Huey Newton or support for the demands of black students their *primary* political activity is to recreate at a higher level of struggle the friends-of-SNCC psychology of the early 1960s, and to program a new generation of activists into the functional equivalent of going South.

III

All of this brings us to the question of what the Resistance shall become. My intuition is that the movement will eventually come down on a political perspective intermediate between middle-class moralism, on the one hand, and Leninism, on the other, and that the Resistance, as a current in the movement intermediate between traditional pacifism and Marxism-Leninism is uniquely situated to affirm that perspective.

Let me give three illustrations of this perspective. Noam Chomsky has described the revolution-from-below created by peasants and workers in the midst of the Spanish Civil War and uniformly neglected by the war's elitist historians.

Second, Daniel Cohn-Bendit offers another illustration: the current within the Russian Revolution known as the Workers' Opposition which insisted that socialism must mean workers' control, and which was crushed by the Bolshevik government at Kronstadt and elsewhere. Even in translation Cohn-Bendit evokes eloquently the vision of a revolution growing from decentralized resistance. What we need, he says, is "not organization with a capital O, but a host of insurrectional cells," "spontaneous resistance to all forms of domination," "the multiplication of nuclei of confrontation." And Cohn-Bendit is clear that this ultimate vision means that during the revolutionary process minorities within the revolution must have, not only the rights of free speech suppressed by the Bolsheviks, but the right to act out their minority convictions. Cohn-Bendit calls this "the right of independent action," a right, it seems to me, which the Resistance has hitherto practiced, and which it should not abandon in the quest for a more coherent political perspective.

Finally, there are the Wobblies. At point after point, as we intuitively perceive, the spirit of the Resistance is akin to the spirit of the IWW. Their insight that change must come about through direct action at what they called "the point of production" is akin to the Resistance axiom that people must change the circumstances of their own daily lives. Their affirmation of the maxim that "an injury to one is an injury to all" is exactly the sense of solidarity with which the Resistance has sought to overcome the atomization created by the Selective Service System. Their belief in building "the new society within the shell of the old" overlaps what, in a more middle-class way, the Resistance has been feeling its way toward through alternative institutions.

This view is brilliantly laid out in an article by Dan Tilton in the *Journal of Resistance* for October 1968 entitled "Socialism and Human Freedom." Tilton asserts that "the time has come for the Resistance to seriously consider definite alternatives to capitalism. . . . It is time . . . for the Resistance to state clearly that not only is capitalism insane, but more importantly that socialism is the only possible alternative." What Tilton means by socialism, however, is libertarian socialism or anarcho-syndicalism. He feels that the Resistance should carry over into its new commitment to socialism its old awareness of the evils of militarism and the nation state:

> Our struggle in the Resistance has been up to now a struggle against governmental bureaucracy and illicit power. In this we have shown more wisdom than our Old Left counterparts with their ideas of nationalization of industry or the dictatorship of the proletariat. We have always realized that political power is suspect not just in capitalist

nations but also in so-called socialist nations and that any solution to capitalism that involves socialism must answer the anarchist's questions concerning the nature of power and concerning its legitimacy. It must answer why "socialism" has not brought about human freedom.

Unlike many elements in the movement Tilton affirms rather than repudiates participatory democracy. "What needs to be done now," he writes, "is to carry the concept of participatory democracy to its ultimate conclusion."

Tilton's attitude toward participatory democracy is the attitude which people in the Resistance should have toward their original intentions. When we are told to abandon nonviolence so as to join in working-class struggle, we can respond that historically that struggle has expressed itself through the nonviolent means of strike, boycott, and sit-in. When advised to put away childish things and become politically "serious," we should remember that the characteristic Resistance conceptions of existential commitment, and the encounter between man and man, were created, not by armchair theorists, but by Albert Camus, Dietrich Bonhoeffer, Martin Buber, Ignazio Silone, in the furnace of resistance to fascism. I think it is possible to become politically serious without giving up the values which drew us into politics in the first place.

IV

Radicals familiar with Marx are suspicious of talk about the good society of the future. Such talk is associated with the Utopian socialists who preceded the "scientific socialism" of Marx and Engels. According to this critique, speculation about the future implies that the speculator expects to convert the existing society by his reasoning, and thus bring about fundamental social change peacefully and gradually. To this naive revolutionary strategy the Marxist counterposes the idea that the future is imminent in the materially conditioned class struggles of the present. In Marx's famous metaphor, the revolutionary acts as midwife to a new society which already exists within the womb of the old.

Yet I persist in believing that it is important for radicals to think about the good society they wish to build. Here are four reasons:

(I) One of the secrets to the success of men who have actually led revolutions is that they had a vision of the future. A North Vietnamese historian told Herbert Aptheker, Tom Hayden, and myself that Ho Chi Minh attracted support partly because he had an "ideal for the time after independence." Fidel Castro's speech, "History Will Absolve Me," projected the picture of a democratic Cuba free of Batista's oppression. Even Fanon, Barbara Deming has observed, questioned the thesis that revolutionary movements can be built on hatred and the desire to destroy. "Racialism and hatred and resentment—'a legitimate desire for revenge'—cannot sustain a war of liberation," Fanon wrote. And he asked that his comrades resolve not to imitate Europe but to "turn over a new leaf . . . work out new concepts, and try to set afoot a new man." Why is it that so many successful twentieth-century revolutions have come to power through guerrilla warfare? Isn't part of the reason that a guerrilla army is obliged to begin running schools and dividing crops and making communal decisions from the moment it creates a liberated zone? And thus perforce to build a new society while tearing down the old? And so wins support, not by rhetoric, but by practically demonstrating a qualitatively different way of life?

In short, one argument for accentuating the positive is that it seems to work.

(2) It seems to me, too, that American radicals frequently "burn out" not merely because of objective obstacles but because we lose psychological contact with the potentiality for fundamental change. One of the lessons of the concentration camps, apparently, is that those who best endured them were Jehovah's Witnesses or socialists or individuals like the therapist Victor Frankl who were able to keep vivid in their imaginations a possible future in which they believed.

Right now, black radicals in this country are much more psychologically "together" than white radicals, partly, I think, because black power has a positive vision. In the writings of black power spokesmen from DuBois to Carmichael one finds the concept of a peaceful and communal traditional African society ethically superior to the dog-eat-dog violence of capitalism. African socialism has its psychological counterpart in an ideal of black manhood (and womanhood) which touches and transforms every aspect of daily life. White radicals lack such a sociological vision and psychological ideal. We have tended to respond to black power by discarding the positive ideology of participatory democracy as sentimental, and filling the empty space with talk of guerrilla warfare. My question is whether this alone can give radicals who wish to be "serious" the emotional staying-power they will have to have.

Thus my second argument for the utility of "Utopian" envisioning is that it speaks to a psychological need to live toward the future.

(3) I feel the need for an image of a good society as an ethical regulator. The trend in the movement is away from "being moral" toward "being

political." But can we not all agree that there are dangers in this tendency? When I read [in recent Guardians] (in columns written by movement activists) of the importance of a "correct" ideology and of opponents as "mad dogs" to be exterminated, I confess to the response that it was exactly such doctrinaire, rhetorical radicalism in reaction to which the new left came into being. I think I understand why younger members of the movement feel that their historical task is to destroy U.S. imperialism by any means necessary. I think I also understand that the vibrant revolutionary societies of Cuba and North Vietnam make old concerns about the perversion of revolution in Russia seem irrelevant. Nevertheless, I sense a hardness and bitterness growing in the movement which not only turns me off, but which I think will prove politically self-defeating. Is it not the tone of one who feels himself to belong to a doomed, impotent minority, but who will take-one-or-two-of-them-with-him-before-he-goes? And understandable as it is that we all feel this way from time to time, is it really more politically effective than a style which seeks to empathize with the feelings of those who do not yet stand with us, but who may stand with us, especially if we make some effort compassionately to grasp their situation?

In terms of Marxist theory, the argument for the future as ethical regulator follows from the awareness that men have more freedom to make history than Marx (or at least the later Marx) supposed (or is often interpreted as supposing). Paul Sweezy and Leo Huberman, for example, emphasize in their assessment of the Bolshevik revolution (Monthly Review, November, 1967, pp. 18 ff.) that in a period of revolution "determinism recedes into the background, and voluntarism seems to take over," and that the policies of the Bolshevik revolution "were deliberately decided upon and in no sense a mere reflex of an objective situation. They could have been different." This means that before, during, and after a revolution one cannot rely on the objective situation alone to prevent a departure from minimal norms of humane behavior. The message of the Chinese cultural revolution, it would seem, is that struggle against bureaucratization and a spirit of self-seeking must continue for decades after a revolutionary seizure of power.

Men who keep clearly in the mind's eye that future toward which they strive will be less likely, I should think, to permit the daily practice of their movement to develop in a different direction.

(4) I believe that in our specific American situation we have a particular, political need to talk to our fellow Americans about the future. This arises from the negative images which have accrued around the word "socialism."

For the past quarter-century, roughly since the publication of Burnham's "Managerial Revolution" and Orwell's "1984," American radicals have tended to concede the thesis of their opponents that a society in which the means of production are publicly owned and the economy is centrally planned is also likely to become dehumanized, undemocratic. So deeply has this cliche taken hold that we of the new left often speak of decentralized self-determination in a rhetoric difficult to distinguish from that of the far right. Belligerently anti-imperialist we may have become, yet I notice a peculiar hesitancy forthrightly to identify ourselves as socialists.

Surely this hesitancy must be overcome. And surely to do this we must show ourselves capable of concrete imagining about a democratic socialist society which breaks through abstract stereotypes. If we mean a decisive change away from the economy which underlies imperialist foreign policy, can this be any other than a change toward socialism? Simply because Sidney Webb confused socialism with the British civil service or Stalin used that term for the Russia of the purges, we should not be dissuaded from reasserting the fundamental radical conception that a society can be both socialist and humane.

V

So these are four reasons why, in general, we should not dismiss thinking about the future as petty-bourgeois Utopianism. Now consider a specific problem: how socialist society in this country would make political decisions.

We have to face this problem now if only because much of our energy in coming months will be spent, perforce, in defending our rights to speak, to assemble, to organize, to travel, to refuse to fight in unjust wars. What is our fundamental attitude toward these "bourgeois democratic" rights? On the one hand, in American courts we will be demanding freedoms which few, if any, societies have ever conceded to their citizens: that draft-card burning and obstruction of induction centers be considered "symbolic speech," that public advocacy of violent revolution be protected, and so on. On the other hand, it is a fact (if it is not a fact, I would appreciate having it proved to me) that not only the Soviet Union, but also Cuba, North Vietnam and China do not protect the rights we demand for ourselves: the right to travel freely, the right publicly to advocate the overthrow of the government, the right not to be required to carry a draft card or other "internal passport," and so on. In any existing Communist society, Karl

Marx—who entered political life as a passionate advocate of freedom of the press, who hated above all things a servile obsequiousness toward bureaucracy—would be in jail.

I think we must find the intellectual and emotional balance to act in solidarity with overseas revolutionaries without making a total commitment to the societies which they are building. I think it would be not only ethically questionable but politically ineffective were we cynically to regard First Amendment freedoms merely as tactical opportunities for ourselves. We can use the freedoms we defend as a means of conveying to others the kind of society we are trying to create, but we can only do so if we believe in those freedoms as fundamental to that good society.

Given agreement as to the value of personal liberties, the question of group decision-making still remains. We began as a movement by asking that democracy be broadened both quantitatively (all adults should vote) and qualitatively (the citizen should do more than vote for representatives, he should participate personally in making the daily decisions which affect his life). These aspirations were reflected in the way the movement made its own decisions. Both SNCC and SDS made decisions by consensus. Both in SNCC and SDS there was and is widespread resentment of even those nominal powers vouchsafed "the Atlanta Office" and "the National Office." Recently, however, the mood has grown that "serious" politics requires more disciplined forms of organization. Participatory democracy is still projected as a model for the future, but the grim work of revolutionary transition is felt to require stronger tools.

In my opinion, one reason the movement vacillates between extremes of anarchism and Bolshevik centralization is that few of us ever sought to imagine what participatory democracy might mean in a large society or even in a large organization. Nor is Marxism of any particular help here. Like ourselves, Marx sometimes referred to a transitional dictatorship but also hailed the Paris Commune as a prototype of the decentralized organs of popular authority which would govern the society of the future. The early Marx believed, just as did SDS when it began, that the election of representatives "must not be understood as the people's only, exceptional civic act"; he thought, just as we did, that when the contradiction between political democracy and capitalist autocracy was overcome, "the significance of the *legislative* power as a *representative* power disappears wholly. The legislative power is representative in the same sense that *every* function is representative, in the sense, for instance, that the cobbler, insofar as he fulfills a social need, is my representative . . ." These insights were never developed. Hence it became possible not only for prerevolutionary Communist parties, but also for postrevolutionary societies which (like Cuba) have no national elected legislature at all, to present themselves as valid expressions of what Marx really meant.

If we took seriously the task of imagining how we, had we the power, would manufacture automobiles and settle priorities concerning allocation of resources and synthesize local and national decision-making, I believe it would help us find our way through current organizational dilemmas. And it might just help to persuade other Americans that we are capable of governing.

VI

The gist of my argument up to this point was this: it is true that the society of the future will emerge, not from Utopian speculation, but from the historically conditioned struggles of the present; but it is also true that our picture of what we want to achieve will help to determine the character of those struggles, and of the society which emerges from them.

Even if one were to argue that in any given period the tasks of the movement are historically inevitable, there would remain variations in style of work. This is not a small thing. For instance, remember Bob Moses. Perhaps it was inevitable for the Southern civil rights movement to focus on voter registration. Was it equally inevitable for the Student Nonviolent Coordinating Committee (SNCC) to register voters in rural counties and Mississippi, and for Moses to work in that state's most resistant region, the southwest? And given the fact that these choices required SNCC people to operate in quasi-underground conditions, isn't it clear that there was more than one way to move in that medium? A common generalization holds that underground work demands rigid centralization. Yet Moses' style was one long battle against the concentration of power in his own hands. Asked to speak at a meeting, he would decline, or speak without standing from his seat at the back of the room; if he could be induced to come to the front of a meeting, he might ask questions rather than make a speech. Bob left Mississippi, so he once told me, because he came to feel that his presence made it difficult for other people and groups (SNCC, Congress of Federated Organizations, Mississippi Freedom Democratic Party) to act freely.

I believe that even in underground work or in guerrilla struggle important options remain open and personality makes a difference. Thus Ernesto Guevara writes somewhere that during the months in the Cuban mountains everyone had a name: so few were involved, under such desperate circumstances, that every aspect of each one's being was significant. The case can be made that repression demands a more decentralized, personalized kind of political work than normal times. In Czarist Russia, Allan Wildman writes, "Ambitious organizational undertakings were extremely vulnerable and short-lived, even when guided by skilled conspirators, whereas a small circle of intimate acquaintances engaging in a limited sphere of activity had the best chance of survival" ("The Making Of A Workers' Revolution," pp. 199–200). Similarly, John Cammett, in his biography of Gramsci, quotes a founder of the German workers' councils in World War I to the effect that these localized institutions resulted "from the repression of all freedom of movement in the working class because of the state of siege and the total incapacity of the unions and political parties" ("Antonio Gramsci And The Origins Of Italian Communism," p. 73). My impression is that instances of this kind can be multiplied indefinitely: Burchett's description of the decentralization of repair work in North Vietnam because of the bombing is another example. In sum, political work under conditions of repression requires discipline (witness the elaborate security procedures which prevailed in Mississippi in 1964) but this does not necessarily mean that choices are fewer, decentralized initiative less required or the consequences of personal style of work less grave.

All right, then. For purposes of these columns it will be assumed that in the most exigent objective situations the question of what we want remains relevant. Let's move on.

I think the movement wants to build a society both communal and libertarian, both fraternal and free. The inarticulate major premise of Cold War ideology is that you have to choose between brotherhood and freedom. If you want brotherhood, *gemeinschaft,* a sense of common purpose, then you must take totalitarianism with it; if you want to be free, then you must put up with its necessary institutional basis, private property, and with its inevitable accompanying atmosphere, competition. We deny that this choice is necessary. We affirm that it is not beyond the wit of man to make a society characterized by both love and liberty.

I have stressed the necessity of individual liberties. Perhaps I did so because I grew up among adults who explained away Stalin's purges, the Nazi-Soviet pact, forced labor camps and, later, Hungary. But I believe I have also been influenced by the experience of living for three years in a cooperative community. Those were the best years of my life. One reason we felt so close to one another, though, was that we faced common adversities. We

were desperately poor. The Southern white society around us was usually
hostile. It is clear to me that affluence and the absence of external pressure
would have obliged us to deal with differences in personal vision which
could remain latent as we labored to meet our production quotas and safeguard our buildings from neighborhood vandalism. Am I wrong to find in
those years a microcosm of the experience of developing socialist societies?
I have read, for example, that great difficulties developed in the kibbutzim
when Arab encirclement eased and the standard of living rose. It became a
question: if my grandmother in Tel Aviv sends me a radio, should I keep it
and invite a few friends to my room for music over tea, or should I turn it
over to the community so that we may dance after supper in the community
dining room? Or: if I have the talent to make a career in music or physics,
should I resolve to practice my skill only to that extent possible in the
unspecialized social world of the kibbutz? Socialism must make sense not
only as war communism, as a form of society appropriate for periods of
forced industrialization and capitalist encirclement, but as a recipe for quiet
times when individuals will choose to live and think in multitudinously
different ways.

It may serve some purpose to give that happy state a name. In April,
1965, at the march sponsored by Students for a Democratic Society on
Washington, Paul Potter urged naming the society we opposed. Clarity
might also be furthered were a name attached to the society we espouse.
One reader of the first installment of "A Good Society" suggested "participatory socialism."

The term would seem to have advantages when compared to the obvious
alternatives. "Democratic socialism" (or "social democracy") has acquired
some unfortunate historical associations. Moreover, the term "democratic
socialism" has usually signified the idea that while the U.S. economy is run
in a way that is undemocratic and bad, the U.S. government is democratic
and good, and so the government should take over the economy. The New
Left, however, rightly insists that U.S. institutions of government are as
much the products of capitalism as its economic institutions. We are no
longer content to imagine socialism as the management of the economy by
professional politicians who from time to time obtain the formal consent of
the populace for their continuance in power.

Another possible name for the new society is "communism." My fundamental objection to this term is not its obvious political liabilities in the
U.S. The more serious question is that in Marxist literature (the initial formulation was Marx's critique of the Gotha program of the German socialist

movement), communism is envisioned as a higher stage which will succeed socialism only when the productive forces are sufficiently developed. This conception has opened the door to monstrosities of many kinds. Dictatorship is permissible in a socialist society because only at the higher stage of communism will it dialectically wither away. Material incentives are appropriate in a socialist society because only at the higher stage of communism can men be motivated by the public good. And so on.

I flatly reject the conception that good human relationships require any particular level of economic abundance. Obviously, abundance eases certain kinds of social strain; but it also creates new temptations, new opportunities for selfish individualism. The fact of the matter is that the most communal societies in history have been extremely poor ones. Barrington Moore writes convincingly in "The Critical Spirit: Essays In Honor Of Herbert Marcuse," p. 402: "There is a tendency to think of past ages as ones in which rich and poor struggled to divide up a supply of goods closely limited by brute scarcity and inadequate techniques. Marxists tell us in effect that a decent society became a realistic possibility only after mankind had passed through the purgatory of the industrial revolution. That is highly doubtful. By the time human societies had accumulated enough technical knowledge to acquire the label civilized, roughly at the point of using a written language, they already possessed the physical bases for establishing societies in which most of their members could have had enough to eat and enough shelter from the elements to prevent outright physical suffering. For some reason or other they did not arrange matters that way. The suspicion remains that a decent society has indeed been a possibility all along." So far as the U.S. is concerned, perhaps what should be said is simply that it can move directly to the moneyless economy and decentralized decision-making which Marxists associate with communism. But in that case, "communism," traditionally conceptualized as a sequel to "socialism," may not be the most useful term.

"Participatory democracy" fails because of its vagueness. The intent of the adjective is to clarify the noun; the result is that the economic side of the good society is neglected. Participatory democracy was a useful term because it made clear that we intended to change the U.S. government, not merely extend it into new areas of social life. The time has come for a new phrase which compactly explains both the politics and economics of what we are about. "Participatory socialism" may do that.

Revulsion and Revolt:
Revolution in Our Times
John R. Seeley

The word "revolution" has been so loosely used—like so many other words from "love" to "democracy"—as almost to have lost its force. (We even have an automobile manufacturer peddling his wares under that title—or the closely similar word "rebellion.")

A word that should make us tremble in the very hidden deeps and remotest recesses of the soul, a word that should call up images of a measureless, sweeping flood of change, obliterating all landmarks and leaving us lost and bewildered we know not and no longer sense where, this word has been (characteristically) attached to everything from electric can-openers—"a revolutionary change in kitchen design"—to the defeat of the horse by the wheeled mustang—"the automotive revolution;" it is applied equally to such relatively petty events as the partial separation of these United States from Great Britain—"the American Revolution"—and such large sweeps as are caught by indicators—like "the Industrial Revolution," "the Agricultural Revolution."

Nothing is meant by such use of the word except a desire to put it about that some large event has occurred; and since there is no scale for largeness —anything is large in *some* scale and small in another—whether or not something is to be called a revolution seems to depend on what particular scale or scheme the person happened to be thinking of or trapped in at the moment of speaking.

Three odd and non-essential ideas are, for many, unreflectively taken to be implicit in the very term : violence, suddenness, and some peculiar eye on the fate of political government. In the sense in which I use the term here, none of these ideas is relevant. The ejection of the British from India was neither more nor less a revolution because violence was held well below its customary brutal minimum; the Russian Revolution, so-called, would have been no less a revolution—and no more—had the Czar yielded to massive non-violent sit-ins rather than to the logic of force culminating in that blood-stained scene in the cellar. As for "suddenness," that too is a subjective term: men call sudden whatever they would have wished to have more time to contain, cope with or resolve to abandon themselves to. Nor is the concentration on government justified, though in a revolution governments, like all else, will be profoundly affected. Not when Rome fell but when over the whole Hellenic world:

> Fire for light and hell for heaven and psalms for paeans
> Felled the clearest eyes and lips most sweet of song
> When for the chant of Greeks, the wail of Galileans
> Made the whole world moan with hymns of wrath and wrong

then was that simultaneous transformation of the way of life and man's mode of consciousness that we ought to call "the Christian Revolution" so well begun that all that follows is mere filling-out, the dotting of i's and crossing of t's almost into our own time.

No. What is revolutionary about a revolution is its range and depth. When, almost over the whole vast ambit of everything, and most particularly in those deepest foundations that sustain alike the order between men and the order within them, there is change, then the change is to be called a revolution. For no longer will tinkering in soul or society suffice, or even aid; and indeed the very flame of life, the inner and the outer, flickers close to extinction as the hitherto known and shared and warming and sustaining world grows "cold as a winter wave, In the wind from a wide-mouthed grave." We should not speak seriously of revolution unless and until we see a way of life and a way of being in the world, a major incarnation of man and men, in the very maw of that grave and then returned from it—or perhaps all but dead and all but resurrected-and-transfigured. Little else in the large sweep of human history rises above mere event and episode.

It is in this sense that I want to speak of revolution, and with this force that I want to characterize what is happening in our times. And if what I say is true—or close to truth—then we should greet our recognition with shock and trembling, for death is in it as near as life or nearer, and a final darkness is at least as imminent as the flash that could—just could—herald the bright new dawn. The spirit that might bring form from chaos is less near than the specter that haunts a sometime order into its last decay.

And worse. For while it might look as though I were going to say that it is ours to choose—which would be frightening enough—that is precisely what I cannot say, or can only say in the most roundabout sense. For that

illusion of free choice—alternating fashionably with intellectual love
affairs with "radical determinism"—is in part what has brought us to our
present pass, and I should not wish to resurrect that myth.

Some political scientists define a revolution as the relatively rapid substitution of one elite for another—our appointees for King George's men,
presumably, or Lenin's people for the mad monk and all the more decora-
tive sons of the great Little Father. That substitution is likely and perhaps
necessary but is not. A revolution is in being when a new, sufficiently com-
manding, sufficiently far-reaching, sufficiently different myth, governing
what it is to be men and do as men, begins to set a new world newly afire.

One such transformation in Western history was the relatively rapid
emergence of the myth of man as predominantly agent over the previously
prevailing myth of man as predominantly patient. I have deliberately left
the event undated, but the shift marks the beginning of what we call "the
modern world," the world that man lives *over* as master rather than *under*
and *in* as subject and child. Do not drive the images too far. Never under
Christian myth (even, strangely, under the myth of predestination) was
man viewed as wholly patient; indeed, a proper consequence of his overall
patienthood was supposed to be a modest but energetic agency—just as a
child terrified in the bad old days into a vision of himself as properly putty
in his schoolmaster's hands was supposed, as the sign of it, to work energet-
ically and "independently" at his allotted studies. And never under neo-
Christian myth, the current paganism that still uses the old symbols, was
man openly and in so many words said to be omnipotent and omniscient.
But, just short of these poles—for every myth needs a penumbra to shield it
from too patent a collision with common sense and experience—the shift
is clear from a world properly governed by non-Man in a manner forever to
be mysterious to a world governed by men with unlimited capacity to
master the "mystery," learn the state secrets of the alleged but non-existent
Governor, and put them to plain, practical and everyday uses. The knife that
rent the veil, showing that behind it lay not mysteries but an engine whose
throttle could in the consummation be commanded, was what we call science. There was a brief flurry in which man sought to save the appearances
—to act seemly—by allowing that a Great Inventor might have made the
machine, set it going, and gone away, but, if so, obviously his purpose (or
permission)was that man should master and manage the machine.

That revolution ran its familiar and rapid course. Life was no longer a
problem of learning and performing the duties of the station in life to which
God had called one, and finding therein one's fulfillment. The moral man-

date was, at its least and lowest, to find, seize, occupy, and exploit the highest station to which society would let one attain. "Highest" here meant most controlling—at its limit, having the capacity to control what controls: the law, political or natural. What "society"—meaning the aggregate of men similarly so minded—would let one attain was a function of the approved struggle of each to get into the same or a similar key position of control over all—at the limit and in principle—all men and all things.

The theme of the revolution was conquest, and all else was subordinate to it. Its watchword was Mastery. To be subdued were, in succession, the inanimate world, the non-human animate world, and the human (and animate) world. The method of conquest was that of the cancer: infiltration followed by proliferation followed by domination (and death). The tools might have been roughly designated as Physics (and its henchman Engineering), Biology (and its henchman chiefly Medicine) and Sociology (and such henchmen as Social Work, "Administrative Science" and such). Things and other animals were to be brought under the sign of man's everenlarging will and in a sense thought to be common-sense clear into his service. And how, given the heady successes in the other two spheres, could men not conclude that the same method, with the same aim, carried out in the same spirit, with equal energy, would yield the same result in reference to men? Indeed, the method was intended to yield control in two probably contradictory senses: the notion of the individual person having control over himself, and the notion of mankind—or society—having control over itself.

The words seem to have an evident and commonsense meaning. Yet it is so far from the case that it is difficult to discover what the words do mean. If we take the terms literally, what is a something that "controls itself," controller or controlled? If it is self-conscious, which does it feel itself to be: slave-master or slave? But the phrase cannot mean that. If I hope that I may "control" me, the first "I" and the second "I" and the "me" must refer to different objects. What is usually meant when we talk of self-control is expressive of some desire to yield rather to prudential than gratificatory considerations, to elevate means above ends. The preference doesn't mean very much, although if pressed very far is not only not very good but dangerously evil advice. We should, if we are prudent, be very prudent about prudence. In any case there is no way to accomplish the mission that meets the test of the vision. The jailer who does aim to, who is mandated to control other men as their prisoner (usually a lifer), as every guard and warden can tell you; he is "controlled" by those he "controls." And if this is true, as it universally must be, for the relations between persons, it is *a fortiori* true for the more intimate and enduring ones within a person. So far as a person "controls" himself, he is controlled by the absorbing necessities of that supervision, and both as subject and object, enslaved. The very notion that between people—let alone within any one of them—there is a possible relation of controller and controlled, similar to the one presumed between man and thing and man and animal, though a most powerful myth, productive in embracement of measureless evil, points to an impossibility. Indeed it is not even valid between man and thing or man and fellow-animal. In our commitment to that enterprise, however, we have had to denature ourselves, each other, the human community, and, indeed, nature itself. No society in history has found so many so deeply enslaved to the effort to maintain and promote a control apparatus over so much. And the enterprise cannot yield satisfaction—the presumed object of controlling—because of the very nature of the basic posture. Just imagine yourself determined (and in some sense able) to control your wife or child, and then ask who would be the slave and what satisfaction would be left (without your own utter corruption). The case is no different in reference to anything else at all. Nevertheless, this is our controlling myth that has shaped and given us the world we "see," or, rather, fail to see.

The costs have been tremendous and in some quarters are being correctly sensed as fatal. Our entrapment in our own normal technology is in a sense a minor—though, perhaps, fatal—sign, symptom and symbol. We *can* clearly put men in the outer reaches of space: what is not at all clear is whether we can *not* do so. "Technological logic dictates. . . ." We can have virtually instantaneous communication with anyone, anywhere—but the silence in which men grow and in which consummation is to be had is hardly to be bought at any price. We can get faster and faster to more and more places; but these are thus everywhere more and more the same, so that in that sense we cannot get anywhere at all for we are everywhere, qualitatively, where we started from. We live longer, but the very instrumentalities that purchase that longevity, assure that there is nothing to live for, either side of the veil, so that strictly speaking we do not live at all but pointlessly endure.

What is problematic is not just the technology, but with the philosophy or primal set that underlies it. For what all this requires and presupposes is so particular, peculiar and precarious a view (or willed image) of the self, of man, and of the Universe that its endurance this long is a matter for wonder—just like the perpetuation of a psychosis whose secondary gains can be understood even while one marvels that the psychotic can continue daily to buy them at such exorbitant, manifest primary costs.

For prerequisite to this view is a setting of man separate from and against nature, separate from and against the biosphere, separate from and against other men severally and society together, separate from and against any new spheres of knowledge and appreciation and even separate from and against God for those who, nevertheless, hold Him to exist.

So conceived and conceiving, we crown the structure with a final irony which, were there gods to laugh, must cause the very heavens to rupture with their laughter. For the alienation of man from his Universe, from his society, from his "product," from other men, from himself, from his activity (whether work or play)—the very alienation or othering that is implicit in and central to this view of oneself in the world is suddenly recognized as a "problem!" And the problem is held to be adventitious, like a sudden and unexpected threat from a new and resistant strain of virus. And seen so— seen so, naturally and necessarily—it is seen as *another* problem "out there," to be remedied or coped with by more of the same methods that created it and brought it into being. It is as though a man sawing himself off a limb could think only of a maybe gravity-suspending machine to deal with his odd and unexpected problem.

And what is true for the "mysterious" problem of alienation is true for the equally "mysterious" problem of aggression. It is not clear whether we are on the brink of blowing up the world and ending all the life we know about because we do not know how to "manage" our aggression or (it may be the same thing) simply because the world is there to be blown up, as space is there to be explored, and what technologically we can do, *ipso facto,* we must do. (That, too, is a curious effect of the control mentality—that "can" comes to mean "must," and hence there is, in the end, no control at all.) But the very essence of the self-conception, of the way it *implies* of being in the world *is* aggression. Aggression is not something that comes in at the end, out of nature or out of nowhere, as a problem to be coped with, like hail or locusts: it is in the act of self making one's conception of self. And the attempt to deal with it as a "fact of nature"—or of "human na- ture"—is not simply fallacious; it contributes to its exacerbation. For that approach requires *more* control, more of that which is in one sense the origin of the aggression, and in another sense only another name for it. A stated aim to control something is a declaration of war. And an aim to control something in its own best interest—the usual and more palatable form of the statement—is a declaration of war coupled with a plea for complicity on the part of the victim.

Alienation and aggression, unmanageable finally in degree and limitless in scope, are thus built into the very presuppositions of the civilization. And even the ways of knowing that can be recognized and accredited in the attempt to extricate ourselves only entangle us further. For the set here—in the attempt to deal with the defects of the doctrine of mastery—continues to be mastery: "We must master *that* problem too." Most particularly, we will again resort to the strategy and tactics which allowed us to reach the galaxies and plunder the atomic treasure-vault. We will have, by presupposition, an active and independent knower and a passive and independent to-be-known. We will cool, set aside the "interfering" passions so that we may clearly see what is to be seen in the frigid light of "objectivity." We will discredit in general what even a child senses in close-as-breathing particular with reference to people in his own family: first, that they are not data independent of his every-moment creative acts; and, second, that any attempt to study them in the only way alleged to be a reliable path to knowledge would destroy the family—and, if he is young enough, the ground of his being, and him with it. In fact, of course, there is no family to be studied independently of his posture toward it. His posture is co-constituent of what is meant by the family. If he alters his posture he is studying a different and denatured object, and has so become a different and denatured person. And what I assert to be true for this family situation is, I believe, essentially true for all situations from self-examination to advanced physics.

We are reaching a realization that we have painted ourselves into a corner. And by "realization" I do not mean mere cognition, but the awful, shaking, engulfing, conversion-like awareness that a man sometimes has when it becomes evident to him, say, that his whole life has been lived on false premises or given to values that are worthless, or dedicated to acts whose consequences are the polar opposites of his conscious intents. When one's world thus falls apart, there comes next the frantic process analogical to the peeling of an onion—layer after layer peeled off, examined, discarded, and followed by a fresh search for a retainable core. At the end, the alternatives emerge as annihilating despair or the search for a non-onion, another object in which to invest faith and love and energy, bringing life to it and life back to the life-giver.

We are, I think, there or somewhere near there.

A specter now stalks the western world whose magnitude makes Marx's specter stalking Europe, even at full growth, as a puling infant. For *that* specter of Marx's is a familiar spirit, a brother of our own flesh and substance, an alternative scheme of control, which is why Marxist-Leninism or Maoism or even Castroism seem as bogus to the modern young as reform liberalism or state welfarism or Reaganism or Great Societism. For they are more all of a piece than not. All propose to cure the defects of mass organization by more organization, of bureaucracy by another layer of bureaucracy, of dehumanization by still another soulless super-machine. The young sense that no amount of horticultural tinkering will allow the gathering of figs from thistles, no matter which variety of thistle. Nor are they lightly to be convinced that this is a universe in which only the thistle is a possible fruit-bearer.

What has brought them to this state? Broadly, two connected developments: Western practices and Western thought-ways are each reaching a climax, simultaneously. Ironically, as the shape of their perfection comes into sight, the utter revulsion with what has been perfected, the *nausée générale,* begins relentlessly and irreversibly to set in.

It is hard to doubt that if the Western practice of civilization is not at its climax, it is so nearly so, that the shape of its fulfillment may be seen. Its logic is, to use Mannheim's terms, the minute and all-embracing pervasion of functional rationality accompanied by the attenuation to infinitesimal scope or to extinction, of all substantive rationality. We—a population of senseless size—will be organized almost perfectly to do with perfect efficiency what makes as nearly as possible no sense and provides as closely as may be no satisfaction.

Again, I believe, we are almost there now.

But the thought-ways have, even more, come to dead-end. Philosophy, which once represented an attempt to express in the discursive mode the principal things worth saying about man-among-men-and-in-nature, has recognized its own end, and become a special kind of discourse about discourse. Its former concerns—what it is to be a man among men, and what it is to be a man at all—have been abandoned to two orphans, psychology and sociology.

Each of these has its scientistic and humanistic branches, the former better developed than the latter. But "better" here—with all the fierce logic of paranoia—means "worse," as is so throughout the civilization. The two sciences that make of man a scientific object, so far as they are successful, assure that he shall be that. And, given the set in which they originate and to which they feed back, they render first possible and then necessary—

"what we can, we must"—a technology of man. Man is now a technifact—so far as we have, in this direction, been successful—and among the names of the burgeoning sub-technics are "management," "administrative science," "social engineering," "advertising," "public relations," "brainwashing," "news management," and so on. Many varieties of what is called "psychotherapy" must, sadly, be added to that somber list. Their posture is that they state the conditions and provide the means through which some men may enduringly control other men, or—not much better—through which a man may control himself meaning, so far as I understand it, procure out of the constituents of his natural harmony some "pyramid of control" analogous to that in the technifact society "outside." These tremendous achievements of the human mind, anticipated with the same mindless glee as those by which we have begun to pollute the entire biosphere, are now, happily, evoking the first stirrings of that holy horror that one might have hoped would attend their initiation.

It is on the humanistic sides of these orphaned sciences that we find some clue to the way to our escape—not always clearly disentangled from scientistic trappings—both disciplines have reluctantly been driven to resurrect as concepts and reaccredit the common coin of the ancient wisdoms: love, grace, oneness, the unity of opposites. And the inclusion of these seemingly irrational phenomena in the spectrum forces us to seek a radically different epistemology. Man as knower hovering and looking down *at* the man-to-be-known yields nothing of what we most want to know of man. For what we desire to know emerges only in what "science" rejected: the embroilment of the knower with the to-be-known—more like Jacob wrestling with the angel than a bystander observing the Crucifixion. But at the outset, such embroilment alters both man as knower and man as known. And the knowledge that emerges alters both. Indeed, the knower-known concept fails, for it suggests an independence that the conditions of knowing deny metaphysically: there is now knower and one to-be-known "out there" and "as such." There can be at most momentary snapshots, cognitive flashes, appreciations appropriate only instantaneously, of the *relatively* other in the *we* that is simultaneously knowing, creating and recreating itself. I must apologize for the words: our very vocabulary is shot through with conventions that exclude by their structure what we are here trying to grasp and invite the intrusion of the basic perceptual and conceptual errors we are trying to escape. I do not know how to state it more simply without inviting further distortion. Let me try once more. There is no non-violative way for me to know you in any respect that matters except inside some "we" that involves a different "I" and "you," initially and socially, than the separate pronouns suggest. And the we-ing that is the way of "knowing" is so much more nearly related to what are commonly distinguished as faith and will, that it would be more adequate to say we create each other, and know each other in creation. But that being so, there is no finite you, me or us to be known, for as what is created at this instant is co-known or co-appreciated, there is a re-creation. Thus, what is opened in principle is an infinite expansion—not in the trivial sense in which no description can exhaust what might be said of a given hunk of wood—but in the radical sense in which, in reference to persons, the "knowing" alters so significantly the "to be known" that "knowing" and "growing" someone are virtual functional equivalents. And what is true for the pair-relation used here only for illustration is *a fortiori* true for the kindred process called self-knowing. The self that "learns" anything significant about the self is *in that act* an irreversibly transforming self. So that the knowing is the history, and the history is the constitution of the self. And it is not that you cannot step into the same river twice simply because time has passed and water has gone by, or because your stepping in itself alters the river, but because, most profoundly, there is no sharply distinguished "you" and "river." Even for very rough purposes the abstraction of "you" from "the river" begins to falsify what most needs appreciation: your co-constituence, your co-emergence.

And having made mutual embroilment both the condition of knowing and the act of creation and recreation of anything human to be known, we may immediately infer that the nature of the embroilment will be to decide the nature of the embroiled. If man is "known" into existence, as I am maintaining, then he is a result (as, alas for simplicity, he will also be a cause) of the manner of knowing. And I can only here point to that manner of knowing that "causes" the known to be (infinitely, or in increments increasing indefinitely) worth knowing. The point I should like to use comes from an exhortation in the Book of Common Prayer: "The peace of God which passeth all understanding, keep your hearts and minds in the knowledge and love of God." The force of the words is to my mind perfectly general, whether God, another man or the self is to be "understood." The function of what is here called "heart" and "mind" is inseparable, distinguishable but not distinct; the knowledge and love are not two effects, but one, a loving knowledge, a knowing love; and something (call it peace, if you respond to the term fully) which "passeth understanding" or dies under definition, precedent and consequent and accompaniment of that loving-knowing which is at once just that and also the continuous instantaneous sustention and creation and recreation of the human world.

I think it is to some such "understanding"—no words truly catch it—that we are led by humane reflection in the yield of that part of the social sciences that retains any contact at all with its subject: man as man.

And that knowledge (if not knowledge of the sources of it) is also now so widespread among the moving young that they are not merely tempted, but driven as they wrestle for integrity to attempt simultaneously to reposition themselves and to begin so to act that speech, act and thought may have at least a minimum congruence. At every turn they face dead-on the sign-universal of our civilization: dead end! A massively moving force, with dead-end everywhere ahead and some sense for or terrains in which alternatives might lie is likely to burst over the civilizational banks, to take an historic turn in the large sense of that term, to set off a revolution in that word's largest reach and meaning.

The threat here, for those who feel charged to preserve the continuities and whose faith is that they can and should be preserved, is not from those labeled "revolutionaries." These—Maoists, Castroists, Stalinists, Trotskyites, Birchers, Kluxers, Debrayists, New Leftists, Old Leftists, Anarchists, Democratic Socialists, National Socialists, Fascists, the whole bag, kit and caboodle—are mainstream mutual friends squabbling family-fashion (perhaps to death) with each other. All share theme, and idolize variations. They are all New Dealers in a sense wider than Roosevelt's; but they are, like him, new dealers in the same game.

It is those who call for and begin to play a new game who feed the revolutionary flame.

And their flame begins to lick at the pillars of the civilizational edifice. The pillars are the fundamental elements that, under all variations, determine a structure that, everywhere, everywhen, everyhow, serves one aimless aim: control. The pillars are designed and engineered desires, systems of rewards and punishments, rules and laws, social structures and organizations generating and generated by these, and all their value schemes, signs and symbols, myths and icons, powers, influences, principalities, and pomps. It is on these that the assault is ordered.

The over-used phrase that points to the beginning of the natural history of the new revolutionary is "opting out." Opting out has, as its readily contemptuous critics note, practical limits: the reproof seems to be that since some revolutionaries must sometimes eat if there is to be a revolution, therefore the revolutionary thrust is also all hypocrisy and pretense. Nonsense! Opting-out defines a vector; the direction is out; the distance is the limit each individual may discover by all-out effort.

What is to be opted-out of (so far, *of course,* as possible) is the "inner" and "outer" systems of self and society. It is of the essence that the process is one two-sided process—"Finding your head" is alike the measure, cause, condition and result of opting out. Both are long, slow, painful pilgrimages of extrication and reconstruction—though the first word is too weak and the second too strong for what occurs. The first and most evident manifestation of extrication lies in self-removal, physical and spiritual, so far as possible from the reward-punishment situation. Beginning with a notion of mere refusal, one moves rapidly through renunciation, to enhanced counter-cathexis or disgust, and then to putting oneself so far as possible beyond the risks of re-addiction. The stifling and suffocating skein or caul from which disentanglement is to be effected, is not merely the extrinsic material donation-deprivation system, but the much subtler parallel system of "spiritual" extrinsic rewards and disawards, external and "internalized." The caul falls away: "And as for the gods of your fashion that take and that give, in their pity and passion, that scourge and forgive—they are worms that are bred in the bark that falls off; they shall die and not live."

But with that apostasy the whole system in its two correlatives—the organization of person and society—begins to come unstuck at all its crucial seams. What begins to collapse is the embodiment of the society's major principle of sustension: the division of labor. It is the division of labor that makes the various games—the army game, the political game, the family game—possible and necessary, as well as the sub-games of subordination, one-upmanship, status competition, and the like. And with games—or, if you prefer the image, plays—go the role-playing, the tests or criteria (such as "efficiency," smoothness and the like), and the supporting practices in "child-raising," "education," self-manipulation and so on, that these permit and require. Not the particular institutional structure or set of institutions that characterizes this particular society at this particular moment, but the whole place, duration and value of institutions is under radical question and subject to eliminative experiment. Except in the most attenuated sense and under the most marginal use and minimum-evil perpetual razoring institutions find small place in the speculations and practices emerging and beginning to flourish.

With the shift in those idea-feeling-attitude complexes, there begins a massive transformation of the personality that is nakedly visible not simply in dress and adornment, but in posture, muscular set, and mien. It is probably not so much beards, beads and locks that panic brave policemen who could readily face a mad gunman at need; what flips them out—and teachers and principals and parents—is the very set of the face which, as the straight folk correctly apprehend, are in themselves the mark of how far their world has been subverted and how fast and far its further subversion may yet go. One begins to understand why Romans must kill Christians, and churches burn St. Joans. The offense is not really in what they say or do, though these are convenient grounds for persecution; their very being-ness in radically different fashion is what is beyond tolerance, for such existences shake the going orders to their depths. This process is also now, I think, well begun.

In the nature of the case, there can be no well-articulated theory of such things. On the very contentions advanced, a way would have to be found to "get out of the culture" in order to find as a new person a new and different direction. Indeed, some sort of opening toward the unknown everything that Western culture closes off is of the essence, and what will follow such opening is of its essence unforeknowable.

The first problem is to find the meaning of opting out and the means to do so; the second problem is to begin to "find one's head" in what then is opened to one; the third is to prevent one's reassimilation; and the fourth is so to live in relation to self, man, and all nature in such fashion as to preserve and enhance the new person in the new relatednesses. To look for a formula for such a quest is to fail to understand what is implied in either term.

Some glimpse of what may be before us may be provided by an appreciation of what was till very recently known as the "hippy" phenomenon. Being *"a* hippy," largely a news-media invention, is itself very nearly a contradiction in terms; being "hippy," a way of being in the world, a way of being in a different way, names a mood, a social movement, a movement of religions, a quest at once personal, social and transcendent.

The ontogeny of hippieness is as easy to abstract as it is fatal to adequate appreciation. In our ideal-typical model, the onset is marked by disaffection and disgust in the full and literal sense of those terms: what was libidinally invested is disendowed, one is orphaned, and what had been nurturant is sensed to be poisonous to one's barely apprehended deeper being. These sentiments move toward repudiation, more or less clearly articulated, more and more massive. Extrication and escape distantiation physical and spiritual from the whole fast-woven web of activities, connections, expectations become paramount necessity, touched with the desperate character of

struggle for survival. Co-emergent is the urgent necessity to find an adequate experience sufficient at least to suggest, to intimate what it is in the
self and the world that has been so radically denied, distorted and filtered
out from the rich life of the rich child of the rich West. The search for
experience evolves to the search for one's head, a long, slow, agonizing
quest that moves over a territory having few general and still fewer particular landmarks. Its criteria, recognized in treasured "highs," are the unitive
experiences with self, others, nature, all, that depend upon and give rise to
some diffusion of the already overbounded ego, some journey into the self-
transcendent and return, renewed, into finding and doing one's thing. The
incidentals—location, drug-adjuvants, music, fatigue, fasting,—whether or
not the by-product of voluntary poverty, which is no incidental—costume,
style, special language of word, touch, or gesture—are each less than essential but more than adventitious. They promote and support, as does the
endless rambling talk in pad and commune, the wandering, tentative search
for one's roots and flower. Finding one's thing and doing one's thing mark
stages and are intrinsic; they contribute to a far-reaching transformation of
the personality, whose inward signs are growth into gentleness, trust and
grace. Radically less atomized, deracinated, homogenized, constricted and
truncated, wedded to wisdom instead of mastery, a new population emerges
not merely bearing a new culture, but manifesting, even in mien and posture, its character of revolution. For the first time since the history of the
West became distinctly Western, a powerful movement emerges whose way
is wisdom, and whose hero is the sage. No more powerful transformation
(or revolution) can be imagined for a society or a culture (particularly for
one so single in its monotheon as ours) than a shift in the type of hero and
the mode of self-modeling. From tycoon and bureaucrat-in-chief to sage,
from conquest of whatever is to participation and life in it, from ordered
march to free dance, from possessing to being possessed, from hierarchy to
mosaic, from organization to flow, from perpetuation to happenstance,
from toadying to the tycoon to respect for the sage, from exploitation to
enjoyment and triumph to joy—these are great distances and direly different directions, dire, at least, for a civilization to singularly set as ours on so
narrow and mean a course.

The very question first put commonly to anyone asserting the power of
the movement—"How many hippies, exactly, are there?"—shows where
our heads are at: lost in mindless computation. It is not only that we do not
distinguish between magnitude and greatness, but that the externality, the
management set is implicit in the question. The question means "How

many of *them* are there, so that I may know whether or how to modify my containing plans?"

That they are the response to previous planning—whether totalistic and coercive, or partialistic and manipulative-seductive as practiced in the best homes and schools—is not seen. That they embody a massive "No!" to the very design of all management, that they answer to the designs on them of all designers with a strategy of dialectical escape, that they speak for another and higher order of freedom, and that they threaten by their very existence to call into question and totter the system, is not seen or sensed— indeed so little so that the kindest question asked will be "How can we plan *for* them?" Bob Dylan's answer—"Get out of the way, if you don't understand"—is evidently incomprehensible, for even the word "understand" is only "understood" by us in characteristic fatal fashion: we think we understand something when we "grasp" it, have hold of those particulars that would permit us to put it in its place. That the vital is only "understood" as it grasps you—or, more exactly, as embrace occurs—is not, it appears, in our understanding.

Opting out is more than spiritual; it implies a physical place to opt to. It is not clear that cities, as we know them, or in any form resembling those we know, can be the locus for, let alone at the high-point of, the new voyage of discovery. For it is a voyage, a voy-age, a let's see, a "trip" not in our sense, but theirs, a going to an unforeseen place to return with an unforeseen vision, even as an unforeseen person. We must remind ourselves of the hippy insistence that "finding your head" and finding the appropriate supportive situation for doing so are co-emergents. No one yet has gone beyond pad or commune scale in such a search and not abandoned the one half-aim or the other—though a loose commune of communes, not spatially concentrated, seems emerging. Most such communes now are physically located, by choice not necessity, in the clefts of mountains, on the not-economically arable plains, in the deserts and waste places generally, in the niches and interstices left free or sparse by the present ecological organization. So at least for a while the conscience of the city, and therewith the City, may well have its dwelling-place anywhere but there. Meanwhile, the city for the foreseeable future may become the province and backwoods, filled with and ruled by provincials and backwoodsmen attempting to learn and do what the advance guard of the new civilization is striving to unlearn and undo. For it seems perfectly clear that the internal proletariat at home, like the external one abroad, is bound and determined to go through all the stages we have gone through in our miserable reaching of this now potentially happy place. Those of these most external to our society want most the goods and powers, the games and their yield in differential deference, the penalties and rewards, the conquests and controls that are precisely what is most ashen on our lips and bitter in our mouths. They want precisely and most that alienation from the world and power over it—and us and one another—that is the Dead Sea Fruit we are finding we can bite and choke down but not be fed by. And the arena, the pit for this belated struggle is to be, it seems clear, what at present we call the city. Just as within the city, the poor took on step by step the abandoned neighborhoods and mansions, so now they seem about to seize the cities. And with these, the city ways which epitomize our maladies and miseries. It will be a "learning environment" of a sort, a learning environment to ease the learning of what we must in agony unlearn, a place, like the pre-asepsis hospitals, to acquire the major diseases one did not have in the vain hope of curing the minor ones one did.

For the views and visions earlier adverted to carry with them altogether different implications for the "life of learning" (all life), the manner of learning (all modes) and the environment of learning.

Whatever else is true, given both the general orientation and what it is that is to be learned, the learning must come bearing the personal signature of some fully credible teacher—which is to say someone much more like a guru than our present technicians of information conveyance. No mass process comparable to our present "knowledge" factories in the Universities or person and "skill" factories in the schools could fill any part in any congruous "process of education." Something reminiscent of, though not identical with, discipleship and apprenticeship, must supervene. Unitive experiences—or even precessory experiences to these—may be sought, even cultivated, but not engineered. The very notion of putting soul-sustenance and soul-deepening into the grip of a vast machine, organized like an army, standardized, bureaucratized, governed, purporting to derive its authority from the state will seem among the more tragi-comic departures in the tragicomic history of man.

We must take it, I think, that all large systems—except for the supply of minimum needs at the cost of minimum effort will have largely disappeared. What we have to imagine, apart from this minimum, is virtually a non-system, and that is, of course, for us, almost beyond imagining. To picture the undesigned is almost as difficult as to design it.

The nature of the society contemplated, and the consequent increase in the tempo of discovery both ensure that in most matters that matter learning can no longer occur in any situation of unilateral expertise. For that the relative newcomer to the subject at hand will have part of the information required for any learning about it that the relative oldcomer simply cannot have. And that information will be more and more indispensable, so that all teaching-learning will need the structure of mutuality and the character of a conference. Such teachers as remain must be adept at dialogue. And, in any case, the bulk of the activity entailed will fall increasingly, as it is beginning to do with increasing acceleration now, to the siblingship. The siblingship, as implied in the few words above on the family, will no longer be the intense, tiny group of biological brothers and sisters, nor the till recently current jump-extension to non-intense "peers" (friends and acquaintances), but something in between: the sibs of the extended families, small "tribes" and such that now begin to dot and will presently fill the landscape.

What will need planning for is very little—just enough control over the spread of cities and their ways to permit the conscience of the city to find itself chiefly outside these centers, to spread thence through the society which, by then, may be ready, having reached its fevered climax, to abandon its delirium and search out its new way. That new way, I am confident, will not be, cannot be, in content, organization, aim, spirit, or the characters it furnishes and favors, anything like a continuation or culmination of what we have hitherto nurtured and known.

A Left Wing Alternative
Greg Calvert

When I worked in the national office of Students for a Democratic Society in Chicago, I used to take the bus down West Madison Street in the skid-row area. I used to look out the window at the faces of the alcoholics and think about my experiences bumming around skid row in Portland, Oregon, when I was a high school kid back in the early 1950s. There I ran from time to time into an old Wobbly organizer. Some of us in the radical movement have wondered whether, after so much hope and so much life, we would end like some of those old Wobblies.

I have wondered, very deeply and with great pain, whether the kind of movement which over the years has made it possible for us to live in America—the kind of movement which, out of the obscenity and sterility of this society, has given us new life—whether in fact that movement was going to survive and grow or whether it was going to die and leave us isolated.

I was asked recently whether I thought there was any possibility that we could avoid the Stalinization of the left. I said there is only one response: knowing we are faced with the possibility of the Stalinization of the left, we must do whatever is necessary to see that it does not happen. People from different organizations of the movement must begin to discuss the possibility and the framework for creating the non-Stalinist, the libertarian, the life-giving alternative for the left.

If that alternative is not created, if the life-giving, libertarian spirit of the left is lost in the mechanical, guilt-ridden forms of Stalinism, we will have no one but ourselves to blame. We can no longer elude the problem by reeling off a list of ten forces which militate against the alternative. We simply must be more determined. If the quality of life inside the radical movement is to survive, we must do it, and we can do it.

But we can't do it unless we cling to all of the categories which now end up in phony dichotomies. Someone has said that today it's "ideolog versus activist." In times past it was "nonviolence versus violence," then it was "centralism versus decentralism," or "student power versus racism." All of those were attempts to assume that at any moment in our history we have only one of two choices. That kind of thinking has to be broken down—

especially the phony distinction between "security" and "openness," as though there were any other kind of real security in the movement apart from the trust in openness which develops among people who can count on each other when the heat's on.

It is fashionable in SDS these days to denounce something called personal liberation. If you talk about what you feel or what's meaningful to you in a political forum, you're suddenly one of those personal-liberation people.

I don't quite understand what that's supposed to mean. I do not believe in a two-story universe; I don't think there's going to be some reward out there somewhere. I don't believe in capitalist ideology, which is the ideology of deferred life, of deferred existence, of accumulation for tomorrow. Unless one does believe in that, then I don't understand what motivation there would be for a biological, physical being to get involved except the liberation of that individual.

In Daniel Cohn-Bendit's book, *Obsolete Communism—The Left Wing Alternative,* there's a phrase which I think must be taken seriously. Danny the Red discusses and puts down people who operate on the politics of guilt—the politics of life deferral, the politics of the acceptance of repressiveness, in the hope that some day there'll be a non-repressive future born suddenly and cataclysmically. He says *the only reason for being a revolutionary in our time is because it's a better way to live.*

I don't think I've ever known anyone in the last five to seven years who was in the movement and in it for good who wasn't there knowing that it was a better way to live. If you think that politics and personality can be split apart and still build a revolution, if you think it's possible to be, in this kind of society, in any sense revolutionary without being engaged to the deepest level of your life, if you think any of those things or do any of those things to your movement, then we will not create that alternative history.

I do not mean that I think it is any longer possible for us to deal with our political responsibilities to ourselves, and to that larger America which we must reach, simply on the basis of existentialist language. But, the alternative is not Stalinist ideology. The alternative to understanding that I'm in this because I want to be free is not economic determinism. Certainly Marx is important; but let us not create a movement based on Marxism as ideology. Let us do more justice to Marx himself.

I want now to trace what I perceive to be the history that has led us to this impasse and this possibility, and talk about my experience of the theme of resistance from the inside of SDS.

This takes us back to the summer of 1966, a summer of great possibilities, possibilities which were given to us because the first phase of the movement had definitely come to an end. We could no longer find our constituencies outside ourselves by going South, into the black community. The statement of black power which SDS endorsed in June 1966 came at a time when many white radicals were realizing it was absolutely necessary that we go out and build in our own circumstances our own movement. Because black power threw us back on ourselves and our own lives, our own situations, it offered us the possibility for being sincerely radical, and not the liberal adjunct of the black movement.

It was also in that summer that the first traveling draft resistance work was done. Mendy Samstein, who had been my closest friend in graduate school at Cornell in 1960 to 1961, and who had spent about three years working in the South, came to Chicago and talked about draft resistance and about his projected program. I argued with Mendy very intensely about that program because I was afraid that inherent in his notion about noncooperation was the possibility for perpetuating the politics of masochism. After I talked with Mendy and others, it seemed to me that, though the danger was there, there was another kind of possibility inherent in the Resistance approach. This was the possibility of white radicals beginning to engage the struggle deeply around an issue of their own oppression.

After SDS passed its draft resistance resolution in December 1966, a very interesting set of ideas began to be generated. In their final formulation, these ideas were our attempt to provide some of the theoretical notions for a larger movement in the United States, which would not only be draft resistance but would go beyond draft resistance and talk to the great mass of Americans about struggling over their own oppression, and struggling for their own liberation—not somebody else's—in the context of the conditions of their own lives.

Let me try to trace how those ideas emerged. I think there's been a kind of unrealistic assumption made about where terms like "neo-capitalism" and "new working class" came from, as though we had snatched them from the firmament of Marxist ideology and imposed them on the movement. In January, 1966, we put out the button, "Not With My Life You Don't," to concretize the spirit of, "It's my fight, it's my life." Everyone was talking about strategy for draft resistance, but every time we sat through a three-hour session on strategy for draft resistance, we didn't get anywhere. What we were asking was the impossible: that draft resistance give us the channels for making a total revolution in society.

Then an article called "Manpower Channelling" by Peter Henig was published in *New Left Notes*. That, at least in SDS, was the first time anybody had bothered to read the material that came out of the Selective Service System. It crystallized a lot of vague notions we'd been playing with in our heads about who students are. What it told us was that the 2-S student deferment was less a privilege than another instrument of oppression. It was part of a larger program, a program of manpower channelling for not only the military but for industry.

Henig's article had been written in the 1940s to make clear that the military needs of American capitalist imperialism would not interfere with the continuing supply of manpower for profit at home. Since the period following the Second World War was the period in which the new technology of the coming automation and cybernated production were emerging, it was clear that American capitalism and industry were going to need an enormous number of highly trained, highly skilled workers to plug into those slots in its advanced technological machinery.

It was clear, also, that the university was going to become the training ground for those workers, those scientific, technical and professional workers who were needed by advanced capitalism. The multiversity would become the motor for the transformation of the labor force in the direction of the new technology.

It was out of that set of realizations that we began to see that students are in a tremendously different historical situation than that of Lenin's Russia in 1902, when they were the petty bourgeois intelligentsia. By 1975, one quarter of the labor force in the country will have had some college training—far too large a number to be considered an elite.

We said, then, that the working class was being renewed, expanded; we called these people the "new working class," the university-trained workers.

That was important because it gave us a handle on the long-range question of social change, of revolution in society. It gave us the possibility of a perspective that said students and post-students fighting around the conditions of their own lives are a legitimately revolutionary stratum. As such, they can contribute to a larger movement, which must include other sectors of the population—the blue-collar workers and the poor.

Back to a little history to bring us up to 1968.

After the summer of 1967, the Pentagon action and Stop the Draft Week which preceded it, it seemed to some of us that the time was rapidly approaching when the resistance notion of strategy could become the base for a new kind of radical solidarity among a variety of elements within the movement. I mean by "resistance strategy" a notion which included not only draft resistance and noncooperation, but also resistance to Dow Chemical and other institutions of repression.

Michael Ferber and I talked the other day, trying to dredge out of our unconsciouses the memories of those months from October 1967 to April 1968. What we came up with was a wealth of memories of political events which affirmed what we believed, events in which representatives of the black militant movement were saying, "Yes, now we have a legitimate basis for an alliance, because in the resistance movement there is a truly radical and potentially revolutionary movement among whites."

I believe that that was true. I do not wish to pretend that events exterior to the movement—such as Johnson's dropping out of the race, and a series of events exterior to the white movement, the series of uprisings that followed King's assassination—did not have an importance in reorienting people's outlooks. The reorientation of SDS in that spring of 1968 was to drop draft resistance and resistance themology almost entirely, and to revert to, "We got to support the black movement, racism is our issue. Anti-racism is the radical position."

What you do to a white man in today's society when you tell him he's got to fight the anti-racism struggle is give him a struggle that doesn't have any outside to it. I do not want to deny that racism is a problem, as male chauvinism is a problem inside of us. But I wish to insist that the only way we can finally fight against racism effectively is to be fighting our battles for our own liberation, in alliance with black people fighting their struggle for their own liberation.

In that situation, when the movement should have held strong—despite the fact that LBJ's pulling out and what happened after King's death were going to have an effect—the movement should have held firm and insisted more firmly than ever on the relevance of the resistance strategy. Instead, meetings were beginning to be held to plan for Chicago. Having taken that direction, having decided that, instead of pushing our resources on the legitimate strategy which we had and focusing our resources on the convention, we abandoned strategic leadership for the white movement. The decline of mass, spontaneous kinds of activity around the war movement, which was inevitable, need not have also disoriented the solid core of resistance which was there.

I do not know, but I wonder whether some of the shifting direction from April to the summer in black organizations was not conditioned by our failure. My understanding of the dynamic of the black movement in relation to the other strata in American society is that it has two choices—either it can rely on whites for liberal support, or it can find a radical ally in a radical white movement. When that ally is not there doing his thing, then the black movement, for its own survival, reverts to looking for liberal support. If honky-baiting goes up, it's because we create the dynamic where there's no other response for desperate black militants. I wonder whether once again in that situation we don't have ourselves to blame.

In the ensuing year, having myself left national SDS much disturbed over this question, having opposed the line of racism being our first issue, having opposed the publication of a pamphlet which said liberation will come from a black thing and having called that pamphlet obscene—in the last year I think we have seen what Staughton described, particularly in SDS, a revival of the politics of guilt. There was one major change, however—from 1961 to 1965 the rhetoric was liberal, and in 1968 to 1969, its rhetoric, but only its rhetoric, was revolutionary.

I do not believe that in a society like ours—an advanced capitalist society where mass culture itself is an instrument of oppression, where the repressiveness of all the last 6,000 years of civilization becomes surplus repression, where the authoritarianism of a highly bureaucratized, centralized corporate capitalism requires the inculcation of authoritarian and self-hating values in order to pacify the population—I do not believe we can free ourselves from that society through emotional structures of guilt which were created to kept us from fighting for freedom. No one that I have talked to in this year of isolation has been able to convince me otherwise, either through argument or through political accomplishment.

What's going on in SDS is that, having denied that students have legitimacy as a strata, or that new-working-class people have legitimacy as a revolutionary stratum, we revert to the old Leninist formulations which say that the task of the petit-bourgeois intelligentsia is to form a vanguard party which will relate to the proletarian struggle of the factory worker. I do not deny the importance of 20 to 30 million blue-collar workers in long-range revolutionary strategy for the society. To do so would be foolish and absurd on its face. But, coming from a blue-collar, working-class background, I find it very difficult to believe that the breast beating of white students and white professionals and white technical workers about the fact that they aren't on the production line is going to save my relatives or my high-school classmates from the oppressive institutions of capitalism. Nor do I believe that talking that way to them addresses itself to the real concerns of their lives.

I think what addresses itself to the concerns of the lives of young people and others in my home town, where practically everybody works in the lumber mills, is to talk to people about their lives in the way we talk with others about our lives, to organize in the same spirit of openness and commitment and hopefulness and joyousness.

I would go even so far as to argue that to organize otherwise is not to organize for revolution and liberation, but to run the danger of organizing something very different. I know from my personal upbringing what the authoritarian discipline of factories does to the family lives of workers. Not to fight authoritarianism there in the same spirit that we fight it in the university is, I think, to make a grave error, and finally to be of no use to anyone, neither to ourselves nor to those whom we would pretend to reach.

Will it be possible to create that alternative history? Will it be possible to build a movement which talks about a community of free men, about new selfhood, about new man?

Will it be possible for us to have the courage to say, yes, what we want is beauty and freedom, and that we become freer and more beautiful on the path to getting there?

It seems to me that such a possibility is not only there in what Marxists call objective conditions, but is also there in the recent history of advanced capitalist civilization itself. It is very much there in the events of France in May and June, 1968.

What were *we* doing in May and June 1968 when revolution almost took place in one of the advanced industrial societies of the world? It was the exemplary action of students fighting first around their own demands that catalyzed the situation. Despite the enormous reactionary force of the huge French Communist party and its trade-union bureaucracy, the students were able to create a language of action which spoke to the other sectors of the population about the control and transformation of their lives. A left-wing alternative was not only created but its effectiveness in opposition to the reactionary character of existing communist institutions was proven.

Meanwhile, the SDS national office was trying to grind out an elaborate analysis of racism, couched in the most abstruse and dogmatic language, so that the line would be right at its national convention in June.

It seems to me that one of our real problems, after 50 years of Stalinism, is the problem of models that give hope. Because of the despair of the New Left with the bureaucratic forms of so-called socialism in the Soviet Union, we've always looked and looked for some place where somebody's trying to do it better. It's not so much that we're dumb and unimaginative—although

I think we're dumber and less imaginative than need be—but because the question of twentieth century history has been: is human freedom possible? Was there another stage of civilization, or were we headed towards 1984, no matter what the ruling bureaucracies called themselves?

So we are enthusiastic when we think that maybe Cuba is doing something new, maybe there is real popular involvement, or maybe the Vietnamese are in fact embodying a spirit like that which gives us life. I do not want to denigrate our attachment to the heroism of the Vietnamese or of the Cubans; nor do I think we should in any slavish manner suspend judgment when we look at societies which turn us on. What I'm saying is what France should mean for the New Left is that we now have a concrete set of experiences to look at that can tell us much more than the Cubans or Vietnamese can tell us, because they are experiences of an advanced industrial society.

Over and over again, as I've read the documents and Cohn-Bendit's book, the experiences tell us we were right. The student movement at Nanterre began really in the spring of 1967, when the university had refused to allow guys and girls to sleep together in the dorms. So a sexual liberation front was created, and they reprinted Wilhelm Reich's sexual liberation manifesto of 1934, and talked about the relationship between authoritarianism, sexual repression and fascism. They began to build a movement which obviously had a libertarian spirit. That spirit was obviously at the fore in the events of a year later. It was "movement people" doing "movement things" that made France happen.

It may be because most French students had already heard about Marx, and read through that, put it in perspective, that it was possible for something new to arise, whereas here it seems that every time old Karl's name is mentioned our deep Baptist backgrounds or something out of our repressive pasts come surging to the fore.

One of the things which the French events say to me very deeply and clearly is that most of the traditional conceptions of organization of vanguard parties, of Leninist practice, are not only unpleasant but ineffective. I find myself revising some notions that had been lost as we thought we were getting more radical. We used to talk in the old days about things like parallel institutions. I don't think that was the right language, but the language pointed to the notions that the revolution was not an event on day "X," but a process that we're into now, and that the structures of revolution and of revolutionary society would begin to be created as we did more work, got involved in more scenes, discovered new things.

The French experience says also that Marx was serious when he said socialism would grow out of the womb of capitalism. The deadly serious question to ask, if that's true, is how the embryo is conceived: what are the embryonic forms of revolutionary society which must be created, however embryonically, as we work?

Is it not possible to begin to envisage a movement which builds a variety of forms and structures, and uses those instead of a centralized party? In such structures, the questions of control and transformation could be raised in a way which points toward the historical alternative, in terms of both the form and the content of those embryonic revolutionary institutions.

All of that, I think, is true and possible. All of that requires a great deal of imagination—the imagination which the students at the Sorbonne enthroned in power in those exciting days of May and June. It takes enormous imagination, a willingness to be new, but that is the only way out.

I do not know whether I would or could participate in an organization which did not embody in its immediate present the values and hopes which I have, but I think it no longer, in our society, does any good to say, "I will sacrifice myself to be part of that dehumanizing vanguard for my children in another day." I just don't think there's anything revolutionary in doing that.

Once again, if the new life which has been created in us in this decade is to be more than a footnote to the last chapter of world civilization, we must take very seriously the lesson of trust in ourselves, of not killing what we feel and need to be true, not blaming objective conditions or using them as a pretext for dehumanizing ourselves. People who argue that game are arguing that the reason I can't be free is because all of that stuff is weighing on me. It's true that the authoritarian forms which are anti-life were not created by us, and we do not need to blame ourselves for them. But we also know in scientific and psychological terms that repression in ourselves does not begin when we touch the outside world. Repression in ourselves begins when we interpret an inner impulse as an exterior threat and call it the world. Since so much of our lives has been learning not only to trust those inner impulses but to rediscover the ones that society wishes were dead, we should in fact affirm those feelings.

That means hard work, but work with joy. It means trusting ourselves, being willing to be experimental. It means not accepting simplistic either/or formulations of complicated human situations. I think, finally, it means being concerned with effective activity rather than purity of the line. We have to trust other people in the immediate situation who may differ from us in their analyses of things; we must be willing to be wrong and willing to be critical, but cling to what we know the movement is all about. Only an ideology of puritanism, religion, capitalism—of deferred existence—can argue otherwise for my life.

I remember one of the most moving and unsettling events in the nine months I spent as national secretary of SDS. I had been out on the road for a couple of weeks, and during that time passed my thirtieth birthday. When I came back to the office, comrades younger than myself needed to assert their youthfulness in the face of my coming middle age with something resembling guerrilla theater. In rummaging through my desk, they discovered an old passport photo of me from 1961, when I was leaving to go to Europe. I wore a suit, tie, and very short hair. I looked for all the world like what I was, an Ivy League graduate student. They put next to it a picture from the *New York Times* of this rather scruffy looking, very tired, but younger looking person—myself. Underneath it they wrote, "The good guerrilla in our society must know how to change his identity in order to fit all new situations."

An American
Socialist Community?
William Appleman Williams

In moving about the country a good bit the last four years—from the campuses to the metropolis and through the provinces—I have repeatedly been struck by two things. The first is the accuracy of Harold Cruse's observation: "Americans generally have no agreement on who they are, what they are, or how they got to be what they are. . . . All Americans are involved in an identity crisis." The second is that the New Left, or "the movement" as the jargon has it, is not doing very much that is effective in dealing with that dangerous but potentially creative situation.

There is no persuasive evidence that the movement is in the process of becoming a social movement of the kind that can generate and push through major reforms on a continuing basis—let alone institute structural changes—in American society. Whatever the victories of the New Left, there are a good many indications that the activities of the movement are increasing the willingness within the establishment to reform and rationalize the corporate system according to its own adaptation of our criticisms. And some actions of the New Left are creating growing support for repressive policies (as contrasted with suppression in specific crises).

There are two orthodox comments at this point. One maintains that the revolution is being made by people doing their own thing: that if you leave the system it will collapse. But if that is correct, then we either collapse with it or confront the necessity of a new ruthlessness to build the replacement. The other argument maintains that establishment reforms will not—even cannot—go far enough quickly enough to avert a crisis that will open the way for the movement. I do not rule out that possibility, but I do not think it is probable because the analysis overlooks, or discounts, several major considerations:

(1) While American society is sick, it is not sick to the verge of rolling over dead, or even to the point that a good push will topple it into History. The will to maintain the system is real and visible and consequential.

(2) An establishment trying to reform itself will, for a long period, hold

the loyalty of even the least repressive groups in society. This is particularly true so long as the New Left makes no discriminations among other groups in society, makes no sustained effort to involve them as participating equals in a non-elitist movement, and offers nothing to attract them into such a venture.

(3) Things may get worse as a short run prelude to getting better, but they may instead get worse for an indefinite period.

There simply cannot be an era of radical reform, or structural change, without a living conception of community and a clearly developed approach to alternatives to meet the needs of America in an equitable and effective manner. Much of the New Left is operating—consciously or unconsciously—under the illusion that the United States today is comparable to England between 1660 and 1688, France in 1789, Russia in 1917, or one of the many poor and non-industrial countries of the contemporary world. It has become fashionable to call this the New Romanticism, and defend it with orthodox irrationality. It would be better, for the honor of true Romanticism, and for our own well-being (to say nothing of the millions of poor and powerless), to call it ignorance at best—innocent or arrogantly self-righteous as warranted by the specific case—and at worst the most insidious kind of anti-intellectualism.

It flatly will not do, in the last third of the twentieth century, to pretend that we in the United States can indulge ourselves in an indefinite period of willy-nilly-working-out-of-a-new-order. Nor is it meaningful to talk about anarchy or self-contained communes of mutually compatible couples, or of the underground that can provide you with subsistence for a year. There is no more justification for putting people off in that fashion than there is for putting people down. Yet the movement is doing a good deal of both.

Eldridge Cleaver heated up the soul on the issue of goals, with these words: "We start with the premise that every man, woman and child on the face of the earth deserves the very highest standard of living that human knowledge and technology is capable of providing. Period. No more than that, no less than that." That is not really enough, or at least it is seriously open to the charge of mistaking economism for socialism (or whatever other name for the new order you prefer), but it is more than sufficient to end the explicit and implicit nonsense of the movement that mundane matters will take care of themselves come the revolution. They do not now, which is one of our criticisms, and they will not do so even ten years after the revolution if we do not see to it ourselves.

In one of his classic throw-away lines, Schumpeter once remarked that socialism was a post-economic problem. In a strict sense that is true. Socialism is, or at any rate should be, about the nature and functioning of a community, rather than about the failings of the capitalist system. And a community is not created, let alone maintained, by everyone simply doing their own thing. Adam Smith wrote that prescription for heaven on earth in 1776, and after 200 years we ought to be able to recognize the limitations. But Schumpeter's arrow did not hit the center of the bullseye. For Marx accurately noted that while capitalism created the means for solving the economic problem it could not organize and use those powers to fulfill its avowed reason for being.

Cleaver, Schumpeter, and Marx. All three were correct. Still are correct. Cleaver's proposition, explicitly expanded to include intellectual, cultural, and interpersonal matters, can stand as the "no-less-than-that" of an American radicalism. But to get on with realizing that objective we have to deal with the implications of Schumpeter's point about socialism. We have, that is, to speak to the nature of a new economy and to the philosophic, physiological, and psychic foundations for a man who is not, as Adam Smith maintained, defined by his propensity to barter and trade in the marketplace. The Left, Old or New, has yet to answer either question.

It is no longer relevant to prove that socialists can operate (albeit more fairly and more efficiently) the centralized and consolidated economic system created by mature capitalism. That would have been very helpful if we had come to power between 1894 and 1914, but the challenge today is to maintain and increase productivity while breaking the Leviathan into community-sized elements. And while the hippies have blasted through some of the walls that capitalism erected around true humanism, they are very largely operating as a self-defined interest group in the classic sense of nineteenth century capitalism. It is no answer to Smith to define individualism in Freudian terms, or some other human propensity.

So we come down to Marx. It is so obvious as to be the cliché of the era: capitalism has demonstrated a congenital incapacity to use its literally fantastic powers and achievements to enable untold members of the lower and middle classes—and even many in the upper class—to live as human beings. But Marx also said that the purpose and the responsibility of the movement is twofold: to extend, deepen, and focus the awareness of that failure, and to organize the people of the society to use the powers created by mature capitalism in humane and creative ways.

So far there is less irrelevant about Marx than there is parochial about the movement. The issues here are not the tactics of disruption, provocation, and violence. At least not for many (including myself) who lack the training or guts to be pacifists, or feel morally queasy about righteously provoking the worst in other men we know are not prepared to transcend their prejudices in a moment of crisis, or consider non-violent revolution as a strategy appropriate only for an established socialist society. I do not think it is possible—even under the best of circumstances—to move from mature capitalism to established socialism without considerable disruption and some amount of blood.

The central matter, however, concerns when—in what context and for what purposes—we provoke and disrupt and spill blood. I think there has been a good deal of bloodletting that has not produced any *sustained* deepening and focusing of radical consciousness. It has been my observation, as well as experience, that six months of quiet work in the dormitories, or of going up to the doorbell for a half-hour conversation, has deeper and more lasting consequences than the occupation of a building or the provocation of a bust. It was, after all, the teach-ins rather than the marches that played the major role in generating the now widespread opposition to the Vietnam War.

And of course that brings us to the nut-crackers: we do not have a meaningful conception of what it is to be an American. We have instead a collection of disjointed notes on what it does not mean, and a vague assertion that all things will be beautiful and lovely come the revolution.

We have never realized that in America the only way to deepen and focus the radical social consciousness of the large numbers of women and men of our time is to tell them in concrete and specific terms how their lives can be richer and purposeful. There is simply not any time or justification for us to be vague like Marx, technocratically optimistic like Lenin, romantically irresponsible like Trotsky, or latter-day agrarians like Mao and Castro.

If we are going to have a social movement, we will have to build it on the basis of a workable answer to the eminently fair demand from our potential constituency among the lower and middle classes: explain how will socialism be any better than a capitalism without the Vietnam War and with a continuing (and improving) pattern of permissive welfarism. We have, that is, to convince those vast numbers of Americans that we can take the productive apparatus of mature capitalism and reorganize it for their benefit. That means erasing two primary lines in their image of the Left. One is the line that connects radical structural change with things getting worse than they are. The other line connects radicalism with radicals doing their own things at the expense of large numbers of other people.

I am very skeptical that we can meet that challenge through a strategy based on the declining age of the majority of the population; at least not as it is now being attempted by various campus groups. For one thing, most Americans do not define their hopes for a better society in terms of university reform. To use the jargon, that is not relevant to them. Frankly, I sympathize with that for, while campus reform is important to me personally in the short-run and to me as a socialist in the long-run, it is not nearly as central as building an inclusive social movement capable of forcing the Establishment to give large chunks of ground on primary issues affecting the majority of my fellow citizens. Secondly, as presently organized and conducted, the campus wing of the movement is not making any serious reach to its own constituency—witness the rush of student activists to McCarthy and Kennedy.

I think another strategy warrants serious consideration. It has three parts.

(1) We must use the campus as a base for reaching the community. This means, in connection with campus action, preparing the ground in the city and the state for the ultimate confrontations on campus. It means, in the broader sense, using the campus as what it is—a generator of ideas— and as a center of serious intellectual activity dealing with the problems of the general society. A radical movement that weakens, or even destroys, the university to gain secondary and symptomatic reforms is not demonstrating a convincing case for general leadership of the society.

(2) We must respond to legitimate demands for clear and convincing proposals for the new American community. If we cannot, then we are irrelevant. Evasion of these demands is at best a disingenuous way of putting people down; it is at worst hard evidence of intellectual incompetence. We ought to be able to learn from Russia and China that the lack of clear ideas and programs can lead to all kinds of serious moral and practical troubles.

(3) We must start dealing with the large numbers of Americans, who have been misled or brutalized as human beings rather than as racists and boobs to be jammed up against the wall. For the self-righteous arrogance in the movement is at least as dangerous to its future as the establishment.

NOTES ON THE AUTHORS

C. George Benello taught sociology at Goddard College and is now a Fellow of the Cambridge Institute, where he is directing research into new town development. He is an editor of both *Our Generation* and *Current Magazine*. He is author of *Wasteland Culture* and other articles on social theory.

Dimitrios Roussopoulos is a long time activist in the peace and New Left movements in Canada. A political economist by profession, he has authored many articles on social questions and movement problems. He has lectured widely throughout Canada and is the editor of *The New Left in Canada*. He is also editor of the Canadian New Left quarterly journal, *Our Generation,* and a member of the Council of the International Confederation for Disarmament and Peace (London).

George Woodcock is editor of *Canadian Literature,* and taught in the English Department of the University of British Columbia. He is author of numerous books and articles on anarchism, George Orwell, the Doukabors, and literary criticism.

Don Calhoun is a professor of sociology at the University of Miami, Florida. He is the editor with Arthur Nartalin, Andreas Papandreou, and others, of recognized texts in social science for college students. He formerly taught at Black Mountain College and lives in Melbourne Village, Florida, an international community.

Stewart E. Perry is a Fellow of the Cambridge Institute and is Director of the Center for Community Economic Development, where his work involves research and planning for community development corporations. Previously, he was a research sociologist with the Office of Economic Opportunity. His publications include *The Human Nature of Science,* (Free Press, 1966) and *Personality and Political Crisis* (Free Press, 1951).

Rosabeth Moss Kanter is Assistant Professor of Sociology at Brandeis University. She has specialized in the study of utopian and intentional communities, and has written articles on the subject, including an article on contemporary American intentional communities which appeared in "Psychology Today." She is completing a book on utopian communities for Harvard University Press.

James Gillespie is an English management consultant (retired) who at various times has been a day laborer, shop steward, strike leader, and works manager. He has written a number of books on industrial organization, including *Free Expression in Industry,* a book whose radical approach and originality virtually ended his career as management consultant.

Gerry Hunnius is a Fellow at The Praxis Corporation (Research Institute for Social Change) in Toronto, Canada, Consultant to the Center for Community Economic Development, in Cambridge, Massachusetts, Associate editor of the international quarterly journal, *Our Generation* (Montreal) and a member of the Council of the International Confederation for Disarmament and Peace (London, England). He is presently working on a book, with the tentative title: *The Politics of Participation and Control: The Yugoslav Experience in Decentralization and Self-Management.*

Murray Bookchin is the author of numerous articles on urbanism, ecology and the nature of post-scarcity society. He teaches at the Alternative University in New York and is associated with the magazine *Anarchos*.

John D. McEwan is a computer expert and programming diagnostician who has studied the applications of anarchist theory to modern organizations. He is a graduate of the University of St. Andrews, where he studied in both the Arts and Science faculties, and holds a degree in mathematics.

Arthur Chickering is at present Program Director for the Project on Student Development in Selected Small Colleges. Before that he was Coordinator of Evaluation and Professor of Psychology at Goddard College. He has written extensively on institutional size and student development. His book, *Education and Identity,* published by Jossey-Bass, appeared in 1969.

Martin Oppenheimer is with the Department of Anthropology and Sociology at Lincoln University. He is a co-author of the *Manual on Direct Action* and author of *Urban Guerrilla Warfare.*

Christian Bay is chairman of the Department of Political Science at the University of Alberta, Edmonton, Canada. Professor Bay has also taught at the University in Berkeley and at Stanford.

Colin Ward is the editor of the British monthly *Anarchy*. He is also a school teacher.

Sidney Lens is an editor of *Liberation* and has been a trade unionist for many years. He is the author of a number of books, including *Radicalism in America.*

Staughton Lynd is a historian who has taught at several universities including Yale. He has authored several books including *Intellectual Origins of American Radicalism* and *A Documented History of Non-Violence in America*. He is also an editor of *Liberation*.

John Seeley has written extensively in the field of education, psychiatry and mental health, and community sociology. His most recent position has been as Dean at the Center for the Study of Democratic Institutions. Before that he was Chairman of the Department of Sociology at Brandeis University. His better known books include *Crestwood Heights,* and *The Americanization of the Unconscious.*

Greg Calvert was a full-time organizer with the National Office of the Students for a Democratic Society. He is now writing a book with his wife on the nature of neo-capitalism.

William Appleman Williams is a distinguished American historian whose published works include *The Contours of American History* and *The Tragedy of American Diplomacy*. He is now teaching at Oregon State University, Corvallis.

This book was set on the linotype in Times Roman.
The display is Perpetua.
The composition, printing, and binding is by
H. Wolff Book Manufacturing Company, New York.
The design is by Jacqueline Schuman.